EISE

MALLEUS

More tales of the Inquisition from Black Library

• EISENHORN •
Dan Abnett

XENOS
MALLEUS
HERETICUS
THE MAGOS

• RAVENOR •
Dan Abnett

RAVENOR
RAVENOR RETURNED
RAVENOR ROGUE

PARIAH: RAVENOR VS EISENHORN
Dan Abnett

THE HORUSIAN WARS: RESURRECTION
John French

VAULTS OF TERRA: THE CARRION THRONE
Chris Wraight

AGENT OF THE THRONE: BLOOD AND LIES (audio drama)
John French

More Warhammer 40,000 from Black Library

• GAUNT'S GHOSTS •
Dan Abnett

THE FOUNDING
THE SAINT
THE LOST
BLOOD PACT
SALVATION'S REACH
THE WARMASTER

SABBAT CRUSADE
Various Authors

• SPACE MARINE CONQUESTS •

THE DEVASTATION OF BAAL
Guy Haley

ASHES OF PROSPERO
Gav Thorpe

WAR OF SECRETS
Phil Kelly

OF HONOUR AND IRON
Ian St Martin

APOCALYPSE
Josh Reynolds

EISENHORN

MALLEUS

DAN ABNETT

BLACK LIBRARY

A BLACK LIBRARY PUBLICATION

'Missing in Action' first published in *Inferno!* magazine in 2001.
Malleus first published in Great Britain in 2001.
This edition published in Great Britain in 2019 by
Black Library,
Games Workshop Ltd.,
Willow Road,
Nottingham, NG7 2WS, UK.

10 9 8

Produced by Games Workshop in Nottingham.
Cover illustration by Alexander Ovchinnikov.

A CIP record for this book is available from the British Library.

ISBN 13: 978 1 84970 961 3

See Black Library on the internet at

blacklibrary.com

Find out more about Games Workshop
and the world of Warhammer 40,000 at

games-workshop.com

Printed and bound by CPI Group (UK) Ltd, Croydon, CR0 4YY

For Kyle Foster and the Taken, wherever you may be.

It is the 41st millennium. For more than a hundred centuries the Emperor has sat immobile on the Golden Throne of Earth. He is the Master of Mankind by the will of the gods, and master of a million worlds by the might of His inexhaustible armies. He is a rotting carcass writhing invisibly with power from the Dark Age of Technology. He is the Carrion Lord of the Imperium for whom a thousand souls are sacrificed every day, so that He may never truly die.

Yet even in His deathless state, the Emperor continues His eternal vigilance. Mighty battlefleets cross the daemon-infested miasma of the warp, the only route between distant stars, their way lit by the Astronomican, the psychic manifestation of the Emperor's will. Vast armies give battle in His name on uncounted worlds. Greatest amongst His soldiers are the Adeptus Astartes, the Space Marines, bioengineered super-warriors. Their comrades in arms are legion: the Astra Militarum and countless planetary defence forces, the ever-vigilant Inquisition and the tech-priests of the Adeptus Mechanicus to name only a few. But for all their multitudes, they are barely enough to hold off the ever-present threat from aliens, heretics, mutants – and worse.

To be a man in such times is to be one amongst untold billions. It is to live in the cruellest and most bloody regime imaginable. These are the tales of those times. Forget the power of technology and science, for so much has been forgotten, never to be re-learned. Forget the promise of progress and understanding, for in the grim dark future there is only war. There is no peace amongst the stars, only an eternity of carnage and slaughter, and the laughter of thirsting gods.

CONTENTS

MISSING IN ACTION

I lost my left hand on Sameter. This is how it occurred. On the thirteenth day of Sagittar (local calendar), three days before the solstice, in the mid-rise district of the city of Urbitane, an itinerant evangelist called Lazlo Mombril was found shuffling aimlessly around the flat roof of a disused tannery lacking his eyes, his tongue, his nose and both of his hands.

Urbitane is the second city of Sameter, a declining agro-chemical planet in the Helican subsector, and it is no stranger to crimes of cruelty and spite brought on by the vicissitudes of neglect and social deprivation afflicting its tightly packed population. But this act of barbarity stood out for two reasons. First, it was no hot-blooded assault or alcohol-fuelled manslaughter but a deliberate and systematic act of brutal, almost ritual mutilation.

Second, it was the fourth such crime discovered that month.

I had been on Sameter for just three weeks, investigating

the links between a bonded trade federation and a secession-
ist movement on Hesperus at the request of Lord Inquisitor
Rorken. The links proved to be nothing – Urbitane's economic
slough had forced the federation to chase unwise business
with unscrupulous shipmasters, and the real meat of the case
lay on Hesperus – but I believe this was the Lord Inquisitor's
way of gently easing me back into active duties following the
long and arduous affair of the Necroteuch.

By the Imperial calendar it was 241.M41, late in that year. I
had just finished several self-imposed months of recupera-
tion, meditation and study on Thracian Primaris. The eyes of
the daemonhost Cherubael still woke me some nights, and I
wore permanent scars from torture at the hands of the sadist
Gorgone Locke. His strousine neural scourge had damaged
my nervous system and paralysed my face. I would not smile
again for the rest of my life. But the battle wounds sustained
on KCX-1288 and 56-Izar had healed, and I was now itching
to renew my work.

This idle task on Sameter had suited me, so I had taken it
and closed the dossier after a swift and efficient investigation.
But latterly, as I prepared to leave, officials of the Munitorum
unexpectedly requested an audience.

I was staying with my associates in a suite of rooms in the
Urbitane Excelsior, a shabby but well-appointed establishment in the high-rise district of the city. Through soot-stained,
armoured roundels of glass twenty metres across, the suite
looked out across the filthy grey towers of the city to the
brackish waters of the polluted bay twenty kilometres away.
Ornithopters and biplanes buzzed between the massive city
structures, and the running lights of freighters and orbitals
glowed in the smog as they swung down towards the landing
port. Out on the isthmus, through a haze of yellow, stagnant

air, promethium refineries belched brown smoke into the perpetual twilight.

'They're here,' said Bequin, entering the suite's lounge from the outer lobby. She had dressed in a demure gown of blue damask and a silk pashmeena, perfectly in keeping with my instruction that we should present a muted but powerful image.

I myself was clad in a suit of soft black linen with a waistcoat of grey velvet and a hip length black leather storm-coat.

'Do you need me for this?' asked Midas Betancore, my pilot and confidant.

I shook my head. 'I don't intend to be delayed here. I just have to be polite. Go on to the landing port and make sure the gun-cutter's readied for departure.'

He nodded and left. Bequin showed the visitors in.

I had felt it necessary to be polite because Eskeen Hansaard, Urbitane's Minister of Security, had come to see me himself. He was a massive man in a double-breasted brown tunic, his big frame offset oddly by his finely featured, boyish face. He was escorted by two bodyguards in grey, armour-ribbed uniforms and a short but handsome, black-haired woman in a dark blue bodyglove.

I had made sure I was sitting in an armchair when Bequin showed them in so I could rise in a measured, respectful way. I wanted them to be in no doubt who was really in charge here.

'Minister Hansaard,' I said, shaking his hand. 'I am Inquisitor Gregor Eisenhorn of the Ordo Xenos. These are my associates Alizebeth Bequin, Arbites Chastener Godwyn Fischig and savant Uber Aemos. How may I help you?'

'I have no wish to waste your time, inquisitor,' he said, apparently nervous in my presence. That was good, just as I had intended it. 'A case has been brought to my attention that I believe is beyond the immediate purview of the city Arbites.

Frankly, it smacks of warp-corruption, and cries out for the attention of the Inquisition.'

He was direct. That impressed me. A ranking official of the Imperium, anxious to be seen to be doing the right thing. Nevertheless, I still expected his business might be a mere nothing, like the affair of the trade federation, a local crime requiring only my nod of approval that it was fine for him to continue and close. Men like Hansaard are often over-careful, in my experience.

'There have been four deaths in the city during the last month that we believe to be linked. I would appreciate your advice on them. They are connected by merit of the ritual mutilation involved.'

'Show me,' I said.

'Captain?' he responded.

Arbites Captain Hurlie Wrex was the handsome woman with the short black hair. She stepped forward, nodded respectfully, and gave me a data-slate with the gold crest of the Adeptus Arbites on it.

'I have prepared a digested summary of the facts,' she said.

I began to speed-read the slate, already preparing the gentle knock-back I was expecting to give to his case. Then I stopped, slowed, read back.

I felt a curious mix of elation and frustration. Even from this cursorial glance, there was no doubt this case required the immediate attention of the Imperial Inquisition. I could feel my instincts stiffen and my appetites whetten, for the first time in months. In bothering me with this, Minister Hansaard was not being over careful at all. At the same time, my heart sank with the realisation that my departure from this miserable city would be delayed.

* * *

All four victims had been blinded and had their noses, tongues and hands removed. At the very least.

The evangelist, Mombril, had been the only one found alive. He had died from his injuries eight minutes after arriving at Urbitane Mid-rise Sector Infirmary. It seemed to me likely that he had escaped his ritual tormentors somehow before they could finish their work.

The other three were a different story.

Poul Grevan, a machinesmith; Luthar Hewall, a rug-maker; Idilane Fasple, a mid-wife.

Hewall had been found a week before by city sanitation servitors during routine maintenance to a soil stack in the mid-rise district. Someone had attempted to burn his remains and then flush them into the city's ancient waste system, but the human body is remarkably durable. The post could not prove his missing body parts had not simply succumbed to decay and been flushed away, but the damage to the ends of the forearm bones seemed to speak convincingly of a saw or chain-blade.

When Idilane Fasple's body was recovered from a crawlspace under the roof of a mid-rise tenement hab, it threw more light on the extent of Hewall's injuries. Not only had Fasple been mutilated in the manner of the evangelist Mombril, but her brain, brainstem and heart had been excised. The injuries were hideous. One of the roof workers who discovered her had subsequently committed suicide. Her bloodless, almost dessicated body, dried out – smoked, if you will – by the tenement's heating vents, had been wrapped in a dark green cloth similar to the material of an Imperial Guard-issue bedroll and stapled to the underside of the rafters with an industrial nail gun.

Cross-reference between her and Hewall convinced the Arbites that the rug-maker had very probably suffered the removal of his brain stem and heart too. Until that point, they had ascribed the identifiable lack of those soft organs to the almost toxic levels of organic decay in the liquiescent filth of the soil stack.

Graven, actually the first victim found, had been dredged from the waters of the bay by salvage ship. He had been presumed to be a suicide dismembered by the screws of a passing boat until Wrex's careful cross-checking had flagged up too many points of similarity.

Because of the peculiar circumstances of their various post mortem locations, it was pathologically impossible to determine any exact date or time of death. But Wrex could be certain of a window. Graven had been last seen on the nineteenth of Aquiarae, three days before his body had been dredged up. Hewall had delivered a finished rug to a high-rise customer on the twenty-fourth, and had dined that same evening with friends at a charcute in mid-rise. Fasple had failed to report for work on the fifth of Sagittar, although the night before she had seemed happy and looking forward to her next shift, according to friends.

'I thought at first we might have a serial predator loose in mid-rise,' said Wrex. 'But the pattern of mutilation seems to me more extreme than that. This is not feral murder, or even psychopathic, post-slaying depravity. This is specific, purposeful ritual.'

'How do you arrive at that?' asked my colleague, Fischig. Fischig was a senior Arbites from Hubris, with plenty of experience in murder cases. Indeed, it was his fluency with procedure and familiarity with modus operandi that had convinced me to make him a part of my band. That, and his ferocious strength in a fight.

Wrex looked sidelong at him, as if he was questioning her ability.

'Because of the nature of the dismemberment. Because of the way the remains were disposed of.' She looked at me. 'In my experience, inquisitor, a serial killer secretly wants to be found, and certainly wants to be known. It will display its kills with wanton openness, declaring its power over the community. It thrives on the terror and fear it generates. Great efforts were made to hide these bodies. That suggest to me the killer was far more interested in the deaths themselves than in the reaction to the deaths.'

'Well put, captain,' I said. 'That has been my experience too. Cult killings are often hidden so that the cult can continue its work without fear of discovery.'

'Suggesting that there are other victims still to find...' said Bequin casually, a chilling prophecy as it now seems to me.

'Cult killings?' said the minister. 'I brought this to your attention because I feared as much, but do you really think–'

'On Alphex, the warp-cult removed their victims' hands and tongues because they were organs of communication,' Aemos began. 'On Brettaria, the brains were scooped out in order for the cult to ingest the spiritual matter – the anima, as you might say – of their prey. A number of other worlds have suffered cult predations where the eyes have been forfeit... Gulinglas, Pentari, Hesperus, Messina... windows of the soul, you see. The Heretics of Saint Scarif, in fact, severed their ritual victims' hands and then made them write out their last confessions using ink quills rammed into the stumps of–'

'Enough information, Aemos,' I said. The minister was looking pale.

'These are clearly cult killings, sir,' I said. 'There is a noxious cell of Chaos at liberty in your city. And I will find it.'

* * *

I went at once to the mid-rise district. Grevan, Hewall and Fasple had all been residents of that part of Urbitane, and Mombril, though a visitor to the metropolis, had been found there too. Aemos went to the Munitorum records spire in high-rise to search the local archives. I was particularly interested in historical cult activity on Sameter, and on date significance. Fischig, Bequin and Wrex accompanied me.

The genius loci of a place can often say much about the crimes committed therein. So far, my stay on Sameter had only introduced me to the cleaner, high-altitude regions of Urbitane's high-rise, up above the smog-cover.

Mid-rise was a dismal, wretched place of neglect and poverty. A tarry resin of pollution coated every surface, and acid rain poured down unremittingly. Raw-engined traffic crawled nose to tail down the poorly lit streets, and the very stone of the buildings seemed to be rotting. The smoggy darkness of mid-rise had a red, firelit quality, the backwash of the flares from giant gas processors. It reminded me of picture-slate engravings of the Inferno.

We stepped from Wrex's armoured speeder at the corner of Shearing Street and Pentecost. The captain pulled on her Arbites helmet and a quilted flak-coat. I began to wish for a hat of my own, or a rebreather mask. The rain stank like urine. Every thirty seconds or so an express flashed past on the elevated trackway, shaking the street.

'In here,' Wrex called, and led us through a shutter off the thoroughfare into the dank hallway of a tenement hab. Everything was stained with centuries of grime. The heating had been set too high, perhaps to combat the murky wetness outside, but the result was simply an overwhelming humidity and a smell like the fur of a mangy canine.

This was Idilane Fasple's last resting place. She'd been found in the roof.

'Where did she live?' asked Fischig.

'Two streets away. She had a parlour on one of the old court-habs.'

'Hewall?'

'His hab about a kilometre west. His remains were found five blocks east.'

I looked at the data-slate. The tannery where Mombril had been found was less than thirty minutes' walk from here, and Graven's home a short tram ride. The only thing that broke the geographical focus of these lives and deaths was the fact that Graven had been dumped in the bay.

'I hasn't escaped my notice that they all inhabited a remarkably specific area,' Wrex smiled.

'I never thought it had. But "remarkably" is the word. It isn't just the same quarter or district. It's a intensely close network of streets, a neighbourhood.'

'Suggesting?' asked Bequin.

'The killer or killers are local too,' said Fischig.

'Or someone from elsewhere has a particular hatred of this neighbourhood and comes into it to do his or her killing,' said Wrex.

'Like a hunting ground?' noted Fischig.

I nodded. Both possibilities had merit.

'Look around,' I told Fischig and Bequin, well aware that Wrex's officers had already been all over the building. But she said nothing. Our expert appraisal might turn up something different.

I found a small office at the end of the entrance hall. It was clearly the cubbyhole of the habitat's superintendent. Sheaves of paper were pinned to the flak-board wall: rental dockets, maintenances rosters, notes of resident complaints. There was a box-tray of lost property, a partially disassembled mini-servitor in a tub of oil, a stale stink of cheap liquor. A faded ribbon and paper rosette from an Imperial shrine was pinned over the door with a regimental rank stud.

'What you doing in here?'

I looked round. The superintendent was a middle-aged man in a dirty overall suit. Details. I always look for details. The gold signet ring with the wheatear symbol. The row of permanent metal sutures closing the scar on his scalp where the hair had never grown back. The prematurely weathered skin. The guarded look in his eyes.

I told him who I was and he didn't seem impressed. Then I asked him who he was and he said 'The super. What you doing in here?'

I use my will sparingly. The psychic gift sometimes closes as many doors as it opens. But there was something about this man. He needed a jolt. 'What is your name?' I asked, modulating my voice to carry the full weight of the psychic probe.

He rocked backwards, and his pupils dilated in surprise.

'Quater Traves,' he mumbled.

'Did you know the midwife Fasple?'

'I sin her around.'

'To speak to?'

He shook his head. His eyes never left mine.

'Did she have friends?'

He shrugged.

'What about strangers? Anyone been hanging around the hab?'

His eyes narrowed. A sullen, mocking look, as if I hadn't seen the streets outside.

'Who has access to the roofspace where her body was found?'

'Ain't nobody bin up there. Not since the place bin built. Then the heating packs in and the contractors has to break through the roof to get up there. They found her.'

'There isn't a hatch?'

'Shutter. Locked, and no one has a key. Easier to go through the plasterboard.'

Outside, we sheltered from the rain under the elevated railway.

'That's what Traves told me too,' Wrex confirmed. 'No one had been into the roof for years until the contractors broke their way in.'

'Someone had. Someone with the keys to the shutter. The killer.'

The soil stack where Hewall had been found was behind a row of commercial properties built into an ancient skin of scaffolding that cased the outside of a toolfitters' workshop like a cobweb. There was what seemed to be a bar two stages up, where a neon signed flicked between an Imperial aquila and a fleur-de-lys. Fischig and Wrex continued up to the next scaffolding level to peer in through the stained windows of the habs there. Bequin and I went into the bar.

The light was grey inside. At a high bar, four or five drinkers sat on ratchet-stools and ignored us. The scent of obscura smoke was in the air.

There was a woman behind the counter who took exception to us from the moment we came in. She was in her forties, with a powerful, almost masculine build. Her vest was cut off at the armpits and her arms were as muscular as Fischig's. There was the small tattoo of a skull and crossbones on her bicep. The skin of her face was weathered and coarse.

'Help you?' she asked, wiping the counter with a glass-cloth. As she did so I saw that her right arm, from the elbow down, was a prosthetic.

'Information,' I said.

She flicked her cloth at the row of bottles on the shelves behind her.

'Not a brand I know.'

'You know a man called Hewall?'

'No.'

'The guy they found in the waste pipes behind here.'

'Oh. Didn't know he had a name.'

Now I was closer I could see the tattoo on her arm wasn't a skull and crossbones. It was a wheatear.

'We all have names. What's yours?'

'Omin Lund.'

'You live around here?'

'Live is too strong a word.' She turned away to serve someone else.

'Scary bitch,' said Bequin as we went outside. 'Everyone acts like they've got something to hide.'

'Everyone does, even if it's simply how much they hate this town.'

The heart had gone out of Urbitane, out of Sameter itself, about seventy years before. The mill-hives of Thracian Primaris eclipsed Sameter's production, and export profits fell away. In an effort to compete, the authorities freed the refineries to escalate production by stripping away the legal restrictions on atmospheric pollution levels. For hundreds of years, Urbitane had had problems controlling its smog and air-pollutants. For the last few decades, it hadn't bothered any more.

My vox-earplug chimed. It was Aemos.

'What have you found?'

'It's most perturbatory. Sameter has been clear of taint for a goodly while. The last Inquisitorial investigation was

thirty-one years ago standard, and that wasn't here in Urbitane but in Aquitane, the capital. A rogue psyker. The planet
has its fair share of criminal activity, usually narcotics traffick-
ing and the consequential mob-fighting. But nothing really
markedly heretical.'

'Nothing with similarities to the ritual methods?'

'No, and I've gone back two centuries.'

'What about the dates?'

'Sagittar thirteenth is just shy of the solstice, but I can't make
any meaning out of that. The Purge of the Sarpetal Hives is
usually commemorated by upswings of cult activity in the
subsector, but that's six weeks away. The only other thing I
can find is that this Sagittar fifth was the twenty-first anniversary of the Battle of Klodeshi Heights.'

'I don't know it.'

'The sixth of seven full-scale engagements during the sixteen month Imperial campaign on Surealis Six.'

'Surealis... that's in the next damn subsector! Aemos, every
day of the year is the anniversary of an Imperial action somewhere. What connection are you making?'

'The Ninth Sameter Infantry saw service in the war on
Surealis.'

Fischig and Wrex had rejoined us from their prowl around
the upper stages of the scaffolding. Wrex was talking on her
own vox-set.

She signed off and looked at me, rain drizzling off her visor.

'They've found another one, inquisitor,' she said.

It wasn't one. It was three, and their discovery threw the
affair wide open. An old warehouse in the mill zone, ten
streets away from Fasple's hab, had been damaged by fire
two months before, and now the municipal work-crews had

moved in to tear it down and reuse the lot as a site for cheap,
prefab habitat blocks. They'd found the bodies behind the
wall insulation in a mouldering section untouched by the
fire. A woman and two men, systematically mutilated in the
manner of the other victims.

But these were much older. I could tell that even at a glance.

I crunched across the debris littering the floorspace of the
warehouse shell. Rain streamed in through the roof holes,
illuminated as a blizzard of white specks by the cold blue
beams of the Arbites' floodlights shining into the place.

Arbites officers were all around, but they hadn't touched
the discovery itself.

Mummified and shrivelled, these foetally curled, pitiful
husks had been in the wall a long time.

'What's that?' I asked.

Fischig leaned forward for a closer look. 'Adhesive tape,
wrapped around them to hold them against the partition.
Old. The gum's decayed.'

'That pattern on it. The silver flecks.'

'I think it's military issue stuff. Matt-silver coating, you know
the sort? The coating's coming off with age.'

'These bodies are different ages,' I said.

'I thought so too,' said Fischig.

We had to wait six hours for a preliminary report from the
district Examiner Medicae, but it confirmed our guess. All
three bodies had been in the wall for at least eight years, and
then for different lengths of time. Decompositional anomalies showed that one of the males had been in position for
as much as twelve years, the other two added subsequently,
at different occasions. No identifications had yet been made.

'The warehouse was last used six years ago,' Wrex told me.

'I want a roster of workers employed there before it went out of business.'

Someone using the same m.o. and the same spools of adhesive tape had hidden bodies there over a period of years.

The disused tannery where poor Mombril had been found stood at the junction between Xerxes Street and a row of slum tenements known as the Pilings. It was a fetid place, with the stink of the lye and coroscutum used in the tanning process still pungent in the air. No amount of acid rain could wash that smell out.

There were no stairs. Fischig, Bequin and I climbed up to the roof via a metal fire-ladder.

'How long does a man survive mutilated like that?'

'From the severed wrists alone, he'd bleed out in twenty minutes, perhaps,' Fischig estimated. 'Clearly, if he had made an escape, he'd have the adrenalin of terror sustaining him a little.'

'So when he was found up here, he can have been no more than twenty minutes from the scene of his brutalisation.'

We looked around. The wretched city looked back at us, close packed and dense. There were hundreds of possibilities. It might take days to search them all.

But we could narrow it down. 'How did he get on the roof?' I asked.

'I was wondering that,' said Fischig.

'The ladder we came up by...' Bequin trailed off as she realised her gaffe.

'Without hands?' Fischig smirked.

'Or sight,' I finished. 'Perhaps he didn't escape. Perhaps his abusers put him here.'

'Or perhaps he fell,' Bequin said, pointing.

The back of a tall warehouse over-shadowed the tannery to the east. Ten metres up there were shattered windows.

'If he was in there somewhere, fled blindly, and fell through onto this roof...'

'Well reasoned, Alizebeth,' I said.

The Arbites had done decent work, but not even Wrex had thought to consider this inconsistency.

We went round to the side entrance of the warehouse. The battered metal shutters were locked. A notice pasted to the wall told would-be intruders to stay out of the property of Hundlemas Agricultural Stowage.

I took out my multi-key and disengaged the padlock. I saw Fischig had drawn his sidearm.

'What's the matter?'

'I had a feeling just then... like we were being watched.'

We went inside. The air was cold and still and smelled of chemicals. Rows of storage vats filled with chemical fertilisers lined the echoing warehall.

The second floor was bare-boarded and hadn't been used in years. Wiremesh had been stapled over a doorway to the next floor, and rainwater dripped down. Fischig pulled at the mesh. It was cosmetic only, and folded aside neatly.

Now I drew my autopistol too.

On the street side of the third floor, which was divided into smaller rooms, we found a chamber ten metres by ten, on the floor of which was spread a sheet of plastic smeared with old blood and other organic deposits. There was a stink of fear.

'This is where they did him,' Fischig said with certainty.

'No sign of cult markings or Chaos symbology,' I mused.

'Maybe not,' said Bequin, crossing the room, being careful not to step on the smeared plastic sheet. For the sake of her shoes, not the crime scene, I was sure. 'What's this? Something was hung here.'

Two rusty hooks in the wall, scraped enough to show something had been hanging there recently. On the floor below was a curious cross drawn in yellow chalk.

'I've seen that before somewhere,' I said. My vox bleeped. It was Wrex.

'I've got that worker roster you asked for.'

'Good. Where are you?'

'Coming to find you at the tannery, if you're still there.'

'We'll meet you on the corner of Xerxes Street. Tell your staff we have a crime scene here in the agricultural warehouse.'

We walked out of the killing room towards the stairwell.

Fischig froze, and brought up his gun.

'Again?' I whispered.

He nodded, and pushed Bequin into the cover of a door jamb.

Silence, apart from the rain and the scurry of vermin. Gun braced, Fischig looked up at the derelict roof. It may have been my imagination, but it seemed as if a shadow had moved across the bare rafters.

I moved forward, scanning the shadows with my pistol.

Something creaked. A floorboard.

Fischig pointed to the stairs. I nodded I understood, but the last thing I wanted was a mistaken shooting. I carefully keyed my vox and whispered, 'Wrex. You're not coming into the warehouse to find us, are you?'

'Negative, inquisitor.'

'Standby.'

Fischig had reached the top of the staircase. He peered down, aiming his weapon.

Las fire erupted through the floorboards next to him and he threw himself flat.

I put a trio of shots into the mouth of the staircase, but my angle was bad.

Two hard round shots spat back up the stairs and then the roar and flash of the las came again, raking the floor.

From above, I realised belatedly. Whoever was on the stairs had a hard-slug side arm, but the las fire was coming down from the roof.

I heard steps running on the floor below. Fischig scrambled up to give chase but another salvo of las fire sent him ducking again.

I raised my aim and fired up into the roof tiles, blowing out holes through which the pale light poked.

Something slithered and scrambled on the roof.

Fischig was on the stairs now, running after the second assailant.

I hurried across the third floor, following the sounds of the man on the roof.

I saw a silhouette against the sky through a hole in the tiles and fired again. Las-fire replied in a bright burst, but then there was a thump and further slithering.

'Cease fire! Give yourself up! Inquisition!' I bellowed, using the will.

There came a much more substantial crash sounding like a whole portion of the roof had come down. Tiles avalanched down and smashed in a room nearby.

I slammed into the doorway, gun aimed, about to yell out a further will command. But there was no one in the room. Piles of shattered roofslates and bricks covered the floor beneath a gaping hole in the roof itself, and a battered lasrifle lay amongst the debris. On the far side of the room were some of the broken windows that Bequin had pointed out as overlooking the tannery roof.

I ran to one. Down below, a powerful figure in dark over-alls was running for cover. The killer, escaping from me in just the same way his last victim had escaped him – through the windows onto the tannery roof.

The distance was too far to use the will again with any effect, but my aim and angle were good. I lined up on the back of the head a second before it disappeared, began to apply pressure – and the world exploded behind me.

I came round cradled in Bequin's arms. 'Don't move, Eisen-horn. The medics are coming.'

'What happened?' I asked.

'Booby trap. The gun that guy left behind? It exploded behind you. Powercell overload.'

'Did Fischig get his man?'

'Of course he did.'

He hadn't, in fact. He'd chased the man hard down two flights of stairs and through the main floor of the warehall. At the outer door onto the street, the man had wheeled around and emptied his autopistol's clip at the chastener, forcing him into cover.

Then Captain Wrex, approaching from outside, had gunned the man down in the doorway.

We assembled in Wrex's crowded office in the busy Arbites Mid-Rise Sector-house. Aemos joined us, laden down with papers and data-slates, and brought Midas Betancore with him.

'You all right?' Midas asked me. In his jacket of embroi-dered cerise silk, he was a vivid splash of colour in the muted gloom of mid-rise.

'Minor abrasions. I'm fine.'

'I thought we were leaving, and here you are having all the fun without me.'

'I thought we were leaving too until I saw this case. Review Bequin's notes. I need you up to speed.'

Aemos shuffled his ancient, augmetically assisted bulk over to Wrex's desk and dropped his books and papers in an unceremonious pile.

'I've been busy,' he said.

'Busy with results?' Bequin asked.

He looked at her sourly. 'No, actually. But I have gathered a commendable resource of information. As the discussion advances, I may be able to fill in blanks.'

'No results, Aemos? Most perturbatory,' grinned Midas, his white teeth gleaming against his dark skin. He was mocking the old savant by using Aemos's favourite phrase.

I had before me the work roster of the warehouse where the three bodies had been found, and another for the agricultural store where our fight had occurred. Quick comparison brought up two coincident names.

'Brell Sodakis. Vim Venik. Both worked as warehousemen before the place closed down. Now they're employed by Hundlemas Agricultural Stowage.'

'Backgrounds? Addresses?' I asked Wrex.

'I'll run checks,' she said.

'So... we have a cult here, eh?' Midas asked. 'You've got a series of ritual killings, at least one murder site, and now the names of two possible cultists.'

'Perhaps.' I wasn't convinced. There seemed both more and less to this than had first appeared. Inquisitorial hunch.

The remains of the lasrifle discarded by my assailant lay on an evidence tray. Even with the damage done by the overloading powercell, it was apparent that this was an old model.

'Did the powercell overload because it was dropped? It fell through the roof, didn't it?' Bequin asked.

'They're pretty solid,' Fischig answered.

'Forced overload,' I said. 'An old Imperial Guard trick. I've heard they learn how to set one off. As a last ditch in tight spots. Cornered. About to die anyway.'

'That's not standard,' said Fischig, poking at the trigger guard of the twisted weapon. His knowledge of guns was sometimes unseemly. 'See this modification? It's been machine-tooled to widen the guard around the trigger.'

'Why?' I asked.

Fischig shrugged. 'Access? For an augmetic hand with rudimentary digits?'

We went through to a morgue room down the hall where the man Wrex had gunned down was lying on a slab. He was middle-aged, with a powerful frame going to seed. His skin was weatherbeaten and lined.

'Identity?'

'We're working on it.'

The body had been stripped by the morgue attendants. Fischig scrutinised it, rolling it with Wrex's help to study the back. The man's clothes and effects were in plasteen bags in a tray at his feet. I lifted the bag of effects and held it up to the light.

'Tattoo,' reported Fischig. 'Imperial eagle, left shoulder. Crude, old. Letters underneath it... capital S period, capital I period, capital I, capital X.'

I'd just found the signet ring in the bag. Gold, with a wheatear motif.

'S.I. IX,' said Aemos. 'Sameter Infantry Nine.'

The Ninth Sameter Infantry had been founded in Urbitane twenty-three years before, and had served, as Aemos had already told me, in the brutal liberation war on Surealis Six. According to city records, five hundred and nineteen veterans of that war and that regiment had been repatriated to Sameter after mustering out thirteen years ago, coming back from the horrors of war to an increasingly depressed world beset by the blight of poverty and urban collapse. Their regimental emblem, as befitted a world once dominated by agriculture, was the wheatear.

'They came back thirteen years ago. The oldest victim we have dates from that time,' said Fischig.

'Surealis Six was a hard campaign, wasn't it?' I asked.

Aemos nodded. 'The enemy was dug in. It was ferocious, brutal. Brutalising. And the climate. Two white dwarf suns, no cloud cover. The most punishing heat and light, not to mention ultraviolet burning.'

'Ruins the skin,' I murmured. 'Makes it weatherbeaten and prematurely aged.'

Everyone looked at the taut, lined face of the body on the slab.

'I'll get a list of the veterans,' volunteered Wrex.

'I already have one,' said Aemos.

'I'm betting you find the names Brell Sodakis and Vim Venik on it,' I said.

Aemos paused as he scanned. 'I do,' he agreed.

'What about Quater Traves?'

'Yes, he's here. Master Gunnery Sergeant Quater Traves.'

'What about Omin Lund?'

'Ummm... yes. Sniper first class. Invalided out of service.'

'The Sameter Ninth were a mixed unit, then?' asked Bequin.

'All our Guard foundings are,' Wrex said proudly.

'So, these men... and women...' Midas mused. 'Soldiers, been through hell. Fighting the corruption... your idea is they brought it back here with them? Some taint? You think they were infected by the touch of the warp on Surealis and have been ritually killing as a way of worship back here ever since?'

'No,' I said. 'I think they're still fighting the war.'

It remains a sad truth of the Imperium that no virtually no veteran ever comes back from fighting its wars intact. Combat alone shreds nerves and shatters bodies. But the horrors of the warp, and of foul xenos forms like the tyranid, steal sanity forever, and leave veterans fearing the shadows, and the night and, sometimes, the nature of their friends and neighbours, for the rest of their lives.

The guards of the Ninth Sameter Infantry had come home thirteen years before, broke by a savage war against mankind's arch-enemy and, through their scars and their fear, brought their war back with them.

The Arbites mounted raids at once on the addresses of all the veterans on the list, those that could be traced, those that were still alive. It appeared that skin cancer had taken over two hundred of them in the years since their repatriation. Surealis had claimed them as surely as if they had fallen there in combat.

A number were rounded up. Bewildered drunks, cripples, addicts, a few honest men and women trying diligently to carry on with their lives. For those latter I felt especially sorry.

But about seventy could not be traced. Many may well have disappeared, moved on, or died without it coming to the attention of the authorities. But some had clearly fled. Lund, Traves, Sodakis, Venik for starters. Their habs were found abandoned, strewn with possessions as if the occupant had left in a hurry. So were the habs of twenty more belonging to names on the list.

The Arbites arrived at the hab of one, ex-corporal Geffin Sancto, in time to catch him in the act of flight. Sancto had been a flamer operator in the guard, and like so many of his kind, had managed to keep his weapon as a memento. Screaming the battlecry of the Sameter Ninth, he torched four Arbites in the stairwell of his building before the tactical squads of the judiciary vaporised him in a hail of gunshots.

'Why are they killing?' Bequin asked me. 'All these years, in secret ritual?'

'I don't know.'

'You do, Eisenhorn. You so do!'

'Very well. I can guess. The fellow worker who jokes at the Emperor's expense and makes your fragile sanity imagine he is tainted with the warp. The rug-maker whose patterns suggest to you the secret encoding of Chaos symbols. The midwife you decide is spawning the offspring of the arch-enemy in the mid-rise maternity hall. The travelling evangelist who seems just too damn fired up to be safe.'

She looked down at the floor of the land speeder. 'They see daemons everywhere.'

'In everything. In every one. And, so help them, they believe they are doing the Emperor's work by killing. They trust no one, so they daren't alert the authorities. They take the eyes, the hands and the tongue... all the organs of communication, any way the arch-enemy might transmit his foul lies. And then they destroy the brain and heart, the organs which common soldier myth declares must harbour daemons.'

'So where are we going now?' she asked.

'Another hunch.'

* * *

The Guildhall of the Sameter Agricultural Fraternity was a massive ragstone building on Furnace Street, its facade decaying from the ministrations of smog and acid rain. It had been disused for over two decades.

Its last duty had been to serve as a recruitment post of the Sameter Ninth during the founding. In its long hallways, the men and women of the Ninth had signed their names, collected their starchy new fatigues, and pledged their battle oath to the God-Emperor of mankind.

At certain times, under certain circumstances, when a proper altar to the Emperor is not available, guard officers improvise in order to conduct their ceremonies. An Imperial eagle, an aquila standard, is suspended from a wall, and a sacred spot is marked on the floor beneath in yellow chalk.

The guildhall was not a consecrated building. The founding must have been the first time the young volunteers of Urbitane had seen that done. They'd made their vows to a yellow chalk cross and a dangling aquila.

Wrex was leading three fireteams of armed Arbites, but I went in with Midas and Fischig first, quietly. Bequin and Aemos stayed by our vehicle.

Midas was carrying his matched needle pistols, and Fischig an auto shotgun. I clipped a slab-pattern magazine full of fresh rounds into the precious bolt pistol given to me by Librarian Brytnoth of the Adeptus Astartes Deathwatch chapter.

We pushed open the boarded doors of the decaying structure and edged down the dank corridors. Rainwater pattered from the roof and the marble floor was spotted and eaten by collected acid.

We could hear the singing. A couple of dozen voices voicing up the Battle Hymn of the Golden Throne.

I led my companions forward, hunched low. Through the crazed windows of an inner door we looked through into the main hall. Twenty-three dishevelled veterans in ragged clothes were knelt down in ranks on the filthy floor, their heads bowed to the rusty Imperial eagle hanging on the wall as they sang. There was a yellow chalk cross on the floor under the aquila. Each veteran had a backpack or rucksack and a weapon by their feet.

My heart ached. This was how it had gone over two decades before, when they came to the service, young and fresh and eager. Before the war. Before the horror.

'Let me try... try to give them a chance,' I said.

'Gregor!' Midas hissed.

'Let me try, for their sake. Cover me.'

I slipped into the back of the hall, my gun lowered at my side, and joined in the verse.

One by one, the voices died away and bowed heads turned sideways to look at me. Down the aisle, at the chalk cross of the altar, Lund, Traves and a bearded man I didn't know stood gazing at me.

In the absence of other voices, I finished the hymn.

'It's over,' I said. 'The war is over and you have all done your duty. Above and beyond the call.'

Silence.

'I am Inquisitor Eisenhorn. I'm here to relieve you. The careful war against the blight of Chaos that you have waged through Urbitane in secret is now over. The Inquisition is here to take over. You can stand down.'

Two or three of the hunched veterans began to weep.

'You lie,' said Lund, stepping forward.

'I do not. Surrender your weapons and I promise you will be treated fairly and with respect.'

'Will... will we get medals?' the bearded man asked, in a quavering voice.

'The gratitude of the God-Emperor will be with you always.'

More were weeping now. Out of fear, anxiety or plain relief.

'Don't trust him!' said Traves. 'It's another trick!'

'I saw you in my bar,' said Lund, stepping forward. 'You came in looking.' Her voice was empty, distant.

'I saw you on the tannery roof, Omin Lund. You're still a fine shot, despite the hand.'

She looked down at her prosthetic with a wince of shame.

'Will we get medals?' the bearded man repeated, eagerly.

Traves turned on him. 'Of course we won't, Spake, you cretin! He's here to kill us!'

'I'm not–' I began.

'I want medals!' the bearded man, Spake, screamed suddenly, sliding his laspistol up from his belt with the fluid speed only a trained soldier can manage.

I had no choice.

His shot tore through the shoulder padding of my storm coat. My bolt exploded his head, spraying blood across the rusty metal eagle on the wall.

Pandemonium.

The veterans leapt to their feet firing wildly, scattering, running.

I threw myself flat as shots tore out the wall plaster behind me. At some point Fischig and Midas burst in, weapons blazing. I saw three or four veterans drop, sliced through by silent needles and another six tumble as shotgun rounds blew them apart.

Traves came down the aisle, blasting his old service-issue lasrifle at me. I rolled and fired, but my shot went wide. His face distorted as a needle round punched through it and he fell in a crumpled heap.

Wrex and her fireteams exploded in. Flames from some spilled accelerants billowed up the wall.

I got up, and then was throw back by a las shot that blew off my left hand.

Spinning, falling, I saw Lund, struggling to make her prosthetic fingers work the unmodified trigger of Traves's lasgun.

My bolt round hit her with such force she flew back down the aisle, hit the wall, and tore the Imperial aquila down.

Not a single veteran escaped the Guildhall alive. The firefight raged for two hours. Wrex lost five men to the experienced guns of the Sameter Ninth veterans. They stood to the last. No more can be said of any Imperial Guard unit.

The whole affair left me sour and troubled. I have devoted my life to the service of the Imperium, to protect it against its manifold foes, inside and out.

But not against its servants. However misguided, they were loyal and true. However wrong, they were shaped that way by the service they had endured in the Emperor's name.

Lund cost me my hand. A hand for a hand. They gave me a prosthetic on Sameter. I never used it. For two years, I made do with a fused stump. Surgeons on Messina finally gave me a fully functional graft.

I consider it still a small price to pay for them.

I have never been back to Sameter. Even today, they are still finding the secreted, hidden bodies. So very many, dead in the Emperor's name.

MALLEUS

BY ORDER OF HIS MOST HOLY MAJESTY
THE GOD-EMPEROR OF TERRA

SEQUESTERED INQUISITORIAL DOSSIERS
AUTHORISED PERSONS ONLY

CASE FILE 442:41F:JL3:Kbu

Please enter your authority code > ●●●●●●●●●●●●●●

Validating...

Thank you, Inquisitor.

You may proceed.

CLASSIFICATION: *Primary Level Intelligence*
CLEARANCE: *Obsidian*
ENCRYPTION: *Cryptox v 2.6*
DATE: *337.M41*
AUTHOR: *Inquisitor Javes Thysser, Ordo Xenos*
SUBJECT: *A matter for your urgent consideration*
RECIPIENT: *Lord Inquisitor Phlebas Alessandro Rorken, Inquisition High Council Officio, Scarus Sector, Scarus Major*

Salutations, lord!

In the name of the God-Emperor, hallowed be his eternal vigil, and by the High Lords of Terra, I commend myself, your Highness, and hope I may speak plainly, in confidence, of a delicate matter.

To begin generally, my work on Vogel Passionata is now complete and my noble duty to the Great Inquisition of Mankind discharged successfully. My full, documented report will follow in a few days, once my savants have finished compiling it, and I trust that your Highness will find it satisfactory reading. To summarise, for the purpose of this brief missive, I am proud to declare that the malign influence of the so-called wyrd-kin has been expunged from the hive cities of Vogel Passionata, and the inner circle of that obscene xenophile order broken forever and put to cleansing flame. Their self-proclaimed messiah, Gaethon Richter, is himself dead by my hand.

A matter, however, has arisen from this. I am troubled by it, and unsure as to the best course of action. For this reason I am writing to you, Highness, in the hope of receiving guidance.

Richter did not go without a fight, as you might expect. In the final, bloody throes of the battle, as my combined forces stormed his fastness beneath the main hive, he called forth to oppose us a being of dreadful power. It slaughtered nineteen of the Imperial Guardsmen assigned to my purge-team, as well as Inquisitor Bluchas, Interrogators Faruline and Seetmol, and Captain Ellen Ossel, my pilot. It would have slain me too, but for the strangest mischance.

The being was an unholy thing, made like a man, but gleaming with an inner light. Its voice was soft, its touch was fire. I believe it was a daemonhost of unfathomable power, with the most vile propensity for spite and cruelty. My report will recount in detail the particular abominations this being subjected Seetmol and Ossel to before it destroyed them. I will spare you those dreadful facts here.

Having disposed of Bluchas, it cornered me on an upper landing in the fastness as I was penetrating the inner sanctum of the wyrd-kin 'messiah.' My weapons did no harm to it, and it laughed gleefully as it threw me backwards down the length of the staircase with a casual flick of its wrist.

Dazed, I looked up as it descended towards me, unable to conceive of a defence against it. I believe I may have clawed around to find my fallen weapon.

That gesture caused it to speak. I report the words exactly. It said, 'Don't worry now, Gregor. You are far too valuable to waste. Indulge me, just a little scar to make it look authentic.'

Its talons tore across my chest and throat, and ripped away my rebreather mask. The wounds will heal, they tell me, but they were deep and excruciating. The being then paused, as it saw my face properly for the first time, free from the mask set. Dreadful dark anger flared in its eyes. It said – forgive me, Highness, but this is the fact of it – it said, 'You are not Eisenhorn! I have been tricked!'

I believe that it would have killed me there and then, but for the frontal assault of the Adeptes Astartes Aurora Chapter, which tore into the hall at that precise moment. In the mayhem,

44 DAN ABNETT

the being fled, though I cannot even now say how. Whatever the terrifying strength of the Adeptus Astartes, this thing was a hundredfold more powerful.

Later, on his knees, with my weapon to his head, seconds before his execution, Gaethon Richter begged for 'Cherubael' to return. He wailed he could not understand why 'Cherubael' had abandoned him. I believe he was speaking of the daemonhost.

I trust your Highness can see my trouble. Mistaking me for another of our kind – and an unimpeachably worthy example, I might add – this thing spared my life. It seemed to me, indeed, that it did so with pre-arranged connivance.

Inquisitor Gregor Eisenhorn is highly regarded, numerously honoured and justly praised as an example of all that is good, strong and dogmatic about our brotherhood. However, since this circumstance, I have begun to wonder, to fear that–

I feel I cannot say what I wonder or fear. But I thought you should know of this, and know it soon. It is my belief that the Ordo Malleus should be informed, if only as a precaution.

I hope and pray this matter will be found empty of truth and consequence. But, as you taught me, sir, it is always better to be sure.

Sealed as my true word by this, my hand, this 276th day of the year 337.M41.

The Emperor Protects!
Your servant,

Thysser

[Message ends.]

ONE

I discover I am dead
Under dark fire, the lair of Sadia
Tantalid, unwelcome

As I grow older, may the Emperor protect me, I find I measure my history in terms of milestones, those occurrences of such intense moment they will never pass from one's memory: my induction into the blessed ordos of the Inquisition; my first day as a neophyte assigned to the great Hapshant; my first successful prosecution; the heretic Lemete Syre; my elevation to full Inquisitorial rank at the age of twenty-four standard years; the long-drawn out Nassar case; the affair of the Necroteuch; the P'glao Conspiracy.

Milestones, all of them. Marked indelibly onto the engrams of my memory. And, alongside them, I remember the Darknight that came at the end of the month of Umbris, Imperial year 338.M41, with particular clarity. For that bloody end was the start of it. The great milestone of my life.

I was on Lethe Eleven under instruction from the Ordo Xenos, deep in work, with the accursed xenophile Beldame

Sadia almost in my grasp. Ten weeks to find her, ten hours to close the trap. I had been without sleep for three days; without food and water for two. Psychic phantoms triggered by the Darknight eclipse were roiling my mind. I was dying of binary poison. Then Tantalid turned up.

To appraise you, Lethe Eleven is a densely populated world at the leading edge of the Helican sub-sector, its chief industries being metalwork and shield technologies. At the end of every Umbris, Lethe's largest moon matches, by some cosmological coincidence, the path, orbit and comparative size of the local star, and the world is plunged into eclipse for a two week period known as the Darknight.

The effect is quite striking. For the space of fourteen days, the sky goes a cold, dark red, the hue of dried blood, and the moon, Kux, dominates the heavens, a peerlessly black orb surrounded by a crackling corona of writhing amber flame. This event has become – students of Imperial ritual will be unsurprised to learn – the key seasonal holiday for all Letheans. Fires of all shape, size and manner are lit as Darknight begins, and the population stands vigil to ensure that none go out until the eclipse ends. Industry is suspended. Leave is granted. Riotous carnivals and firelit parades spill through the cities. Licentiousness and law-breaking are rife.

Above it all, the dark fire of the eclipsed sun haloes the black moon. There is even a tradition of fortune-casting grown up around the interpretation of the corona's form.

I had hoped to catch the Beldame before Darknight began, but she was one step ahead of me. Her chief poisoner, Pye, who had learned his skills in early life as a prisoner of the renegade dark eldar, so the story went, managed to plant a toxin in my drinking water that would remain inert until I ingested the second component of its binary action.

I was a dead man. The Beldame had killed me.

My savant, Aemos, accidentally discovered the toxin in my body, and was able to prevent me from eating or drinking anything further. But graceless death beckoned me inexorably. My only chance of survival was to capture the Beldame and her vassal Pye and extract the solution to my doom from them.

Out in the dark streets of the city, my followers did their work. I had eighty loyal servants scouring the streets. In my rooms at the Hippodrome, I waited, parched, unsteady, distant.

Ravenor came up trumps. Ravenor, of course. With his promise, it wouldn't be long before he left the rank of interrogator behind and became a full inquisitor in his own right.

He found Beldame Sadia's lair in the catacombs beneath the derelict church of Saint Kiodrus. I hurried to respond to his call.

'You should stay here,' Bequin told me, but I shook her off.

'I have to do this, Alizebeth.'

Alizebeth Bequin was by that time one hundred and twenty-five years old. She was still as beautiful and as active as she had been in her thirties, thanks to discreet augmetic surgery and a regime of juvenat-drugs. Framed by the veil of her starch-silk dress, her handsome face and dark eyes glared at me.

'It will kill you, Gregor,' she said.

'If it does, then it is time for Gregor Eisenhorn to die.'

Bequin looked across the gloomy, candlelit room at Aemos, but he simply shook his ancient, augmented skull sadly. There were times, he knew, when there was simply no reasoning with me.

I went down into the street, where canister fires blazed and masked revellers capered and caroused. I was dressed all in black, with a floor length coat of heavy black leather.

Despite that, despite the flames around me, I was cold. Fatigue, and the lack of nourishment, were eating into my bones.

I looked at the moon. Threads of heat around a cold, black heart. Like me, I thought, like me.

A carriage had been called for. Six painted hippines, snorting and bridled, teamed to a stately landau. Several members of my staff waited nearby, and hurried forward when they saw me emerge onto the street.

I assessed them quickly. Good people all, or they wouldn't have made the cut to be here. With a few wordless gestures I pulled out four to accompany me and then sent the rest back to other duties.

The four chosen mounted the carriage with me. Mescher Qus, an ex-Imperial Guardsman from Vladislav; Arianrhod Esw Sweydyr, the swordswoman from Carthae; and Beronice and Zu Zeng, two females from Bequin's Distaff.

At the last moment, Beronice was ordered out of the carriage and Alizebeth Bequin took her place. Bequin had quit active service with me sixty-eight standard years before in order to develop and run her Distaff, but there were still times she didn't trust her people and insisted on accompanying me herself.

I realised this was just such a time because Bequin didn't expect me to survive and wanted to be with me to the end. In truth, I didn't expect to survive either.

The carriage started off with a whipcrack, and we rumbled through the streets, skirting around ceremonial fires and torchlit processions.

None of us spoke. Qus checked and loaded his autocannon and adjusted his body armour. Arianrhod drew her sabre and tested the cutting edge with one of her own head hairs.

Zu Zeng, a native of Vitria, sat with her head down, her long glass robes clinking with the carriage's motion.

Bequin stared at me.

'What?' I asked eventually.

She shook her head and looked away.

The church of Saint Kiodrus lay in the waterfowlers' district, close to the edge of the city and the vast, lizard-haunted salt-licks. The darkness throbbed with insect rhythms.

The carriage stopped in a street of blackly rotting stone pilings, two hundred metres short of the church's wrecked silhouette. The sky was amber darkness. Behind us, the city was alive with bright points of fire. The neighbourhood around us was a dead ruin, slowly submitting to the salty hunger of the marshes.

'Talon wishes Thorn, rapturous beasts within,' Ravenor said over the vox-link.

'Thorn impinging multifarious, the blades of disguise,' I responded. My throat was dry and hoarse.

'Talon observes moment. Torus pathway requested, pattern ebony.'

'Pattern denied. Pattern crucible. Rose thorn wishes hiatus.'

'Confirm.'

We spoke using Glossia, an informal verbal code known only to my staff. Even on an open vox-channel, our communications would be impenetrable to the foe.

I adjusted my vox-unit's channel.

'Thorn wishes aegis, to me, pattern crucible.'

'Aegis arising,' Betancore, my pilot, responded from far away. 'Pattern confirmed.'

My gun-cutter, with its fabulous firepower, was now inbound. I looked to the others in the shadows as I drew my weapon.

'Now is the time,' I told them.

* * *

We edged into the gloomy, slime-swathed ruins of the church. There was a heady stink of wet corruption in the air and sheens of salt clung to every surface. Clusters of maggot-like worms ate into the stones, and flinched back as the fierce beams of our flashlights found them.

Qus ran point, his autocannon swinging from side to side, hunting targets with the red laser rangefinder that projected from the corner of his bionically enhanced left eye. He was a stocky man, rippling with muscle under his harness of ceramite armour. He had painted his blunt face in the colours of his old regiment, the 90th Vladislavan.

Arianrhod and I tailed him. She'd dulled her sabre's blade with brick dust but still it hooked the light as she turned it in her hands. Arianrhod Esw Sweydyr was well over two metres tall, quite the tallest human woman I have ever met, though such stature is common amongst the people of far away Carthae. Her long-boned frame was clad in a leather bodysuit embossed with bronze studs, over which she wore a long, tasselled cloak of patchwork hide. Her silver hair was plaited with beads. The sabre was called Barbarisater and had been carried by women of the Esw Sweydyr tribe for nineteen generations. From the braided grip to the tip of the curved, engraved blade, it measured almost a metre and a half. Long, lean, slender, like the woman who wielded it. Already I could sense the vibration of the psychic energies she was feeding into it. Woman and blade had become one living thing.

Arianrhod had served with my staff for five years, and I was still learning the intricacies of her martial prowess. Ordinarily I'd be noting every detail of her combat trance methods, but I was too fatigued, too drawn out with hunger and thirst.

Bequin and Zu Zeng brought up the rear, side by side, Bequin in a long black gown with a ruff of black feathers around the shoulders, and Zu Zeng in her unreflective robes of Vitrian glass. They stayed back far enough so the aura of their psychic blankness would not conflict with the abilities of Arianrhod or myself, yet close enough to move forward in defence if the time came.

The Inquisition – and many other institutions, august or otherwise – has long been aware of the usefulness of untouchables, those rare human souls who simply have no psionic signature whatsoever and thus disrupt or negate even the most strenuous psychic attack. When I met her on Hubris, a century before, Alizebeth Bequin had been the first untouchable I had ever encountered. Despite her unnerving presence – even non-psykers find untouchables difficult to be around – I had added her to my staff and she had proved to be invaluable. After many years of service, she had retired to form the Distaff, a cadre of untouchables recruited from all across the Imperium. The Distaff was my own private resource, although I often loaned their services to others of my order. They numbered around forty members now, trained and managed by Bequin. It is my belief that the Distaff was collectively one of the most potent anti-psyker weapons in the Emperor's domain.

The ruins were festering with shadows and dank salt. Rot-beetles scurried over the flaking mosaic portraits of long-dead worthies that stared out of alcoves. Worms crawled everywhere. The steady chirrup of insects from the salt-licks was like someone shaking a rattle. As we probed deeper, we came upon inner yards and grave-squares where neglect had shaken free placestones and revealed the smeared bones of the long interred in the loamy earth below. In places, rot-browned skulls had been dug out and piled in loose pyramids.

It saddened me to see this holy place so befouled and dreary. Kiodrus had been a great man, had stood and fought at the right hand of the sacred Beati Sabbat during her mighty crusade. But that had been a long time ago and far away, and his cult of worship had faded. It would take another crusade into the distant Sabbat Worlds to rekindle interest in him and his forgotten deeds.

Qus called a halt and pointed towards the steps of an undercroft that led away below ground. I waved him back, indicating the tiny strip of red ribbon placed under a stone on the top step. A marker, left by Ravenor, indicating this was not a suitable entry point. Peering into the staircase gloom, I saw what he had seen: the half buried cables of a tremor-detector and what looked like bundles of tube charges.

We found three more entrances like it, all marked by Ravenor. The Beldame had secured her fastness well.

'Through there, do you think, sir?' Qus whispered, pointing towards the columns of a roofless cloister.

I was about to agree when Arianrhod hissed 'Barbarisater thirsts...'

I looked at her. She was prowling to the left, towards an archway in the base of the main bell-tower. She moved silently, the sabre held upright in a two-handed grip, her tasselled cloak floating out behind her like angelic wings.

I gestured to Qus and the women and we formed in behind her. I drew my prized boltpistol, given to me by Librarian Brytnoth of the Adeptus Astartes Deathwatch Chapter on the eve of the Purge of Izar, almost a century before. It had never failed me.

The Beldame's minions came out of the night. Eight of them, just shadows that disengaged themselves from the surrounding darkness. Qus began to fire, blasting back a shadow that pounced at him. I fired too, raking bolt rounds into the ghostly opposition.

Beldame Sadia was a heretic witch and consorted with xenos breeds. She had a particular fascination with the beliefs and necromancies of the dark eldar, and had made it her life-cause to tap that foul alien heritage for power and lore. She was one of the only humans I knew of who had struck collaborative pacts with their wretched kabals. Rumour had it she had been recently initiated into the cult of Kaela Men-sha Khaine, in his aspect as the Murder-God beloved of the eldar renegades.

As befitted such a loyalty, she recruited only convicted murderers for her minions. The men who attacked us in that blighted yard were base killers, shrouded in shadow fields she had bought, borrowed or stolen from her inhuman allies.

One swung at me with a long-bladed halberd and I blew off his head. Just. My body was tired and my reactions were damnably slow.

I saw Arianrhod. She was a balletic blur, her beaded hair streaming out above her flying cloak. Barbarisater purred in her hands.

She severed the neck of one shadow with a backward slash, then pirouetted around and chopped another in two from neck to pelvis. The sabre was moving so fast I could barely see it. She stamped hard and reversed her direction of move-ment, causing a third shadow to sprawl as he overshot her. His head flew off, and the sabre swept on to impale a fourth with-out breaking its fluid motion. Then Arianrhod swept around, the sword held horizontally over her right shoulder. The steel haft of the fifth shadow's polearm was cut in two and he stag-gered back. Barbarisater described a figure of eight in the air and another shadow fell, cut into several sections.

The last minion turned and fled. A shot from Bequin's laspistol brought him down.

A pulse was pounding in my temple and I realised I had to sit down before I passed out. Qus grabbed me by the arm and helped me down onto a block of fallen wall stone.

'Gregor?'

'I'm all right, Alizebeth... give me a moment...'

'You shouldn't have come, you old fool! You should have left this to your disciples!'

'Shut up, Alizebeth.'

'I will not, Gregor. It's high time you understood your own limits.'

I looked up at her. 'I have no limits,' I said.

Qus laughed involuntarily.

'I believe him, Mistress Bequin,' said Ravenor, stepping from the shadows. Emperor damn his stealth, even Arianrhod had not seen him coming. She had to force her sabre down to stop it slicing at him.

Gideon Ravenor was a shade shorter than me, but strong and well-made. He was only thirty-four years old. His long black hair was tied back from his sculpted, high cheek-boned face. He wore a grey bodyglove and a long leather storm coat. The psycannon mounted on his left shoulder whirred and clicked around to aim at Arianrhod.

'Careful, swordswoman,' he said. 'My weapon has you squarely.'

'And it will still have me squarely when your head is lying in the dust,' she replied.

They both laughed. I knew they had been lovers for over a year, but still in public they sparred and sported with each other.

Ravenor snapped his fingers and his companion, the

festering mutant Gonvax, shambled out of hiding, drool stringing from his thick, malformed lips. He carried a flamer, the fuel-tanks strapped to the hump of his twisted back.

I rose. 'What have you found?' I asked Ravenor.

'The Beldame – and a way in,' he said.

Beldame Sadia's lair was in the sacrarium beneath the main chapel of the ruin. Ravenor had scouted it carefully, and found an entry point in one of the ruptured crypts that perhaps even she didn't know about.

My respect for Ravenor was growing daily. I had never had a disciple like him. He excelled at almost every skill an inquisitor is meant to have. I looked forward to the day when I supported his petition to Inquisitorial status. He deserved it. The Inquisition needed men like him.

Single-file, we entered the crypt behind Ravenor. He drew our attention carefully to every pitfall and loose flag. The stench of salt and old bones was intolerable, and I felt increasingly weak in the close, hot air.

We emerged into a stone gallery that overlooked a wide subterranean chamber. Pitch-lamps sputtered in the darkness and there was a strong smell of dried herbs and fouler unguents.

Beings were worshipping in the chamber. Worshipping is the only word I can use. Naked, daubed in blood, twenty depraved humans were conducting a dark eldar rite around a torture pit in which a battered man was chained and stretched.

The stink of blood and excrement wafted to me. I tried not to throw up, for I knew the effort would make me pass out.

'There, you see him?' Ravenor whispered into my ear as we crawled to the edge of the gallery.

I made out a pale-skinned ghoul in the distant shadows.

'A haemonculus, sent by the Kabal of the Fell Witch to witness the Beldame's practices.'

I tried to make out detail, but the figure was too deep in the shadows.

I registered grinning teeth and some form of blade device around the right hand.

'Where's Pye?' asked Bequin, whispering too.

Ravenor shook his head. Then he seized my arm and squeezed. Even whispers were no longer possible.

The Beldame herself had entered the chamber.

She walked on eight, spider legs, a huge augmetic chassis of hooked arachnid limbs that skittered on the stones. Inquisitor Atelath, Emperor grant him rest, had destroyed her real legs one hundred and fifty years before my birth.

She was veiled in black gauze that looked like cobwebs. I could actually feel her evil like a fever-sweat.

She paused at the edge of the torture pit, raised her veil with withered hands and spat at the victim below. It was venom, squirted from the glands built into her mouth behind her augmetic fangs. The viscous fluid hit the sacrificial victim full in the face and he gurgled in agony as the front of his skull was eaten away.

Sadia began to speak, her voice low and sibilant. She spoke in the language of the dark eldar and her naked brethren writhed and moaned.

'I've seen enough,' I whispered. 'She's mine. Ravenor, can you manage the haemonculus?'

He nodded.

On my signal, we launched our attack, leaping down from the gallery, weapons blazing. Several of the worshippers were punched apart by Qus's heavy fire.

Whooping the battlecry of Carthae, Arianrhod flew at the haemonculus, way ahead of Ravenor.

I realised I had pushed it too far. I was giddy as I landed, and stumbled.

Her metal spider legs striking sparks from the flagstones, Beldame Sadia reared up at me, ululating. She pulled back her veil to spit at me.

Abruptly, she reeled backwards, thunderstruck by the combined force of Bequin and Zu Zeng who flanked her.

I gathered myself and fired at her, blowing one of the augmetic limbs off her spider-frame.

She spat anyway, but missed. The venom sizzled into the cold stone slabs at my feet.

'Imperial Inquisition!' I bellowed. 'In the name of the hallowed God-Emperor, you and your kind are charged with treason and manifest disbelief!'

I raised my weapon. She flew at me.

Her sheer bulk brought me down.

One spider limb stabbed entirely through the meat of my left thigh. Her steel fangs, like curved needles, snarled into my face. I saw her eyes, for an instant, black and without limit or sanity.

She spat.

I wrenched my head around to avoid the corrosive spew, and fired my bolt pistol up into her.

The impact threw her backwards, all four hundred kilos of wizened witch and bionic carriage.

I rolled over.

The haemonculus had met Arianrhod's attack face on, the glaive around his right hand screaming as the xenos-made blades whirled. He was stick-thin and clad in shiny black leather, his grin a perpetual consequence of the way the colourless skin of his face was pinned back around his skull. He wore metal jewellery fashioned from the weapons of the warriors he had slain.

I could hear Ravenor crying out Arianrhod's name.

Barbarisater sliced at the darting eldar monster, but he evaded, his physical speed unbelievable.

She swung again, placing two perfect kill strokes that somehow missed him altogether. He sent her lurching away in a mist of blood. For the first time since I had known her, I heard Arianrhod yelp in pain.

Flames belched across the chamber. Gonvax shambled forward, forever loyal to his master... and his master's lover. He tried to squirt flames at the haemonculus, but it was suddenly somehow behind him. Gonvax shrieked as the glaive eviscerated him.

With a howl, Arianrhod threw herself at the dark eldar. I saw her, for a moment, frozen in mid-air, her sabre descending. Then the two bodies struck each other, and flew apart.

The sabre had taken off the eldar's left arm at the shoulder. But his glaive...

I knew she was dead. No one could survive that, not even a noble swordswoman from far Carthae.

Bequin was pulling me up. 'Gregor! Gregor!'

Beldame Sadia, her spider carriage limping, was fleeing towards the staircase.

Something exploded behind me. I could hear Ravenor bellowing in rage and pain.

I ran after the Beldame.

The upper chapel, above ground, was silent and cold. Darknight flares glimmered through the lines of stained glass windows.

'You can't escape, Sadia!' I shouted, but my voice was thin and hoarse.

I glimpsed her as she skittered between the columns to my left. A shadow in the shadows.

'Sadia! Sadia, old hag, you have killed me! But you will die by my hand!'

To my right now, another skuttling shadow, half-seen. I moved that way.

I was stabbed hard from behind, in between my shoulder blades. I turned as I fell, and saw the manic face of the Beldame's arch-poisoner, Pye. He cackled and giggled, prancing, a spent injector tube clutched in each hand.

'Dead! Dead, dead, dead, dead, dead!' he warbled.

He had injected me with the secondary part of the poison.

I fell over, my muscles already cramping.

'How does it feel, inquisitor?' Pye chuckled, capering towards me.

'Emperor damn you,' I gasped and shot him through the face.

I blacked out.

When I came round, Beldame Sadia had me by the throat and was shaking me with her augmetic mandibles.

'I want you awake!' she hissed, her veil falling back and the toxin sacs in her wizened cheeks bulging. 'I want you awake to feel this!'

Her head exploded in a spray of bone shards and tissue. The spider carriage went into convulsions and threw me across the chapel. It continued to scuttle and dance, her corpse jerking slackly from it, for a full minute before it collapsed.

I was face down on the floor, and I tried to turn, but the advancing effect of the poison was shutting me down.

Shutting me down hard.

Massive feet strode into my field of vision. Armoured feet, plated with ceramite.

I rolled as best I could and looked up.

Witchfinder Tantalid stood over me, holstering the bolt-gun he had used to kill Beldame Sadia. He was encased in gold-encrusted battle armour, the pennants of the Ministorum suspended over his back plate.

'You are an accursed heretic, Eisenhorn. And I claim your life.'

Not Tantalid, I thought as my consciousness spun away again. Not Tantalid. Not now.

TWO

Something so typically Betancore
My fallen
The summons

From the moment I slipped into unconsciousness at the feet of the vicious Witchfinder Tantalid, I knew nothing more until I woke, twenty-nine hours later, aboard my gun-cutter. I remembered nothing about the seven attempts to shock my system back to life, the cardiac massages, the anti-venom shots injected directly into my heart muscle, the fight to make me live again. I learned all about it later, as I slowly recovered. For days, I was as weak as a feline whelp.

Most particularly, I knew nothing about the way Tantalid had been denied. Bequin told me, a day or two after my first awakening. It had been something so typically Betancore.

Alizebeth had been hard on my heels up the stairs from the sacrarium, in time to see Tantalid's arrival. She had known him at once. The Witchfinder is notorious throughout the sub-sector.

He'd been about to kill me, and I was unconscious at his

feet, going into anaphylactic shock with the venom bonding and seething in my veins.

She'd cried out, fumbling for her weapon.

Then light – hard, powerful light – had streamed in through the stained glass windows. There was a roaring sound. My gun-cutter, its lamps on full beam, rose to a hover over the ruined chapel, lighting up the night. Guessing what was about to follow, Bequin had thrown herself down.

Betancore's voice had boomed out from the hull tannoy of the hovering gunship.

'Imperial Inquisition! Step away from the inquisitor now!'

Tantalid had squinted up into the glare, his stringy tortoise head turning in the rim of his massive carapace armour.

'Ministorum officer!' he had yelled back, his voice amplified by his suit's vox-unit. 'Back off! Back off now! This heretic is mine!'

Bequin grinned as she told me Betancore's response. 'Never argue with a gun-cutter, you asshole.'

The slaved servitors in the cutter's blunt wingtips opened fire, hosing the chapel with autocannon shells. The stained glass windows had all shattered, statues had been decapitated, flagstones had disintegrated. Hit at least once, Tantalid had fallen backwards into the dust and debris. His body had not been found, so I presumed the bastard had survived. But he had been smart enough to flee.

My prone body had not been touched, even though the chapel around me had been peppered with fire.

Typical Betancore bravado. Typical Betancore finesse.

She was just like her damned father.

'Send her to me,' I told Bequin as I lay back in my cot, half-dead and feeling terrible.

Medea Betancore looked in a few minutes later. Like her father, Midas, she was clad in the red-piped black suit of a Glavian pilot, and she proudly wore his old cerise, embroidered jacket.

Her skin, like Midas's, like all that of all Glavians, was dark. She grinned at me.

'I owe you,' I said.

Medea shook her head. 'Nothing my father wouldn't have done.' She sat on the foot of my cot.

'He'd have killed Tantalid, though,' she decided.

'He was a better shot.'

That grin again, pearl white teeth framed by ebony skin.

'Yeah, he was that.'

'But you'll do,' I smiled.

She saluted and left.

Midas Betancore had been dead for twenty-six years. I missed him still. He was the closest thing to a friend I had ever had. Bequin and Aemos, they were allies, and I trusted them with my life. But Midas...

May the God-Emperor rot Fayde Thuring for taking him. May the God-Emperor lead me to Fayde Thuring one day so that I and Medea may avenge Midas.

Medea had never known her father. She'd been born a month after his death, raised by her mother on Glavia, and had come into my service by chance. I was her godfather, a promise to Midas. Duty bound, I had visited Glavia for her ascension to adulthood, and watched her drive a Glavia long-prow through the vortex rapids of the Stilt Hills during the Rites of Majority. One glimpse of her skills had convinced me.

* * *

Arianrhod Esw Sweydyr was dead. So were Gonvax and Qus. The battle in the sacrarium had been fierce. Ravenor had killed the raging haemonculus, but only after it had ripped open his belly and taken off Zu Zeng's left ear.

Gideon Ravenor was in intensive care in the main city infirmary of Lethe. We would collect him once he was out of danger.

I wondered how long that would be. I wondered how he would be. He had loved Arianrhod, loved her dearly. I prayed this loss would not set him back too far.

I mourned Qus and the swordswoman. Qus had been with me for nineteen years. That Darknight in the chapel had robbed me of so much.

Qus was buried with full honours in the Imperial Guard Memorial Cenotaph at Lethe Majeure. Arianrhod was burned on a bare hill west of the salt-licks. I was too weak to attend either service.

Aemos brought the sabre Barbarisater to me after the pyre. I wrapped it in a vizzy-cloth and a silk sheet. I knew I was duty bound to return it to the tribal elders of the Esw Sweydyr on Carthae before long. That would mean a round trip of at least a year. I had no time for it. I put the wrapped sword in my safebox.

It barely fitted.

As I worked my way back to health, I considered Tantalid. Arnaut Tantalid had risen from the rank of confessor militant in the Missionaria Galaxia seventy years before to become one of the Ministorum's most feared and ruthless witch-hunters. Like many of his breed, he followed the doctrines of Sebastian Thor with such unswerving precision it bordered on clinical obsession.

To most of the common folk of the Imperium, there would be blessed little to choose between an Ordo Xenos inquisitor such as myself and an ecclesiarchy witchkiller like Tantalid. We both hunt out the damning darkness that stalks mankind, we are both figures of fear and dread, we are both, so it seems, laws unto ourselves.

Twinned though we may be in so many ways, we could not be more distinct. It is my personal belief that the Adeptus Ministorum, the Imperium's vast organ of faith and worship, should focus its entire attention on the promulgation of the true church of the God-Emperor and leave the persecution of heretics to the Inquisition. Our jurisdictions often clash. There have, to my certain knowledge, been two wars of faith in the last century provoked and sustained by just such rivalry.

Tantalid and I had locked horns twice before. On Bradell's World, five decades earlier, we had faced each other across the marble floor of a synod court, arguing for the right to extradite the psyker Elbone Parsuval. On that occasion, he had triumphed, thanks mainly to the strict Thorian mindset of the Ministorum elders of Bradell's World.

Then, just eight years ago, our paths had crossed again on Kuuma.

Tantalid's fanatical hatred – indeed, I would venture, fear – of the psyker was by then insurmountable. I made no secret of the fact that I employed psychic methods in the pursuit of my work. There were psychic adepts in my staff, and I myself had worked to develop my own psychic abilities over the years. Such is my right, as an authorised bearer of the Inquisition's seal.

In my eyes, he was a blinkered zealot with psychotic streak. In his, I was the spawn of witches and a heretic.

No courtroom argument for us on Kuuma. A little war

instead. It lasted an afternoon, and raged through the tiered streets of the oasis town at Unat Akim.

Twenty-eight latent psykers, none older than fourteen, had been rooted out of the population of Kuuma's sprawling capital city during a purge, and sequestered prior to their collection by the Black Ships. They were recruits, a precious resource, untainted and ready to be shaped by the Adeptus Astropathicus into worthy servants of the God-Emperor. Some of them, perhaps, would have the ultimate honour of joining the choir of the Astronomican. They were frightened and confused, but this was their salvation.

Better to be found early and turned to good service than to remain undetected and become tainted, corrupt and a threat to our entire society.

But before the Black Ships could arrive to take them, they were spirited away by renegade slavers working in collusion with corrupt officials in the local Administratum. Vast sums could be made on the black market for unregistered, virgin psychic slaves.

I followed the slavers' trail across the seif dunes to Unat Akim with the intention of liberating the youngsters. Tantalid made his way there to exterminate them all as witches.

By the end of the fight, I had driven the witchfinder and his cohorts, mostly foot soldiers of the Frateris Militia, out of the oasis town. Two of the young psykers had been killed in the crossfire, but the others were safely transferred into the hands of the Astropathicus.

Tantalid, fleeing Kuuma to lick his wounds, had tried to have me declared heretic, but the charges were swiftly overturned. The Ministorum had, at that time, no wish to court conflict with their allies in the Inquisition.

I had expected, known even, that Tantalid would return

sometime to plague me. It was a personal matter now, one which his fanatical disposition would fix upon and transform into a holy calling.

But the last I had heard, he had been leading an ecclesiar-chy mission into the Ophidian sub-sector in support of the century-long Purge Campaign there.

I wondered what had brought him to Lethe Eleven at so inopportune a moment.

By the time I was back on my feet, two weeks later, the Darknight was over and I knew the answer, in general if not specific terms.

I was hobbling around on a cane in the private mansion I had rented in Lethe Majeure when Aemos brought me the news. The great Ophidian Campaign was over.

'Great success,' he announced. 'The last action took place at Dolsene four months ago, and the Warmaster has declared the sub-sector cleansed. A famous victory, don't you think?'

'Yes. I should hope so. It's taken them long enough.'

'Gregor, Gregor... even with a force as large as the hal-lowed Battlefleet Scarus, the subjugation of a sub-sector is an immense task! That it took the best part of a century is nothing! The pacification of the Extempus sub-sector took four hundred y-'

He paused.

'You're toying with me, aren't you?'

I nodded. He was very easy to wind up.

Aemos shook his head and eased his ancient body down into one of the leather chairs.

'Martial law still dominates, I understand, and caretaker governments have been established on the key worlds. But the Warmaster himself is returning with the bulk of the fleet in triumph, setting foot in this sub-sector again for the first time in a hundred years.'

I stood by the open windows, looking out from the mansion's first floor across the grey roofs of Lethe Majeure which seemed to coat the hills of the Tito Basin like the scaled hide of some prehistoric reptile. The sky was a magnolia haze, and a light breeze breathed. It was almost impossible now to picture this place beset by the filthy, permanent shadows of the Darknight.

Now, perhaps, I knew why Tantalid had returned. The Ophidian war was over, and his holy mission concluded with it.

'I remember them setting out, don't you?' I asked.

A foolish question. My savant was a data-addict, driven since the age of forty-two standard to collect and retain all manner of information thanks to a meme-virus he had contracted. There was no possibility of him forgetting anything. He scratched the side of his hooked nose where his heavy augmetic eye-pieces touched.

'How could either of us forget that?' he replied. 'The summer of 240. Hunting the Glaw clan on Gudrun during the very Founding itself.'

Indeed, we had played a particular role in delaying the start of the Ophidian Campaign. The Warmaster, or lord militant as he had been back then, had been all but set to launch his purge into Ophidian space when my investigation of the heretic Glaw family had triggered a mass uprising later known as the Helican Schism. To his great surprise and displeasure, the Warmaster had been abruptly forced to redirect his readied forces in a pacification of his very own sub-sector.

Warmaster Honorius. Honorius Magnus they were calling

him. I had never met him, nor had I much wish to. A brutal
man, as are so many of his kind. It takes a special mindset, a
special brutality, to crush planets and populations.

'There is to be a great Jubilation on Thracian Primaris,'
Aemos said. 'A Holy Novena congregated by the Synod the
High Ecclesiarchy. It is rumoured that the Imperial Lord Commander Helican himself will attend, specifically to bestow
upon the Warmaster the rank of Feudal Protector.'

'I'm sure he'll be very pleased. Another heavy medallion to
throw at his officers when he's annoyed.'

'You're not tempted to attend?'

I laughed. In truth, I had thought to return to the Helican
sub-sector capital before long. Thracian Primaris, the most
massive, industrialised and populated world in the sub-sector,
had wrested capital planet status from ancient Gudrun after
the disgrace and foment of the Schism, finally achieving the
preeminence it felt its size and power had long deserved. It
was now the chief Imperial planet of this region.

There was work to be done, reports to be filed and presented, and those things could best be achieved by returning
to my property on Thracian, my base of operations, near to
the Palace of the Inquisition. But I had little love for Thracian
Primaris. It was an ugly place, and I only made my headquarters there out of convenience. The thought of pomp and
ceremony and festivals filled me with quiet dread.

Perhaps I would go to Messina instead, or to the quiet of
Gudrun, where I maintained a small, comfortable estate.

'The Inquisition is to attend in great strength. Lord Rorken
himself...'

I waved a hand in Aemos's direction. 'Does it appeal to you?'
'No.'

'Are there not better uses for our time? Pressing matters?

Things that would be more easily achieved away from such overblown distractions?'

'Most certainly,' he said.

'Then I think you know my mind.'

'I think I do, Gregor,' he said, rising to his feet and reaching into the pocket of his green robe. 'And therefore I'm fully prepared for the fact that you're going to curse me when I give you this.'

He held out a small data-slate, an encrypted message-tile whose contents had been received and stored by the astropaths.

The official seal of the Inquisition was stamped across its front.

THREE

**Capital world
The Ocean House
Intruders, past and present**

Thracian Primaris, capital world of the Helican sub-sector, seat of government, Helican sub-sector, Scarus sector, Segmentum Obscurus. You can read that description in any one of a hundred thousand guidebooks, geographies, Imperial histories, pilgrimage primers, industrial ledgers, trade directories, star maps. It sounds impressive, authoritarian, powerful.

It does no justice at all to the monster it describes.

I have known hellholes and death-planets that from space look serene and wondrous: the watercolours of their atmospheres, the glittering moons and belts they wear like bangles and jewels, the natural wonders that belie the dangers they contain.

Thracian Primaris is no such dissembler. From space, it glowers like an oozing, cataracted eye. It is corpulent, swollen, sheened in grey veils of atmospheric soot through which the billion billion lights of the city hives glimmer like rotting stars. It glares balefully at all ships that approach.

And, oh! But they approach! Shoals of ships, flocks of them, countless craft, drawn to this bloated cesspit by the lure of its vast industrial wealth and mercantile vigour.

It has no moons, no natural moons anyway. Five Ramilies-class starforts hang above its atmosphere, their crenellated towers and buttressed gun-stations guarding the approaches to and from the capital world. A dedicated guild of forty thousand skilled pilots exists simply to guide traffic in and out of the jostling, crowded high-anchor reaches. It has a planetary defence force, a standing army of eight million men. It has a population of twenty-two billion, plus another billion temporary residents and visitors. Seven-tenths of its surface are now covered by hive structures, including great sections of the world's original oceans. City-sprawl fills and covers the seas, and the waters roll in darkness far beneath.

I loathe the place. I loathe the lightless streets, the noise, the press of bodies. I loathe the stink of its re-circulated air. I loathe its airborne grease-filth adhering to my clothes and skin.

But fate and duty bring me back there, time and again.

The encrypted Inquisitorial missive had been quite clear: I, and a great number of my peers, was summoned to Thracian Primaris to attend the Holy Novena, and wait upon the pleasure of the Lord Grandmaster Inquisitor Ubertino Orsini. Orsini was the most senior officer of the Inquisition in the entire Helican sub-sector, a status that made him equal in rank and power to any cardinal palatine.

I was not about to decline.

* * *

The voyage from Lethe Eleven took a month, and I brought my entire entourage back with me. We arrived just four days shy of the start of the Novena. As a tiny pilot boat led my ship in to anchor through the massed ranks of orbiting starships, I saw the dark formations of Battlefleet Scarus, suckling at a starfort as if they were its young. This was their heroic home-coming. There was a taste of victory in the air. An Imperial triumph on this scale was something to be savoured, some-thing the Ministorum could use to boost the morale of the common citizenry.

'Your itinerary has been prepared,' said Alain von Baigg, a jun-ior interrogator who served as my secretary. We were aboard the gun-cutter, dropping towards the planet.

'Oh, by whom?'

He paused. Von Baigg was a diffident and lustreless young man who I doubted would ever make the rank of inquisitor. I'd accepted him to my staff in the hope that service along-side Ravenor might inspire him. It had not.

'I would have presumed that the preparation of my itiner-ary might have included my own choices.'

Von Baigg stammered something. I took the data-slate he was holding. The list of appointments was not his handiwork, I saw. It was an official document, processed by the Minis-torum's nunciature in collaboration with the Office of the Inquisition. My timetable for all nine days of the Holy Novena was filled with audiences, acts of worship, feasts, presenta-tion ceremonies, unveilings and Ministorum rites. All nine days, plus the days before and after.

I was here, damn it! I had responded to the summons. I would not allow myself to be subjected to this round of jun-kets too. I took a stylus and quickly marked the events I was prepared to attend: the formal rites, the Inquisitorial audience, the Grand Bestowment.

'That's it,' I said, tossing it back to him. 'The rest I'm skipping.'

Von Baigg looked uncomfortable. 'You are expected at the Post-Apostolic Conclave immediately on arrival.'

'Immediately on arrival,' I told him sternly, 'I'm going home.'

Home, for me, was the Ocean House, a private residence I leased in the most select quarter of Hive Seventy. On many hive worlds, the rich and privileged dwell in districts high up in the top-most city spires, divorced as far as possible from the dirt and crowding of the mid and low-hab levels. But no matter how high you climbed on Thracian Primaris, there was nothing to find but smog and pollution.

Instead, the exclusive habitats were on the underside of the hive portions that extended out over and into the hidden seas. There was at least a tranquillity here.

Medea Betancore flew the gun-cutter down through the traffic-thick atmosphere, threaded her way between the tawdry domes, dingy towers, rusting masts and crumbling spires, and laced into the seething lanes of air vehicles entering a vast feeder tunnel which gave access to the hives' arterial transit network.

Bars of blue-white light set into the walls of the huge tunnel strobed by the ports. In under an hour we had reached a great transit hub, three kilometres down in the city-crust, where she set the cutter down on a massive elevator platform that sedately lowered us and a dozen other craft into the sub-levels of Hive Seventy. The cutter was then berthed in a private lifter-drome and we transferred to a tuberail for the final stretch to the maritime habitats.

I was already weary of Thracian Primaris by the time I
reached the Ocean House.

Built from plasma-sealed grandiorite and an adamite frame,
the Ocean House was one of a thousand estates built along
the submarine wall of Hive Seventy. It was nine kilometres
beneath the city crust and another two below sea level. A
small palace by the standards of most common Imperial citizens, it was large enough to house my entire retinue, my
libraries, armoury and training facilities, not to mention a private chapel, an audience hall and an entire annex for Bequin's
Distaff. It was also secure, private and quiet.

Jarat, my housekeeper, was waiting for us in the entrance
hall. She was dressed, as ever, in a pale grey gown-robe and
a black lace cap draped with a white veil. As the great iron
hatch-doors cycled open, and I breathed the cool, purified
air of the house, she clapped her plump hands and sent servitors scurrying forward to take our coats and assist with the
baggage train.

I stood for a moment on the nashemeek rug and looked
around at the austere stone walls and the high arched roof.
There were no paintings, no busts or statuary, no crossed
weapons or embroidered tapestries, only an Inquisitorial crest
on the far wall over the stairs. I am not one for decoration or
opulence. I require simple comfort and functionality.

The others bustled around me. Bequin and Aemos went
through to the library. Ravenor and von Baigg issued careful
instructions to the servitors concerning some baggage items.
Medea disappeared to her private room. The others in my retinue melted away into the house.

Jarat greeted them all, and then came to me.

'Welcome, sir,' she said. 'You have long been from us.'

'Sixteen months, Jarat.'

'The house is aired and ready. We made preparations as soon as you signalled your intentions. We were saddened to hear of the losses.'

'Anything to report?'

'Security was of course double-checked prior to your arrival. There are a number of messages.'

'I'll review them shortly.'

'You are hungry, no doubt?'

She was right, though I hadn't realised it.

'The kitchen is preparing dinner. I took the liberty of selecting a menu that I believe you will approve of.'

'As ever, I have faith in your choices, Jarat. I'd like to dine on the sea terrace, with any who would join me.'

'I'll see to it, sir. Welcome home.'

I bathed, put on a robe of grey wool, and sat for a while alone in my private chambers, sipping a glass of amasec and looking through the messages and communiqués by the soft light of the lamp.

There were many, mostly recent postings from old acquaintances – officials, fellow inquisitors, soldiers – alerting me to their arrival on the planet and conveying respects. Few needed more than a form reply from my secretary. To some, I penned courteous, personal responses, expressing the hope of meeting them at some or other of the Novena's many events.

There were three that drew my particular attention. The first was a private, coded missive from Lord Inquisitor Phlebas Alessandro Rorken. Rorken was the head of Ordo Xenos in the Helican sub-sector, my immediate superior and part of the triumvurate of senior inquisitors who answered directly to Grandmaster Orsini. Rorken wanted to see me as soon as I was back on Thracian. I responded immediately that I would come to him at the Palace of the Inquisition the follow morning.

The second was from my old friend and colleague, Titus Endor. It had been a long time since I had set eyes on him. His message, uncoded, read: 'Gregor. My greetings to you. Are you home?'

The brevity was disarming. I sent an affirmative response that was similarly brief. Endor clearly did not want to converse in writing. I awaited his reponse.

The third was also uncoded, or at least lacked electronic encryption. It said, in Glossia: 'Scalpel cuts quickly, eager tongues revealed. At Cadia, by terce. Hound wishes Thorn. Thorn should be sharp.'

The sea terrace was probably the main reason I had leased the Ocean House in the first place. It was a long, ceramite-vaulted hall with one entire wall made of armoured glass looking into the ocean. The industrialisation of Thracian Primaris had killed off a great part of the world's sea-life, but at these depths, hardy survivors such as luminous deep anglers and schools of incandescent jellies could still be glimpsed in the emerald nocturnal glow. The candlelit room was washed by a rippling green half-light.

Jarat's servitors had set the long table for nine and those nine were already taking their seats and chatting over preprandial drinks as I arrived. Like most of them, I had dressed informally, putting on a simple black suit. The kitchen provided steamed fubi dumplings and grilled ketelfish, followed by seared haunches of rare, gamey orkunu, and then pear and berry tarts with a cinnamon jus. A sturdy Gudrunite claret and sweet dessert wine from the vineyards of Messina complemented the food perfectly. I had forgotten the excellent qualities of the house Jarat ran for me, so far away from the hardship of missions in the field.

Around the table with me were Aemos, Bequin, Ravenor, von Baigg, my rubricator and scribe Aldemar Psullus, Jubal Kircher, the head of household security, a trusted field agent called Harlon Nayl, and Thula Surskova, who was Bequin's chief aide with the Distaff. Medea Betancore had chosen not to join us, but I knew the intensity of the piloting chores down through Thracian airspace had undoubtedly worn her out.

I was pleased to see that Ravenor was present. His injuries were healing, the physical ones at least, and though he was quiet and a little withdrawn, I felt he was beginning to come through the shock of Arianrhod's death.

Surskova, a short, ample woman in her forties, was quietly briefing Bequin on the progress of the newer Distaff initiates. Aemos chuntered on to Psullus and Nayl about the events on Lethe Eleven and they listened intently. Psullus, enfeebled and prematurely aged by a wasting disease, never left the Ocean House and devoted his life to the maintenance and preservation of my extensive private libraries. If Aemos hadn't related the story of our last mission to him, I would have made sure I did. Such tales were his only connection to the active process of our business and he loved to hear them. Nayl, an ex-bounty hunter from Loki, had been injured on a mission the year before and had not been able to join us for the Lethe endeavour. He too lapped up Aemos's account, asking occasional questions. I could tell he was itching to get back to work.

Von Baigg and Kircher chatted idly about the preparations for the Novena that were now gripping the hives of Thracian, and the security consequences they brought. Kircher was an

able man, ex-Arbites, and dependable if a little unimagina-
tive. As dessert was served, the discussion broadened across
the table.

'They say the Bestowment will be the making of the Warmaster,' Nayl said, his loaded spoon poised in front of his mouth.

'He's made already, I'd say,' I retorted.

'Nayl's right, Gregor. I heard that too,' said Ravenor. 'Feudal
Protector. That's as good as Imperial Lord Commander Helican admitting the Warmaster is on an equal footing with him.'

'It's a sinecure.'

'Not at all. It makes Honorius the favourite to become
warmaster-in-chief in the Acrotara theatre now that Warmaster Hiju is dead, and Hiju was being groomed for a place on
the Senatorum Imperialis, perhaps even to sit amongst the
High Lords of Terra.'

'Honorius may be "Magnus", but he's not High Lord material,' I ventured.

'After this he might be,' said Nayl. 'Lord Commander Helican must think he has potential, or he wouldn't be giving
him such an almighty hand up.'

Politics left me cold, and I seldom empathised with political ambitions. I only studied the subject because my duties
often demanded a detailed working knowledge. Imperial
Lord Commander Helican, which is to say Jeromya Faurlitz
IV of the noble Imperial family Faurlitz, was the supreme
secular authority in the Helican sub-sector, for which reason
he styled himself with the sub-sector's name in his appella-
tion. On paper, even the cardinals of the Ministorium, the
Grandmaster of the Inquisition, the senior luminaries of the
Administratum and the Lords Militant had to answer to him,
though as with all things in Imperial society, it was never as
easy as that. Church, state and military, woven together as

one, yet constantly inimical. In favouring Warmaster Honorius with the Bestowment, Lord Helican was throwing his lot in with the military – an overt signal to the other organs of government – and clearly expected the Warmaster to return the favour when he rose to levels of government beyond those of a single sub-sector. It was a dangerous game, and rare for so senior an official to play openly for such an advantage, though the battle-glory that surrounded Honorius made a perfect excuse.

And that made it a dangerous time. Somebody would want to redress that balance. My money would be on the Ecclesiarchy, though it's fair to say I'm biased. However, history has shown the Church to be chronically intolerant of losing power to the military or the state. I said as much.

'There are many other elements,' Aemos chuckled, accepting a refill of dessert wine. 'The Faurlitz line is weak and lacks both support in the Adeptus Terra and a ready ear at the Senatorum Imperialis and the courts of the Golden Throne. Two powerful families, the De Vensii and the Fulvatorae, are seeking to make gains against the Faurlitz, and would take this as an open show of defiance. Then there's the House of Eirswald, who see their own famous son, Lord Militant Strefon, as the only viable replacement for Hiju. And the Augustyn dynasty, let's not forget, who were ousted from power when High Lord of Terra Giann Augustyn died in office forty years ago. They've been trying to get back in with feverish determination these last few years, pushing their candidate, Lord Commander Cosimo, with almost unseemly impudence. If Nayl's right and the Bestowment makes Honorius a certainty as Hiju's successor, he'd become a direct competitor with Cosimo for the High Lord's vacant position.'

Down the table, Bequin yawned and caught my eye.

'Cosimo's never going to make it,' Psullus put in candidly. 'His house is far too unpopular with the Adeptus Mechanicus, and without their consent, however tacit, no one ever makes it to High Lord rank. Besides, the Ministorum would block it. Giann Augustyn made no friends there with his reforms. They say it was a Callidus of the Officio Assassinorum, under orders from the Ecclesiarcy, that took old Giann off, not a stroke at all.'

'Careful what you say, old friend, or they'll be sending one after you,' Ravenor said. Psullus held up his bony hands in a dismissive gesture as laughter rippled around the table.

'It is, still, most perturbatory,' Aemos said. 'This Bestowment could lead to a House war. Quite apart from all the obvious opponents, Lord Helican and the Warmaster could find themselves tasked by Imperial families who are thus far neutral. There are many who are quite comfortable with their situation, and who would strike with astonishing ruthlessness simply to avoid being drawn into an open bloody clash.'

There was silence for a moment.

'Psullus,' said Ravenor quickly, changing the subject with a diplomat's deftness, 'I have a number of works for you that I collected on Lethe, including a palimpsest of the Analecta Phaenomena...'

Psullus engaged the young interrogator eagerly. Aemos, von Baigg and Nayl continued to debate the Imperial intrigue. Bequin and Surskova made their goodnights and withdrew. I took my crystal balloon of amasec to the glass wall and looked out into the oceanic depths. Kircher joined me after a moment. He smoothed the front of his navy blue jacket and put on his black gloves before speaking.

'We had intruders last month,' he said quietly.

I looked round at him. 'When?'

'Three times, in fact,' he said, 'though I didn't realise that until the third occasion. During night cycle about six weeks ago, I had what seemed to be a persistent fault on the alarms covering the seawall vents. There was no further sign, and the servitors replaced that section of the system. Then again, a week later, on the service entrance to the food stores, and the outer doors of the Distaff annex, both on the same night. I suspected a system corruption, and planned an overhaul of the entire alarm net. The following week, I found the security code on the outer locks of the main door had been defaulted to zero. Someone had been in and left again. I scoured the building and found vox-thieves buried in the walls of six rooms, including your inner chambers, and discreet farcoders wired into three communication junction nodes, spliced to vox and pict lines. Someone had also tried, and failed, to force their way into your void-vault, but they didn't know the shield codes.'

'And there were no traces?'

'No prints, no microspores, no follicles. I washed the air itself through the particle scrubber. The in-house pict recorders show nothing... except a beautifully disguised time-jump of thirty-four seconds. The astropaths sensed nothing. In one place, the intruder must have walked across four metres of under-floor pressure pads without setting them off. In retrospect, I realised the two prior incidents, far from being system faults, were experimental tests to probe, gauge and estimate our security net. Trial runs before the actual intrusion. For that, they used a code scrambler on the main doors. If they'd actually been able to crack it, they could have reset the code and I'd never have known they'd been in.'

'You've double-checked everything? No more bugs to be found?'

He shook his head. 'Lord, I can only apologise for–'

I held up a hand. 'No need, Kircher. You've done your job. Show me what they left.'

Kircher unrolled a red felt cloth across the top of a table in the quiet of the inner library. He was nervous, and beads of sweat were trickling down from his crest-like shock of white hair.

I hadn't wanted to alarm anyone, so I had asked only Ravenor and Aemos to join us. The room smelled of teak from the shelves, must from the books, and ozone from the suspension fields sustaining especially frail manuscripts.

The felt was laid out. On it lay nine tiny devices, six vox-thieves and three farcoders, each one set in a pearl of solid plastic.

'Once I'd stripped them out, I sealed them in inert gel to make sure they were dead. None were booby trapped.'

Gideon Ravenor stepped in and picked up one of the sealed vox-thieves, holding it up to the light.

'Imperial,' he said. 'Unmarked, but Imperial. Very high grade and advanced.'

'I thought so too,' said Kircher.

'Military? Secular?' I asked.

Ravenor shrugged. 'We could source them to likely manufacturers, but they likely supply all arms of the Imperium.'

Aemos's augmetic optics clicked and turned as he peered down at the objects on the cloth. 'The farcoders,' he began, 'similarly advanced. It takes singular skill to patch one of these successfully into a comm-node.'

'It takes singular skill to break in like they did,' I countered.

'They have no maker markings, but they're clearly refined models from the Amplox series. Much more refined than the heavy-duty units the military use. It's just conjecture, but I'd say this was beyond the Ministorum too. They're notoriously behind when it comes to tech advancements.'

'Who then?' I asked.

'The Adeptus Mechanicus?' he ventured. I scowled.

He shrugged, smiling. 'Or at least a body with the power and influence to secure such advanced devices from the Adeptus Mechanicus.'

'Like?'

'The Officio Assassinorum?'

'Who would break in to kill, not listen.'

'Noted. Then a powerful Imperial house, one with clout in the Senatorum Imperialis.'

'Possible...' I admitted.

'Or...' he said.

'Or?'

'Or the one Imperial institution that regularly employs such devices and has the prestige and determination to make sure it is using the best available equipment.'

'That being?'

Aemos looked at me as if I was stupid.

'The Inquisition, of course.'

I slept badly, fitfully. Three hours before the end of the night cycle, I sat up in my bed, suddenly, coldly awake.

Dressed only in the sheet I had wrapped around me, I stalked out into the hall, my grip firm on the matt-grey snub pistol that lived in a holster secured behind my headboard.

Dim blue light filtered through the hallway, softening the edges of everything. I crept forward.

I was not mistaken. Someone was moving about down below, in the lower foyer.

I edged down the stairs, gun braced, willing my eyes to accustomise to the gloom.

I thought to hit a vox and alert Kircher and his staff, but if someone was inside, skillful enough to get past the alarms, then I wanted to capture him, not scare him off with a full blown alert. In the few hours since I had arrived back at the Ocean House, a nasty taste of treachery had seeped into my world. It might be largely paranoia, but I wanted an end to it.

A beam of white light stabbed across the foyer floor from the half open kitchen doors. I heard movement again.

I sidled to the doorframe, checked the safety was off, and slid, weapon first, through the gap in the doors.

The outer kitchen, a realm of marble-topped workbays and scrubbed aluminium ranges, was empty. Metal pots and utensils hung silently from ceiling racks. There was a smell of garlic and cooked herbs in the still air. The light was on in the inner pantry, near the cold store, and the illuminated backwash filled the room.

Two steps, three, four. The kitchen's stone floor was numb-ingly cold under my bare feet. I reached the door to the inner pantry. There was movement inside.

I kicked the door open and leapt inside, aiming the com-pact sidearm.

Medea Betancore, clad only in a long, ex-military under-shirt, roared out in surprise and dropped the tray of leftover ketelfish she had been gorging on. The tray clattered on the tiled floor in front of the open larder.

'Great gods alive, Eisenhorn!' she wailed in outrage, jump-ing up and down on the spot. 'Don't do that!'

I was angry. I didn't immediately lower my aim. 'What are you doing?'

'Eating? Hello?' She sneered at me. 'Feel like I've been asleep for a week. I'm famished.'

I began to lower the gun. A sense of embarrassment began to filter into my wired state.

'I'm sorry. Sorry. You should... maybe... get dressed before you come down to raid the larder.' It sounded stupid even as I said it. I didn't realise how stupid until a moment later. I was too painfully aware of her long, dark legs and the way the singlet top was curved around the proud swell of her bust.

'You should take your own advice... Gregor,' she said, raising one eyebrow.

I looked down. I had lost the sheet kicking open the door. I was what Midas Betancore used to call 'very naked'.

Except, of course, for the loaded gun.

'Damn. My apologies.' I turned to scrabble for the fallen sheet.

'Don't stand on my account,' she sniggered.

I froze, stooped. The muzzle of a Tronsvasse parabellum was pointing directly at my head from the darkness behind me.

It lowered. Harlon Nayl looked me up and down for a moment in frank dismay and then raised a warning finger to his lips. He was fully clothed, damn him.

I retrieved my sheet.

'What?' I hissed.

'Someone's in. I can feel it,' he whispered. 'The noise you two were making, I thought it was the intruder. Didn't know you were so keen on Medea.'

'Shut up.'

The two of us fanned out back through the outer kitchen. Nayl pulled up the hood of his vulcanised black bodyglove to cover his pale, shaved head. He was a big man, a head taller than me, but he melted away into the darkness. I watched carefully for his signals.

Nayl waved me left down the hall. I trusted his judgment completely. He had stalked the galaxy's most innovative and able scum for three decades. If there were intruders, he'd find them.

I entered the Ocean House's main hall, and saw the front entry was ajar. The code display on the main lock was blinking a default of zeros.

I swung round as a gun roared behind me. I heard Nayl cry out and sprinted back into the inner foyer. Nayl was on the floor, grappling with an unidentifiable man.

'Get up! Get up! I'm armed!' I shouted.

In reply, the unknown intruder smacked Nayl's head back against the floor so hard he knocked him out, and then threw Nayl's heavy sidearm at me.

I fired, once, and blew a hole in the wall. The spinning gun clipped my temple and knocked me over.

I heard a series of fleshy cracks and impacts, a guttural gasp and then Medea Betancore's voice shouting, 'Lights up!'

I rose. She was standing astride the intruder, one hand braced in a fierce fist, the other pulling down her undershirt for modesty.

'I got him,' she said, glancing round at me.

The dazed intruder was clad in black from head to foot. I wrenched off his hood.

It was Titus Endor.

'Gregor,' he lisped through a bloody mouth. 'You did say you were home.'

FOUR

Between friends
An interview with Lord Rorken
The Apotropaic Congress

'Grain joiliq, with shaved ice, and a sliver of citrus.'

Seated in my sanctum chamber, Endor took the proffered drink and grinned at me. 'You remembered.'

'Many were the nights, in those fine old days. Titus, I've mixed your drink of choice too many times to count.'

'Hah! I know. What was that place, the one off Zansiple Street? Where the host used to drink the profits?'

'The Thirsty Eagle,' I replied. He knew full well. It was as if he was testing me.

'The Thirsty Eagle, that's it! Many were the nights, as you say.'

He held up his tumbler of clear, iced spirits.

'Raise 'em and sink 'em and let's have another!'

I echoed the old toast and clinked my lead-crystal of vintage amasec against his glass.

For a moment, it was indeed like the fine old days. Both of us, nineteen years old, full of piss and promethium, newly promoted interrogators ready to take on the whole damn galaxy, students of old Inquisitor Hapshant. Five years later, almost simultaneously, we would both be elected full inquisitors, and our individual careers would begin in earnest.

Nineteen years old, drunk on our feet, carousing in an armpit of a bar off Zansiple Street after hours, mocking our illustrious mentor and bonding for life, bonding with that unquestioning exuberance that seems to me now only possible in youth.

It was like regarding a different life, so far away, almost unrecoverable. I was not that Gregor Eisenhorn. And this man, with his long, braided grey hair and scarred face, sitting in my sanctum dressed in a body-heat masking stealth suit, was not that Titus Endor.

'You could have called,' I began.

'I did.'

I shrugged. 'You could have joined us for dinner tonight. Jarat excelled herself again.'

'I know. But then...' he paused, and rattled the ice around in his drink thoughtfully. 'But then, it might have become known that Inquisitor Endor had visited Inquisitor Eisenhorn.'

'It is well known that those two are old friends. Why would that have been a problem?'

Endor set down his drink, unpopped the fasteners around his waistband and pulled the top half of his stealth suit up over his head. He cast the garment aside.

'Too hot,' he remarked. His undershirt was dark with sweat. The jagged saurapt tooth still hung around his neck on a black cord. That tooth. Years ago, I'd dug it out of his leg after he had driven the beast off. Brontotaph, twelve decades ago and more. The pair of us, alongside Hapshant, in the mist-meres.

'I've come for the Novena,' he said. 'I was summoned to attend by Orsini's staff, like you I imagine. I wanted to talk to you, talk to you as far off the record as was possible.'

'So you broke into my house?'

He sighed deeply, finished his drink and walked over to the spirit stand in the corner of the room to fix another.

'You're in trouble,' he said.

'Really? Why is that?'

He looked round, peeling strips of citrus rind off a fruit with a paring knife.

'I don't know. But there are rumblings.'

'There are always rumblings.'

He turned to face me fully. His eyes were suddenly very hard and bright. 'Take this seriously.'

'Very well, I will.'

'You know what the rumour-mill is like. Someone's always got a point to make, a score to settle. There were stories. I dismissed them at first.'

'Stories?'

He sighed again and returned to his seat with his refreshed drink.

'There is talk that you are... unsound.'

'What talk?'

'Damn it, Gregor! I'm not one of your interview suspects! I've come here as a friend.'

'A friend who broke in wearing a stealth suit and–'

'Shut up just for a minute, would you?'

I paused.

'Gladly. If you cut to the chase.'

'The first I heard, someone was bad-mouthing you.'

'Who?'

'It doesn't matter. I waded in and told them just what I

thought. Then I heard the story again. Eisenhorn's unsound. He's lost the plot.'

'Really?'

'Then the stories changed. It was no longer "Eisenhorn's unsound", it was, "The people who matter think Eisenhorn's unsound". As if somehow suspicion of you had become official.'

'I've heard nothing,' I said, sitting back.

'Of course you haven't. Who'd say it to your face but a friend... or a convening judge from Internal Prosecution?'

I raised my eyebrows. 'You're really worried, aren't you, Titus?'

'Damn right. Someone's gunning for you. Someone whose got the ear of the upper echelon. Your career and activities are under scrutiny.'

'You get that all from rumours? Come on, Titus. There are plenty of inquisitors I can think of who'd like to score points off me. Orsini's a closet Monodominant, and the puritan idealists are forming a power block around him. They are radicals, in their way. You know that. Us Amalathians are too louche for their tastes.'

I mentioned before how I hated politics. Nothing is more fruitless and wearying than the internal politics of the Inquisition itself. My kind is fractured internally by belief factions and intellectual sectarianism. Endor and myself count ourselves as Amalathian inquisitors, which is to say we hold an optimistic outlook and work to sustain the integrity of the Imperium, believing it to be functioning according to the divine Emperor's scheme. We preserve the status quo. We hunt down recidivist elements: heretics, aliens, psykers, the three key enemies of mankind – these are of course our primary targets – but we will set ourselves against anything that we perceive to be destabilising Imperial society, up to and including factional infighting between the august organs of our culture. It has always struck me as ironic that we had to become a faction in order to fight factionalism.

We profess to be puritans, and certainly are so compared to the extreme radical factions of the Inquisition such as the Istvaanians and the Recongrenators.

But equally alien to us are the extreme right wing of the puritan factions, the Monodominants and the Thorians, some of whom believe even the use of trained psykers to be heretical.

If I was in trouble, it would not be the first time an inquisitor of tempered, moderate beliefs had run foul of either extreme in his own organisation.

'This goes beyond simple faction intrigue,' Titus said quietly. 'This isn't a hardliner deciding to give the moderates a going over. This is particular to you. They have something.'

'What?'

'Something concrete on you.'

'How do you know?'

'Because twenty days ago on Messina, I was detained and questioned by Inquisitor Osma of the Ordo Malleus.'

I suddenly realised I was up out of my seat.

'You were what?'

He waved dismissively. 'I'd just finished a waste-of-time matter, and was preparing to pack up and ship for Thracian. Osma contacted me, polite and friendly, and asked if he could meet with me. I went to see him. It was all very civil. He made no effort to restrain me... but I don't think I could have left before he had finished. He was guarded, but he made it clear that if I decided to walk out... his people would stop me.'

'That's outrageous!'

'No, that's Osma. You've met him surely? One of Orsini's. Bezier's right-hand man. Thorian to the marrow. He makes a point of getting what he's after.'

'And what did he get?'

'From me?' Endor laughed. 'Not a thing, except for a glowing character reference! He allowed me to leave after an hour. The bastard even suggested we might meet and dine together, socially, during the Novena.'

'Osma is a skilled operator. Slippery. So... that begs the question, what did he want?'

'He wanted you. He was interested in our friendship and our history. He asked me about you, like he wanted me to let something personal and damning slip. He didn't give away much of anything, but it was clear he had dirt. Some report had been filed that compromised you, directly or indirectly. By the end of it, I knew that the rumours I had been hearing were just the surface ripples of a secret inquiry. I knew then that I had to warn you... without anyone knowing we'd spoken.'

'It's all lies,' I told him.

'What is?'

'I don't know. Whatever they think. Whatever they fear. I've done nothing that deserves the attention of the Ordo Malleus.'

'I believe you, Gregor,' Endor said, in a way that suggested to me he undoubtedly did not.

We took fresh drinks onto the sea terrace. He looked out at the kalaedoscopic swirls of luminous plankton and said, 'They've only just begun.'

I nodded and looked down at the drink cradled in my hands.

'On Lethe... Tantalid came after me. I supposed at the time

it was old scores, but from what you've said tonight, I doubt that now.'

'Be careful,' he murmured. 'Look, Gregor, I should go. This should have been a better reunion of old friends.'

'I want to thank you for the chance you took. The effort you made to bring this to me.'

'You'd do the same.'

'I would. One last thing... how did you get in?'

He looked round at me sharply.

'What?'

'In here? Tonight?'

'I used a code scrambler on the door.'

'You diverted the alarms.'

'I'm not a novice, Gregor. My scrambler was set to trigger a nulling cascade effect through the system.'

'That's quite a piece of kit. May I see it?'

He took a small black pad from his hip-pocket and passed it to me.

'An Amplox model,' I noted. 'Quite advanced.'

'I only use the best.'

'Me too. I've employed these before. They seem... just in my experience... to work best after a few tests.'

'How so?'

'A dry run or two, I mean. To assess the system you're try-ing to penetrate. A few soft passes to gauge the security and let the scrambler assimilate and learn what it's up against.'

'Yeah, I've done that, when I've had the luxury of time. These suckers learn fast. Still, they do the job on the spot when time is tight.'

'Like tonight?' I handed the device back to him.

'Yes... what do you mean?'

'It got you in tonight from cold? No test runs necessary?'

'No, of course not. This visit was spur of the moment. And until that pretty bitch of yours kicked me in the face, I had thought myself very lucky to have gotten so far.'

'So you haven't been here before? You haven't been in before?'

'No,' he said sharply. Either I had offended him or...

'Go if you have to,' I said.

'Goodnight, Gregor.'

'Goodnight, Titus. I'd offer to show you out, but I think you know the way well enough.'

He grinned, raised his glass and finished it in a single swig.

'Raise 'em and sink 'em and let's have another!'

'I hope so,' I replied.

The Palace of the Inquisition on Thracian Primaris is high in the cloud tiers of Hive Forty-Four. The size of a small city itself, it is the chief office of the Inquisition in the Helican sub-sector, maintaining a permanent staff of sixty thousand. I make no excuses for its black staetite facings, its darkened windows, its protective spines of iron spikes. Critics of the Inquisition may regard its architecture as almost comically overdone, playing directly to the general public's worst fears about the nature of the Inquisition with its deliberate, black menace. That, I would say, is precisely the point. Fear keeps the populace in line, fear of an institution so terrible it will not hesitate to punish them for transgressions.

At the start of the next day cycle, I went to the Palace, escorted by Aemos, von Baigg and Thula Surskova. Ironically, I felt vulnerable with only three companions at my side. I had grown too used to a large retinue these last few decades. I had to remind myself that there had been a time when my entire retinue would have numbered three such people.

The Palace of the Inquisition is not a place for casual or accidental meetings. Inside, it is a dark maze of shadowy halls, void screens and opaquing fields. The staff and visitors move privately behind masking energy fields, their business confidential. On entry to the echoing main hall, my party was issued with a drone cyber-skull that hovered at our shoulders and projected an insulating cone of silence around us. We were offered an astropath adept too to further ensure our privacy, but I declined. Surskova, with her untouchable quality, was all I needed.

The hooded Inquisitorial guards, their burgundy armour threaded with gold leaf and emblazoned with the seal of our Office, led us across the black marble floor, their double-handed powerblades held upright before them. Glinting brown opaquing fields swirled into being on either side, forming a solid, buzzing corridor of energy that divorced us from our surroundings.

Alain von Baigg played with his high collar distractedly as we walked. He was nervous. The oppressive threat of the palace affected even its own servants.

Lord Rorken awaited us in his private chambers. A void shield dissipated to allow us through the circular doorway and flickered back to life once we were inside. The guards did not accompany us. I told my trio to wait for me in the austere vestibule where there were two cast iron benches piled with white satin bolsters.

I went in through the inner door.

I had come wearing black, with a three-quarter cloak of dark brown leather. My Inquisitorial crest was pinned at my throat. My companions were all formally robed too. One did not call on Master of the Ordo Xenos in casual attire.

The reception chamber was dazzlingly bright. The walls were mirrors, framed in ormolu gilt, and the floor was a polished cream marble. Thousands of candles burned all around, on stands, on forked candelabras, or simply placed directly on the floor. The mirrors reflected their glare. It was like standing in a prism that was catching golden sunlight.

I blinked, and raised my hand to shield my eyes. I saw a hundred other men in cloaks do the same. My reflections. Multiplied Gregor Eisenhorns, framed by twinkling candles. I saw I looked edgy.

That would not do.

'None may escape the penetrating glare of the Inquisition's light,' said a voice.

'For to do so means perforce they embrace the outer darkness,' I finished.

Rorken strode towards me. 'You know your Catuldynas, Eisenhorn.'

'His apopthegms please me. I have never much liked his later allegories.'

'Too dry?'

'Too arch. Too mannered. For my taste, Sathescine has a superior voice. Less... bombastic.'

Rorken smiled and took my hand. 'So you rate poetic beauty over content?'

'Beauty is truth, and truth beauty.'

He raised an eyebrow. 'What is that?'

'A pre-Imperial fragment I once read. Anonymous. As to your first question, I would read Sathescine over Catuldynas for pleasure, and insist that my neophytes read Catuldynas repeatedly until they can quote it as well as I.'

Rorken nodded. He was a compact man, his head shaved but for a short goatee, and he wore crimson robes over black clothes and gloves. It was impossible to guess his age, but he must have been at least three hundred years old, for he had held his high office for a century and a half. Thanks to augmentation and juvenatus processes, he looked like a man in his late forties.

'Can I offer you refreshment?' he asked.

'Thank you, no, sir. The nunciature has organised a busy schedule for me through the Novena, so I would be grateful if we could deal with things directly.'

'The Ministorum's nuncios have set busy schedules for us all. The Lord Commander has charged them with arranging as much pomp as possible for this celebration. And the Gregor Eisenhorn I know won't be sticking to their appointments if he can help it.'

I made no reply. That was a telling remark.

I became wary. Rorken and I had a good working relationship, and I felt he had trusted me ever since the affair with the Necroteuch ninety-eight years before. Since then he had been pleased to lead me, guide me, and oversee my cases personally. But one did not become anything like friends with the Master of the Ordo Xenos Helican.

'Have a seat. You can spare me a little time, I think.'

We sat on high-backed chairs either side of a low table, and he gave me chilled water imported from the chalybeate springs of Gidmos.

'A restorative tonic. I understand the Beldame tested you hard on Lethe Eleven.'

I slid a data-slate out of my cloak.

'A preliminary draft of my full report,' I said, handing it to him. He took it and put it, unread, on the table.

'Do you know why I have asked to see you?'

I paused, and took a calculated gamble.

'Because of the stories that I am unsound.'

He cocked his head in interest. 'You've heard them?'

'They've been brought to my attention. Recently.'

'Your reaction?'

'In all honesty? Puzzlement. I don't know the matter of the stories themselves. I feel someone must have a grudge.'

'Against you?'

'Against me personally.'

He sipped his water. 'Before we go any further, I must ask you... Is there any reason, any reason at all, that you think this story has arisen?'

'As I said, a grudge is the–'

'No,' he said quietly. 'You know what I'm asking you.'

'I've done nothing,' I said.

'I'll take your word for that. If at a later time I discover you're lying, or even hiding something from me, I will... be displeased.'

'I have done nothing,' I repeated.

He steepled his hands and looked out across the sea of candles. 'Here is the way of it. An inquisitor – who, it does not matter – reported to me in confidence a disturbing encounter. A daemonhost made a show of sparing a man's life, because it thought he was you.'

I was fascinated and horrified at the thought.

'I am not able to confirm it, but the daemonhost has been identified as Cherubael.'

Now my blood ran cold. Cherubael.

'You've had no contact with that entity since 56-Izar?'

I shook my head. 'No, sir. And that was almost a century ago.'

'But you've been looking for it ever since?'

'I've made no secret of that, sir. Cherubael is the agency of an invisible enemy, one whose machinations involved even a member of our Office.'

'Molitor.'

'Yes, Konrad Molitor. I have spent a great deal of time and effort trying to uncover the truth about Cherubael and its unseen master, but it has been fruitless. Ten decades, and only the barest few hints.'

'The matter of Cherubael's involvement in the Necroteuch affair was passed to the Ordo Malleus, as you know. They too have failed to turn up a trace of it.'

'Where was this alleged encounter?'

He paused. 'Vogel Passionata.'

'And it thought it was sparing me?'

'The implication was the daemonhost had better things in mind for you. There was a strong suggestion of... a compact between you and it.'

'Nonsense!'

'I hope so–'

'Really, nonsense, sir!'

'I hope so, Eisenhorn. Grandmaster Orsini has no time for radical elements in the Inquisition. Even if he wasn't so hard-line, I'd not stand for it. Ordo Xenos Helican has no place for those who consort with Chaos.'

'I understand.'

'Make sure you do.' Rorken's face was dark and stern now. 'Your search for this entity continues?'

'Even now I have agents in the field hunting for it.'

'With any signs of success?'

I thought of the Glossia-coded message I had received the night before. 'No,' I said, my first and only lie in the conversation.

'The inquisitor in question urged me to take the matter to the Ordo Malleus. I'll not throw one of my best men to the mercy of Bezier's dogs. I kept the matter internal to our ordo.'

'Then why the stories?'

'That's what troubled me too. Word has got out anyway. I thought it prudent to advise you that the Ordo Malleus might be scrutinising you.'

A second warning in twelve hours.

'I'd like to suggest you leave Thracian and get on with other work until the matter blows over,' he said. 'But your presence is required for the Apotropaic Congress.'

Pieces now fell into place. The sheer scale of the triumph celebrations, the magnitude of the Novena, were appropriate enough, but the number of senior inquisitors summoned to attend was heavy handed to say the least. Military and Ecclesiarch luminaries may be ordered around to swell such events, but inquisitors are a different breed, more aloof, more... independent. It is unusual for us to be called together in any great gathering, particularly by such incontestable orders. I had presumed Orsini was throwing his weight around to impress the Lord Commander Helican.

But that was not the case. There was to be an Apotropaic Congress. That is why we had been called here.

Apotropaic studies are conducted all the time by the Inquisition, and usually involve one or perhaps as many as three inquisitors. On a larger scale, they are named Councils, and require a quorum of at least eleven inquisitors. Larger than that, they become a Congress. Such assemblies are extremely rare. I knew for a fact that my late master Hapshant had served on the last such Congress held in the sub-sector. That was two hundred and seventy-nine years in the past.

The purpose of these studies, even at their smallest level, is the acute examination and assessment of unusually valuable captives. Once in the custody of the Inquisition, a rogue psyker, a charismatic heretic, an alien warlord... whatever... undergoes a sometimes lengthy formal examination quite separate from the dissection of his or her actual crimes. They are often already condemned and only waiting for sentence to be carried out. At that stage, the Inquisition wishes to expand its own learning, to understand more precisely the nature of the enemies of mankind. The subjects are dissected, usually intellectually, sometimes psychically and occasionally literally, in order to discover their strengths, weaknesses, beliefs and drives. Vital truths have in this way been discovered by Apotropaic councils, truths that have armoured the servants of the Imperium for later clashes. To illustrate, the Imperial Guard's famous victory over the Ezzel meta-breed was only successful thanks to methods of detecting their presence discovered by the examination of an Ezzel scoutform by the Apotropaic Council of Adiemus Ultima in 883.M40.

The size of the inquiry depends on the number or magnitude of the subject.

'Thirty-three heretic psykers of level alpha or above were captured by the Warmaster at Dolsene, during the final major engagement of the Ophidian Suppression,' Rorken told me, showing me a data-slate. The security clearance on the slate was so high that even I was impressed. 'Trained, somehow, to control and master the warp-spawned filth they channel, they formed the backbone of the Enemy's high command defence, the beating heart of the adversary.'

'How were they taken? Alive, I mean?' It was astonishing. Untrained psykers are terrifying enough, their minds always carrying the horrendous potential to open up a gate into the immaterium, to let its daemons flood through into our universe. But these... these fiends, they had somehow learnt – or been trained – to focus their warp-spawned talents, to contain the daemons within themselves and use their damnable strength. My mind reeled at the threat they had posed, and posed still, though they were our prisoners.

Rorken gestured to the slate in my hands. 'You'll find a summary of the incident there, appended to the main list. In brief, it was luck... luck, and the amazing courage of the Adeptus Astartes, working in conjunction with Inquisitors Heldane, Lyko and Voke.'

'Voke... Commodus Voke.'

'I forgot, you're old friends, aren't you? He was involved with the Glaw affair on Gudrun, just before the Schism.'

'Old friends is probably pushing it. We worked together. We generated a mutual respect. I've seen him infrequently since then. I'm amazed the old dog is still alive.'

'Alive, despite the prognoses of several generations of medicae experts. And still powerful. To achieve this, in his twilight years...'

I nodded. Even a speed-reading of the incident suggested an act of near mythical valour. Voke's service to the Emperor was, as ever, above and beyond any reasonable expectation of duty.

'I know Heldane too. He was Voke's pupil. So he's finally made it to inquisitor rank too?'

'For sixty years now... Eisenhorn, you lead a solitary life, don't you?'

'If you mean I don't keep up with the comings and goings of elections and the businesses of other inquisitors, sir, yes. I do. I focus on my work, and the needs of my staff.'

He smiled, as if indulging me. In truth, my attitude was not uncommon. As I have said, we of the Inquisition are an aloof, independent kind, and have little interest in the affairs of our colleagues. I saw another difference between myself and Rorken. Whatever my seniority, I was still an agent of the field, a worker, an achiever, who might be gone into the distant gulfs of the Halo Stars for months or even years at a time. His rank tied him to his palace, and wrapped him in the intrigues and mechanisms of the Imperial ruling classes in general and the Inquisition in particular.

I remembered Commodus Voke as a poisonous old viper, but a determined ally. During the affair of the Necroteuch, believing himself to be on his deathbed, he had implored me to stand reference for his pupil Heldane. I had promised him that, though when Voke then proceeded to stay alive, I had never followed it through. He had been around to see that Heldane got his rosette.

Heldane... I had never liked him at all.

I'd never met Lyko, the third member of the glorious trio, but I knew him by reputation as an inquisitor whose star was very much in the ascendant. Their spectacular achievement on Dolsene would further all their careers magnificently.

I read through the list of inquisitors summoned to form the Council, a list which included my name. There were sixty in all. Titus Endor was amongst them. So was Osma, and so was Bezier. Some names, like Schongard, Hand and Reiker, leapt out as men I had little wish to be in the same room with. Others – Endor, naturally, and Shilo, Defay and Cuvier – were individuals it would be a pleasure to see again.

Some names I'd barely heard of, or never heard of at all; others were famous or infamous inquisitors who I knew only by reputation. It was quite an assembly, drawn from all over the sector.

'My inclusion on this list?' I began.

'Is no surprise. You are a senior and respected member of our office.'

'Thank you, sir. But I wonder, did Voke request me personally?'

'He was going to,' Rorken told me, 'but you had already been nominated.'

'By whom?'

'Inquisitor Osma,' he replied.

FIVE

The Triumph
At the Spatian Gate
The line breaks

For all my condemnations of the overzealous pageantry of the Novena, I will admit that the Great Triumph of the first day filled me with a sense of pride and exhilaration.

Across Hive Primaris, the largest and most powerful hive on Thracian, dawn brought a chorus of klaxons and a cacophony of bells. Ministorum services, relayed live from the Monument of the Ecclesiarch, were broadcast on every crackling pict channel and public vox service. The phlegmy intonations of Cardinal Palatine Anderucias rolled across the street levels of the great hive city, overlapping like some gigantic choral round due to the echoes of doppler distortion.

Civilians and pilgrims flooded into the streets of Hive Primaris in their millions, clogging the arterial routes and feeder tunnels, and blackening the sky with their craft. Many were turned back to surrounding hives to watch the proceedings on vast hololithic screens raised in stadiums and amphitheatres for the event.

The Arbites struggled to control the flow of people and keep the route of the Triumph clear.

The day cycle began brightly. In the night, flocks of dirigibles from the Officium Meteorologicus had seeded the smog fields and upper cloud levels with carbon black and other chemical precipitants. Before dawn, sixteen hundred-kilometre wide rainstorms had washed the clouds away and drenched the primary hives, sluicing the dirt and grime away. For the first time in decades, the sky was clear. Not blue exactly, but clear of yellow pollution banks. The sun's light permeated the atmosphere and the steepled ridges and high towers of the hives glowed. I had heard, from informal sources, that this radical act of weather control would have profound ill consequences for the planet's already brutalised climate for decades to come. Reactive hurricane storms were expected in the southern regions before the week was out, and the drainage system of the primary hives was said to be choked to bursting by the singular rainfall.

It was also said that the seas would die quicker, thanks to the overdose of pollutants hosed into them so suddenly by the rain-clearance.

But the Lord Commander Helican had insisted that the sun shone on his victory parade.

I arrived early to take my place, fearing the great flow of traffic into the hive. I brought Ravenor with me. We were both dressed in our finest garb, emblems proudly displayed, and wore ceremonial weapons.

Medea Betancore flew us in, and landed us at a reserved Navy air-station just south of the Imperial armour depot. By

the time she'd got us on the ground, the air routes were so thick
she had no choice but to stay put there for the day. There was
no flying out. She bade us a good day, and strolled away across
the pad to chat with the ground crew servicing a Marauder.

A private car, arranged by the Nunciature, took Ravenor
and myself to the hive's old Founding Fields at Lempenor
Avenue, where the Inquisition was expected to gather to join
the march. Outside the windows of the speeding lifter limou-
sine, we saw steam rising from the empty, rain-washed streets.
Despite his best efforts, the Lord Commander Helican would
have clouds before noon.

I leant forward in the car's passenger bay and straightened
Ravenor's interrogator rosette. He looked nervous, a look I
didn't associate with him. He also looked the very image of
an inquisitor. I realised he didn't look nervous so much as just
very young. Like a man hurrying to join his drinking friends
in the Thirsty Eagle off Zansiple Street.

'What is it?' he asked, smiling.

I shook my head. 'This will be quite a day, Gideon. Are you
ready for it?'

'Absolutely,' he said.

I noticed he had added the tribe badge of clan Esw Sweydyr to the decoration of his uniform.

'An appropriate touch,' I remarked, pointing to it.

'I thought so,' he said.

At ten, the Triumph began. A deafening roar of hooters and
sirens blasted across the hive, followed by a mass cheer that
quite took my breath away. By then, the streets were packed
with close on two billion jubilant citizens.

Two billion voices, raised as one. You cannot imagine it.

* * *

In sunlit air vibrating with colossal cheering, the Great Triumph moved out from the Armour depot. It was to follow an eighteen kilometre route straight down the kilometre-wide Avenue of the Victor Bellum, right into the heart of the hive and the Monument of the Ecclesiarch. Millions lined the way, cheering, applauding, waving banners and Imperial flags.

At the front rolled eighty tanks of the Thracian Fifth, pennants quivering from their aerial masts. Behind them, the colours band of the Fiftieth Gudrunite Rifles, pumped out the stately *March of the Primarchs*.

Next, the standard bearers: five hundred men carrying aloft the many regimental guidons and emblems representing the units and regiments that had participated in the Ophidian Suppression. It took an hour for them alone to all pass.

On their heels came the Great Standard of the Emperor, a vast aquila symbol like a clipper's mainsail, so big it took a stocky, lumbering, unbelievably ancient dreadnought of the White Consuls to lift it and stop it being carried away by the wind. The dreadnought was escorted by five Baneblade super-heavy tanks.

Behind that, rolled the dead. Every Imperial corpse recovered from the closing stages of the war, loaded in state into fifteen hundred Rhino carriers painted black for the duty. One hundred mighty Space Marines of the Aurora Chapter marched beside the trundling machines, holding up black-ribboned placards on which the names of the dead were etched in gold leaf.

It was noon by the time the marching ranks of the rest of Aurora Chapter, all in full, polished imperator armour, moved by. The massive cheering had not yet diminished. After the Space Marines came sixty thousand Thracian troops, thirty thousand from Gudrun, eight thousand from Messina, four

thousand from Samater. Breastplates and lances glittered in
the sun. Then the Navy officers from Battlefleet Scarus in neat
echelons. Then the White Consuls, glittering and terrifying.

Then the endless files of the Munitorum and the Administratum, followed by the slow-moving trains of the Astropathicus.
A dull psychic discharge, like corposant, slithered and crackled around their carriages and their heads, and left a metallic
taste in the air.

The Titans of the Adeptus Mechanicus followed them. Four
Warlords, blotting out the sun, eight grinding Warhounds,
and a massive Super-Titan called *Imperius Volcanus*. It was
as if significant sections of the hive itself had detached and
begun walking. The vast crowds hushed as they thumped past;
man-shaped mechanisms as tall as a steeple, taller yet in the
case of Volcanus. Their massive legs rose and fell in perfect
synchronisation. The ground shook. Unperturbed, six hundred tech-priests and magos of the Adeptus paraded casually
between their feet.

The tank brigades of the Narmenians and the Scuterans followed the god-machines. Five thousand armour units, rolling
forward under a haze of exhaust, barrels raised in salute. Tractors towed Earthshaker cannons behind them, three abreast,
and then a seemingly endless flow of Hydra batteries, traversing their multiple barrels from left to right, like sun-following
flowers.

The Ecclesiarchy followed, led by Cardinal Rouchefor, who
srode ahead of his two thousand hierarchs barefoot. Cardinal Palatine Anderucias awaited us all for the blessing at the
monument.

From its muster point at the old Founding Fields, the Inquisition fell in line behind the priesthood, six hundred strong.
We were the only part of the Triumph not to march in

ordered ranks. We simply strode behind the Ecclesiarch in a sombre wedge. We were not uniform. All manner of men and women filled our ranks, all manner of appearances and aspects. Individuals walking, dressed in dark robes or leather capes, some with great entourages holding up the trains of gaudy robes, some on lifter thrones, some alone and dignified, some even hidden by personal void shields. Ravenor and I walked together in the press, behind the extravagant ensemble of Inquisitor Eudora.

Lord Orsini, the grandmaster, led us, his long purple vestments trained out behind him and supported by thirty servitors. At his side strode Lord Rorken of the Ordo Xenos, Lord Bezier of the Ordo Malleus and Lord Sakarof of the Ordo Hereticus, Orsini's triumvirate.

Sonic booms sounded over the hives as honour escorts of Thunderhawks flashed down above us. Fireworks banged and fizzed, staining the sky with quick blooms of colour and light.

At our backs came the triumphal procession of the Warmaster himself. Honorius rode with Lord Commander Helican, standing in a howdah built upon the humped back of the largest and most venerable aurochothere warbeast. Ten thousand men from their personal retinues marched together. Two hundred grunting, snuffling behemoths from the aurochothere cavalry. Eight hundred Conqueror tanks. Lifter bikes skimmed alongside their line. The frenzied crowd strewed thousands of flowers in their path.

Behind them all came the prisoners.

Like the honoured dead in the funereal Rhinos, the prisoners were an open show of Imperial heroism in general, and the Warmaster's heroism in particular. Honorius delighted in displaying their torment to the adoring populace. The sight of these great, potent creatures cowed and submissive made his own power manifest.

There were several hundred foot soldiers, chained together at the hands and feet, shambling along in two wretched lines. Veterans of the Thracian Guard marched around them, lashing out with force-poles and neural-whips to drive them on. The crowd booed and howled, and pelted the subjugated foe with bottles and rocks.

Six Trojan tank-tractors, painted in the Warmaster's colours and teamed together like horses pulling a state landau, came behind the chained prisoners, towing a vast flatbed trailer designed to transport a super-heavy tank. On the flatbed, shackled in adamite and encased in individual void shield bubbles, were the thirty-three psykers, the greatest trophies of all. They were dim, contorted shapes, barely human, swimming in the milky green cocoons of the imprisoning shields. Along with the White Consuls guarding the tractor-team, two hundred astrotelepaths strode alongside it, mentally reinforcing the void bubbles that were damping the psychic fury of the captives. Frost coated the metal of the flatbed. More psychic ball-lightning drifted overhead.

Twenty thousand men and five hundred armoured machines of the Thracian Interior Guard formed the tail of the Great Triumph, marching under the dual standard of Thracia and the Warmaster.

After barely fifteen minutes of walking in the immense procession, I was utterly numb. The noise of the crowd alone vibrated me to the very marrow. My diaphragm shook every time the flypast came in low or when the great siege sirens of the Titans blasted. The scale of the occasion was overwhelming, the sensory assault bewildering. Seldom have I been so in awe of the power of my species.

Seldom have I been so forcibly reminded of my place as a tiny cog in the workings of the holy Imperium of Mankind.

Following the mighty Avenue of the Victor Bellum, the Triumph passed under the Spatian Gate, a monolithic structure of glossy white aethercite. The memorial gate was so cyclopean, even the Titans passed under it without difficulty.

It had been raised to commemorate Admiral Lorpal Spatian, who had been killed in the early years of the Ophidian Suppression during the magnificent fleet action that had taken Uritule IV.

The inner part of the arch was painted with majestic murals depicting that event, and rose to a dome so high, a microclimate of clouds regularly formed under the apex. I had known Spatian personally, and like several others in the procession, I paused under the giant gate to pay my respects to the eternal flame.

No, that is not true. I had known Spatian, during the Helican Schism, but not at all well. For reasons I could not explain, I felt compelled to stop. I certainly had no great urge to honour him.

'Sir?' Ravenor asked as I stepped aside.

'Go on, I'll catch up shortly,' I told him.

Ravenor moved on with the procession while I lit a votive candle and set it amongst the thousands of others around Spatian's tomb. The vast tide of the Triumph moved slowly by behind me. Other figures had detached themselves from the procession and stood nearby, paying silent homage to the admiral.

'Eisenhorn?'

I looked round, the voice breaking my reverie. An elderly but powerful Navy officer stood before me, splendidly austere in his white dress jacket.

'Madorthene,' I said, recognising him at once.

We shook hands. It had been a few years since I'd seen Olm Madorthene – Lord Procurator Madorthene, as he was now. We'd first met at Gudrun during the Necroteuch affair when he had been a mid-ranking officer in the Battlefleet Disciplinary Detachment, the Navy's military police. Now he ran that detachment. He'd been a useful and reliable ally over the years.

'Quite an event,' he said, with a reserved smile. Outside, the horns of the immense Titans blared again and the noise from the crowd swelled.

'I find myself sufficiently humbled,' I said. 'The Warmaster must be loving it.'

He nodded. 'Uplifting, good for public morale.'

I agreed, but in truth my heart was not in it. It wasn't just the overwhelming cacophony of it, or my deep-seated reluctance to be here at all. Since Ravenor and I had stepped out to take our place in the Triumph, I had nursed a sense of foreboding that was growing with each passing minute. Was that what had made me pause here, under the great arch?

'There's a look on your face,' said Madorthene. 'This isn't really your thing, is it?'

'I suppose not.'

'What is it, old friend?'

I paused. Something...

I strode back to the south arch of the Spatian Gate and looked back down the huge river of the Triumph. Madorthene was with me. The Warmaster's retinue was just then beginning to pass under the Gate. Cymbals and horns clashed and blared. The noise of the crowd boomed in like a tidal wave surging down.

There were petals in the air. I remember that clearly. A

blizzard of loose petals gusting up from the flowers the crowd was strewing.

A formation of twelve Lightnings was swooping in low from the south, coming down the length of the Triumph parade, following the Avenue of the Victor Bellum. Coming towards the Gate. They were in line abreast, the tips of their forward-swept wings almost touching. A display of perfect formation flying from the Battlefleet's best pilots. Sunlight glinted on their canopies and on the raked double-vanes of their tailplanes.

The sense of foreboding I had felt now became oppressively real. It was like heavy clouds had passed in front of the sun.

'Olm, I–'

'Emperor's mercy! He's in trouble, look!' Madorthene cried.

The fighters were half a kilometre from the Gate, moving at a high cruising speed. The left hand wingman suddenly wobbled, bucked...

...and veered.

The flier directly inside of him pulled hard to avoid a collision, and his starboard wing clipped the wingtip of the next Lightning in line. There was a bright puff of impact debris.

One by one, like pearls coming off a necklace, each aircraft was knocked out of the formation. The once-sleek line broke in utter disarray.

Madorthene hurled me to the ground as the jets shrieked overhead, rattling the world with their afterburners.

The two that I had seen strike each other were spinning in the air, somersaulting like discarded toys, splintering trails of metal scrap behind them. In the confusion, it seemed to me as if several others had also accidentally collided.

One Lightning, over ten tonnes of almost supersonic metal, cartwheeled down and went into the crowd on the west side of the Avenue. It bounced at least once, showering human debris into the air. At its final impact, it became a massive fireball that belched up a blazing mushroom cloud a hundred metres into the air. Shock and berserk panic filled the crowd. The stench of flame and heat and promethium washed over me.

There was a flash and the ground shook as a second stricken Lightning spiralled in under the shadow the Gate. Then, almost simultaneously, a third and louder blast came as a third aircraft, sent lurching out of control, sheared off a wing on the top corner of the Spatian Gate itself, right above us, and began tumbling down, end over end.

In the face of this calamitous accident, the soldiers in the Triumph were scattering in all directions. I dragged Madorthene back in under the arch as shattered chunks of the stricken aircraft avalanched down.

A catastrophe. A terrible, terrible catastrophe.

And it was just beginning.

SIX

Doom comes to Thracian
Chaos unslipped
Headshot

Even at that stage, gripped by horror and outrage, I knew that a great hollow part of me deep in my soul could not, would not believe that this had simply been a tragic accident.

There were fire and explosions all around, mass panic, screaming.

And another sound. An extraordinary low moaning, a swelling, surging susurration that I realised was the sound two billion people make when they are panicking and in fear for their lives.

The crowds had spilled over onto the Avenue, quite beyond the measure of the Arbites to contain them, fleeing both the dreadful crash sites and the fires, and also the imagined risk that to stand still somehow invited more Imperial warcraft to fall upon their heads.

The crowd moved as one, a fluid thing, like water. There was no decision making process, no ringleader. Mass instinct simply compelled the people who swamped the vast street, in awful, trampling tides, overwhelming the ranks of the Triumph, much of which was already breaking up in shocked dismay. There was no sound of music any more, no cheering, no drums or sirens. Just a braying insanity, a world turned on its head.

I saw people die in their hundreds, trampled underfoot or crushed in the sheer press of bodies. In some cases, the dead were so squeezed by their neighbours, they were carried along for many metres before being freed to slither to the ground.

I saw troopers from the retinues, and Arbites, firing into the crowd in terror before they were run down. Barricades collapsed. Standards swayed and toppled. Walkways over the drain canals alongside the Avenue cracked and fell in, spilling hundreds down into the rockcrete trenches.

I'd lost sight of Madorthene in the pandemonium. I tried to push out from the arch into the sunlight, but fleeing bodies slammed into me. The entire approach to the Spatian Gate was a mass of twisted wreckage and fire from the impact high above. Several dozen Guardsmen lay twisted and dead amid the wreckage, killed by falling metal and stone, their dress uniforms dusted white with powdered aethercite or scorched by fire.

Through the sea of screaming humanity, I could see several of the massive aurochotheres stampeding out of control, rearing up, shaking their riders from their backs, trampling into the multitude. Lifeless bodies were tossed high into the air by their swishing tails.

I managed to slide along the outer edge of the gate until I could look north, towards the distant Monument of the Ecclesiarch. Right along the wide Avenue, the scene was repeated. The procession of the Triumph was overrun by the sheer numbers of the terrified public.

There was fire too, great plumes of it, rising from the crowd spaces on either side of the road in three places and on the Avenue of the Victor Bellum itself, about seven hundred metres beyond the Gate. It also seemed to me that fire also rose from other open areas beyond the next spire, off the roadway into the artisans' quarter. By my estimation, at least five more of the stricken Lightnings had fallen from the sky, ripping into the mass of the citizenry teeming in panic on the Avenue.

Soot and ash fogged the air. Distantly, above the milling nightmare of bodies, I could see the vast shapes of the Titans, turning on their metal hips, hesitant, as if utterly confused.

I doubt I saw the other Lightnings before anyone else. But I was transfixed. They were all I could see. There were four more of them, presumably the only survivors of the disastrous flyby. They had turned, and were sweeping back down the Avenue. Their formation was nothing like as precise or pretty as it had been just before the accident.

But they were much lower. And much faster.

And I knew what that meant, for I had seen it before.

An attack run.

Emperor spare me, my heart almost stopped as I saw the insane intention taking shape before me.

I screamed out something, but it was futile. One voice against two billion.

Streams of tracer rounds spat from the heavy cannons under their noses. Wing-mounted lascannons sparkled soundlessly.

Two went low over the crowd, slaughtering thousands. The other two followed the Avenue itself, raking the Great Triumph.

The destruction was extraordinary, as if invisible, white-hot ploughs had been set into the sea of bodies, slicing long, straight, explosive furrows out of the Imperial citizenry below. Or as if some fast-moving, burrowing force was scattering them from below. Stippled lines of explosions sawed through the populace, casting up both human and mechanical wreckage. There was an actual fog of liquefied tissue in the air. I saw tanks struck on the highway, detonating in the mob. Hundreds of Guarsdmen and Space Marines in the ruined cavalcade opened fire into the air, chasing the planes, churning the sky with bright, criss-crossed lines.

A Lightning swept by almost overhead, cutting to the left of the Spatian Gate. Its strafing firepower explosively mangled hundreds of people perilously close to me, showering me and the white stone of the Gate's side face with cooked blood.

Hundreds of batteries in the procession were now firing into the sky, the Hydras blitzing the air. Even tanks were firing – out of anger, I suppose, for they hadn't a hope in hell of hitting the fast-moving aircraft.

Yet something must have struck. A second Lightning tilted as it passed over the Gate, tiny explosions shredding its left wing and tail section. It dove straight down into the Avenue itself. It hit what seemed to me to be the heart of the Warmaster's section of the Triumph. The blast wake blew out across the wide roadway, killing as many with its concussive effects as with the impact fireball itself.

The three remaining Lightnings banked again down over the far end of the Avenue and made for a third pass. I was struck by the way they didn't turn as a pack. They flew individually, as if divorced from the world. Were their pilots possessed, insane? My mind span. Two of them banked into each other and almost hit. One didn't veer, and carried on up the Avenue, hungry for more carnage. The other was forced to swing wide, corrected, and turned over the wailing crowd mass to the west of the Avenue.

The third overshot and almost disappeared. I saw it loop faraway, out over the river haze, its wings glinting in the sun. Then it too came back for us. Like the others, straight back heedlessly into the teeth of the firestorms that the tanks, Hydras and infantry were throwing up at them.

Several hundreds more died in that final run. Loyal citizens whose exciting day out had turned to horror; proud Guardsmen back from the war, thinking only to enjoy this special hour of praise; mysterious Space Marines, who were there only because they had been invited to be there, as an expression of honour, who perhaps greeted this death as just an alternative to their expected fate. Imperial nobles and dignitaries died in their hundreds. Several noble households never recovered from the losses at the Triumph of Thracian.

The last three Lightnings fell in this manner.

One, crossing the Spatian Gate and beyond, was blown apart in an airburst by tracking Hydras on the chaotic street.

A second flew the gauntlet of anti-air salvos without adjusting its height and then, struck by one of the guns almost as an afterthought, turned upside down in a lazy yaw. Streaming smoke, it tilted down towards the ground but exploded against the Monument of the Ecclesiarch.

The third came in, guns chattering, and actually flew under the arch of the Spatian Gate. By then, the Titans themselves had turned to engage, and my guts convulsed with the subsonic roar of their weapons. I could see them, three kilometres away, weapon mounts pumping and flashing, high above the crowd.

Excelcis Gaude, one of the Warlord Titans, caught it dead on, and killed it in the air, but not cleanly enough. The tumbling

Lightning, ablaze from end to end, hit the immense Warlord Titan square on and decapitated the colossus as it exploded.

I was lost. I was stupefied. I was speechless.

I felt as if I should fall to my knees amid the tumult and beg the God-Emperor of Mankind for salvation.

But my part in this was only just beginning.

Pellucid blue flame, like a searing wall of acid, suddenly washed through the churning mob behind the Gate. Men, women, soldiers, civilians, were caught in it and shuddered, melting, resolving into skeletons that turned to dust and blew away.

I felt the pain in my sinuses, the throb in my spine. I knew what it was.

Psyker-evil. Raw Chaos, loosed on this world.

The prisoners were loose.

The warriors did not matter. A vast pitched battle was already raging across the Avenue behind Spatian's broken Gate. The Thracian Guard, the Aurora Marines and the Arbites were striving to contain the outbreak of enemy prisoners, many of whom had taken the opportunity to break free and grab weapons. A ferocious, point-blank war had seized the great approach.

But what concerned me were the psykers. The captured heretics. The thirty-three. They had broken free.

I drew my power sword and my boltgun, plunging into the milling bodies, crunching over the calcified bones of those slaughtered by the psychic wave.

An inhuman thing, a Chaos prisoner, leapt at me, and I struck its head off with my blade. I leapt over a dead Space Marine, who was leaking blood onto the rockcrete from splits in his imperator armour, and pushed through the howling civilians.

Four Thracian Guardsmen were directly ahead of me, using

the charred corpse of a fallen aurochothere for cover as they blasted into the press.

I was a few steps away from them when the gigantic dead animal reanimated, a psychic puppet, killing them all.

My weapons were useless. I focussed my mind and blew the thing apart with a concussive mental wave.

An Aurora Marine flew through the air over me, ten metres up, his legs missing.

I ran on, scything my blade at the escaped prisoners who menaced me.

The road was covered with the dead. Humans, on fire from head to foot, stumbled past me and collapsed on their faces.

The Trojan tractor team was on fire, its massive trailer slewed around. Three of the enemy pyskers lay dead on the payload space, and four void shields remained intact, their occupants frantic within.

But the others...

Upwards of twenty-five alpha-level enemy psykers had escaped.

I saw the first, a stumbling, emaciated wretch of a man, near the end of the trailer. Corposant flickered around his head and he was trying to eat a screaming astropath novitiate.

My boltgun stopped his daemonic work.

I dropped to my knees, gasping and crying as the second found me. She was a stringy female, clad in a gauzy white veil, her fingernails like talons.

She cowered behind the end of the trailer, sobbing and lashing out at me with her foul power. She had no eyes.

I am not alpha-class. My brain was broiling and bubbling.

A Thracian Guardsman ran at her from the left, and instinctively, she turned her attention to him. His head popped like a blister.

I shot her through the heart and knocked her flat on her back. Her limbs continued to thrash for over a minute.

Electrical discharge spat out at me from nearby in the crowd. People, screaming and burning, tumbled frantically back from a male psyker who was striding, head down, towards the hives. He was a dwarf, with stunted limbs and an enlarged cranium. Ball lightning crackled around his pudgy fingers.

I stabbed at him with my mind, just to get his attention and then exploded his face with a pin-point bolt.

Emperor save me, he kept coming. I had blown the front off his skull, but he kept coming. Blind, his features a gory mess. He stumbled across the ground towards me, his still-active mind boring into mine.

I fired again, almost panicking myself, and blew off one of his arms. Still he came on. My jacket, hair and eyelashes caught fire. My brain was about to explode out of my skull.

A Space Marine in the colours of the Aurora Chapter came at him from behind and shredded him into pulp with his boltgun.

'Inquisitor?' the Space Marine asked me, his voice distorted by his helmet mic. 'Are you all right?'

He helped me up.

'What insanity is this?' he rasped.

'You have a vox-channel? Alert Lord Orsini!'

'Already done, inquisitor,' he crackled.

Behind us, the tractors exploded en masse, flinging fire and debris high into the air.

A scalded child ran past us, shrieking.

The Space Marine grabbed the child in his massive arms.

'This way, this way, out of danger...'

'No,' I said slowly. 'Don't... don't...'

His visored face swung up at me in confusion, the child cradled in his arms.

'Don't what?' he asked.

'Look at the brand! The mark there!' I yelled, pointing to the Malleus rune burned into the child's ankle. The hammer of witches. The brand-mark of the psyker.

The Chaos child looked up at me and grinned.

'What mark?' asked the Space Marine. 'What mark are you talking about?'

'I... I...'

I tried to fight it, please know that. I tried to repel the unholy power of the child's mind as it groped into my head. But this thing, this 'child', was far beyond my powers to contain.

Kill him, it said.

My hand was shaking, resisting, as I swung the boltgun around and shot the Space Marine through the head. A searing white agony flooded my horrified being.

Now kill yourself, it suggested, chortling.

I put the smoking muzzle of the boltgun against my own temple, my vision filled with the giggling face of the child, perched on the knee of the collapsed, headless Space Marine.

That's it... go on...

My finger tightened on the trigger.

'No... n-no...'

Yes, you stupid fool... yes...

Blood streamed out of my nose. I wanted to fall to my knees, but the monster wouldn't let me. It wanted me to do one thing, and one thing only. It implored me, ripping my consciousness apart.

It was strident and it was undeniable.

I pulled the trigger.

SEVEN

Voke, and speculations
Esarhaddon
Through the Void

But I did not die.

The boltgun, that gift from Librarian Brytnoth, which had never failed me in ten decades of use, failed to fire.

The child-thing shrieked and leapt away into the smoke and flames and struggling shapes around me. The dead Space Marine toppled over. The air frothed with psychic discharge and three figures ran past me in pursuit of the tiny abomination. Inquisitors. All three were inquisitors, or interrogators at least. One, I was sure, was Inquisitor Lyko.

I lowered my shaking hand. Both it, and the boltgun it clutched, were cased in psionic ice, the mechanism jammed and locked out.

I turned and found Commodus Voke standing a few paces behind me. His ancient face was contorted with internal pressure. Crusts of psipathetic frost glittered on his long black gown.

'Point. It. Aside.' His words came out as halting gasps. 'I. Cannot. Hold. It. Much. Longer.'

Swiftly, I turned the boltgun aside and up into the air. With a barking gasp, he convulsively relaxed and the weapon bucked and fired. The deadly round whined away harmlessly into the sky.

Voke was sagging, the gyros in the augmetic exo-skeleton that cradled his frail body straining to manage his balance. I gave him my hand in support.

'Thank you, Commodus.'

'No matter,' he said, his voice a whisper. His strength began to return and he peered up at me with his bird-bright eyes. 'Only a brave man or a fool tangles with a plus-alpha psyker.'

'Then I am both or neither. I was closest to the emergency. I could not just stand by.'

We were assailed by extraordinary noises from the charnel ground behind us. Gunfire, grenades, screams and the popping, surging sounds of minds fracturing reality, compressing matter, boiling atmosphere. I saw a robed man, an inquisitor or an astropath, rising slowly into the sky in a pillar of green fire, burning, shredding inside out. I saw geysers of blood like waterspouts. Squalls of hail and acid rain, localised to this small stretch of the Avenue, blustered across us, triggered by the ferocity of the psychic war.

Figures were rushing in to join that battle. Many from the ordos with their expert bodyguards, and dozens of the Adeptus Astartes. There was a vibration underfoot, and I saw that one of the towering Warhound Titans was stalking past the Spatian Gate, spitting its turbo lasers at ground targets. A series of withering explosions, mainly psyker-blasts, tore through the habitats and hive structures on the eastern side of the wide – and now infamous – Avenue.

Imperial Marauders flashed low overhead. The sky was black with smoke, all sunlight blotted out. Wisps of ash fell on us like grey snow.

'This is... a great crime,' Voke said to me. 'A black day in the Imperial annals.'

I had forgotten how much Commodus Voke loved understatement.

The greater part of Hive Primaris remained lawless and out of control for five days. Panic, rioting, looting and civil unrest boiled through the streets and hab-levels of the wounded megapolis as the Arbites and the other organs of the Imperium struggled to impose martial law and restore order.

It was a desperate task. The indigenous population alone was vast, but it had been swelled to an unimaginable extent by pilgrims and tourists for the Novena. Sympathetic panic riots broke out in other hives too. For a day or two, it seemed like the entire planet was going to collapse in blood and fire.

Small sections of Hive Primaris had managed to insulate themselves: the elite spire levels; the noble houses, built like fortresses; the impregnable precincts of the Inquisition, the Imperial Guard, the Astropathicus, the various bastions of the Munitorum and the Royal Palace of the Lord Commander. Elsewhere, especially in the common and general hab levels, it was like a war zone.

The Ecclesiarchy suffered particularly gravely. With the Monument of the Ecclesiarch in flames, the common masses regarded the nightmare as some holy curse, and turned in their frenzy on all the churches, temples and sacerdotal orders they could find. We learned within the first few hours that Cardinal Palatine Anderucias had been killed in the destruction of the Monument. He was far from the only great hierarch to perish in the orgy of carnage that followed.

The recapture or extermination of the remaining rogue psykers was the first and most fundamental task facing the authorities. Ten were known to have escaped the initial battle on the Avenue of the Victor Bellum, and these had fled into the hive, sowing carnage as they went, hunted by the forces of the Inquisition and all the Imperial might that could be brought to bear in support.

Two of them made it only a kilometre or two from the route of the procession, hounded every step by Imperial forces from the Avenue battle, and were neutralised by nightfall on that terrible first day. Another went to ground in a vegetable cannery in an eastern sector outhab, and was laid to siege. It cost three days and the lives of eight hundred Imperial Guardsmen, sixty-two astropaths, two Space Marines and six inquisitors to blast it out and burn it. The cannery, and the outhab for three square kilometres around it, was flattened.

There was little or no central control for our forces. Admiral Oetron, who had remained with the orbiting battlefleet as watch commander, managed to move four picket ships into geo-synchronous orbit above Hive Primaris, and for a while succeeded in providing comprehensive vox and astropathic communications for the ground forces. But by nightfall on the first day, psychic storms had blown up across the hive and all relayed reception was lost.

* * *

It was a dark and frightening period. Down in the burning streets, we sub-divided as best we could into small units, functioning autonomously. Simply by dint of being with Voke, I became part of a group that made its headquarters in an Arbites section house on Blammerside Street in the mercantile district. Desperate groups of citizens flocked to us, craving aid and mercy and sanctuary, and much larger gangs attacked the section house time and again, driven by fear, by rage against the Imperial machine or simply because we wouldn't let them in.

We couldn't. We were overflowing with injured and dead, far too many for the Arbites surgeons and morgue attendants to manage. There was very little food, medical supplies or ammunition left, and we were also rationing water as the mains supply had been cut.

The power was down too, but the section house had its own generator.

All through the night, bottles and missiles and promethium bombs splintered off the shielded windows, and fists pounded on the doors.

By merit of his seniority, Voke was in command. Aside from myself, there was Inquisitor Roban, Inquisitor Yelena, Inquisitor Essidari, twenty interrogators and junior servants of the Inquisition, sixty troopers from the Interior Guard, several dozen astropaths and four White Consul Space Marines. The Arbites themselves numbered around one hundred and fifty, and the section house was also sheltering about three hundred nobles, ecclesiarchs and dignitaries from the Great Triumph, as well as a few hundred common citizens.

* * *

I remember standing alone in a ransacked office of the Arbites commander just after midnight, looking out through shielded windows at the burning streets and the blossoms of psyker storm that were wrenching the sky apart. I had received no word or sign of Ravenor since the catastrophe had begun. I remember my hands were shaking even then.

In truth, I believe I was in shock. From the event itself, naturally, and also from the psychic assaults I had suffered in the course of it. I pride myself on a sharp mind, but there was no sharpness to me then.

Numb, my brain kept returning to the idea that this outrage had been deliberate.

'There is no question,' Voke said from behind me, clearly reading my surface thoughts without my permission. He lifted and straightened a steel chair and sat down on it.

'Accidents happen, warplanes crash!' he cried. 'But these turned and attacked. Their assaults were deliberate.'

I nodded. At least one of the Lightnings had crashed into the Warmaster's entourage and another had come down amongst the files of the Inquisition. No one yet knew how many of my institution had been slain, but Voke had seen enough of it to know that as many as two hundred of our fellow inquisitors had been obliterated.

I remembered the conversation that had turned around my dining table, the speculations about those powerful forces who would oppose Honorius's bestowment.

'Is this the first act in a House war?' I said. 'The Ecclesiarchy, or perhaps great dynasties, trying to thwart Lord Commander Helican's advancement of the Warmaster? His elevation to Feudal Protector would not have been popular with many, powerful factions.'

'No,' he said. 'Though I'm sure that's what many will think. What many will be supposed to think.'

Voke looked at me intently. 'Freeing the psykers was the point,' he said. 'There is no other explanation. The Archenemy struck to cause mayhem and allow the prisoners to escape, and to wound the section of the parade that was most able to contain their escape.'

'I won't argue with that in principle. But was freeing the psykers the point itself, or simply a means to an end?'

'How so?'

'Was it an attempt to liberate the psykers... or was this just an act of extreme violence against the Imperium that the release of dangerous psykers was meant to exacerbate?'

'Until we know what was behind it, we can't answer that.'

'Could the psykers themselves have done it? Manipulated the minds of the pilots?'

He shrugged. 'We can't know that either. Not yet. The War-master might have been guilty of bravado in displaying his prisoners, but he would have made certain security around them was seamless. I must suspect an outside hand.'

We said nothing for a moment. Honorius Magnus him-self had barely survived the crash-blast and was undergoing emergency surgery aboard a medical frigate at the Navy-yard. No one yet knew if Lord Commander Helican was alive. If he was dead, or if the Warmaster died of his injuries, then Chaos would have won a historic victory.

'I suspect an outside hand too,' I told Voke. 'Perhaps another psyker or psykers, trailing their colleagues here to stage an escape.'

He pursed his lipless mouth. 'The greatest triumph of my life, Gregor, capturing those monsters in the name of the Emperor... and look what it becomes.'

'You can't blame yourself for this, Commodus.'

'Can I not?' He squinted at me. 'In my place, how would you feel?'

I shrugged. 'I will make amends. I will not rest until every one of these wretches is destroyed, and order restored. And then I will not rest until I find who and what was behind it.'

He stared at me for a long time.

'What?' I asked, though I had a feeling I knew what was coming.

'You... you were close to the scene, as you said to me. Closer than many, and shielded from the worst of the destruction by the bulk of the Spatian Gate.'

'And?'

'You know what I want to ask you.'

'You thought you'd start with me. I'm too tired, Voke. I stopped to honour the admiral's tomb.'

He raised one eyebrow, as if he sensed I didn't really believe it myself. But at least he did me the courtesy of not ripping into my mind with his much more powerful psychic abilities to scour out what truth might be there. We had reached an understanding through our encounters over the years, and were now even when it came to owing each other our lives.

He knew me well enough not to press this.

Not now, at least.

An interrogator hurried into the room.

'Sirs,' she said. 'Inquisitor Roban wishes you to know that we have made contact with one of the heretics.'

As far as could be learned, the rogue was an alpha-plus psyker called Esarhaddon, one of the leaders of the coven. Sowing tumult and woe in his wake, he had fled into the hive with a group led by Lyko and Heldane in pursuit. Heldane had managed to contact one of Voke's astropaths with a scrambled summons for help.

Voke, Roban and I headed out into the hive streets with a kill team of sixty that included the four White Consuls. Their squad leader was a particularly large sergeant called Kurvel. We travelled on foot through the debris and smoke. Gangs of citizens jeered and pelted missiles at us, but the sight of four terrible Space Marines kept them at bay.

Esarhaddon, Voke warned me, was a being of dreadful intellect and not to be underestimated. When we saw the monster's choice of bolt-hole, I understood what Voke meant.

The noble family of Lange was prominent in the aristocracy of Thracian Primaris, and kept an ample summer palace in the east sector of Hive Primaris, near to the mercantile quarter where they had made their fortunes.

The palace rose proud of the lowhab streets around it, swathed in its own force bubble.

This had been one of the city areas we had supposed to be secure. With their power and resources, noble houses should have been able to protect themselves for the duration of the unrest.

But not against Esarhaddon. He was inside, with all the resources of the palace to protect him.

We met Heldane on the western approach road to the palace. He had a team of about twenty with him. The street itself was littered with bodies, most of them citizens.

'He's controlling the crowds as if they were puppets,' Heldane said curtly, with no word of greeting. 'Waves of them keep coming at us, preventing us getting to the garden walls and the servants' annex along there.'

As I may have said, I had little time for Inquisitor Heldane. A very tall, grim man, his face an unsightly mass of scar tissue since an encounter with a hungry carnodon back on Gudrun.

He'd been Voke's pupil when I had first met him; now he was a full inquisitor, with mental powers, it was said, that exceeded even his old master's. As I saw him there, I shuddered. He had undergone extensive surgery, not to disguise the damage to his face, but to exaggerate it. His skull seemed to have been extended into an almost equine shape, with a snout-like mouth full of blunt teeth, and dark, murky eyes. Fibre-wires and fluid tubes braided his cranium in place of hair. He wore plasteel body armour the colour of blood and carried a segmented power glaive.

'Eisenhorn,' he nodded, noticing me. It was like having a warhorse shake its head in my direction.

'They're coming again!' The cry went up from Heldane's men. Down the street, moving through the fire spills, figures were lurching towards us.

Weapons! Stand ready! Heldane had spoken, but not with his voice. His psychic command shook through our skulls and some of our own troopers looked dismayed.

Missiles rained down on us, and the Interior Guardsmen raised an umbrella of riot shields. Small arms fired at us too, and an Arbites near me fell with his knee buckled the wrong way.

Our attackers, some hundred or more, were hive citizens, blank faced and moving like marionettes. As Heldane had reported, some monumental psychic force was making puppets out of them. The smoky night air ionised with the psionic backwash.

I take no pleasure in actions like the one that followed. The beast Esarhaddon was forcing us to fight innocent civilians just to protect ourselves.

Maybe he thought we'd shrink from the task and leave him alone.

We, however, were the Inquisition.

Kurvel led his White Consuls at the front, banging their weapons against their chest-plates and howling defiance through their helmet speakers. I saw a promethium bomb strike one and shatter, swathing him in liquid flame. He simply strode on.

We fired over the mob's heads, trying to break them, but they had no will of their own. Our firing became kill-shots. In ten minutes, we had reluctantly added a fair number to the planet's rising death toll.

That brought us to the corner of the street, facing the high walls of the garden and the edge of the palace's iridescent force shield itself.

I could hear a low chuckling in my head.

Esarhaddon.

Where's Lyko? I heard Voke ask Heldane psychically.

He took a team around the front to try and disable the force wall.

'You idiot!' I said, out loud, looking over at Heldane. 'This monster can control a crowd that big and you mind-speak this close to him?'

'This monster,' Heldane replied, 'can read every mind in the city and beyond. He knows what we're all doing. There is no point in secrecy. Just effort. Is that beyond you?'

'How long until the next attack?' Kurvel asked, reloading his weapon.

'They've become less frequent since we first arrived,' replied Heldane. 'However long it takes Esarhaddon to mind-search the surrounding habs and recruit another puppet force. He's having to cast his net wider each time.'

'How did he get in there?' Roban asked.

Heldane simply shook his head and shrugged. Roban, a

robust inquisitor of middle years dressed in brown and yellow layered robes, was a good man, though I didn't know him well. But he was an outspoken Xanthanite and the ultra-puritan Heldane had little time for him.

Voke and Heldane fell to discussing possible assault plans with Kurvel as the soldiers around us formed a defensive position.

'This is a damned thankless task,' Roban said to me. 'I don't even know why we're here!'

'Cannon fodder,' said his youthful interrogator, Inshabel, bluntly, and it made us both laugh.

'There has to be something...' I said. I took out my pocket scope and tried to read the energy patterns and spectrums.

'You!' I called to one of the Arbites in our party, a grizzled precinct commander in full riot gear.

'Inquisitor?'

'What's your name?'

'Luclus, sir.'

'Dear God-Emperor!' I sighed again and Roban laughed once more.

'Okay, Luckless – this palace must come into your precinct's patrol area.'

'Yes, sir.'

'So street security around it is your responsibility.'

'Again, yes sir.'

'So... just as a matter of procedure, your section house will have on file the shield type and harmonics for the palace, in case of emergencies.' In my experience, it was standard protocol for any Arbites precinct to know such things about key structures within their purview.

'It's classified, sir.'

'Of course it is,' I sighed again. 'But now would be a good time...'

He got on his vox-link and after a lot of effort, managed to get a channel open to the section house.

'You're on to something, aren't you?' Roban asked me.

'Maybe.'

'The wily Inquisitor Eisenhorn–'

'The what?'

'No offence. Your reputation precedes you.'

'Does it now? In a good way?'

Roban grinned and shook his head, like a man who might have heard something, but who had decided to make up his own mind.

'It's an old type-ten conical void,' Arbites Commander Luclus reported presently. 'Tangent eight-seven-eight harmonic wave. We don't have an override code. Lady Lange wouldn't permit it.'

'I bet she wishes she had now,' said Interrogator Inshabel, caustic and to the point once again. I was beginning to like him.

'Thank you, Luckless,' I said.

'It's... Luclus, sir.'

'I know.'

I tried to remember everything Aemos had counselled me about shields over the years. I wished I had his recall. Better still, I wished I had him here.

'We can collapse it,' I said, with fair confidence.

'Collapse a void shield?' Roban asked.

'It's conical... super-surface only. And it's old. Voids shrug off just about anything, but they don't retain their field if you take out one or more of the projectors.

'That buttress there, the one the garden wall is built around, that's got to be one of the projector units, seated down into the ground.'

Roban nodded, apparently impressed. 'I see the logic, but not the practice.'

I walked over to Brother-Sergeant Kurvel, interrupting his conversation with Heldane without apology, and explained what I wanted to do.

Heldane scoffed at once. 'Lyko's already trying that!'

'How?'

'He's located the outer controls at the front gate and is trying to break their coding...'

'Coding and controls that will be dead and locked out thanks to Esarhaddon. Lyko's wasting his time. We can't switch this off. We can't break Esarhaddon's control over its system. But we can undermine the system itself.'

Heldane was about to speak again, but Voke shut him up. 'I think Gregor may be on to something.'

'Why?'

Voke pointed. Close to five hundred citizens were now advancing towards us from streets on all sides.

'Because as you pointed out, Heldane, the monster can hear us, and he clearly doesn't like the sound of this plan.'

It took Kurvel about ten minutes to gouge out the pavement and a section of garden wall with his lightning claw, and all the while we were under attack from the growing mob of puppets.

'Sewer!' Kurvel announced.

I turned to the others as shots and missiles rained down. 'Commodus... you have to hold them off a while longer.'

'Count on it,' he said.

'Roban, get a small squad and follow me.'

Heldane wasn't happy. But by then, Heldane wasn't calling the shots any more. I believe he took his rage out on the enslaved citizens.

I dropped into the sewer hole with Kurvel, Roban, Inshabel and three troopers of the Interior Guard. The defence on the street above could barely spare any of them.

The filthy sewer tube went in under the wall itself before dropping sharply away. Old, patched stone swelled around the base of the buttress. The stone was warm, and foamy clumps of fungus were growing on it.

Inshabel trained a spotbeam in so I could see.

Kurvel could see in the dark. He took out his last two krak grenades and fixed them to the stonework with smears of adhesive paste from a tube he carried in his pack.

'I wish we had more. We could blow the wall right through.'

'We could, brother-sergeant, but this might be better.'

'Why?'

'Because if we can simply make this projector fail, the energies of the shield will short out before they collapse. Rather than blowing outwards, that'll cause an electromagnetic pulse within the field itself. And I think an EM pulse is the last thing Esarhaddon wants right now.'

As if to prove my suspicions right, a stabbing sheet of psychic power lashed at us. Esarhaddon had realised his vulnerability, and was turning his immense power on us now. The puppets had been sport, but now it was time to control or blast out the minds of his hunters before they stopped being playthings and became a danger.

The psyker attack was devastating. Two of the Interior Guardsmen simply died. Another started firing, hitting Kurvel twice and wounding Inshabel. Regretfully, Roban blasted the trooper down with his laspistol.

Our minds were harder to attack, especially given the shield formed by the rock above us and our proximity to the energy flux of the shield.

But Roban, Inshabel, Kurvel and I would be dead or homicidal in seconds.

How I wished for Alizebeth, or any of the Distaff right then.

'Trigger it! Trigger it!' I gasped, the blood vessels in my nose and throat opening yet again that day.

'We're right on top of the–'

'Just do it, brother-sergeant! In the name of the God-Emperor!'

The blast took out the projector. It filled the sewer tunnel with flickering destruction. It would have killed us but for the fact that Brother-Sergeant Kurvel shielded us with his massive armoured body.

It cost him his life.

I have made a point to have his name and memory celebrated by the White Consuls.

With the generating projector killed, the void shield collapsed in on itself, blacking out the palace systems with the thunderclap of electromagnetic rage.

Blacking out Esarhaddon's seething mind too.

My research into untouchables, through Alizebeth and then through the Distaff she created and ran, had indicated to me that perhaps psychic power, no matter how potent, relied in the final analysis on the electrical workings of the human mind, the firing of impulse charges between synapses. Untouchables somehow blanked this, and triggered a disturbing and disarming vacancy in the natural and fundamental processes of the human brain. That, I had initially concluded, was why psykers don't work around untouchables... and why forgetfulness and unease is prevalent in their company. And, ultimately, why they disturb and upset humans so, and psykers doubly so.

I'd turned the old void shield into a brief, bright untouchable event.

And now, Emperor damn him, the heretic psyker Esarhaddon, temporarily rendered deaf, blind and mute, was mine.

EIGHT

Esarhaddon's lair
Lyko the victor
A vestige

We went into the grounds of the Lange palace over the wall. There was a harsh stink of ozone from the ruptured shield, and the trimmed fruit trees and laraebur hedges of the gardens were singed and smouldering.

With Roban and Inshabel, I ran down a flint-chip path between the servants' wing and the east portico. Flashlights and under-muzzle torches bobbed in the gardens behind us as Heldane led the main force of our troop round to the garden terrace.

The house was dead and dark, all power killed by the pulse. The main doors on the east portico lay splintered on the mosaic floor where the accompanying wave of overpressure from the void collapse had blown them in. All of the windows were smashed holes too.

Photo-receptors and climate controls in the portico's polished bluewood panels were fused and charred. Smoke and the glow of flames issued from deeper in the palace.

We pushed further in, finding dead house staff and inert servitors. A whole suite of state rooms on the first floor was burning where ornate promethium lamps had been knocked over.

We checked the rooms on each side as we progressed. Roban led the way, sweeping his braced laspistol from side to side.

'How long?' Inshabel asked me.

'Until?'

'Until he recovers from the pulse?'

I didn't know. There was no telling how badly we'd hurt Esarhaddon, or how resilient his mind was. We hadn't got long.

On the second floor, a flight of aethercite steps brought us up into a grand banqueting hall. The roof, a turtleback of toughened glass, had fallen in and the psi-storms crackled and surged in the sky far above. Every step crunched glass or disturbed debris.

There were bodies here too, the bodies of nobility and servants intermingled.

I heard movement and sobbing from an adjoining antechamber.

The wretched occupants of the room gasped in terror as our flashlights found them. A handful of survivors from the household, cowering in fear in the dark. Many displayed signs of psychic burns or telekinetic welts.

'Imperial Inquisition,' I said firmly but quietly. 'Stay calm. Where is Esarhaddon?'

Some flinched or moaned at the sound of the name. A regal dowager in a torn pearlescent gown curled up in the corner and began weeping.

'Quickly... there's little time! Where is he?' I thought to use my will to spur them into an answer, but their minds had been tortured enough already that night. Even a mild mental probe might kill some of them.

'W–when the lights went out, he ran... ran towards the west exit,' said a blood-soaked man dressed in what I presumed was the uniform of the House Lange bodyguard.

'Can you show us?'

'My leg's broken...'

'Someone else then! Please!'

'Frewa... you go. Frewa!' The bodyguard gestured to a terrified page boy crouching behind a column.

'Come on, lad, show us the way,' Roban said encouragingly.

The boy got to his feet, his eyes white with fear. I wasn't sure if he was more afraid of Esarhaddon or the inquisitors looming over him.

A communicating hallway ran from the rear of the banquet hall west towards the house's private landing platform. Specks of blood and glass twinkled along its tiled floor.

I felt what seemed to me a breath of wind on my skin. An exit to the outside, perhaps?

Heavy blast shutters were prised open in the entrance to the gloomy loading dock. Past the shadowy shapes of several slumped, dormant cargo servitors, stood a main hatchway through which cold exterior light flickered.

My weapon raised, I waved Roban and Inshabel round to the right. The page boy cowered back in the doorway. The air quality was changing, as if the atmosphere itself was stiffening and drawing tight. Like some great force gathering its breath.

Esarhaddon was recovering, I was certain.

Livid green light suddenly bathed the loading dock, a psychometric flare accompanying a burst of savage psionic power.

Roban and I staggered, our lungs squeezed and fingers of tele-kinesis thrusting at our minds. Inshabel cried out as he was bowled over from behind by the page boy, Frewa. Dull-eyed and frothing at the mouth, the boy had been reduced, in an instant, to a mindless puppet. Inshabel fought, but the boy was feral, and despite the interrogator's superior bulk he was pinned.

The pain in my head was intense, but I knew Esarhaddon must still be way below full strength. I raised the strongest mind shield my abilities were able to conjure and moved forward.

There was a sudden grind of servo-gears. A large steel paw swung at my head and I dived back.

A cargo servitor, its metal carapace caked with verdigris, rose up to its full height of three metres and clanked across the deck towards me on squat hydraulic legs. Plumes of steam squirted from its broad shoulder joints as it pistoned its arms at me again. Hot yellow dots of light burned in the eye sockets of its dented visor.

Despite its mechanical appearance, the cargo drone, like all servitors, was built around human organic components: brain, brain-stem, neural network, glands so Esarhaddon could control it just like a standard human.

It swung at me again, and missed. The slicing limb had cut the air with a distinct whistle.

It was built like a great simian: squat legs, barrel chest, wide shoulders and long, thick arms. Ideal for hefting heavy cargo items into the belly-hold of a liftship.

Ideal for smashing a human body into gory paste.

Roban cried out a warning. A second, larger cargo servitor with a long quadruped body, was also moving. Its body casing was pitted, brown metal and it had a fork-lifter assembly where its head should have been, giving it the appearance of a bull. The greased black forks of the lifter lurched at Roban, who fired six or seven shots that dented or bounced off the machine's chassis.

I ducked two more slow, heavy blows from the ape-servitor. We were losing precious time. With every tick of the clock, Esarhaddon was recovering and becoming more powerful.

I put a bolt round into the thickest part of the servitor's body and rocked it back, the gears and pistons of its legs whining as they compensated for the recoil.

My power sword was out now, the blade burning. Blessed for me by the Provost of Inx, it was my weapon of choice. My swordsmanship had always been good, but Arianrhod had instructed me in the Carthaen *Ewl Wyla Scryi* before her death. *Ewl Wyla Scryi*, literally, 'the genius of sharpness', the Carthaen way of the sword.

I made a figure of eight turn, the *ghan fasl*, and then a back-hand crosscut, the *uin* or reverse form of the *tahn wyla*.

The stroke was good. The energised blade sliced clean through the servitor's left forearm, sending the massive manipulator paw clattering to the deck.

It lurched bodily at me, as if enraged, clawing with its remaining hand and lashing with the fused, smoking end of its recently truncated limb.

I made a head-height horizontal parry called the *uwe sar*, and then left and right block strokes, the *ulsar* and the *uin ulsar*. Sheets of sparks cascaded from each hit against its metal body. I ducked right under the next huge blow, spun round out of the crouch and came up to face it again in time to follow through with the *ura wyla bei*, the devastating diagonal downslash, left to right. My blade edge and tip sawed the servitor's torso plating wide open in an electrical flash.

The exchange had given me long enough to mentally identify the seat of the servitor's brain-stem component, lit up and glowing in my mind's eye with the psionic power that drove it. It lay deep under the carapace between the collar bones.

One more *uwe sar* and then the *ewl caer*, the deathstroke. Tip first, plunging clean through the bodywork, impaling the organic brain. I rested the crackling blade there for a moment while the yellow dot eyes went out and then ripped it clear again, sidestepping as the servitor slammed down onto the flooring.

'Roban!' I called out, leaping over my despatched foe.

But Roban was dead. The servitor's forks had his limp body impaled through the belly and it was shaking it as if trying to dislodge him.

Inshabel was on his feet, tears streaming down his face as he blasted at the servitor with his autogun.

Cursing, I ran forward, raised the power sword with both hands and swung it down over the servitor's back. I doubt the Carthaens, in all their wisdom, have a name in the most hallowed *Ewl Wyla Scryi* for an enraged downstroke that severs the backbone and torso of a servitor.

Inshabel ran to his dead master as the servitor collapsed, trying to pull the corpse clear.

'Later! Later for that!' I said, spiking the command with my will. Inshabel was close to losing his wits to anger and grief, and I needed him.

He snatched up his weapon and ran after me.

'The page boy?' I asked.

'I had to hit him. I hope he's just unconscious.'

We came out into the storm-wracked night on the palace landing pad. Psychic lightning splintered the sky above us and the wind lashed us. There was no one on the pad itself, but a fight was raging on the lawns beyond. I could see eight figures, some robed, some dressed in the body armour of the Interior Guard, closing to surrounding a lone humanoid who crackled and glowed with spectral light. Thorny jags of flame lit out from the cornered figure and dropped one of the Guardsmen as we watched.

Esarhaddon. They had Esarhaddon cornered.

Inshabel and I leapt down from the pad – a three metre drop onto the wet grass – and ran to join the fray.

I could see Esarhaddon clearly now despite the rain. A tall, almost naked man with wild black hair and a lean, stringy body, corposant gleaming and sliding around his capering limbs.

We were just ten metres from the edge of the fight when one of the robed figures raised a bulky weapon and blasted at the rogue psyker.

A plasma gun.

The violet beam, almost too bright to look at, struck Esarhaddon. In his weakened state, he had no defence against it.

He ignited like an incendiary round and burned from head to foot in the middle of the lawn.

Lowering our weapons, Inshabel and I walked to join the ring of figures standing around the white hot pyre. As his robed and hooded acolytes murmured prayers of grace and deliverance, Inquisitor Lyko set down his plasma gun.

'The Emperor will thank you, Lyko,' I said.

He glanced round, seeing me for the first time. 'Eisenhorn.' He nodded. His narrow face was lined and taut and his blue eyes hooded. He was only about fifty years old sidereal, a mere youth by inquisitional standards. Young enough for his promising career to survive the way this day's atrocity would tarnish his achievement on Dolsene.

'I do not serve the Emperor for his gratitude. I do it for the glory of the Imperium.'

'Quite so,' I said. I looked back at the molten heat that had been our quarry. It mattered little to me that I'd made this opportunity for Lyko. He could take the glory. I didn't care. The escape of the psykers had stolen much of the glory he had received of late. Hunting them down was the only way he could make amends.

Planetwide, there was some sense of rejoicing when it was announced that Lord Commander Helican had survived the carnage unscathed, and that Warmaster Honorius would live. That announcement came on the sixth day of unrest, by which time the Imperial authorities had begun to reimpose order on the stricken citizens of Thracian Primaris. But it helped. Common folk who assumed themselves to be lost were calmed into believing law was back in the hands of the great and good. Panics died away. Arbites units unleashed their last few suppression raids against the die-hard recidivist looters in the lowhabs.

My own spirits were not much lifted. For a start I was privy to the confidential fact that Lord Commander Helican had actually died screaming and shitting himself under a crash-diving Imperial Navy Lightning on the Avenue of the Victor Bellum. A double had been arranged by the Ecclesiarchy and the Helican Senatorum, and that double continued to act in his place until, several years later, he 'died naturally of old age' and a successor was established in less-turbulent circumstances.

I can speak of that public deceit now in this private record, but at the time, communicating that secret was a death-crime for even the highest lord of the Imperium. I was not about to break that confidence. I am an inquisitor and I understand how fundamental it is to maintain public order.

In addition to fatigue and the pain of my wounds, what darkened my mood was the news about Gideon Ravenor. Now, of course, we all understand what a priceless and brilliant contribution he was to make to Imperial learning, and how that would never have happened if he had not been confined to a life of mental rumination.

But back then, in that stinking hospice ward off the Street of Prescients, all I saw was a young man, burned and crippled and physically paralysed, a brilliant inquisitor ruined before he could fulfill his potential.

Ravenor, in the eyes of some, had been lucky. He had not been amongst the one hundred and ninety-eight Inquisition personnel killed outright by the crashing fighter that fell into the Great Triumph beyond the Spatian Gate.

He, like fifty others, had been caught on the edge of the explosion and lived.

My pupil was barely recognisable. A blood-wet bundle of charred flesh. One hundred per cent burns. Blind, deaf, mute, his face so melted that an incision had been made in the fused meat where his mouth should have been so he could breathe.

The loss touched me acutely. The waste even more. Gideon Ravenor had been the greatest, most promising pupil I had ever taught. I stood by his plastic-sheeted cot, listening to the suck and drool of his ventilator and fluid drains and remembered what Commodus Voke had said in the Arbites sector house on Blammerside Street.

'I will make amends. I will not rest until every one of these wretches is destroyed and order restored. And then I will not rest until I find who and what was behind it.'

Right then, there, for Ravenor's sake, I made that promise to myself too.

At that time, I had little idea what that would mean or where it would take me.

I returned to the Ocean House at last on what would have been the ninth and final day of the Holy Novena. There was no one to greet me, and the place seemed empty and forlorn.

I stalked into my study, poured a too-large measure of vintage amasec and flopped down into an armchair. It felt like an eternity since I had sat here with Titus Endor, worrying over speculations that seemed now so insignificant and remote.

A door opened. From the instant chill in the air, I knew at once it was Bequin.

'We didn't know you'd returned, Gregor.'

'Well, I have, Alizebeth.'

'So I see. Are you alright?'

I shrugged. 'Where is everybody?'

'When the...' she paused, considering her words. 'When the tragedy occurred, there was a great public commotion. Jarat and Kircher took the staff into the secure bunkers for safety, and I locked myself away with the Distaff in the west wing, waiting, hoping for your call.'

'Channels were out.'

'Yes. For eight days.'

'But everyone is safe?'

'Yes.'

I leaned out of my chair and looked at her. Her face was pale and drawn from too many nights of fear.

'Where's Aemos?'

'Outside, with Betancore, Kircher and Nayl. Von Baigg's around too. Is... is it true what we've heard about Gideon?'

'Alizebeth... it's...'

She crouched down and put her arms around me. It is difficult for a psyker to be hugged by an untouchable, no matter how long and close their personal history. But her intentions were good, and I tolerated the contact for as long as seemed polite. When I gently pushed her back, I said, 'Send them in. In fact, send everyone in here.'

'They won't all fit, Gregor.'

'The sea terrace, then. One last time.'

Sitting or standing around in the lime glow of the sea terrace, the numerous members of my faithful band looked at me expectantly. The place was packed. Jarat had fussed around, bringing out drinks and sweetmeats until I had pressed a glass of amasec into her gnarled hands and forced her down into a chair.

'I'm closing the Ocean House,' I said.

There was a murmur.

'I'm retaining the lease, but I have little wish to live here any more. In fact, I have little wish to be on Thracian any more. Not after this... Holy Novena. There seems no point maintaining a staff here.'

'But, sir, the library?' Psullus said from the back.

I held up a finger.

'I will take up a contract arrangement with one of the hive accommodation bureaux to keep the house in working order with servitors. Who knows, sometime I might have need of a place here again.'

I refilled my glass before turning back.

'But I wish to move my centre of operations. It's compromised, if nothing else.'

At that, Jubal Kircher looked into his cit-juice uncomfortably.

'I wish to relocate the household to the estate on Gudrun. Its environment suits me better than this... hive-hell. Jarat, you and Kircher will supervise the packing and organisation for the move. I would like you to undertake the duties of head of household at the Gudrun estate, if you are willing. I realise you have never been off Thracian.'

She sat forward, her eyebrows raised, considering this sudden change to her life. 'I... I would be honoured to do so, sir,' she said.

'I'm pleased. The country air will do you good. The estate is managed by a caretaker staff, so I'll need a good housekeeper, and a good chief of house security. Jubal... I'd like you to consider that job.'

'Thank you, sir,' said Kircher.

'Psullus... we're going to transplant the library permanently to Gudrun. That task is yours, as is the ongoing duty of being my librarian. Can I entrust you with it?'

'Oh, yes... there will be problems, of course, the handling and care of certain shielded texts and–'

'But I can leave it with you?'

Psullus waved his frail hands at me in a gesture of excitement that made everyone laugh.

'I know this wholesale move will take months to manage and carry out. Alain... I'd like you to supervise and oversee the whole thing.'

Von Baigg looked suddenly awkward. 'Of – of course, inquisitor.'

'This is a weighty task, interrogator. Are you up to it?'

'Yes, sir.'

'Good. I will return to the Gudrun estate no later than ten months from now. I trust it will be the home I expect.'

It was a promise I would fail miserably to keep.

'What of the Distaff, sir?' asked Surskova.

'I want to divide that,' I said. 'I want six of the best Distaff members sent to Gudrun to bide there at my wishes. The future of the Distaff itself I see as separate from my living arrangements. I have a lease on a spire-top residence on Messina. That will be the new official home of the Distaff. Surskova, you will supervise the move and establishment of the untouchable school there.'

She nodded, shocked. Bequin seemed taken aback.

I looked round at the hundred-plus servants, warriors and aides crammed into the room.

'That's it. Until I see you all again, may the God-Emperor protect you.'

I was left alone with Aemos, Bequin, Medea and Nayl.

'Not for us the chores of moving house,' I said.

'I had a hunch not,' smirked Medea.

'For us, two missions.'

'For us?' asked Bequin.

'Yes, Alizebeth. Unless you think you and I are too old for such diversions?'

'No, I– I–'

'I've been too long at the back of things. Too long relying on my capable staff. I yearn for field work.'

'The last field work we were in nearly got you killed,' scolded Bequin darkly.

'Proving that I'm losing my edge, I think.'

'For shame!' muttered Nayl with a smile.

'So we're going to have an adventure, all of us. Just the few of us. Remember what those were like, Aemos?'

'Frankly, I'm still not over them, Gregor, but yes.'

'Alizebeth?'

Bequin crossed her arms ill-humouredly. 'Oh, I'd just love to come and watch you get killed...'

'We're all agreed, then?' I said. I can't help being deadpan. Gorgone Locke made sure of that. But my delivery was good enough to get Nayl and Medea raucous with laughter and Aemos chuckling.

Alizebeth Bequin grinned despite herself.

'Two missions, as I said. After this briefing, I'll allow you to recruit a few personnel from the staff. Nayl – a fighter or two you can count on. Aemos – an astropath we can use without worry. Alizebeth – one or two from the Distaff. A maximum of ten in the party, all told. No more, you understand? Argue it out between yourselves. Don't bring me into it. We leave in two days, and I don't want to even hear about any arguments second hand.'

'So what are the missions?' asked Medea, lounging back in her padded chair and slipping her long legs over the arm. She took a long swig of her weedwine and added, 'You said two, right?'

'Two.'

I pushed a stud on a data wand in my hand and a hololithic screen fogged into life over the table. The words of the message I'd received before the start of the tumult on Thracian were displayed in shimmering letters: 'Scalpel cuts quickly, eager tongues revealed. At Cadia, by terce. Hound wishes Thorn. Thorn should be sharp.'

'Shit!' cried Nayl.

'Is that authentic?' Medea asked, looking at me.

'It is.'

'God-Emperor, he's in trouble, he needs us...' Bequin murmured.

'Very probably. Medea, you have to arrange transit for us to Cadia. That's the first port of call.'

'What's the second?' asked Aemos.

'The second?'

'The second mission?'

I looked at them all. 'We all know how serious the Cadian matter is. But I made a vow to Gideon. I want to find out what was behind the outrage here. I want to find it, hunt it out and punish it.'

You know, it's funny how things turn out.

It was late, and we were devouring a splendid meal Jarat had prepared for us. Nayl was telling a devastatingly crude joke to Aemos, Medea and Bequin and I were talking over the rearrangement of the Distaff and the missions ahead.

I think she was feeling excited. Like me, she'd been taking a back seat for too long.

Kircher came up the terrace, entering the filmy green light.

'Sir, you have a visitor.'

'At this hour, who?'

'He says his name is Inshabel, sir. Interrogator Nathun Inshabel.'

Inshabel was waiting for me in the library.

'Interrogator. Has my staff offered you refreshment?'

'None needed, sir.'

'Very well... so to what do I owe this visit?'

Inshabel, no more than twenty-five, pushed his thick blond hair out of his eyes and looked at me fiercely. 'I... I am masterless. Roban is dead...'

'God-Emperor rest him. He will be missed.'

'Sir, do you ever think what it would be like if you died?'

The notion stopped me in my tracks. I had, in all honesty, never considered it.

'No, Inshabel. I haven't.'

'It's a terrible thing, sir. As Roban's senior acolyte it falls to me to disburse his staff, his fortune, his knowledge. I'm left to tidy up, as it were. I have to make sense of Roban's estate.'

'You will not fail in that duty, interrogator, of that I'm sure.'

He smiled weakly. 'Thank you, sir. I had... I had thought to come to you, and beg you to take me on. I so very much want to be an inquisitor. My master is dead, and I know that your own... your own interrogator is...'

'Indeed. I choose my own staff, of course. I–'

'Inquisitor Eisenhorn. Begging you to take me on as a drift-wood student was not why I came here. As I said, I had to close up Roban's estate. That meant filing and authorising the pathologica statement of his death. Inquisitor Roban was killed by a cargo servitor manipulated by a rogue psyker.'

'Yes?'

'So to complete the papers, I had to review the death notice of Esarhaddon so as to establish causal motive.'

'That is the procedure,' I admitted.

'The statement was very brief. Esarhadon's corpse was burnt from the calves upwards and utterly immolated. As in the incidents of spontaneous human combustion, the relics left by the plasma weapon were little more than the flesh and bones of the feet and ankles. Just bare vestiges.'

'And?'

'There was no Malleus brand on the ankle flesh.'

'It– What..?'

'I don't know who Inquisitor Lyko burned on the lawns of the Lange house... but it wasn't the heretic Esarhaddon.'

NINE

Eechan, six weeks later
A word with the Phant
Knives in the night

The bicephalic minder in the squalid doorway of the twist bar regarded us with one of his lice-ridden heads, while the other glazed out, smoking an obscura pipe.

'Not your place, not your kind. Get on.'

The sap rain was falling heavily on our heads through the rotten awning, and I had little wish to stand in it any longer. I nodded a sidelong glance to my companion, who tugged back his hood and showed the minder the cluster of malformed, winking eyes that mottled his cheek and ran down his pallid throat. I raised my own damp cloak and revealed the knot of stunted tentacles that sprouted from an extra sleeve slit under my right armpit.

The minder got off his stool, one head nodding dozily. He was big, broad and tall as an ogryn, and his greasy skin was busy with tattoos.

'Hnh...' he muttered, limping around us as he sized us up. 'Maybe then. You didn't smell like twists. Okay...'

We went inside, down a few dark steps into a nocturnal club room that was fogged with obscura smoke and pulsing with a brand of harsh, discordant music called 'pound'. Panes of red glass had been put over the lights of the lanterns and the place was a hellish swamp, like the damnation paintings of that insane genius Omarmettia.

Mal-forms, deforms, halfbreeds and underscum huddled or gambled or drank or danced. On a raised stage, a naked, heavy-breasted, eyeless girl with a grinning mouth where her navel should have been gyrated to the pound beat.

We reached the bar, a soiled curve of hardwood under a series of hard white lights. The barkeep was a bloated thing with bloodshot eyes and a black snake tongue that flickered between his wet, slit mouth and rotting teeth.

'Hey, twist. What will it be?'

'Two of those,' I said, pointing to clear grain-alcohol shots that a waitress was carrying past on a tray. She would have been beautiful except for the yellow quills stippling her skin.

Twists. We were all twists here. 'Mutant' is a dirty word if you're a mutant. They delight in referring to themselves by the Imperium's glibbest and most detrimental slang, as a badge of honour. It's a pride thing, a common habit with any under-class. Non-telepaths do it when they call themselves 'blunts'. The tall, slender people of low-grav Sylvan do it when they call themselves 'sticks'. A slur's not a slur if you use it on yourself.

Labour laws on Eechan permit twists to work as indentured labourers in the industrial mill-farms and the sap distilleries, provided they abide by the local regime and keep themselves to the licensed shanty towns huddled in the skirts of the bad end of Eechan mainhive.

The barkeep slapped two heavy shotglasses down on the counter and filled them to the brim with grain liquor from a spouted flask.

I tossed a couple of coins down and reached for my drink. The bloodshot eyes leered at me.

'What's this? 'Perial coins? Come now, twist, you know we ain't allowed to trade in those.'

I paused. A glance down the counter showed me that the rest of the clientele were paying in mill-authorised coupons or nuggets of base metal. And that they were all staring and scowling at us. A basic mistake, right off the bat.

My companion leaned forward and sipped his drink. 'Don't get fret with two thirsty twists who's happened to have lucked into a good black score, eh?'

The barkeep smiled and his black tongue flickered. He scooped up the coins. 'Ain't no fret, twist. You earn 'em, I'll take 'em. Just sayin' you might not want to go flashing 'em, s'all.'

We took our drinks away from the bar, looking for a table. It had taken six weeks to reach Eechan, and I was impatient for a lead.

The beat changed. Another pound number began pumping through the underfloor speakers, which to my untutored ears was simply a variation in auditory assault. But the crowd clapped and roared approval. The naked girl with the grinning stomach began rotating her hips the other way.

'I have a feeling I should be leaving this to you,' I whispered to my companion.

'You're doing fine.'

'"Don't get fret, twist...". for God-Emperor's sake... where did you learn to talk like that?'

'You never hung with twists?'

'Not like this...'

'So I'm guessin' you don't s'love that genejack pound beat, twist?'

'Stop it or I'll shoot you.'

Harlon Nayl grinned and blinked with all his sixteen eyes in mock offence.

'Sup up, twist. If that ain't Phant Mastik, I'll poke my eyes out.'

'Oh, let me,' I hissed, and slugged back my shot. 'Raise 'em and sink 'em and let's have another!' I grimaced to myself as the burning spirit scalded down my oesophagus, and then scooped two more drinks from the tray of the porcupine girl as she sashayed past.

Phant Mastik sat with his cronies in a side booth. Generations of rad-storm mutation had made him an obese thing with wrinkled flesh and enlarged features. His ears were frayed fan-like swathes of veiny skin and his nose was a drooping proboscis. An incongruous tuft of thick red hair decorated his neanderthal brow.

His eyes were deep-set and black.

And sad, I thought. Tremendously sad.

He was drinking from a big tankard by snorting the alcohol up through his dangling nose. His mouth, distorted by tusk-like jags of tooth, was useless. A twist whore, with an unnecessary number of arms, was sipping her drink, smoking an obscura stick, retouching her make-up and doing something to Phant under the table that he was clearly enjoying.

We approached.

Phant's minders got up immediately to block us. A horned brute and a twist whose entire head was a wrinkled skin hood for an outsized eye. They both reached into their robes.

'How you tonight, twists?' puffed Horn-brute.

'We fine. No fret, Just s'gotta talk to the Phant,' said Nayl.

'Ain't not gonna happen,' said Big-eye, his voice muffled by his clothing. God-Emperor knew where his mouth was.

'I s'think so, when we have us such a scalding black score, him to enjoy.' Nayl didn't shrink back.

++Let them through++ Phant said, his voice conveyed by an augmetic carry-sound unit. A vox-implant. Few twists had the money for that. Phant was certainly a player.

The minders stepped aside and allowed us into the booth. We sat.

++Go on++

'Twist, I s'tell ya, we be in the market for section-alpha brainjobs. We s'hear you got one for the begging.'

++Hear? Where?++

'Round and around,' said Nayl.

++Uh huh. And you are?++

'Just two twists s'gonna earn us a deal,' I said.

++That right?++

We sat in silence for a moment as Phant called for more drinks. The girl was now combing and fixing her hair and doing her make-up. One of her many hands was on my knee under the table.

She winked at me.

With an eye growing from the end of her tongue.

++What I got, ain't no section-alpha, twists. S'section-alpha-plus++

'That is s'why we came to you, Phant! S'why! No upper limit for our buy!'

++How you gonna pay?++

Nayl dropped one of the ingots onto the table.

'Pure mellow-yellow. And we got the bars. Much as it takes. So...? S'when-where?'

++I gotta talk to some people++

'Kay.'

++Where can I reach you?++

'The Twist and Sleep.'

++You sleep tight. Maybe I call you++

The audience was over. We took a table of our own near the raised stage and stayed for a couple more rounds, making a show of appreciating the indecent writhings of the girl with the belly mouth.

After an hour or so, we saw Phant and his retinue leave by a side door. 'Let's go,' I said. We finished our drinks and rose. Nayl gave porcupine girl a handful of coins and patted her bottom. Her quills bristled, but she smiled.

The minder didn't spare us a look with either of his heads as we left. Out of sight, round the corner of the dreary barstoop, I handed Nayl one of a pair of brass stimm-injectors and we detoxed quickly to rid our bodies of the alcohol dulling our systems.

It was the dead of night, but there was little darkness. The great curve of Eechan's ring systems glowed with reflecting sunlight and shone like bands of diamond-crusted platinum.

The main street of the shanty was a rutted, water-logged morass, and flaking boardwalk pavements edged the rows of slumping, dingy buildings. Glowing signs and the few street lamps reflected in the street puddles.

Beyond the shanty, to the west, the alpine slopes of the mainhive rose against the stars, like a dark mountain of trash decorated with a million little lights. To the east were the stacked, grubby mushrooms of the mill-farms and the distilleries, venting brown steam and yellow pollutants into the wind.

To the south, in the verdant farm lands, plains of thick,

rubbery growth, we could see the running lights of several vast harvesters. They were segmented juggernauts: beetle-like machines the size of small starships, chewing up the green-belt with massive reaping mandibles and digesting it through vast interior vats and worklines. Flues lined their backs like spines and spewed moisture waste and atomised sap up high into the atmosphere, where it drifted and fell again like rain. Everything in the twist shanty was sticky with sap-fall. The rain was tacky and thick like syrup. The street puddles were viscous. Downpipes glugged and throbbed rather than pouring. Everywhere, there was a stench of decomposing plantfibre and liquefied cellulose.

'Do you think he took the bait?' I asked.

Nayl nodded. 'You could see he was interested. Gold's rare on Eechan. His eyes lit when I showed him that ingot.'

'He'll want to check us, though.'

'Of course. He's a businessman.'

We walked along the street, hoods raised against the sticky rain. There were a few mutants around, all of them dressed in rancid tatters. They shambled along, lurked in doorways around covered braziers, or shared obscura bottle-pipes out of the rain in dim breezeways.

A squirt of sirens warbled down the main street and Nayl pulled me into an alley-end. A black armoured land speeder with blazing grilled lamps crept past.

I saw the crest motif of the mainhive Arbites on the side and an armoured officer sat in the top hatch manipulating a spotlight.

The beam played across us and passed along. Another flute of siren-noise sounded and we heard a vox-amplified voice demand, 'Idents and papers, you five. Now!'

Moaning and grumbling, a pack of twists moved out into

the street, lit by the spot-beam, as the officers dismounted to shake them down and run their gene-prints through the system.

Something we couldn't afford to let happen. Not if we wanted to maintain our position as anonymous mutants. One flash of my credentials would speed us past any Arbites red-tape. But it might also alert Lyko.

I'd insisted on full concealment for the mission. No one knew we were here, officially. Aemos had done some surreptitious checking, and there was no official trace of Lyko either. But that was to be expected, and there was no telling how many mainhive officials he might have back-handed to alert him of any Inquisitorial presence.

Nayl and I turned west at the next junction, and followed the maze of alleys and breezeways between the rents and mill-habs to reach the Twist and Sleep by a circuitous route that would keep us off the main thoroughfares and away from Arbites patrols.

And, as it turned out, bring us right into trouble.

It didn't look like trouble at first. A short, flat-browed runt in rags stepped into our path, grinning like a salesman. He held his hands open, as if he was going to curtsy.

'Twists, my twists, my friends... spare a few 'perials for a poor badgene down on his luck.'

I heard Nayl begin to say, 'Not tonight, twist. S'get you to one side.'

But I had already tensed. How had this scabscum known to ask for Imperial coins if he hadn't seen us at the bar and followed us on purpose?

His accomplices came out of the gloom and sap-rain behind us.

I rammed the word *Evade!* hard into Nayl's mind with a 'pathic surge and dropped.

A massive, spiked weapon sailed through the space our heads had just been occupying and connected with nothing but air.

The runt who had waylaid us uttered quite the most obscene series of curses I have ever, ever heard and dived on me. He had a double-headed dagger with a nurled hand-guard.

I caught his upflung wrist as he made to gouge at me, broke his elbow and kicked him through a nearby fence while he was still screaming in pain.

'Boss! Move!' I heard Nayl sing out and I rolled hard aside in the mud as the spiked weapon slammed down into the mire.

It was a thick length of timber with dozens of nails and knife blades hammered through it.

The friendly end of it was held by two amazingly large paws. The paws belonged to a hulk, a two hundred kilo monster covered with blistered fish-scales and bony scutes. It wore only a pair of ragged blue trousers held in place around its midriff, almost comically, by a pair of red braces.

It swung the spike-post at me again, and I had to dive and shoulder-roll to escape it.

Nayl was going toe-to-toe with two others: a snouted female in black leather whose mouth and nose were hideously combined into one drooling, snarling organ, and a tall, thin male with a face peculiarly distorted by bone and gristle.

The female had a reaping sickle in each hand, and the tall male was armed with a mace made out of a reinforced strut toothed with the rusting blades of two wood saws.

Nayl had drawn his serrated shortsword and duelling knife and was fending off thrusts and strikes from both of them.

A power sword, a boltgun, a lascarbine... they would all

have finished this unnecessary encounter fast enough. But we had agreed to carry nothing that would mark us out from the twist population. Tech-levels were low in the shanty. A plasma gun might have ended this quickly, but stories would have got round.

The scaly giant was on me again, and I fell through the rotting flakboard of a fence in my efforts to evade his swing. I found myself lying amid the debris in the back yard of one of the loathsome hab-rents. A light went on in an upper window and abuse, stones and the contents of a chamber pot were hurled at me.

The giant came on, swinging his club from side to side. The nails and blades were darkly caked with dried blood.

He backed me towards the rear of the rent dwelling and made to swing again.

No! I commanded, using the will. He stopped dead. The rain of abuse and excrement from above stopped too.

It would take him a moment to reconfigure his mind and find his anger again. I moved right at him, punching a knuckle-curved fist at the place where his nose should have been. There was a crack of bone and a spray of blood.

The giant went down hard on his back, his nasal bone slammed back into his brain.

Nayl seemed to be enjoying his uneven duel. He was jeering at his attackers, deflecting the sickles with his sword and blocking the strenuous attacks of the mace with his knife. I saw him spin and belly-kick the male away, then turn to give the ghastly, snorting female his full attention.

But more figures were emerging from the night.

Ugly, abhuman scum dressed in rags. Three, four of them.

I called a warning out to Nayl and pulled out my blackpowder pistol. It was a clumsy antique I'd acquired from the black market on Front's Planet, but even so I'd dumbed it down to Eechan tech levels by replacing the engraved furniture with a shaped piece of packet-wood.

The flintlock mechanism was in good order, though. It cracked loudly with a fizz and a flash, the recoil punishing my wrist, and the ball went point-blank through the forehead of the nearest twist, exploding the rear of his cranium in a surprisingly messy fountain.

But it was a one-shot piece and there was no time for reloading.

Two of the remaining outlaws came right at me, the other turning to come in on Nayl's flank.

I broke the teeth of the first one to reach me with the rounded butt of the pistol, and ducked the second's poorly judged slice with a rapier.

Backing away, I drew my own blade. Also a rapier. Shorter by a good ten centimetres than my opponent's but balanced and guarded with a hand-net of articulated metal struts.

Our blades clashed. He was good, trained to his skill by a life of slaughter in the underhive. But I... I had me on my side.

I dazzled him with the *ulsar* and the *uin ulsar*, and then drove him back with a four-stroke combination of *pel ighan* and *uin pel ihnarr* before ripping the blade out of his dazed fingers with a swift *tahn asaf wyla*.

Then the *ewl caer*. My blade transfixed his torso. He looked confused for a second and then fell down, sliding dead off my blade.

His broken-faced accomplice, blood spilling from my pistol whipping, flew at me and I span, decapitating him with the edge of my blade. The Carthaens believe side-blade work is lazy, and stress the use of the point.

But what the hell.

Nayl had killed the third attacker with a bodypunch, and as I turned, he locked both of the female's sickles around his twisting knife and ran her through with his main blade.

He turned to me and raised his bloody shortsword to his nose in a salute. I returned it with my rapier.

The siren of an Arbites groundcar was wailing along the alley.

'Time to be gone,' I said to Nayl.

'I thought you were dead!' Bequin cursed as Nayl and I burst in to the room in the Twist and Sleep.

'We had some fun on the way home,' Nayl said. 'Don't worry, Lizzie, I brought the boss back safe.'

I smiled and fixed myself a small amasec from the bureau. Bequin hated to be called 'Lizzie'. Only Nayl had the balls to do it.

Aemos was hovering by the window. Somehow, the rags of his twist disguise suited him.

'Most perturbatory... the Arbites are coming this way.'

'What?'

Nayl moved to the window.

'Aemos is right. Three land cruisers pulled up outside. Officers coming in.'

'Hide yourselves, now!' I ordered.

Aemos hurried through the communicating door into the other bedchamber and threw himself down on the cot. Nayl blundered into the adjoining bathroom and used a tooth mug and loud groans to suggest he was busy throwing up.

Alizebeth looked at me frantically.

'Into bed! Hurry!' I ordered.

The Arbites kicked open the door and played their flashlights over the bed. 'Hive Arbites! Who's in here?'

'What is this?' I asked, dragging the sheets back.

'Streetfight killers... witnesses said they came in here,' said the Arbites sergeant, advancing towards the bed.

'Me, I been here all night. Me and my friends.'

'They gonna vouch for you, twist?' asked the sergeant, raising his weapon.

'Wass goin' on? Too much light!' said Bequin, emerging from the dirty linen on the bed. Somehow she had removed her dress beneath the sheets. Clad in brief underwear, she slithered on top of me.

'Wass you doin'? Stoppin' a girl makin' her way? Shame on you!'

The sergeant ran his flashlight beam up and down the length of her body as it clung to me. I smiled the inane smile of the lucky or well-oiled.

He snapped the light off. 'Sorry to interrupt you, miss.' The door closed and the Arbites thumped away.

I looked down at Bequin with a wink. 'Good improvisation,' I said.

She leapt off me and grabbed her clothes. 'Don't get any funny ideas, Gregor!'

I'd had funny ideas about her for years, truth be told. She was beautiful and sublimely sexy. But she was also an untouchable. It hurt me to be close to her, physically hurt.

I hate that fact. I feel a lot for Bequin and I long to be with her, but it was never going to happen. Never, ever.

That's one of the truly great sadnesses of my life.

And hers too, I hope, in my more self-aggrandising moments.

I lay in bed and watched her drag on her dress again, and I felt the pang of desire.

But there was no way. No way in the galaxy.

She was untouchable. I was a psyker.

That way pain and madness lay.

TEN

Ruminations on Lyko
The Chew-after
The highest bidder

Tumultuous sap-storms hammered the twist-town in the pre-dawn, blanketing the sky with swirling vapours and shaking the tiles and shutters with the gross weight of their heavy pelting goop. Thunder rolled. In the aftermath, veils of mist swathed the countryside, and the stillness was alive with gurgling and dripping and the swarming scurry of sap-lice and storm-bugs.

Nayl went out early with Aemos and bought paper pails of warm food from the twist-town commissary just down the street, which was already serving the work lines forming for the shift change in the mills. By the time they returned, we had been joined by Inshabel and Husmaan, who had slept through the night's altercation with the Arbites in a shared room down the hall.

I'd yet to formally notify the ordo that Inshabel had joined my band, but he was now very much part of it. I felt he had the right to be here on this mission, for Roban's sake, and for his own. He had brought the news of Esarhaddon to me, directly and selflessly. Few of my team yet referred to him by his rank – it would be a long while until anyone eclipsed the memory of Interrogator Ravenor – but he had meshed well, with his bright mind and healthy, caustic wit. He was already providing me with more solid service than Alain von Baigg had ever managed.

Duj Husmaan had been a skin-hunter on his homeworld of Windhover when Harlon Nayl had first met him. That was back in Nayl's bounty-chasing days, before he'd joined my cause. I'd recruited Husmaan eight years before on Nayl's recommendation, and he'd proved to be a resourceful, if superstitious, warrior with a great sense for pathfinding. Nayl had personally selected him from the individuals in my retinue as muscle for this venture, and I had no quibble with the choice.

Husmaan was a slender man of medium height with coppery skin and white, sun-scorched hair and goatee. Here on Eechan, like all of us, he'd drabbed down his clothing to ragged black twist robes. He ignored the bundle of disposable wooden forks that Aemos had brought back from the commissary and started to eat the hot food from his paper pail with his fingers.

I picked at my own food idly, wondering how close we were to Lyko.

Lyko had been a fool and had damned himself. The damaging revelation that it hadn't been Esarhaddon who had been torched on the lawns of the Lange palace could have been circumvented if Lyko had kept his head. He could have claimed it a mistake, another example of the heretic psyker's treachery.

But Lyko had run. Out of fear, or chasing some timetable, I didn't know. But he'd run and, in so doing, incriminated himself.

I'd gone to his residence, a rented hab high in the spires of Hive Ten, the moment Inshabel had alerted me to the deceit. But Lyko had cleared out, taking his people with him. His hab was empty and abandoned, with just a few scatterings of trash left behind in the stripped rooms.

I had set my staff to work tracing him, a tall order given the planet-wide data-access problems in the wake of the rioting. I had decided almost at once to pursue him alone, without informing the Inquisition. You may see this as odd, almost reckless. In a way, it was. But Lyko was an inquisitor of good repute, held in high regard, and with many friends. There was scant chance I could tell the ordos I was undertaking a hunt for him on the basis he was harbouring a notorious rogue psyker without the fact reaching him, or without his friends making trouble for me.

Those friends of his, of course, included Heldane and Commodus Voke: the stalwart trio that had captured the thirty-three rogues on Dolsene in the first place. How empty that 'heroic' action now seemed to me. I had been so impressed when Lord Rorken had shown me the report. Perhaps the 'capture' had been easy, or even staged, if Lyko was secretly in league with Esarhaddon. Perhaps it had all been part of an elaborate conspiracy to perpetrate the atrocity of Hive Primaris.

I was dogged by grim, unanswerable speculations. I had no way to prove Lyko was corrupt, not even now, though I certainly suspected it. He might have been an unwitting pawn on Dolsene, or at the Lange palace, or he might have been in it all along. It was possible too that his departure from Thracian was a coincidence that I had misinterpreted. It wouldn't have been the first time an inquisitor had moved undercover without announcement.

It was even possible that he too had discovered the deceit after the event, and was moving fast following some lead to make amends for his mistake. Or that he was fleeing the shame... or...

So many possibilities. I had to play the odds the safest way. I was sure Lyko was guilty to a greater or lesser extent, so I would follow him. Even if he was simply chasing Esarhaddon too, it would lead me in the right direction.

And I couldn't inform the Inquisition, or talk to Voke or Heldane. My uncertainty was such that I couldn't even trust them not to be part of it.

A complex trail of almost subliminal clues had put me on his tail. I'll spare you the bulk of the details, for they would merely document the painstaking tedium that is often the better part of an inquisitor's work. Suffice to say, we searched and processed vox logs, and the broadcast archives of the local and planetary astropathic guilds. We watched ship transfers, orbital traffic, departure lists, cargo movements. I had personnel in the streets, watching key locations, asking off-the-record questions in trader bars, calling in favours from friends of friends, acquaintances of acquaintances, even one or too old adversaries. I hired trackers and bloodhounders, and took every scent trace I could from Lyko's apartment. I had pheromone codes programmed into servitor skulls that I released into up-ports and orbital stations.

I had well over a hundred personnel on my staff, many of them trained hunters, researchers or surveillancers, but I swear the sheer load of data would have burned out our brains.

We would have failed without Aemos. My old savant simply rose to the challenge, never put off, never fatigued, his
mind soaking in more and more information and making a
thousand mental cross checks and comparisons every hour,
tasks I couldn't have managed in a day with a codifier engine
and a datascope.

He seemed, damn his old bones, to enjoy it.

The clues came in, one by one. A shipment of cargo put
into long-term storage in a holding house in Hive Eight and
paid for by a debit transfer from one of Lyko's known associates. A two-second pheromone trace in the departure halls
of a commercial port down on the coast at Far Hive Beta. A
fuzzy image captured from a Munitorum pict-watcher on the
streets of Hive Primaris.

A passenger on a manifest listing making an unnecessary
number of interconnecting flights between up-ports before
moving off planet, as if trying to lose pursuit.

Then the key ones: a cursory excise exam of freight that registered the presence of psi-baffling equipment in an off-world
shipment. A series of clumsily disguised and presumably
hasty bribes to key longshoremen at the Primaris starport. A
rogue trader vessel – the *Princeps Amalgum* – staying a day
longer at high-anchor than it had logged permission to do,
and then a sudden change in its course plans.

Instead of a long run to the Ursoridae Reef, it was heading
spinwards, via Front's World, to the twist farms of Eechan.

There was a knock at the room door just after dawn, and I
sent everyone except Nayl into the adjoining room. Bequin
and Inshabel had the presence of mind to scoop up all the
food pails except two. I went over to the window, and Nayl
sat down in a chair, with his arm casually over the back so

anyone coming in couldn't see the autopistol in his hand.

I focussed my mind for a moment to make sure our twist disguises were live, and then said, 'Enter.'

The door opened and the porcupine girl from the twist bar came in. She was dressed in a glistening sap-cloak, and she looked at us curiously as she pushed back her hood.

'You take your time, twists,' she said.

'You got something, sweetgene, or you simply s'got to check the good stuff you passed on last night?' Nayl asked with a lascivious smile.

She scowled, and a head crest of spines rose in a threat posture.

'I s'got a message. You know who from.'

'The Phant?'

'I ain't saying, genesmudge. I just bring it.'

'Then s'bring it.'

She reached into her cloak and produced an old, low-tech tracker set, battered and worn. Holding it up briefly, she thumbed it on long enough for us to see the green telltale winking, and then switched it off again and dropped it with a clatter onto the peeling tabletop.

'S'gonna be an auction. Bidder's market, so bring lotsa yellow, he says. Lotsa.'

'Where? When?'

'Today at shift two, in the chew-after. That s'tell you where.'

'That it?' I asked.

'S'all I have. I just bring it.' She hesitated at the door. 'You s'might wanna make my worth while.'

I put my hand into my coat pocket and pulled out a single, large denomination Imperial coin.

'You take these?'

Her eyes lit up. 'I take anything.'

I tossed it over to her and she caught it with one hand.

'Thanks,' she said. She went out through the door and then looked back at us, as if my generous contribution to her immediate happiness had shifted her opinion of us.

Which, sadly, given this miserable place, it probably had.

'S'don't trust him,' she advised, then closed the door and left.

The chew-after was the local name given to the tracts of farmland laid waste after the harvesters had been through. Wrecklands of shredded vegetation that began to regrow within days of a harvest, such was the speed and fecundity of Eechan's floral growth. At any one time, there were several thousand square kilometres of chew-after in the farmlands round the mainhive.

We headed south, into the most recent areas of thresh-wake, following the signal of the tracker.

Noon. That was what she had meant by shift two. The second shift change of the day. We gave ourselves two hours to get there.

On top of all my speculations about Lyko, things still didn't add up. It had been easy enough for Nayl to identify Phant Mastik as the local slaver, with a specialisation in mindjobs, but why was Lyko using him? Why was Lyko selling Esarhaddon at all?

Aemos had suggested it was part of a final trade now that Esarhaddon had completed his part of their pact. That supposed Lyko was in control, which I doubted. And if he was simply cutting the heretic loose now the work was done, why sell him? Why, indeed, come all this way to do that? Inshabel supposed that maybe Lyko was now anxious to get rid of the rogue-psyker because he was afraid of him.

I had my own theory. Lyko had brought Esarhaddon to Eechan for some other purpose, and arranging a mock sale through the Phant was simply bait to draw anyone who might have followed him out into the open.

As it turned out, I was right. I wasn't surprised. It's what I would have done.

The chew-after was a miasmal waste. As far as the eye could see, which wasn't far at all given the clinging sap-mists from the night before, the land was a gouged, punished ruin of ripped shoots, shredded plant-fibre, wrenched-up root balls and pressure-flattened soil. The massive trackmarks of the harvesters had left wide ruts the depth of a man's waist, at the bottom of which plant material and soil was layered into a glassy flatness like they had been set in aspic.

The misty air was wet with sap and everything was crawling with lice motes and storm-bugs. They swarmed in the air, settled all over us, and we could feel them in our clothes.

By then, although we maintained our twist disguises, we were all armed and armoured at full strength. One doesn't walk into a likely trap with a blackpowder pistol and a sharp stick. I wore body armour, and carried my power sword and boltpistol. The others were similarly heavy with battlegear. If we were caught now, maintaining the pretence we were twists would be the last of our problems.

Ten kilometres south, through the swirling, sticky mists, we could hear the chugging, rending sounds of the harvesters as they moved on their way. Every few metres there was another bloody smear or furry pulp, the remains of crop rodents caught in the reaping blades of the factory machines.

'You'd think,' said Inshabel, pausing to wipe the gooey sweat from his face, 'that the wildlife would have got used to the farm-factories by now. Learned to get out of the way.'

'Some things never learn,' Husmaan muttered. 'Some things always come back to the source.'

'He means food. He always means food,' Nayl chuckled to me. 'To Duj, everything comes back to food.'

'According to mill statistics,' said Aemos, 'there are four billion crop-rats in every demitare of field space. Rivers of them flee before the harvesters. We've seen one rat-corpse for every twenty-two metres, which suggests only two-point-two per cent of them were unlucky enough to be caught in the blades. That means the vast percentage fled. They're smarter than you think.'

He paused. Everyone had stopped and was staring at him.

'What?' he asked. 'What? I was only saying...'

'That old geezer fantisises about maths and stats more'n I fantisise about the lay-dies,' Nayl told Bequin as we moved forward again.

'I'm not sure which of you I'm supposed to feel more sorry for,' she said.

Husmaan held up the tracker the Porcupine-girl had given us and shook it. Then he slapped it a couple of times for good measure.

We waded through the plant fibre and came level with him.

'Problem?' I asked.

'Damn thing... too old.'

'Let me see it.'

Husmaan handed it to me. It was a piece of crap, all right. Battered by a lifetime of hard knocks, with a nearly flat powercell. A nice touch that, I thought, noting Lyko's careful planning. An unreliable tracker made this seem so much more genuine. A brand new or well-powered unit would have been as good as a written invitation beginning 'Dear people chasing me, please come here and get killed...'

I shook the device myself and got a good return. Just enough juice to lead us to our deaths.

'That way,' I said.

It was close to noon. The sun was up, but the sap-mists hadn't dissipated. We were bathed in a warm, yellow, filmy glare. According to the tracker, we were about half a kilometre from the auction site.

'They're expecting me and Nayl, so we'll go in with Bequin.' I wanted an untouchable close to me. 'Inshabel, cut east with Aemos. Husmaan, west. Covering positions. Don't move in unless you hear me vox a direct command. Understand?'

The three nodded.

'If you find anything, keep it Glossia and keep it brief. Go.'

Nathun Inshabel armed his lascarbine and moved away to the left with Aemos along a harvester track-bed, leaving tacky footprints in the glassy, crushed residue at the bottom of the huge rut. Husmaan's hempcloth-wrapped long-las was already armed. He darted away to the right, quickly lost in the mist.

'Shall we?' I said to Bequin and Nayl.

'After you,' Nayl grinned.

I made one last command by vox, in Glossia code, and we trudged into the ripped thickets of the chew-after.

The Phant's people had used flamers to clear a wide space in the morass of the chew-over. We could smell the burnt pulp-fibre from several dozen metres away.

The mist was still close, but I could make out several

crop-runner trucks, skimmers and land speeders parked in the blackened clearing. People bustled around them.

'What do you see?' I asked Nayl.

He played his magnoculars round again. 'Phant... and his twist cronies. The horned guy, and that eyeball creep. Maybe a dozen, some of whom think they're hidden around the perimeter. Plus the prospective buyers. I make... three... no, four, all hive-types, with minders. Sixteen other bodies, all told.'

I yanked up my hood. 'Come on.'

'There's an alarm strand round the site.'

'We'll trip it. That's what it's there for.'

The alarm strand was an ankle-high wire-cord tied taut between the churned root clumps. Every metre or so, the air-dried shell case of a storm bug was carefully tied to it, forming a little, hollow-sounding bell. They rattled and jangled as we deliberately plucked the wire.

In a moment, ragged-robed twist muscle loomed out of the murdered undergrowth, aiming matchlocks and blades at us.

'We're s'here for the auction,' I told them, holding up Phant's tracker. 'S'invited.'

'Name?' croaked a frog-headed thing with a crossbow and a spittle problem.

'Eye-gor, from off. With his twists.'

Frog-head waved us into the site. The others assembled before the low, flak-board stage on which Phant Mastik stood, looking round at us.

'Eye-gor! Off-world twist, with two others,' Frog-head announced.

Phant nodded his heavy, tusked head and Frog-head and his men backed off, putting up their weapons.

++S'glad you could make it, twist++

'You the Phant. You the twist with the stuff. But... I s'hear my own name loud, not these others.'

++Let's all be known, then the sale can begin++

Phant looked down at the other buyers. One, a stunning female up-spire hiver in a tight bodyglove nodded. 'Frovys Vassik,' she said through a pan-lingual servitor-skull drone that floated at her shoulder.

She was clearly speaking some high-caste dialect cant which the drone was translating. I assayed her and her two male bodyguards quickly: dilettante wealthers, would-be cult-ist types, well-armed and armoured with all the wargear spire money could afford.

'Merdok,' said the next, a frail, white-suited, elderly man leaning on a cane and wiping perspiration from his brow with a japanagar lace kerchief that had cost more than the lowly Phant's entire outfit. He had four minders, squat females in rubberised war-rena suits, each with an electronic slave-leash collar around her throat.

'Tanselman Fybes,' said the bland-faced man to Merdok's left, stepping forward with a courteous nod. He was dressed in a bright orange cooler-suit, with large, articulated exchanger vanes sprouting from his shoulders. His breath smoked in the personal veil of cold air the suit was generating around him.

He was also alone, which made him instantly more danger-ous than the hive retards who had brought muscle.

'You may address me as Erotik,' said the last, a bitch-faced crone who had inadvisably wedged her ancient body into a close-fitting, spiked, black bodyglove, the mark of a death-cultist.

Or would be death-cultist, I thought. She had five masked and harnessed slaves with her, all of them sweating in the

misty heat. I saw at once they were out of their depth. They
played at death-cult, up in the eyries of the mainhive, maybe
cutting their skin and drinking blood once in a while. The
closest they had come to a real death-cult was watching some
blurry, fake snuff-pict to impress their friends after a banquet.

'S'greet you all. I'm Eye-gor. S'off world, and twisted as they
come.'

I bowed. Fybes and Vassik returned the motion. Merdok
mopped his brow and Erotik gestured a very ham-fisted sign
of the True Death which nearly made Nayl laugh out loud.

'Can we get started, my friend Phant?' Merdok asked, dab-
bing his kerchief around the sweat runs on his face. 'It's
midday and bloody hot out here.'

'And I have murders to do and blood to drink!' Erotik cried.
Her plump and unhealthy minders oohed and aahed and tried
to get their nipple-spikes and bondage straps comfortable.

'Oh dear God-Emperor... they're never going to make it out
alive...' whispered Bequin.

'More fool them...' I whispered back.

Phant's men used force-poles and electrolashes to goad the
sale item from the back of a crop-runner truck onto the stage.
It was a rangy human, straitjacketed and bindfolded, with a
heavy psychic-damper muzzle buckled around his head.

++Alpha-plus quality. One only. S'bids, now?'++

'Ten bars!' cried Erotik at once.

'Twenty,' said Vassik.

'Twenty-five!' cried Merdok.

Fybes cleared his throat. His cough blew cold steam out
from the private atmosphere generated by his suit. 'I think
that's established the common level here. I do hate mixing
with proles. One thousand bars.'

Erotik and her minders gasped.

Merdok looked pale.

Vassik glanced round at Fybes with a curt look.

'Ahh. At least someone sees the true worth of the item on sale. Good. We can begin serious bidding.' Vassik cleared her throat and her cyber-skull dutifully issued white noise. 'Twelve hundred bars,' she said.

'Thirteen hundred!' Erotik cried out, desperately.

'Fifteen,' said Merdok. 'My best offer. I had no idea this meet would be so hungry... or so rich.'

'Two thousand,' said Vassik's hovering skull.

'Three,' said Fybes.

Merdok was already shaking his head. Erotik was walking away towards the edge of the site, complaining loudly to her pudgy sex-toys, who bustled around her.

'Three five,' said Vassik.

'Four,' said Fybes.

'Anything?' I whispered to Bequin.

'Not even the slightest latent push. But those baffles could be doing their job.'

'So it could be Esarhaddon?'

'Yes. I doubt it. But it could.'

'Nayl?'

Harlon Nayl looked round at me.

'Nothing. The Phant's minders are getting edgy because the old witch and her sad hump-muffins are trying to leave before the auction's finished. But nothing else...'

'Five five,' Vassik's servitor-skull rasped.

'Six,' said Fybes.

Merdok had withdrawn to one side of the site with his minders, and was taking a sustaining puff of obscura from a portable water-pipe one of the war-rena slave fems was holding for him. Erotik and her chubby concubines were arguing with Horn-head and another couple of twists on the other side of the burned acre.

'Eight five!' Vassik was announcing.

'Nine!' returned Fybes.

'Fifty!' I said quietly, tossing a huge pile of ingots down onto the stained soil.

There was a pause. A long, damned pause.

++Fifty bid++

Phant looked down at us all.

Merdok and Erotik and all their people were simply dumb-struck. Vassik turned away, screaming, and her minders had to hold her down as she went into fits of rage.

Fybes just looked at me, his breath coming slow and short in clouds.

'Fifty?' he said.

'S'fifty, count 'em. You got better?'

'What if I have, Eye-gor? And please... stop it with the "s'stupid s'twist" talk. It's getting on my nerves.'

Fybes walked towards me. He reached up and pulled his face off. The flesh disintegrated like gossamer as he pulled it away, revealing his blank, piercing eyes.

'Oh, Gregor. You do so like to make an entrance, don't you?' said Cherubael.

ELEVEN

**Face to face
No witnesses
Death along the line**

His was the last face I had expected to see here, though it had been in my mind and my nightmares for nearly a hundred years.

'It's been a while, hasn't it, Gregor?' the daemonhost said softly, almost cordially. 'I've thought of you often, fondly. You bested me on 56-Izar. I... held a grudge for a while, I must admit. But when I learned you had survived after all, I was quite delighted. It meant there would be a chance for us to meet again.'

The orange cooler-suit began to burn and collapse off him in molten hanks until he was naked. He rose gently, arms by his side, like a dancer, and hovered on the wind a few metres above the churned soil. He was still tall, and powerfully made, but the aura that shone from him was more sickly green than the gold I remembered.

Unhealthy bulging veins corded his body, and the nub-horns on his brow had grown into short, twisted hooks.

'And so we meet again. Aren't you going to say anything?'

I could feel Bequin shaking in terror beside me.

'Stay calm, stay still,' I told her.

The daemonhost glanced at her and his smile widened. 'The untouchable! How wonderful! An almost exact repeat of our first encounter. How are you, my dear?'

'What do you want?' I asked.

'Want?'

'You always want something. On 56-Izar, it was the Necroteuch. Oh, I forgot. You never want anything, do you? You're just a slave, doing another's bidding.'

Cherubael frowned slightly. 'Don't be uncivil, Gregor. You should treasure the fact that I have taken a personal interest in you. Most things that cross me get destroyed very quickly. I could have hunted you out years ago. But I knew... there was a bond.'

'More of your riddles. More nothings. Tell me something real. Tell me about Vogel Passionata.'

He laughed, an ugly sound. 'Oh, you heard about, that did you?'

'Reports of the incident have made me suspect in the eyes of many.'

'I know. Bless you, that wasn't my intention. It was just a tiny error on my part. I'm sorry if it's inconvenienced you.'

'I have no wish to be seen as a man who would form a compact with daemons.'

'I'm sure you haven't. But that is what's happening, whether you like it or not. Destiny, Gregor. Our destinies are entwined, in ways you cannot even begin to see. Why else would you dream about me?'

'Because it has become a central goal of my life to hunt you down and banish you.'

'Oh, this is a lot more than simple professional obsession. Think, why do you really dream of me? Why do you search for me so diligently, even hiding the extent of that search from your masters?'

'I...' My mind was racing. This thing knew so much.

'And why did I spare you? If it had been you on Vogel Passionata, I would have let you live. I let you live on Thracian.'

'What?'

'You stopped to pay homage at Spatian's tomb, and the Gate shielded you from the disaster. Why did you stop? You don't know. You can't explain it, can you? It was me. Watching over you. Planting the suggestion in your mind. Making you pause for no reason. We've been working together all along.'

'No!'

'You know it, Gregor. You just don't know you know it.'

Cherubael floated away a short distance, and looked around. The auction site was frozen, all eyes on him. No one dared move, not even the most weak-willed twist guard. Even those present who didn't know what he was recognised the extraordinary evil and power he represented.

'What are you waiting for?' a voice yelled from nearby. Several armed men stepped out of their cover in the chew-after tangles and approached. It was Lyko, with six gristly examples of hired muscle.

'Look who I found, Lyko. I sprung this trap, just like you suggested, to discover if anyone was on your tail, and look who it turned out to be.'

'Eisenhorn...' Lyko murmured, fear crossing his face for a second. He looked over at Cherubael.

'I said, what are you waiting for? Kill them and we can be gone.'

It was suddenly clear to me Lyko wasn't the daemonhost's master. Like Konrad Molitor all those years before, Lyko was another pawn, a corrupted agent of someone... something... else.

'Must I?' asked the hovering figure.

'Do it! No witnesses!'

'Please!' cried the elderly Merdok. 'We only meant t–'

Lyko whipped around and incinerated the old man with his plasma gun.

That broke the impasse. Phant's people and the other buyers broke in panic, drawing weapons, shouting. Indiscriminate shooting began. Lyko's gunmen, all ex-military types with autocannons, hosed the staging area and cut down the fleeing twists. I saw Phant Mastik hit by a burst of fire and collapse in rough sections backwards off the platform.

His horn-headed minder ran at Cherubael, firing a grubby old laspistol.

Cherubael hadn't moved. He was simply watching the murder around him. The las-shots sizzled off his skin, and he glanced down at the twist, as if his reverie had been broken.

The daemonhost didn't even move a hand, a finger. There was just a slight nod in the direction of the horned minder, and the miserable twist was somehow filleted where he stood, waves of force stripping off his flesh and popping out his skeleton, parts of it still articulated.

I felt the warp churning around that dismal place as Cherubael went to work. Once he had started, his fury was unstinting. Merdok's war-rena fems disappeared in a sudden vortex and died, fused together. The mud beneath Vassik's feet boiled, and she and her bodyguards sank, screaming and thrashing, into it.

I was frozen, rigid. I felt Bequin pulling at me.

Shots seared past my face. I snapped round, and saw two of Lyko's men charging us. One dropped suddenly, headshot by what could only have been a sniping round from Husmaan out in the torn undergrowth.

Nayl flew past me and gunned the other down with his Tronsvasse parabellum.

'Come on! We've got to get out of here!' he yelled at me.

There was blood and filth and swirling plant-fibre in the air. A warp storm was crackling around us, so dense and dark we could barely see, barely stand against its churning force. But I could make out the glowing shape of Cherubael through it all.

I drew my power sword and ran towards him.

'Gregor! No!' Bequin screamed.

I had no choice. I had waited the best part of a hundred years. I would not let him go again.

He floated around to face me, smiling down.

'Put that away, Gregor. Don't worry. I won't kill you. Lyko has no power over me. I'll deal with his complaints later, and–'

'Who does have power over you? Who is your master? Tell me! You caused the atrocity on Thracian, didn't you! Why? On whose orders?'

'Just go away, Gregor. This is not your concern now. Go away.'

I think he was honestly surprised when I hacked the power sword into his chest.

I don't really know if I had imagined I could do him any harm.

The blessed blade almost disembowelled him before it exploded and hurled me backwards.

He looked down in dismay at the wound across his torso. Warp energies, bright and toxic, were spilling out of it. In a second, the wound closed as if it had never been.

'You little fool,' said Cherubael.

I found myself flying backwards through the air, blood in my mouth.

The impact of landing shook my bones and smashed the breath out of me. My head swam. The daemonhost's power had thrown me a good thirty metres across the site, into the underbrush.

Furious psychic detonations went off all round. Screaming, semi-sentient winds from the deepest warp snaked around the field, destroying the last of the twists and the fleeing buyers.

I tried to rise, but consciousness left me.

When I came to, the chew-after was on fire. There was no sign of Cherubael. Inshabel and Aemos were pulling me to my feet.

'Bequin! Nayl!' I coughed.

'I'll find them,' Inshabel said.

'Where's Lyko?' I asked Aemos, as Inshabel ran off, weapon drawn.

'Fled, with his men, in two of the land speeders.'

'And the daemonhost?'

'I don't know. It seemed to just vanish. Maybe it had a displacer field.'

I started to run back into the site, though my body was burning with pain. Aemos cried out after me.

Most of the vehicles were smashed or overturned, but a couple were still intact.

I scrambled into a small, black speeder; a sleek, up-hive sports model that had presumably belonged to Vassik. I cued the thrusters, lifting off before I'd even strapped on the seat harness.

The craft was powerful and over-responsive. It took a moment to master the lightness of touch needed to accelerate without sudden blurts of speed. I turned it unsteadily in the air as I climbed too fast above the blasted site. Below, I could see Nayl, ragged and bloody, shouting up at me to come back.

Banking out of the cone of smoke at a hundred metres, I got my bearings. On every side, the acreage of the chew-after spread out until it became lush greencover again. There was the mainhive, looming in the distance. Where were they? Where were they?

I saw two dots in the air three kilometres to the west and gunned the machine after them. Heavy land speeders, making towards the bulk of the nearest harvester factory.

I pushed the turbines to their limit, coming in low and fast behind the slower lift-machines. I knew they'd seen me the moment autofire chattered back in my direction, wildly off target.

I began to jink, the way Midas had taught me, before they got their aim in. I thought about shooting back at them, but it took both hands on the stick just to keep the sports speeder level.

We were passing over green crop land now, an emerald sea that raced away below in an alarming blur. More tracer shots howled back past me.

A big shadow passed across the sun.

'Want them splashed?' crackled from the vox.

Downjets flaring, the streamlined bulk of my gun-cutter settled in beside me, matching my speed. It seemed huge compared to my insignificant little speeder; one-fifty tonnes, eighty metres from beak nose to finned tail, landing gear lowered like insect legs. I could see Medea grinning in the cockpit.

I daren't lift my hands from the jarring stick to activate the vox.

Instead, I opened my mind directly to hers.

Only if you have to. Try and get them to land.

'Ow!' answered the vox. 'Warn me next time you're gonna do that.'

The great bulk of the cutter suddenly surged forward, afterburners incandescent and landing gear raising, and banked away to the right. Its thrust wake wobbled me hard. I watched it turn out in a wide semi-circle, low over the crops, furrowing them with its downwash. It looked like a vast bird of prey swooping round for the kill.

With its interplanetary thrust-tunnels, it easily outstripped the racing speeders, and came in towards them, head on.

I felt a surge of psychic power. My enemies had nothing but their minds with which to combat the gun-cutter.

The cutter suddenly broke left, dipped and then righted itself. They'd got to Medea, if only for a moment.

She was angry now. I could tell that simply from the way she flew. With a wail of braking jets, she turned the cutter on a stall-hover as the speeders flashed past.

The chin-turret crackled, and heavy-gauge munitions tore the second of the two speeders into a shower of flames in the air.

Hitting the throttle, I zipped in behind the hovering gun-cutter, chasing down the other speeder.

No more! I sent to Medea. *I want them alive if possible!*

The remaining speeder was close ahead now. I could feel Lyko's mind aboard it.

He was closing on the armoured bulk of the harvester, which now dominated the landscape ahead. It was a giant, six hundred metres long and ninety high at the peak of its humped, beetle-back. It was kicking a vast wake of sap-spray and smoke out behind it. The rattle of its threshing blades was audible above the scream of my speeder's engines.

My quarry dipped, and flew in along the spine of the huge factory machine, heading for a rear-facing docking hangar raised like a wart on the hull's back. Warning hails were beeping at me over the speeder's vox-set, the alarmed challenges of the harvester.

The heavy speeder braked hard and landed badly in the mouth of the docking hangar. Turning in to follow it, I saw figures scrambling out. They disappeared, into the hangar, all except one man, who dropped to his knees on the approach slip and began firing back at me with his autocannon.

Streams of high-velocity rounds whipped past on either side. Then a bunch of them went into my port intake with a clattering roar that shook the speeder and threw shards of casing out in a belch of sparks.

Warning lights lit up across the control board.

I dropped ten metres, put the nose in.

And bailed.

I broke my left wrist and four ribs hitting the topside of the harvester. With hindsight, I was lucky not to have been killed outright, lucky even to have hit the harvester's hull at all. It was a long way down. I managed to grab a stanchion cable as I began to slither down, and wrapped my right arm around it.

My speeder glanced once off the approach slip, and bounced up again, tail up, beginning to tear apart. Trailing debris, the machine cartwheeled in, vapourised the gunman, hit Lyko's parked land speeder, and shunted it right into the hangar, which exploded a second later in a sheet of fire and metal.

I limped along the approach slip, sidestepping chunks of burning wreckage, and climbed over the smashed, smouldering speeders into the hangar. Impact klaxons were rasping out, and automatic fire-fighting sprays were still squirting out dribbles of retardant foam.

At the back of the hangar, a hatch was half open, next to the cages of the service and cargo elevators.

I pushed through the hatch. A metal staircase descended into the factory. At the bottom, it opened out into a companionway that ran the length of the harvester. Stunned work-crews, most of them twists in sap-stained overalls, gazed at me.

I produced my rosette.

'Imperial Inquisition. Where did they go?'

'Who?'

'Where did they go?' I snarled, enforcing my will without restraint.

The effect was so powerful, none of them could speak, and several passed out. All the others pointed down the companionway towards the head of the factory.

Another hatch, another staircase. The noise of the internal threshers was now shudderingly loud. I came down into the vast internal work line, a long chamber that ran the length of the harvester. It was a huge, deafening place, the air thick with sap mist. A massive processing conveyor carried the harvested produce along from the reaping blades at the harvester's mouth, at a rate of several tonnes every second. Twist workers in masks and aprons worked the front part of the line with chaintools and cutting lances which were attached to overhead power systems by thick rubber-trunked hoses. They sorted and cut the larger sections of root and stalk before the crop went through the great vicing rollers and stamping presses into the macerating vats further back down the factory.

With the alarms sounding and warning lights flashing, the

line had come to a halt, and the workers were looking around, liquid cellulose and sap dripping off their gauntlets, overalls and work tools.

I blundered through them, overseers shouting at me from gantry stations far above. I could see Lyko, thirty metres away down the line, pushing through with one last gunman and a bound, visored figure that could only be Esarhaddon.

The gunmen turned and fired at me down the length of the line vault. Three workers crumpled, one spilling over onto the belt. The shots spanged sparks off the metal walkways and machinery.

As the other workers dived for cover, I dropped to my knee and reached for my boltgun. It wasn't there. In fact, the entire holster was ripped open. I wasn't sure when I lost it: during Cherubael's assault or slamming off the hull of the harvester, but it was long gone. And my beloved power sword had been disintegrated on contact with the daemonhost.

More shots whizzed down the work-line and dented the metal facings of the belt-drivers. I crawled into cover behind a drum of hydrobac tool-wash.

I pulled my back-up weapon from the ankle-holster built into the side of my boot. It was a compact, short-frame auto with a muzzle so short it barely extended beyond the trigger guard. The handgrip was actually longer than the barrel, and contained a slide-magazine of twenty small-calibre rounds.

Selecting single-fire, I cracked off a couple of shots. The aim was lousy and the power poor. It really was meant to be a close-range last ditch.

The gunman down the line, undeterred by my pathetic display, switched over to full auto and raked the deck area and working space beside the stationary belt. Workers, all pressing themselves into cover, began to scream and yell.

The shooting stopped. I dared a look out. There was a clunk and a whirr and the conveyor started moving again.

The gunman was following his departing master again. Lyko was almost out of sight, pushing his captive ahead of him.

Why was Esarhaddon a captive, I wondered? I still didn't understand the relationship between Lyko, the psyker and Cherubael.

I ran on. The gunman, Lyko and his captive psyker had all disappeared through a bulkhead door. To follow them, I'd have to go in blind. And if I'd been in Lyko's place, I'd have used the bulkhead as a point to turn and wait.

My gut readings of his actions had not been wrong so far.

I leapt up onto the wide conveyor belt, ignoring the shouts of the cowering work crew, and slithered across it through the matted, sticky crop load. The sap and the moving belt made it nigh on impossible to stay upright. For a moment, I thought I might slip and be carried along under the nearest roller press.

I leapt off the far side onto the solid deck, dripping with green mush and vegetal fluid. Now I was following the work-line down the other side of the wide conveyor, which divided the harvester centrally.

There was a bulkhead door on this side, too.

I went through it, low.

The gunman was waiting behind the other door on the far side of the moving belt. He saw me, cursed, and turned with his autocannon. I was firing already. Even at this shorter range, the pathetic stopping power of my auto was evident. His drum-barrelled autocannon was about to roar out my doom.

I dived headlong, thumbing my weapon to auto and ripped off the entire clip of small slugs in a shrill, high-pitched chatter.

What I lacked in power I made up for in numbers. I hit him six or seven times in the left arm and collar and staggered him backwards, his bonded armour torn open. The heavy cannon flew out of his hands and landed on the moving belt between us to be carried out of view.

He was far from dead, though he was bleeding profusely from the multiple small calibre grazes and impacts. He was probably glanding some stimm that kept his edge.

Snarling an oath, he drew a military-issue las-pistol from his webbing, and climbed up on the work-line foot rail on his side of the rolling belt to get a better angle at me. I threw the empty gun at him and made him duck, and then grabbed one of the hose-suspended work lances hanging by the line-edge.

He got off a shot that barely missed my shoulder. I swung the lance at him, the chain-blade tip chittering, reaching out across the belt. But it was hard to manipulate it with one wrist smashed.

So I turned the swing into a throw and launched the long tool like a harpoon.

The chain-tip impaled him and he died still screaming and trying to drag the industrial cutter from his chest. As he went limp, the tension in the rubberised power-hose pulled the lance back towards its rest hook on my side of the line, dragging the body onto the conveyor. The belt carried it along as far as the hose would allow, and then it stuck fast, the belt moving under it.

Piles of wet plant fibre began damming up against it and spilling over onto the floor.

Eisenhorn, a voice said in my mind.

I wheeled round and saw Lyko standing on a grilled gantry that formed a walk-bridge over the belt. The plasma gun he had used to burn the fake Esarhaddon was aimed at me. I could see the battered psyker, his head still masked and visored, lashed to a wall-pipe on the far side of the line.

You should have left well alone, Eisenhorn. You should never have come after me.

I'm doing my job, you bastard. What were you doing?

What had to be done. What needs to be done.

He came down the walk-bridge and stepped towards me. There was a hunted, terrified look in his face.

And what needs to be done?

Silence.

Why, Lyko? The atrocity on Thracian... how could you have allowed that? Been part of it?

I... I didn't know! I didn't know what they were going to do.

Who?

He squashed my cheek with the muzzle of his potent weapon.

'No more,' he said, speaking for the first time.

'If you're going to kill me, just do it. I'm surprised you haven't already.'

'I need to know something first. Who knows? Who knows what you know?'

'About you and your little pact with the daemonscum? About your theft of an alpha-plus class psyker? That you stood by while millions died on Thracian? Hah!' *Everyone.* I added the answer psychically for emphasis. *Everyone. I informed Rorken and Orsini himself before I left on your trail*

'No! There would have been more than just you after me...'

'There is.'

'You're lying! You're alone...'

You're doomed.

He stormed his mind into mine, frantic to tear the truth out of me. I think he was truly realising how far into damnation he had cast himself.

I blocked his feverish mind-assault, and countered, driving an augur of psychic rage into his hind brain. It was in there. I could feel it. His true master. The face, the name...

He realised what I was doing, realised that I outclassed him psychically. He tried to shoot me with his plasma gun, but by then I had shut down his nervous system and blocked all autonomous function. I scoured his mind. He was frozen, helpless, unable to stop me ransacking his memory, despite the blocks and engram locks he had placed there. Or someone had.

There. There. The answer.

He uttered an agonised, oddly modulated scream.

Lyko tumbled away from me.

Cherubael hovered above us, high in the roof space of the factory chamber, casting a glow of filthy warp-light.

Choking, twitching, his limbs limp, Lyko was rising up towards him. Smoke was coming out of his mouth and nostrils.

'Now, now, Gregor,' Cherubael said. 'Nice try, but there are some secrets that must remain.'

With a nod of his head, he tossed Lyko aside. The traitor-inquisitor flew down to the front of the factory space, bounced hard off the inner hull and then fell down into the churning reaper blades in the factory harvester's maw.

His body was utterly disintegrated.

Cherubael hovered lower, grabbed the comatose, bound form of Esarhaddon like a child picking up a doll.

'I won't forget what you did,' said the daemonhost, looking back at me one last time. 'You'll have to make it up to me.'

Then he was gone, and Esarhaddon was gone with him.

TWELVE

At Cadia, by terce
The pylons
Talking with Neve

A bitter autumn wind was coming down off the moors, and the turning ribbon-leaves of the axeltrees were beginning to fall. They fluttered past me like dry strands of black kelp, and collected in slowly decomposing drifts on the windward side of the graves and the low stone walls.

Above, the overcast sky was full of racing brown clouds.

I followed the old, overgrown path up the wooded slope, under the hissing axeltrees, and stood for a while alone, looking down at the wide grave field and the little shrine tower that watched over it. There was no sign of life, and, apart from the wind, no movement. Even the air-shay that had brought me here from the landing fields at Kasr Tyrok had departed. I almost missed the driver's grumbles that the place was so far out of town.

Far away, almost out of sight beyond the glowering moors, I saw the nearest of the famed, mysterious pylons, an angular silhouette. Even from this distance, I could hear the strange, moaning note the wind made as it blew through the pylons' geometries, geometries that thousands of years of human scholarship had failed to explain.

This was my first time on the world they called the Gatehouse of the Imperium. So far, it was not endearing itself to me.

'So, Thorn... you were none too sharp, were you?'

I turned slowly. He had arrived behind me, as silent as the void itself.

'Well?' he asked. 'What time do you call this?'

'I consider myself suitably chastened,' I said.

He was impassive, then the scar under his milky eye twitched and he smiled.

'Welcome to Cadia, Eisenhorn,' said Fischig.

Aside from Aemos, Godwyn Fischig was my longest serving companion, though he and Bequin often disputed that record. I'd met them both on Hubris, during my hunt for the Chaos-broker Eyclone, which led in turn to the whole bloody affair of the Necroteuch.

I'd actually encountered Fischig first. He'd then been a chastener in the local Arbites, ordered to keep a watch on me. He became my ally through circumstance. Bequin had crossed my path, if my memory serves, about a day later, but I had co-opted her almost directly into my service, while Fischig had remained, technically, a serving Arbites officer for some considerable time before resigning to join me.

Which is why Bequin claimed the prize, and why they sometimes fell to disputing it when the hour was late and the amasec unstoppered.

His was a big man, of my own age, his cropped blond hair

now turning silver. But he was as robust as ever, clad in a coat
of black fur, a mail surcoat and steel-fronted boots.

He shook my hand.

'I was beginning to think you wouldn't make it.'

'I was beginning to think so too.'

He cocked his head slightly. 'Trouble?'

'Like you wouldn't believe. Let's walk and I'll tell you.'

We wandered back down the tree-shrouded path together.
He knew something of the atrocity on Thracian, which was
by then some seven months past, but he had no idea I had
been caught up in it.

When I told him the details, especially about Ravenor, his
face darkened.

He had admired Gideon – frankly, it had been difficult not
to admire Gideon – and I sometimes felt that Gideon was the
man Fischig would have liked to have been.

Fischig's great strength was his self-knowledge. He understood his own limitations. His strengths were loyalty, physical
power, fine combat skills, observation and a nose for detail.
He was not quick witted, and his abhorrence of book-learning
meant that even the rank of interrogator was beyond him.
Though he would have loved to rise formally through the
ranks of the Inquisition, he had never tried, contenting himself with becoming one of the fundamental components of
my staff.

To try, he knew, would have meant failure. And Godwyn
Fischig hated to fail.

We crossed the narrow funeral lane and went into the grave
field by the old lychgate in the low wall. I told him about Lyko,
and Esarhaddon. I told him of the warnings from Endor and

Lord Rorken. I told him about the bloody, inconclusive mess on Eechan. I told him about Cherubael.

'I would have come as soon as I received your message. But Rorken practically forbade me. And then, as you have heard, matters got out of hand.'

He nodded. 'Don't worry, I'm a patient man.'

We stood for a moment in the middle of the vast field of graves. Several shivering priests in ragged black robes were wandering through the lines of crumbling gravestones, pausing to study each one.

'What are they doing?'

'Reading the names,' he said.

'What for?'

'To see if they can be read.'

'Okay... why?'

'As you might imagine, a martial world like this produces many dead. Long ago, an edict was made by the planetary government that only certain fields of land could ever be used for burial. So cemetery space is at an optimum. Hence, the Law of Decipherability.'

'Which is?'

'The law states that once the eroding hands of time and the elements have made the last names on a field's gravestones illegible, the anonymous dead may be exhumed, the bones buried in a pit, and the field reused.'

'So they tend the field for years until the names can no longer be read?'

He shrugged. 'It's their way. Once the names have vanished, so has the memory, and so has any need for honour. The time's coming for this place. Another year or two, they tell me.'

That struck me as infinitely melancholic. Cadia was a warrior-world, standing guard in the one navigable approach to the warp-tumult of the infamous Eye of Terror. The region, known as the Cadian Gate, is the route of choice for invasions of Chaos, and Cadia is seen by most as the Imperium's first line of defence. It has bred elite troops since it was first colonised, and billions of its sons and daughters have died bravely protecting our culture.

Died bravely... then left to slowly vanish in the desolate fields of their home world.

It was dismal, but probably entirely in keeping with the stoic martial mindset of the Cadians.

Fischig pushed open the heavy axelwood door of the shrine tower and we went inside out of the wind.

The tower was a single chamber, a drum of stone, with weep-hole window slits high up near the summit. A circle of rough wooden pews was arranged around a central altar-piece, above which a massive iron candelabra in the form of a double-headed eagle was suspended on a chain from the beamed roof.

On this dark autumn day, the light from the votive candles fixed amongst the metal feathers of the aquila's unfurled wings was the only illumination. There was a spare, thin, golden light, an atmosphere of frugality and numinous grace.

And a musty stink of rotting axel leaves.

We sat together on a pew, both of us briefly honouring the altar with the sign of the aquila, our hands splayed together against our hearts.

'It's strange,' sighed Fischig after a long pause. 'You sent me out, over a year ago, on yet another quest for signs of that daemonspawn Cherubael. And just when I find a trace, you run into him again, on the other side of the damn sector.'

'Strange is possibly not the word I'd use.'

'But the coincidence. Is it coincidence?'

'I don't know. It seems so much like it. But... that thing... Cherubael... disarms me so.'

'Naturally, old friend.'

I shook my head. 'Not because of his power. Not that.'

'Then what?'

'The way he speaks to me. The way he says he's using me.'

'Daemon guile!'

'Perhaps. But he knows so much. He knows... ah, damn it! He speaks as if our destinies are irrevocably entwined. Like he matters to me and vice versa.'

'He does matter to you.'

'I know, I know. As my goal. My prey. My nemesis. But he talks like it's more than that. Like he can see the future, or can read it, or has even been there. He talks to me like... he knows what I'm going to do.'

Fischig frowned. 'And... what do you think that might be?'

I rose and stalked to the altar. 'I have no idea! I can't conceive of doing anything that would please or benefit a daemon! I can't ever imagine myself that insane!'

'Trust me, Eisenhorn, if I ever thought you were, I'd shoot you myself.'

I glanced back at him. 'Please do.'

I halted and looked up into the flickering flames of the candles, seeing the many shadows and possible shadows of myself they cast, interlapping and criss-crossing the stone floor. Like the myriad possibilities of the future. I tried not to look into the thicker, blacker shadows.

'The warp-spawned bastard's just playing games with you,' said Fischig. 'That's all it is. Games to put you off the scent and keep you at bay.'

'If that's the case, why does he keep saving my life?'

* * *

We went back out into the moorland wind. The moaning of
the pylon seemed louder to me now.

'Who's with you?' Fischig asked.

'Aemos, Bequin, Nayl, Medea, Husmaan... and a lad you've
not met, Inshabel. We came here directly from Eechan.'

'Long ride?'

'Best part of six months. We got as far as Mordia on a free
trader called the *Best of Eagles*, and then came the rest of the
way as guests of the Adeptus Mechanicus. The super-heavy
barge *Mons Olympus*, no less, carrying virgin Titans to the
garrisons of the Cadian Gate.'

'Quite an honour.'

'The inquisitor's rosette carries its benefits. But I tell you,
the tech-priests of Mars are damned surly company for a two
month voyage. I would have gone mad but for Bequin's regicide tournaments.'

'Nayl getting any better?'

'No. I think by now he owes me... what is it? Hmm. His first
born and his soul.'

Fischig laughed.

'Oh, it wasn't all so bad. There was one fellow, a veteran
princeps from the Titan Legion. Old guy, centuries old. At
the point of retirement, like those men ever retire. He was
supervising the transfer of the new war machines. Name of
Hekate. We got to drinking some nights. Remind me to tell
you some of his war-stories.'

'I will. Come on...'

He had a land speeder parked down off the lane under the
swaying axeltrees. We brushed fallen ribbon-leaves off the
hood and got in.

'Let me show you what I found. Then we can all meet and
greet in a safe place.'

'How safe?'

'The safest.'

We flew over the moorlands, into the biting winds, hugging the terrain. The light was fading. The grim glory of Cadia was spread out below us. This was the merciless, windblown wilderness that raised one of the Imperium's hardiest warrior breeds. Here were the scattered islets in the Caducades Sea where they were left naked as pre-pubescents to survive the ritual Month of Making. Here were the hill-forts where the Cadian Youth armies wintered and toughened and waged mock wars on their neighbour forts. Here were the crags, ice-lakes and axel-forests where they learned the arts of camouflage.

Here were the wide, sundered plains where their live firing exercises were staged.

There is a saying: 'If the ammo ain't live, this ain't no Cadian practice'. Right from the time they are issued with their own las-guns, which is about the same time they are given their first primary readers, the young warrior-caste of Cadia are handling live ammunition. Most can fire, and kill, and perform most infantry field drills before they reach the age of ten standard.

Little wonder that the shock troops of Cadia are among the Imperium's best.

But we weren't here to gawp at the rugged crucible of landscape that had formed the Cadians.

We were here to look at the pylons.

'Cherubael's been here,' said Fischig, jockeying the control stick and eyeing the windspeed gauge. 'Far as I know, nine times in the last forty years.'

MALLEUS 217

'You're sure?'

'It's what you pay me for. Your daemonhost – and whatever he's working for – is fascinated by Cadia.'

'Why have the Inquisition not had a hint of it?'

'Come on, Gregor. The galaxy is big. Aemos once told me that the weight of data generated by the Imperium would fry all the metriculators and codifiers on Terra in a flash if it was input simultaneously. It's a matter of making connections. Sifting the data. The Inquisition – and you – have been looking all over for signs of Cherubael. But some things just don't flag. I got lucky.'

'How?'

'I was doing my job. Old friend of mine, Isak Actte, from the old Arbites day. Used to be my boss, in fact. He rose, got promoted, wound up on Hydraphur as an Arbites general and then got stationed here as watch overseer to the Cadian Interior Guard. I contacted him years ago, and got a message I had to check.'

'You're intriguing me.'

He ran us low over a headland and our speeder made a small, sharp shadow on the glittering ice-lake below.

'Actte said the Arbites had closed down a heretical cell here on Cadia about ten years ago. Called themselves the Sons of Bael. A fairly worthless lot, by all accounts. Harmless. But under interrogation, they'd admitted to following a daemon they called Bael or the Bael. The local inquisitor general spent some time with them and had them all burned.'

'What's his name?'

'Gorfal. But he's dead, three years gone. The current incumbent is a she. Inquisitor General Neve. Anyway, the cell has flared up a few times since then. Nothing a good team of riot-officers couldn't handle. Like I said, the Sons of Bael were pretty harmless, really. They were only interesting in one thing.'

'Which was?'

'Measuring the dimensions of the pylons.'

The pylon had been looming in our windscreen for a while now, and Fischig swept us around it, almost kissing the black stone.

The moaning song of the wind as it laced through the geometries of the pylon was now so loud I could hear it over the racing turbines of the speeder.

The pylon was vast: half a kilometre high and a quarter square. The upper facing of the smooth black stone was machined with delicate craft to form holes and other round-edged orifices no bigger than a man's head. It was through these slim, two hundred and fifty metre tubes that the wind moaned and howled.

And the tubes weren't straight. They wove through the pylon like worm tunnels. Tech-magos had tried running tiny servitor probes through them to map their loops, but generally the probes didn't come back.

As we banked up higher for another pass, I could see the distant shape of the neighbouring pylon, across the moors, sixty kilometres away. Five thousand, eight hundred and ten known pylons dot the surface of Cadia, not counting the two thousand others that remain as partial ruins or buried relics.

No two are identical in design. Each one rises to a precise half kilometre height and is sunk a quarter kilometre into the ground. They predate mankind's arrival in this system, and their manner of manufacture is unknown. They are totally inert, by any auspex measure known to our race, but many believe their presence explains the quieting of the violent warp torrents that makes the Cadia Gate the single, calm, navigable route to the Ocularis Terribus.

'They were trying to measure this thing?'

'Uh huh,' Fischig replied clearly over the speeder's drive as we pulled another hard turn. 'This and several others. They had auspex and geo-locators and magnetic plumbs. Finding the exact dimensions... and I do mean exact... was the entire goal of the Sons of Bael.'

'They connect with Cherubael... I mean, beyond the "Bael" part?'

'The interview logs I've read show they name "Bael" fully as a god called Cherub of Bael, who came amongst them and made demands that they measure the pylons in return for great knowledge and power.'

'And the inquisitor general... this Gorfal? He suppressed this?'

'Not deliberately. I think he was just sloppy.'

'I want to speak with the current inquisitor general... Neve, did you say her name was?'

'Yeah. I thought you might.'

While daylight remained, we flew west to Kasr Derth, the largest castellum in the region and the seat of provincial government for the Caducades. Fischig switched on the speeder's voxponder and broadcast the day's access codes to the sentry turrets as we passed the outer ring-ditch. Even so, Manticore and Hydra batteries traversed and tracked us as we went over.

The voxponder pinged fretfully as it detected multiple target-locks.

'Don't worry,' said Fischig, noticing my look. 'We're safe. I think the Cadians enjoy taking every possible opportunity to practise.'

We ran down the line of a slow moving convoy – drab, armoured twelve-wheeler transports escorted by lurching Sentinel walkers – and followed the highway up towards the ridge of the earthwork. Beyond it, and two more like it, the heavy, grey fortifications and shatrovies of Kasr Derth sulked in the twilight.

Watch-lights on skeleton towers stood on the upper slope of the earthwork. More turret emplacements and pillboxes studded the defence berm like knuckles. Again, the voxponder pinged.

Fischig dropped the speed and altitude, and swung us down towards the eastern barbican, a small fortress in its own right, bristling with Earthshaker platforms. A bas-relief Imperial eagle decorated the upper face of the ashlar-dressed structure.

We ran in through the barbican's gate, over the hydraulic bascule that crossed the inner moat, and into the castellum's deliberately narrow and twisting streets.

Cadia's earliest kasrs had been built in the High Terra style, with the wide streets laid out on a grid system. In early M.32, a Chaos invasion had made wretchedly short work of three of them. The broad, ordered avenues had proved impossible to defend or hold.

Since then, the kasrs had been planned in elaborate geometric patterns, the streets jinking back and forth like the teeth of a key. From the air, Kasr Derth looked like an intricate, angular puzzle. Given the Cadians' mettle and their skills at urban-war, a kasr could be held, street by street, metre by metre, for months if not years.

We slunk along the busy, labyrinthine streets as the caged lamps came on and business began to shut for the night. I was about to remark to Fischig that it looked for all the world like a military camp, until I realised that even the civilian fashion was for camouflaged clothing. It soon became easy to pick out locals from visitors. The jag-white and grey of tundra dress or the panelled green and beige of moor fatigues marked out newcomers and off duty soldiery. The population of Kasr Derth wore grey and brown checkered urban camouflage.

We passed the stilted horreums of the Imperial Cadian Granary, and the tight-packed baileys of the rich and successful. Even the townhouses of the wealthy had armouring on their mansard roofs.

To the left lay the brightly-lit aleatorium, to which night crowds were already flocking to gamble away their pay. To the right, Kasr's senaculum with its gleaming, ceramite-plated shatrovy pyramid. Ahead, lay the minster of the Inquisition. The voxponder pinged again as the gun-walls along the deep approach followed us.

Fischig settled the speeder down on the spicae testicae paving of the minster's inner yard, where sunken guide-lights stitched out a winking cross. Inquisitorial guards in gold-laced burgundy armour approached us as we swung back the speeder's canopy and climbed out.

I showed the nearest one my rosette.

He clipped his heels together and saluted.

'My lord.'

'I wish to see the inquisitor general.'

'I will inform her staff,' he said obediently, and hurried away across the herringbone paving, holding up his baldric so his power sword wouldn't trip him.

'You won't like her,' Fischig said as he came round the parked speeder to join me.

'Why?'

'Ah, trust me. You just won't.'

* * *

'It's late. I had finished business for the day,' said Inquisitor General Neve, stabbing her holoquill back into the brass power-well on the desk.

'My apologies, madam.'

'Don't bother. I'm not about to shut my doors to the famous Inquisitor Eisenhorn. We're a long way from the Helican sub, but your fame precedes you.'

'In a good way, I hope.'

The inquisitor general rose from her writing desk and straightened the front of her green flannel robe. She was a short, sturdy woman in her late one tens, if my eye was any judge, with salt and pepper hair plied back tightly into a bourse. She had the typical pale, tight flesh and violet eyes of a Cadian.

'Whatever,' she snapped.

We stood in her sanctum, an octastyle chamber with a black and white cosmati floor and aethercite walls inscribed with a waterleaf design. It was lit with rushlights and the flame glow accented the carved lotus motif.

Inquisitor General Neve clumped around her desk to face us, leaning on an ornate silver crutch.

'You'll want to be reviewing the Bael records, I suppose?'

'How did you guess?' I asked.

She favoured her weight on her sound foot and pointed the rubber-capped toe of the crutch at Fischig.

'Him, I know. He's been here before. One of yours, I suppose, inquisitor.'

'One of my best.'

She arched her spare, plucked eyebrows. 'Hah. Much that says about you. Come on. The archivum.'

A dim screw-stair led down to the basement archivum. The turning steps of the spiral were hard for her to manage, but she shooed me away curtly when I offered to assist her.

'I meant no insult, inquisitor general,' I said.

'Your kind never do,' she snapped. I felt it wasn't the moment to inquire what kind that might be.

The archivum was a long, panelled chamber lit only by the lamps of the double-faced desk-row that ran down its middle.

'Light buoy!' Neve snarled, and a servitor-skull drifted down from the coffered ceiling, hovering at her shoulder and igniting its halogen eyebeams.

'Bael, Sons of. Find,' she told it, and it coursed away, turning and dipping, sweeping the racks of the catalogue with its twin spears of light.

It stopped, eight sections down, and began to buzz around a shelf groaning with data-slates, file tubes and dusty paper books.

Fischig and I followed Neve as she hobbled over to join it.

'Sons of... Sons of... Sons of Teuth, Sons of Macharius, sons of bitches...' She glanced round at me. 'That passes for humour here, Eisenhorn.'

'I'm sure it does, madam.'

Her fingers went back to the stacks, running along the fraying spines and tagged slate-sleeves, following the skull-buoy's light beams.

'Sons of Barabus... Sons of Balkar... Here! Here it is. Sons of Bael.'

She pulled a file case off the shelf, blew the dust off it into my face and handed it to me. 'Put it back where you found it when you've finished,' she said. She turned to go.

'Your pardon, wait,' I said.

Two emphatic thumps of her crutch swung her around to face me again.

'What?'

'Your predecessor... um...'

'Gorfal,' whispered Fischig.

'Gorfal. He burned the members of this cult without examination. Have you never reviewed the case?'

She smiled at me. It wasn't encouraging.

'You know, Eisenhorn... I always imagined roving inquisitors
like you had adventurous, exciting lives. All so very exhilarat-
ing, all that celebrity and heroism and notoriety. To think I
used to dream of being like you. You have no idea, do you?'

'With respect, inquisitor general... of what?'

She gestured at the file case I was clutching. 'The crap. The
nonsense. The bric-a-brac. The Sons of Bael? Why the hell
should I review that case? It's dead, dead and nothing. A
bunch of fools who were pulled off the Westmoorland pylon
in the middle of the night for playing around with geo-locators.
Whoooo! I'm so scared! Imagine that, they're measuring us!
Do you have any idea what this wardship is like?'

'Inquisitor general, I–'

'Do you? This is Cadia, you silly fool! Cadia! Right on the
doorway of Chaos! Right in the heart of everything! The seep-
age of evil is so great, I have a hundred active cults to subdue
every month! A hundred! The place breeds recidivists like a
pond breeds scum. I sleep three or four hours a night if I'm
lucky. My vox chimes and I'm up, called out to another nest
of poison that the Arbites have uncovered. Firefights in the
street, Eisenhorn! Running battles with the foot soldiers of
the archenemy! I can barely keep up with the day-to-day ban-
ishments, forget the past cases my crap-witted predecessor
filed. This is Cadia! This is the Gate of the Eye! This is where
the bloody work of the Inquisition is done! Don't distract me
with stories of some engineering club gone bad.'

'My apologies.'

'Taken. See yourselves out.' She limped away.

'Neve?'

She turned. I dropped the file case on to the reading table.

'They might have been idiots,' I said, 'but they're the only solid link I have to a daemonhost that could destroy us all.'

'A daemonhost?' she said.

'That's right. And the beast that controls it. A beast that, if I'm right... is one of ours.'

She lurched back down the archivum.

'Convince me,' she said.

THIRTEEN

A reunion
War-bells
The long, slow task begins

I don't know if I did convince the inquisitor general. I don't
know if I could. But she heard me out and stayed around for
another two hours, helping to locate the files of connected
cases and other materials. Past nine, she was called away
to a disturbance on an island community in the Caducades.
Before she left, she offered accommodation for me and my
staff in the minster, which I politely declined, and made it
clear that I had her permission to continue my investigation
in Kasr Derth, provided I kept her informed.

'I've heard stories about your... adventures, Eisenhorn. I
don't want anything like that happening on my turf. Do we
understand each other?'

'We do.'

'Good night, then. And good hunting.'

Fischig and I were left alone in the archivum.

'You were wrong,' I told him.

'How's that?'

'I did like her.'

'Hah! That hard-nosed bitch?'

'Actually, I liked her *because* she was a hard-nosed bitch.'

I always took pleasure in meeting a fellow inquisitor who conducted their work fairly and seriously, even if their methods differed from mine. Neve was a thoroughbred puritan, and lacked patience. She was abrupt to the point of rudeness. She was over-worked. But she called things as she saw them, despised sloppiness, and took the threats to our society and way of life completely seriously.

In my opinion, there was no other way for an inquisitor to behave.

We worked on until midnight, studying and collating the contents of hundreds of case-files.

By then, the gun-cutter had arrived from the landing fields at Kasr Tyrok, in response to my vox-summons. Fischig found one of Neve's rubricators and charged him with making data-slate copies of the most promising files ready for our return in the morning. Then we got back into the speeder and flew through the castellum's zig-zag streets to the town field.

The stars were out, and it was cool. Noctule moths fluttered around the landing lights of the waiting cutter.

There was a mauve smudge in the night sky, down low over the eastern horizon. The rising nebula of the Eye of Terror. Even from this great distance, just a blur in the heavens, it put a chill into me. If the two-headed eagle symbolises all that is good and noble and right about the Imperium of Mankind, that rancid blur symbolised all that was abominable about our eternal foe.

* * *

Laughter and warm voices greeted Fischig as we went aboard.
Aemos shook him repeatedly by the hand and Bequin planted
a quick kiss on his cheek that made him blush. He exchanged
a few playful put-downs with Nayl and Medea, and asked
Husmaan if he was hungry.

'Why?' the scout-hunter asked, his eyes widening in
anticipation.

'Because it's supper time,' said Fischig. 'Betancore, get this
crate into the air.'

We were going to that safe place he had mentioned.

I had not been aboard the sprint trader *Essene* for some five
years. A classic Isolde-pattern bulk clipper, the ship was like
a space-going cathedral, three kilometres long, and looked
as majestic holding low anchor above Cadia as it had when
I first saw it, nearly one hundred years before, in the cold
orbit of Hubris.

Medea coasted us in towards the cargo hatch of the gigantic craft.

'A rogue trader?' asked Inshabel cautiously, looking over my
shoulder at the ship ahead.

'An old friend,' I reassured him.

Shipmaster Tobias Maxilla was, I suppose, my most unlikely
ally. He'd made his living shipping luxury goods officially, and
unofficially, along the space lanes of the Helican sub-sector. He
still did. He was a merchant, he maintained, to any that asked.

But he had a pirate's taste for adventure, a yearning for the
halcyon days of early space-faring. I had hired his ship during the affair of the Necroteuch, to provide nothing more than
transport for my team, but he had got involved, with increasing glee, and he'd stayed involved ever since. Every few years
over the last century, I had hired him to run passage for me

or some of my staff, or he had contacted me to ask if his services were needed. Just because he was bored. Just because
he was 'in the neighbourhood.'

Maxilla was an educated, erudite man with a subtle wit
and a taste for the finest things in life. He was also a charming host and a good companion and I liked him immensely.
He was in no way a formal part of my staff. But he was, I
suppose, after all this time and all those shared adventures,
a vital part.

The year before, when it had been decided that Fischig
would embark on this long chase after the Cadian leads, I
had asked Maxilla to provide him with transportation, for as
long as it was needed. He had agreed at once, and not because
of the generous fee I was offering. To him, it sounded like a
true adventure. Besides, it promised a chance to give the old
Essene a proper long run out, beyond its normal route of the
Helican stars.

A genuine voyage. An odyssey. That was what Tobias Maxilla lived for.

He was waiting in the cargo hold to greet us even before the
extractor vents had finished dumping out the cutter's thruster
fumes. He had dressed for the occasion, as was his way: a
blue velvet balmacaan with huge sleeves and a jabot collar,
a peascod doublet of japanagar silk, patent leather sabattons
with gold buckles, and a stupendous fantail hat perched on
his powdered periwig. His face was skin-dyed white and set
with an emerald beauty spot. His cologne was stronger than
the thruster fumes.

'My dear, dear Gregor!' he cried, striding forward and taking my proffered hands with both of his. 'A signal joy to have
you back aboard our humble craft.'

'Tobias. A pleasure, as always.'

'And dear Alizebeth! Looking younger and more fragrant than ever!' He clasped her hand and kissed her cheek.

'Steady now, you'll smudge... your make up.'

'Wise Aemos! Welcome, savant!'

Aemos just chuckled as his hand was shaken. I don't think he ever knew quite what to make of Maxilla.

'Mr Nayl!'

'Maxilla.'

'And Medea! Ravishing! Quite ravishing!'

'You certainly are,' Medea said playfully, allowing one of her circuit-inlaid hands to be kissed.

'You knew we were coming, Maxilla. You might have smartened up a bit,' said Fischig. Amid laughter, they shook hands. I realised their relationship had changed. They had been together for a year on this mission. Fischig had never really connected with Maxilla: their backgrounds and lives were too divergent. But clearly, a year in each other's company had brokered a true friendship at last.

That pleased me too. An inquisitor's band works better when it is close knit.

Maxilla turned to Husmaan and Inshabel.

'You two I don't know. But I will, as that's what dinners are for. Welcome to the *Essene*.'

Maxilla's sculptural gold servitors, each one a work of art, had prepared a late supper for us in the grand dining lounge. A paté zephir of crab, fresh from the Caducades that morning, ontol flowers poivrade in their husks, fillets of Cadian boar hongroise, followed by an ebonfruit talmouse with cream and Intian syrup. The gilded sommelier served petillant Samatan rosé, heavy-bodied Cadian claret, a sweet and sticky Tokay from a lowland clos on Hydraphur, and stinging shots of Mordian schnapps.

Our humours were good, and the impromptu supper gave us time to step back from the work at hand and relax. None of us spoke of the case, or the demands that it was likely to make of us. To rest the mind often clears it.

I was going to need clarity now.

We returned to Kasr Derth the next morning in the gun-cutter. The steel dawn over the wide island group of the Caducades was cut by the rising edge of a burning, red sun. As we swept in over the craggy mainland, the peaks and edges of the moors were caught with a pink alpenglow.

Despite the fact that we were broadcasting the correct clearances, we were challenged six times in the half-hour descent. At one point, a pair of Cadian Marauders rolled in and flanked us as they checked us over.

Military security dominated the Cadian way of life. Every non-military transport, shuttle and starship was placed under acute observation, especially those that behaved suspiciously or wandered from the authorised flight routes. Aemos told me that a pinnace carrying the Deacon of Arnush, visiting Cadia for a promulgation seminar, had been shot down over the Sea of Kansk six months earlier, simply because it failed to give the correct codes. It made me wonder how our unknown foe had got his minions on and off Cadia.

Unless, like us, he had an identity and a rank that easily turned aside routine security checks.

We were diverted sixty kilometres west of Kasr Derth because a war was going on. The dawn light was filled with the flashes and light streaks of a mass rocket attack.

Eight regiments of Cadian Shock, just a few days away from shipping out to a tour of duty on one of the inner fortress worlds of the Cadian Gate, were staging a live firing exercise.

We finally set down on the minster's launch pad over an hour late. The war-bells in every tower and shatrovy in the Kasr were ringing to signal that the roar of battle from the nearby plains and moors was just a practice.

We divided our efforts. Fischig took Aemos to the Minster's archivum to study the records we had ordered copied the night before and do further research. Bequin, escorted by Husmaan, went to search the stacks of the Ecclesiarchy's records in the apostolaeum. Inshabel and Nayl visited the Administratum's catalogue of records.

I went with Medea to the Ministry of Interior Defence.

There are no Arbites on Cadia. A permanent state of martial law governs the world, and as a result, all civil policing duties are overseen by the Interior Guard, a sub-office of the Cadian Imperial Guard itself. In Kasr Derth, the region's administrative capital, their headquarters is the Ministry of Interior Defence, a grey-stone donjon adjoining the fortress of the martial governor, right at the heart of Kasr Derth.

Members of the Interior Guard are chosen at random. Worldwide, one in every ten soldiers recruited into the Cadian forces is transferred into the Interior force at the end of basic and preparatory, whatever their achievements and promise. As a result, some of the most able troopers ever raised on this planet of warriors serve out their time on the home world itself, and Cadia boasts one of the most effective and skilled planetary defence forces of any Imperial world.

We were seen by a Colonel Ibbet, a powerful, lean man in his forties who looked like he should have been leading the charge into the Eye of Terror. He was courteous, but mistrustful.

'We have no files on illegal or suspect immigration.'

'Why is that, colonel?'

'Because it doesn't happen. The system does not permit it.'

'Surely there are unfortunate exceptions?'

Ibbet, his grey and white camoed uniformed starched and pressed so sharply you could have cut yourself on the creases, steepled his fingers.

'All right, then,' I said, changing tack. 'What if someone wanted to get onto the planet anonymously? How could that be managed?'

'It couldn't,' he said. He wasn't giving at all. 'Every identity and visit-purpose is logged and filed and any infractions quickly dealt with.'

'Then I'll start with the files annotating those infractions.'

Resignedly, Ibbet showed us into a codifier room and assigned us a military clerk to take us through the records. We sorted and checked for about three hours, slowly becoming bored with the interminable lists of orbital boardings, air-space interceptions and ground-based raids. I could tell that a thorough review of these records alone was going to take weeks.

So that's what we did. We spent ten and a half weeks scouring the archives and catalogues of Kasr Derth, working in shifts and living out of the quarters on the gun-cutter. Every few days, we returned to the *Essene* for a little rest and reflection.

It was the dead of winter by the time we were finished.

FOURTEEN

Winter brings a chance
The damned has a name
The pylon at Kasr Gesh

Wintertide on Cadia.

There had been glinting ice-floes in the gun-metal waters of the Caducades that morning, and light snow had fallen on the moors. At that time of year, the foul corona of the Eye of Terror was visible even during the fleeting hours of daylight. The unholy mauve radiance of the nights became a violet fuzz in the cold daylight, like a badly-blotted ink stain on white paper.

It made us feel like we were under surveillance all the time. The Eye, bloodshot, angry, peering down at us.

Worst of all were the moor winds, cold and sharp as a Cadian's bayonet, blowing down from arctic latitudes. The high lakes were all frozen now, and lethal pogonip fogs haunted the bitter heaths and uplands. In the Kasr itself, it seemed like the locals had a morbid fear of heaters or window insulation.

Chilly gales breathed down the hallways of the minster and the Administratum building. Water froze in the pipes.

Despite it all, the war-bells sounded every few days, and the moors rolled with the sounds of winter manoeuvres. I began to imagine that the Cadians were simply shooting at each other to keep warm.

Ten and a half long, increasingly cold weeks after we had begun our systematic search of the Kasr's records, I was making my now habitual morning walk from the minster of the Inquisition to the headquarters of the Interior Guard. I wore a thick fur coat against the cold, and spike-soled boots to combat the sheet ice on the roads. I was miserable. The search had left us all pale and edgy, too many fruitless hours spent in dark rooms.

There had been so many promising leads. Links and traces of the Sons of Bael, unauthorised starship traffic, suspicious excise logs.

They had all dwindled away into nothing. As far as we could make out, no living member of the Sons of Bael, or any living associate or family member, remained. There had been no pylon-related cult activity, not even registered xeno-archaeological work. I had interviewed specialist professors at the universitary, and certain tech-priests from the Mechanicus who were shown in the records as having expert knowledge of the pylons.

Nothing.

With Inshabel, Nayl or Fischig, I had travelled the region, as far afield as Kasr Tyrok and Kasr Bellan. A worker in the gunshops of Kasr Bellan, who had been identified as a Bael cult member, turned out to simply have the same name, misfiled. A wasted ten hour round trip by speeder.

Aemos had constructed a codifier model by which we

checked record anomalies against the timetable of past cult activity.

There seemed to be no correlation at all.

I walked up the steps of the Ministry of Interior Defence, and submitted myself to the clearance check in the postern guard-house. It should have been a formality. I had been arriving at the same time almost every day for the last seventy-five. I even recognised some of the Guardsmen by sight.

But still, it was like the first time I had ever been there. Papers were not only stamped, but read thoroughly and run through an anti-counterfeit auspex. My rosette was scruti-nised and tagged. The duty officer voxed my details through to the main building to get authorisation.

'Doesn't this ever bore you?' I asked one of the desk offic-ers as I waited, folding my papers back into my leather wallet.

'Doesn't what bore me, sir?' he asked.

I hadn't seen Ibbet since the first week. I'd been rotated between a number of supervisors. One told me it was because of shift changes, but I knew it was because none of them liked to deal with an inquisitor. Especially a persistent one.

That morning, it was Major Revll who escorted me in. Revll, a surly young man, was new to me.

'How can I assist you, sir?' he asked curtly.

I sighed.

Open log books and data-slates were piled around the work-station where I had abandoned them the night before. Revll was already calling for a clerk to tidy them away and make space for me before I could explain that I'd made the mess in the first place.

He looked at me warily. 'You've been here before?'

I sighed again.

I had two hours. At eleven, I was due to meet Inshabel and Bequin and fly out to a village on one of the islands in the Caducades to investigate a rumour that a man there knew something about smuggling. Another waste of time, I was sure.

I started in on the air-traffic day-book, reading through the lists of orbital transfers for a summer day two years earlier. Halfway down the slate was an entry showing a shuttle transfer from an orbiting ship to a landing field near Kasr Gesh. Gesh was near to one of the pylons frequented by the Sons of Bael. Moreover, on checking, I realised the date put it three days before the last incident of cult activity at the pylon.

I stoked up the data-engine, and requested further information on the entry. I was immediately denied. I used a higher decrypt key, and was shown a report that withheld both the name of the ship and the source of its authority. I began to get excited, and scrolled down. Even the purpose of the visit was restricted.

Now I typed in the teeth of my highest decrypt key. The terminal throbbed and chattered, sorting through files and authorisations.

The name came up. My elation peaked, and plunged away.

Neve. The mysterious entry had been a record of a classified mission by the inquisitor general. Back to square one.

The island was cold and bare. A small fishing community clung to the rim of the western bay. Inshabel swung the speeder down onto the cobbled tideway where spread nets had gone stiff with ice.

'How much longer, Gregor?' Bequin asked me, winding her scarf around her throat.

'How much longer what?'

'Until we give up and leave? I'm so sick of this fate-forsaken world.'

I shrugged. 'Another week. Until Candlemas. If we haven't found anything by then, I promise we'll say goodbye to Cadia.'

The three of us trudged up the icy walk to a grim tavern overlooking the sea wall. Anchor fish, as tall as men, were hung outside, salted and drying in the winter air.

The barman didn't want to know us, but his steward brought us drinks and led us through to a back parlour. He admitted that he had sent the message about the smuggler. The smuggler was here to meet us, he said.

We entered the back parlour. A man sat by the roaring grate, warming his jewelled fingers at its flames. I smelled cologne.

'Good morning, Gregor,' said Tobias Maxilla.

Despite the shouting coming from the back parlour, the steward brought us herb omelettes and bowls of steaming zar-fin broth, along with a bottle of fortified wine.

'Are you going to explain?' asked Inshabel tersely.

'Of course, dear Nathun, of course,' Maxilla replied, pouring a careful measure of wine into each glass.

'Be patient.'

'Now, Tobias!' I snapped.

'Oh,' he said, seeing my look. He sat back. 'I confess I have become despondent these last few weeks. You've been so busy and I've just been waiting up there on the *Essene*... well, anyway, you've said a number of times that the answer you're searching for depended on one key thing. It depended on you establishing a way of getting past this dire planet's obsessively tight security. Anonymously. And I said to myself... "Tobias, that's what you do, even though Gregor doesn't like to think about it. Smuggling, Tobias, is your forte." So I decided to see if I could smuggle myself down here. And guess what?'

He sat back, sipping his glass, looking disgustingly pleased with himself.

'You smuggled yourself onto the planet to prove it could be done?' asked Bequin slowly.

He nodded. 'My shuttle's hidden in the spinneys behind the village. It's amazing how many zipped mouths and blind eyes you can buy with a purse of hard cash round here.'

'I don't know what to say,' I said.

He made an open-handed gesture. 'You told me weeks ago that the Interior Guard recognised no illegal or suspect immigration. Well, I'm here today – literally – to prove that claim wrong. Cadia's a tough nut to crack, I'll admit. One of the toughest I've faced in a long and naughty career. But not impossible, as you see.'

I sank my wine in a single gulp. 'I should sever my links with you for this, Tobias. You know that.'

'Oh, pooh, Gregor! Because I've shown up the Cadian Interior Guard as a bunch of fools?'

'Because you've broken the law!'

'Ah ah ah! No, I haven't. Bent it, possibly, but not broken it. My presence here is entirely legal, under both Cadian local and Imperial general law.'

'What?'

'Come on, my old friend! Why do you think my shuttle wasn't blasted out of the heavens this morning by eager Cadian lightning jockeys? That was a rhetorical question by the way. Answer... because when the interceptors came scrambling up to meet me, I broadcast the right security clearance, and that contented them.'

'But the day codes are privileged! The counter-checks are triple! They are issued only to those with appropriately high credentials. What authority could you possibly have used to get them?'

'Well, Gregor... yours, of course.'

It had been staring me in the face, and it took the grandstanding flamboyance of Maxilla, in his very worst showing-off mode, to reveal it. The reason the Interior Guard had no file on illegal or suspect immigration was because there was nothing of that nature to file. Those that tried to run the strict gauntlet of Cadian security and failed, died. The ones that got through were never noticed.

Because they were using high-level security clearances, masquerading as the sort of official visitor who would not be stopped.

People like me. People like Neve.

'I never made this trip,' Neve said, staring steadily at the data-slate I was showing her. 'Or this.'

'Of course not. But someone borrowed your authority code. Used it to gain trans-orbital access. That's how they were getting in. Look here, your code again, and again. And before that, the code headers of your predecessor, Gonfal. It goes back forty years. Each and every flurry of activity from the Sons of Bael... and other cults... can be matched by space-to-surface transfers cleared as genuine Inquisition flights.'

'Emperor protect me!' Neve looked up. She put down the data-slate and called hoarsely for a servitor to bring more lights into her octastyle sanctum.

'But my authority code is protected. How was it stolen? Eisenhorn, yours was used to prove this. How was that stolen?'

I paused. 'It wasn't, not exactly. One of my associates borrowed it to prove the point.'

'Why doesn't that surprise me? Oh, no matter! Eisenhorn, there's a great deal of difference between you and me. You may have rogue elements in your band who act behind your back in unorthodox, unilateral ways. I do not. My code could not have been abused so.'

'I accept your point, but it could. Who has access to your code?'

'No one! No one below me!'

'But above you?'

'What?'

'I said this could be one of ours. A senior inquisitor, a grandmaster even. Certainly a wily veteran with enough clout to pull the right strings.'

'That would require a direct override at the highest levels.

'Exactly. Let's look.'

In the end, that was my adversary's downfall. All the blood and fury and combat we had gone through was as nothing to this prosaic clue that revealed his identity. To steal Neve's authority code, and the authority codes of her predecessors, my adversary had been forced to use the clout of his own identity get into the files.

The record of that operation was encrypted, of course. Sitting side by side at the codifier in her sanctum's annex, Neve and I quickly found it. It wasn't even hidden. He never thought anyone would look.

But still, it was encrypted.

The cryptology was beyond both me and Neve. But together, combining our ranks, we could request, via the Astropathicus, permission to use the Inquisition's most powerful decryption keys.

It took five hours to approve our joint rating.

Just after midnight, a scribe from the Officio Astropathicus brought us the message slate. Midwinter winds shook the sanctum's casements.

I was alone with Neve. We had felt it inappropriate to have company. This was a matter of the gravest import. We had talked, of this and that, to pass the time, though both of us were restless and edgy. She poured generous glasses of Cadian glayva, which took the edge off the cold.

Her aide announced the scribe, and he entered, bowing low, his augmetic chassis grinding beneath his robes. He held out a slate to her clutched in the mechadendrites that served as his hand. Neve took it and dismissed him.

I rose, and put down my barely touched glass of spirits.

Neve limped over to me, leant on her silver crutch, and held up the slate.

'Shall we?' she asked.

We went into the annex and loaded the slate into the ancient codifier. The limpid green display shifted feverishly with runes. She opened the file we were after and set the key to work.

It took a moment or two.

Then the identity of the veteran who had used his power to manipulate Neve's code was revealed on the small, green-washed screen. At last, the damned had a name.

It shocked even me.

'Glory from above,' breathed Inquisitor General Neve. '*Quixos.*'

* * *

Aemos was arguing with Neve's chief savant, Cutch.

'Quixos is dead, long dead!' Cutch maintained. 'This is clearly a case of someone using his authority...'

'Quixos is still registered as living by the annals of the Inquisition.'

'As an oversight! No body has ever been retrieved. No proof of death–'

'Precisely...'

'But still! There has been no sign or word from Quixos for over a hundred years.'

'None that we've seen,' I said.

'Eisenhorn's right,' Neve said. 'Inquisitor Utlen was presumed dead for over seventy years. Then he reappeared overnight to bring down the tyrants of Esquestor II.'

'It's most perturbatory,' Aemos muttered.

Quixos. Quixos the Great. Quixos the Bright. One of the most revered inquisitors ever to roam the Imperium. His early texts had been required reading for all of us. He was a legend. At the age of just twenty-one he had burned the daemons out of Artum. Then he had purged the Endorian sub-sector of its false goat-gods. He had transcribed the *Book of Eibon*. He had broken the wretched sub-cult of Nurgle that had tainted one of the palaces of Terra itself. He had tracked down and killed the Chaos Marine Baneglos. He had silenced the Whisperers of Domactoni. He had crucified the Witch-king of Sarpeth on the battlements above his incinerated hive.

But there had always been an odour about Quixos. A hint that he was too close to the evil he prosecuted. He was a radical, certainly. Some amongst the ordos said he was a rogue. Others said, in low, private voices, much worse.

To me, he was a great man who had perhaps gone too

far. I simply honoured his memory and his achievements.

Because, as far as I had been concerned, he was long dead.

'Could he still be alive?' Neve asked.

'Madam, not at all...' Cutch began.

'I don't know why you employ him,' I said, pointing dismissively at the Cadian savant. 'His advice isn't sound.'

'Well really!' Cutch huffed.

'Shut up and go away,' Neve told him.

She stalked across to me and took my empty glass from me. 'Go on, then. Your opinion.'

'You want it? From an adventurer like me? Are you sure, inquisitor general?'

She thrust a topped-up glass of glayva into my hand so hard it sloshed. 'Just give me your damned opinion!'

I sipped. Aemos was staring over at me nervously from the settle by the door.

'Quixos could be very much alive. He'd be... what, now, Aemos?'

'Three hundred and forty-two, sir.'

'Right. Well, that's no age, is it? Not given augmetics, or rejuvanat drugs... or sorcery.'

'Dammit!' Neve said.

'He's an incredibly gifted individual, as his career testifies. He has a reputation, however unwarranted, for straying too far to the radical side. He has... dabbled with the warp. We can say that much. Just because we've heard nothing of him these last hundred or more years, doesn't mean he isn't still active.'

'And that activity?' Neve smacked the tip of her crutch down twice on the tiled floor. 'What? What? Utilising daemonhosts? Perverting inquisitors? Hunting for abominated texts like your Necroteuch? Triggering the dreadful atrocity of Thracian?'

'Perhaps? Why not?'

'Because that would make him a monster! The exact antithesis of everything our order is about!'

'Well, yes it would. It's happened before. A powerful man who gets so close to the evil he is sworn to combat he gets dragged into it. Inquisitor Ruberu, for example.'

'Yes, yes! Ruberu, I know...'

'Grandmaster Derkon?'

'Granted. I remember...'

'Cardinal Palfro of Mimiga? Saint Boniface, also called the Deathshead of a Thousand Tears?' intoned Aemos.

'For the Emperor's sake!'

'High Lord Vandire?' I suggested.

'All right, all right–'

'Horus?' Aemos dared to whisper.

There was a long silence.

'Great Quixos,' Neve murmured, slowly turning to face me. 'Will he be added to that unholy list? Is one of our greatest to be condemned so?'

'If he must be,' I replied.

'What do we do?' she asked.

'We find him. We find out if the passing centuries have truly changed him into the being we fear he is. And if they have, Emperor pardon me, we declare him Heretic and Extremis Diabolus, and we destroy him for his crimes.'

Neve sat down hard, staring into her glass. There was a knock at the sanctum's door, which Aemos answered.

It was Fischig.

'Sir... madam...' he said, acknowledging Neve.

'Well, Fischig?'

'Further to your discoveries today, we have been monitoring

inter-orbit traffic. Two hours ago, a craft made planetfall at
Kasr Gesh. It cleared Cadian airspace using the inquisitor
general's authority code.'

Gesh was the site of the last known cult activity.

I gathered up my coat. 'With your permission, inquisitor
general?'

Neve rose with me, her face set hard. 'With *your* permission,
Inquisitor Eisenhorn. I'd like to come with you.'

Kasr Gesh was three hours flight from Kasr Derth. Cruel winter had blown in from the upland heaths, and the gun-cutter
was vibrating its way against powerful ice storms.

My band was all aboard, preparing weapons. So was Inquisitor General Neve and a six-man squad of Cadian Elite
Shock, impassive troopers in winter camo armour, prepping
matt-white lasrifles and stubbers in the crew-bay.

'God-throne, they're tough-ass bastards,' Nayl muttered to
me as I passed him coming out of the bay.

'Impressed?'

'Scared is more like it. Regular Cadian is soldier enough for
me. These are elite. The elite of the elite. The Kasrkin.'

'The what?' It wasn't like an experienced fighter to show
deference to other fighting men.

'The Kasrkin. The Cadian best, and you can imagine what
that means. Holy Terra, they're stone-killers!'

'How do you know?'

'Oh, please... look at their necks. The Caducades sea-eagle
brand. Come to that, just look at their necks. I've seen slim-
mer trees!'

'Good thing they're on our side,' I said.

'I bloody hope so,' Nayl returned, and moved forward.

The deck lurched again. I walked back down the bay,

steadying myself on the overhead handloops, and approached Neve.

She was dressed in Cadian mesh armour, and was adjusting her winter hood. I saw she had exchanged her silver crutch for a lift-assisted cane fitted with a compact cylindrical grenade launcher.

In my fur coat and bodyglove armour, I felt underdressed.

'Your usual attire?' I asked.

'Necessary clothing. You should come out with me sometime, cult-hunting in the islands after dark.'

'My staff are... worried. These men are Kasrkin?'

'Yes.'

'Their reputation precedes them.'

'So did yours.'

'Good point. But, anyway...'

Neve looked round at the row of Cadian elite. 'Captain Echbar!' she shouted, raising her voice above the roar of the buffet and the thrusters.

'Inquisitor general ma'am!' said the warrior on the end.

'Inquisitor Eisenhorn wants reassurance that you are the best of the best and will be careful to watch the backsides of him and his band.'

Six snow-visored faces turned to look at me.

'We've logged the bio-spoors of you and your company into our sighting auspexes, sir,' Echbar announced to me. 'We couldn't shoot them now even if we wanted to.'

'Make sure you don't. My staff and I will be leading the way in. The situation may not call for firepower. If it does, the vox or psyker command is "Rosethorn". Vox-channel is gamma-nine-eight. Are you prepared for a psychic summons?'

'We're prepared for anything.' Echbar told me.

The gun-cutter stopped shaking.

'We've come out of the storm,' Medea voxed me.

A moment later, she crackled, 'I see approach lights. Kasr Geth landing field in two.'

The pylon stood three kilometres outside the earthworks of Kasr Geth. The night was clear and glassy, with a heaven full of stars. The Eye of Terror throbbed dimly at the top of the sky. It seemed to me more lurid and brighter than ever before.

Somewhere up there, I knew, orbital detachments of the Cadian Interior Guard were hunting the hidden starship from which the visitors to Kasr Gesh had come. Neve had scrambled them before we left, with strict orders not to move until we had engaged on the ground.

We didn't want our visitors tipped off.

My team moved in up through the frost-caked scrub of the moorland slope. The pylon was simply a black, oblong, absence of stars. I could hear it moaning.

I slid out my main weapon: a storm-bolter which I had sprayed green in memory of the prize sidearm I had lost somewhere on Eechan, may Librarian Brytnoth forgive me. This storm-gun was slightly larger and more powerful, but nothing like so well engineered as the boltpistol I had treasured.

On my hip I wore a Cadian hanger, a short, curved twin-edged sabre that replaced my beloved power sword. It was just a simple piece of sharp steel, but I'd had the hierarchs at the Ministorum of Kasr Derth make some modifications.

Still, in truth, I felt vulnerable going up that slope.

Nayl was to my left, fielding a combat-cannon. Husmaan to my right with his trustworthy long-las. Inshabel was to his right, armed with a brace of antique laspistols that had belonged to Inquisitor Roban. Fischig, hefting an old and trusted Arbites-issue riot-gun, had gone wide to the far left.

Bequin, a long-barrelled autopistol in her gloved hand, was right beside me.

Behind us, Neve and her Kasrkin lurked, waiting for my signal.

Aemos was aboard the gun-cutter with Medea, hovering above the drop point, lights killed. They, rather than Neve and her elite, were my reassurance.

'What do you see?' I voxed.

'Nothing,' replied Husmaan and Nayl.

'I've got an angle into the seat of the pylon,' said Inshabel. 'I see lights.'

'Confirm that,' crackled Fischig, wide to the left. 'There are men down there. I count eight, no ten. Twelve. Portable lights. They've got machines.'

'Machines?'

'Handheld. Auspexes.'

'Measuring again,' Neve whispered over the link.

'I'm sure,' I said. Then I said, in Glossia: 'Thorn eyes flesh, rapturous beasts at hand. Aegis to arms, crucible. All points cowled. Razor torus pathway, pattern ebony.'

My storm-gun made a loud click as I racked it.

The robed men working in the floodlights around the foot of the pylon froze and slowly turned from their work to look at me.

I walked down from the moor, through the ice-stiffened bracken, bracing my gun in a pose that could kill any one of them.

Bequin followed me a few steps behind, her pistol held loosely, ready to swing up.

I knew we were covered by Husmaan, Inshabel, Nayl and Fischig.

'Who is the leader here?' I asked, panning my weapon around.

'I am,' said one of the robed figures.

'Step forward and identify yourself,' I said.

'To whom?'

I raised the rosette plainly in my left hand. 'Imperial Inquisition.' Some of the robed men moaned with dismay.

The leader did not. He stepped forward. I could suddenly smell a cold, metallic scent, one that was not new to me.

A warning that came too late.

The leader slowly drew back his cowl. His angular, cruel head was hairless and a cold blue light shone out through his skin. Sharpened, steel-tipped horns sprouted from his brow. His eyes were white slits.

A daemonhost!

'Cherubael?' I said, foolishly, stupidly.

'Your witless ally is not here, Eisenhorn,' said the being, baring his teeth and gleaming with light.

'My name is Prophaniti.'

FIFTEEN

Rosethorn
What Cadians are born for
The last thing I expected

There were two ways for this to go. The first was for me to continue talking, and still be talking when the daemonhost killed me and tossed my smoking corpse on the piled bodies of my comrades. The second was for me to say 'Rosethorn' and place my trust in the mettle of my supporters and the ever-vigilant gaze of the holy God-Emperor.

I said 'Rosethorn.'

The thing, Prophaniti, was stepping towards me. I shot at it with my storm-gun, watching in horrid fascination as it caught the white hot bolt rounds out of the air in its outstretched hands, like a man idly catching slow-tossed racquet balls.

The bolts dulled to an ember-red in its palms, and it tossed them aside.

But its entire attention was on me.

Its mistake.

Husmaan's first hot-shot round cracked into the side of

its head, and snapped its skull around. As it was reeling, its robes were ripped across by double laspistol fire from Inshabel. Then Fischig's riot-gun roared and knocked it down in the brittle bracken. Fischig liked to spend his free time hand-moulding the shot for his riot-gun's cartridges. Every pellet was silver, and stamped with a sacred sigil of warding that I had taught him long ago.

Prophaniti writhed in agony, the blessed buck-shot burning into its flesh. It started to rise, wrathful and frenzied, but a grinding whir rose from my left, a sound like a circular saw running up to speed.

Nayl's cycling drum-cannon raked the daemonhost and the earth around it, doing hideous damage. The blizzard of shots twisted it, ripping off one of its legs at the knee and the fingers off its left hand.

Eldritch power, white-cold like frost, spurted from its wounds like lava, and burned the soil.

The other cultists were moving now, pulling weapons and firing wildly into the night. The place lit up with shooting.

Las-fire came from behind us, startlingly close, whipping past our elbows and shoulders. Two of the cultists crumpled, one of them smashing over some of the erected floodlights.

Echbar and his Kasrkin charged in past us to engage.

In truth, I may say now that they were somehow more terrifying than the daemonhost. For Prophaniti was a supernatural thing, and one expected it to be horrifying.

The Kasrkin were just men. It made their actions all the more astonishing. Six white blurs, they fell upon the cultists, lasguns barking at close range. They wasted no shots. One shot, one kill. A cultist fled past me, and a Kasrkin swung to bring him down. His weapon refused to fire as its sight-auspex detected my bio-spoor in the range-field.

A second later, I was no longer blocking the shot and the weapon spat.

The fleeing cultist tumbled over headlong in the brush.

More cultists had emerged from the other side of the pylon, and I could hear rapid exchanges of gunfire in that direction. Nayl's combat-cannon was making its distinctive metallic whir between bursts of fire. Inshabel's las-cracks overlapped themselves.

'Fischig!' I yelled. 'Lead off round the back of the pylon. See what you can find. Maybe take a damn prisoner before the Kasrkin slay them all!'

I turned back to deal with the ruined daemonhost. We had punished it badly, but I had no illusions as to its resilience.

Or rather... I had thought I hadn't.

Prophaniti was already gone, the ground still smoking and congealing where it had lain.

'Damn! Damn!'

Neve limped down the slope to me. 'Eisenhorn?'

'The daemonhost! Did you see it?'

She shook her head. A loud explosion rolled from the far side of the pylon.

'You killed it, didn't you?'

'Not even slightly,' I replied.

'Gregor!' Bequin shrieked.

Prophaniti was behind me, hanging in the air, incandescent with power. It was naked, and wore the terrible wounds we had inflicted like medals. The right leg, frayed at the knee, dribbled glowing white ichor. Entry wounds and burns bubbled and smoked across its chest. Its head hung slack on a neck broken by Husmaan's hot-shot. It spread its arms and a hand that was just a thumb and a mangled palm sprayed lightning into the midnight grass.

'Nice... try...' the slack head gurgled.

With its robe gone, I could see its body was strung with chains, padlocks and bindings. Stitching needles and other iron awls were pierced into its luminous flesh. Various amulets hung from the chains, or from the barbed wire looped around its neck.

'Run,' I said to Neve and Bequin. 'Run!'

Neve raised her silver cane and triggered the launcher.

The grenade hit Prophaniti in the lower torso and blew it back a few metres with a flash of fyceline.

It rushed back towards us, moaning and chattering in a warp-cursed language.

Bequin grabbed both me and Neve. Her untouchable quality was our only defence now, and she knew it.

Prophaniti stopped short of us, just a metre or so away, hovering in the air and shining like a star. I could smell the rank stench of eternal murder about it.

Its broken neck made a sound like snapping twigs as it slowly turned its lolling head to look at us. The light of dead suns billowed from its eyes and mouth.

Bequin's fingers bit into my arm. The three of us looked up at it, hair ruffled by the warp-winds it generated.

'Tenacious,' it said. 'No wonder Cherubael likes you. He said you employed untouchables. A wise move. You can't hurt me with your guns, but with her around, I can't touch you with my mind.'

'Fortunately, I don't have to,' it added.

It lashed out suddenly with its maimed hand. Neve shrieked as she was hurled aside. There was blood on Prophaniti's thumb talon.

Alizebeth's psychic deadness blocked its psychic rage. But not its physical assault.

It lashed out again, and I leapt back, dragging Bequin.

Prophaniti cackled.

'Alizebeth!' I yelled, and grabbed her by the hand. 'Stay with me!'

I drew my hanger. The short curved blade shone in Pro-phaniti's glare. The runes inscribed on the blade by the Ministorum glittered.

I swung hard, skillessly and frantic, the blade of the hunt-ing sword biting into its rib-meat. It howled and flew back, smoke issuing from the gash.

I circled, hanger in my right hand, Bequin clinging to my left.

'You've done your homework. Pentagrammatic runes on your blade. A nice touch. They hurt!'

It lunged at me.

'But nothing like the hurt you will feel!'

Alizebeth screamed. She fell, and I struggled to hold on to her hand. If our contact broke, I would feel the full force of the daemonhost's power.

I blocked with my falcate blade, shredding the flesh off the left part of its chest, exposing the ribs.

Its talons ripped into my left shoulder and down my flank, ripping my body-armour into tatters.

Blood cascaded down inside my clothes.

I swung again, trying for an *uin ulsar*. It gripped my blade fast, in its one good hand. Smoke rose from the clamping fist around the blade.

It clenched its teeth in pain. 'The wards... hurt... but they are no... stronger... than the weapon... you should learn to... make your weapons sounder... next time...'

'Not that there will be... a next time...' it added. The hanger had become so hot, I let it go with a howl. Prophaniti tossed the buckled, molten steel aside. It had burned its hand terri-bly, but it didn't seem to notice.

'Now comes death,' it said, reaching for me.

* * *

The next few seconds are burned in my memory. I will never see such heroism again, I am sure. Captain Echbar and two of his Kasrkin troopers assaulted Prophaniti from the rear. Their lasguns wouldn't fire because Bequin and I were in their range-field.

Echbar body-tackled the daemonhost, smashing it away from us. Prophaniti hurled him aside, and then incinerated the second Kasrkin mid-leap with its eyes. The third jammed his Cadian bayonet up to the hilt in Prophaniti's breastbone. Fire exploded back from the wound, down the trooper's arm and engulfed him.

He fell back screaming as Echbar came in again, a ragged hole in his cheek and throat. His knife, clenched double-handed, split Prophaniti open down the back bone. The warp-energies that boiled out blew Echbar apart.

Screaming, Prophaniti writhed away through the air.

I knew it wasn't dead. I knew it couldn't really die.

But the Cadian elite had given me an opening by sacrificing their lives. They had fallen in the service of the God-Emperor, which is what every Cadian is born to do.

'Aegis! By scarlet inferno! Thorn redux!'

I screamed the words into my vox, clinging on to Bequin's hand.

Prophaniti came hurtling towards us.

Lights blazing, the gun-cutter surged in overhead in a killing run. The downdraft blasted the icy bracken flat and threw us over. Medea was low, so low...

The gun-servitors trained wing and chin turrets on the charging daemonhost.

When they opened up, their firepower was so monumental, they vapourised it.

The light went out.

I pulled Bequin to me as the drizzle of liquidised host-form rained on us out of the cold night.

I could hear Fischig calling my name.

'Help her,' I said to Fischig as I rose, and he scooped Bequin up.

I looked around. The place was littered with dead, most of them cultists. Inshabel had found Neve, lacerated but alive, twenty metres up the slope, and was calling for a medic.

The aft thrusters of the gun-cutter winked hot-white in the night sky as Medea banked around out of her run to come down again.

Nayl, who had taken a flesh wound to the arm, leaned against the pylon and shut off his whirring cannon-drum.

'We... we need to regroup,' I said.

'Agreed,' said Fischig.

'You have no idea what you're up against, do you?' asked Husmaan.

We all turned. The old skin-hunter from Windhover was stalking down the moor slope towards us, his long-las slung over one crooked arm. Fierce graupel had begun to fleck down from the clouding sky.

'Do you?' he hissed again. I felt Bequin tense.

It wasn't Husmaan.

Husmaan looked at me. White light shone from his eyes. His voice was Prophaniti's.

'Not the slightest clue,' he said. 'You can destroy my physical host, but you cannot break the links to the master.'

'Husmaan!' Inshabel cried.

'Not here any more. He was the most open mind, so I took him. He will serve for a while.'

I took a step forward. Husmaan raised a hand. 'Don't bother, Eisenhorn,' said Prophaniti. 'I could kill you all here, now... but what's about to happen is far more interesting.'

Husmaan, his arms held out from his body and his head back, suddenly rose into the air, dropping his prized long-las. Steadily, he floated away into the sky until he had vanished over the moors into the dawn's counter glow.

'What did he mean?' asked Bequin.

'I don't–'

Floodlights mobbed over the rise and we suddenly heard the clank of armoured tracks.

Twenty Cadian APCs crested the brow, their floods beaming down at us. Cadian shock troops scrambled down the slope, covering us with their guns.

'What the hell?' Nayl cried.

I was stunned. This was the last thing I had expected.

'Inquisitor Eisenhorn,' boomed a vox-amped voice from the lead APC. 'For crimes against the Imperium, for the atrocity at Thracian, for consorting with daemonhosts, you are hereby arrested and condemned to death.'

I recognised the voice.

It was Osma.

SIXTEEN

The Hammer of Witches
Three months in the Carnificina
Flight from Cadia

Flanked by six robed interrogators reading aloud from the Books of Pain and the Chapters of Punishment, Inquisitor Leonid Osma came down the moorland slope towards me. Pink dawn light was beginning to spear lengthways across the bleak heath, and the gorse and bracken was stirred by the early morning breeze. Distantly, heath grouse and ptarcerns were whooping and calling to the midwinter sun.

Osma was a well-built, broad-shouldered man in his one fifties. He wore brass power armour that glowed almost orange in the ruddy dawn. Ornate Malleus crests decorated his armour's besagews and poleyns and six purity seals were threaded around his bevor like a floral wreath. A long cloak of white fur played out behind him, brushing the tops of the heather and gorse.

His face was blunt and pugnacious. His eyes were glinting dots set in puffy lids, fringed by heavy, grey eyebrows.

His bowl-cut hair was the colour of sword-metal. Some years before, he had lost his lower jaw during a fight with a Khornate berserker. The augmetic replacement was a jutting chin of chrome, linked into his skull by feed tubes and micro-servos. The emblem of the Inquisition rose above his head on a standard mounted between his shoulder blades. In one hand he carried a power hammer, the mark of his ordo.

In the other, a sealed ebony scroll tube. I recognised it at once. A carta extremis.

'This is insanity!' Fischig growled. The Cadians around us stiffened and jabbed with their weapons.

'Enough!' I warned Fischig. I turned to my companions. They looked so lost, so miserable, so dismayed.

'We will not fight our own,' I told them. 'Surrender your weapons. I will soon have this laughable error resolved.'

Bequin and Inshabel handed their weapons to the Cadian guards. Fischig reluctantly allowed the storm troopers to divorce him from his riot-gun. Nayl unclipped his drum-cannon's ammo feed, slid out the magazine box and passed that to the waiting troops, leaving the disabled heavy weapon strapped around his torso on its harness.

I nodded, satisfied. 'Thorn bids Aegis, by cool water, soft,' I whispered into my vox and then turned to meet Osma.

He raised his power hammer in a brief gesture and the mumbling interrogators fell silent and closed their books. 'Gregor Eisenhorn,' he said in precisely enunciated High Formal Gothic, 'In fealty to the God-Emperor, our undying lord, and by the grace of the Golden Throne, in the name of the Ordo Malleus and the Inquisition, I call thee diabolus, and in the testimony of thy crimes, I submit this carta. May Imperial justice account in all balance. The Emperor protects.'

I slid my storm-gun out of its holster, ejected the clip and handed it to him grip first.

'I hear full well thy charge and thy words, and make my submission,' I responded in the ancient form. 'May Imperial justice account in all balance. The Emperor protects.'

'Dost thou accept this carta from my hand?'

'I accept it into mine, for that I may prove it thrice false.'

'Dost thou state thy innocence now, at the going off?'

'I state it true and clear. May it be so writ down.'

Vox-drones idling by the shoulders of the interrogators had been recording all this, but the youngest interrogator was transcribing it all with a holoquill into a dispositional slate suspended before him on a grav plate. I noted this detail with some satisfaction.

Preposterous though the charges were, Osma was prosecuting with total and precise formality.

'I ask of thee thy badge of office,' Osma said.

'I deny thy asking. By the code of prejudice, I declare my right to retain my rank until due process is concluded.'

He nodded. His language changed from High Formal to Low Gothic. 'I expected as much. Thank you for avoiding unpleasantness.'

'I don't think I've avoided any unpleasantness, Osma. What I have avoided is bloodshed. This is ridiculous.'

'They all say that,' he muttered snidely, turning away.

'No,' I said levelly, stopping him dead. 'The guilty and the polluted fight. They deny. They struggle. In my lifetime, I have brought down nine marked diabolus. None went quietly. Mark that fact in your record,' I said to the scribing interrogator. 'If I was guilty, I would not be submitting to your process so politely.'

'Mark it so!' Osma told his hesitating scribe.

He looked back at me. 'Read the carta, Eisenhorn. You're guilty as sin. This show of understanding and co-operation is exactly what I would have expected from a being as canny and clever as you.'

'A compliment, Osma?'

He spat into the bracken. 'You were one of the best, Eisenhorn. Lord Rorken actually pleaded for you. I acknowledge your past triumphs. But you have been turned. You are Malleus. You are an abomination. And you will pay.'

'This is insane...' Neve muttered, limping towards us.

'And none of your business, inquisitor general,' Osma replied.

Neve faced him, her torn armour wet with her own blood.

'This is my province, inquisitor. Eisenhorn has proved himself to me. This charade is interfering with Inquisition business.'

'Read the carta, inquisitor general,' Osma told her. 'And shut up. Eisenhorn is clever and convincing. He has fooled you, lady. Be thankful that you're not implicated.'

My companions were arraigned at Kasr Derth, under Neve's recognizance. No such luxury for me. I was flown south aboard a Cadian military lighter, through the dawn, to the furthest islet of the Caducades group, to the infamous Cadian prison, the Carnificina.

They had fettered my hands and feet. I sat on a bracket-bench dropped from the wall of the lighter's armoured hold, surrounded by Cadian guards, and read the carta by the shifting light that sheared in through the window slits.

I could scarcely believe what I was reading.

'Well?' grunted Fischig from his seat in the corner. I had been allowed one spokesman, and I had selected Fischig, with his legal background.

'Read it,' I said, holding the carta out to him.

One of the impassive Cadians took it from me and passed it to the scowling Hubrusian.

After a few moments spent reviewing the scroll, Fischig blurted out an incredulous profanity.

'Just what I thought,' I said.

The Carnificina jutted up from the thrashing sea like the molar of a massive herbivore, the gum eaten away.

It had not been built so much as hollowed out of the upthrust crag. There wasn't a wall on the prison isle thinner than five metres.

Vicious plungers broke in white spray around its granite base and the western aspects were open to the worst of the pelagic abuse from the oceans beyond. Icebergs from the calving glaciers at Cadu Sound and the distant Caducades Isthmus jostled and splintered in the open water between the prison isle and the barren atolls opposing it.

Kelp and hardy, lean axel trees decorated its lower slopes.

The lighter swung in over the eastern ramparts and settled on a pad cut from the stone. I was marched under guard out into the cold sunlight, and then into the dank hallways of the rock. The white-washed walls sweated and stank of seawater. Rusting chains ran down from the ceiling to the hatches of forgotten oubliettes.

I could hear the shouts and screams of prisoners. The demented and infected of the Cadians lived here, mostly ex-servicemen who had been driven mad in the wars of the Eye.

The Cadian troops handed me over to a squad of red-uniformed prison guards who reeked of unwashed flesh and carried pain-flails and leather whips.

They opened up a fifty centimetre-thick hatch cover riven with studs, and pushed me into a cell.

It was four paces by four, cut from stone, with no window. It stank of piss. The previous incumbent had died here... and never been removed.

I pushed aside his dry bones and sat on the wooden bunk. I knew nothing. I had no idea if the Cadian Interior had captured that rogue starship, or if anyone had managed to track the flight of the thing that had been poor Husmaan.

The path to Quixos, the path we had been so lucky to strike at last, was disappearing by the second as we played these games. And there was nothing I could do about it.

'When did you first decide to consort with daemons?' asked Interrogator Riggre.

'I have never done so, or decided to do so.'

'But the daemonhost Cherubael knows you by name,' said Interrogator Palfir.

'Is that a question?'

'It–' Palfir stammered.

'What is your relationship with the daemonhost Cherubael?' cut in Interrogator Moyag sternly.

'I have no relationship with any daemonhost,' I replied.

I was chained to a wooden chair in the great hall of the Carnificina, winter sunlight shafting down from the high windows. Osma's three interrogators stalked around me like caged beasts, their robes swirling in the draft.

'It knows your name,' Moyag said testily.

'I know yours, Moyag. Does that give me power over you?'

'How did you orchestrate the atrocity at Thracian Hive Primaris?' asked Palfir.

'I didn't. Next question.'

'Do you know who did?' asked Riggre.

'Not precisely. But I believe it was the being you have referred to. Cherubael.'

'He has been in your life before.'

'I have thwarted him before. One hundred years ago, at 56-Izar. You must have the records.'

Riggre glanced at his colleagues before replying. 'We do. But you have been searching for him ever since.'

'Yes. As a matter of duty. Cherubael is a repellent abomination. Do you wonder that I would seek him out?'

'Not all your contacts with him have been recorded.'

'What?'

'We know some contacts have remained secret,' Moyag rephrased.

'How?'

'The sworn testimony of an Alain von Baigg. He states that you sent an operative code-named Hound out to make contact with Cherubael, one year ago, and that you refrained from telling your ordo master about it.'

'I didn't think to bother Lord Rorken with the matter.'

'So, you don't deny it?'

'Deny what? Hunting for Chaos? No, I don't.'

'In secret?'

'What inquisitor doesn't work in secret?'

'Who is Hound?' asked Palfir.

I had no wish to make Fischig's life more difficult just then. I said, 'I don't know his real name. He works clandestinely.'

I thought they would press me, but instead Moyag said, 'Why did you survive the Thracian horror?'

'I was lucky.'

Palfir walked a circle around me, his polished boots squeaking on the worn floor. 'Let me make it clear. We are just

beginning here. In respect to your rank and career, we are
employing interrogation of the First Action. The First Action is–'

I cut him short. 'I have been an inquisitor for many years,
Palfir. I know what the First Action is. Verbal interview without duress.'

'Then you know of the Third and Fifth Actions?' sneered
Riggre.

'Light physical torture and psychic interrogation. And by
the way, you just utilised the Second Action – verbal threat
of and/or description of Actions that may follow.'

'Have you ever been tortured, Eisenhorn?' asked Moyag.

'Yes, by less squeamish men than you. And I have interro-
gated too. Second Action methods really won't work on me.'

'Inquisitor Osma has authorised us to use any methods up
to and including Ninth Action,' spat Palfir.

'Again, a threat. Second Action. It won't work on me. I told
you that. I am trying to be co-operative.'

'Who is Hound?' asked Riggre.

Ah, there it was, the follow-up, designed to wrong-foot by
coming out of sequence. For a moment, I began to admire
their interrogation skills.

'I don't know his real name. He works clandestinely.'

'Is it not Godwyn Fischig? The man you chose as your second here. The man who waits outside this chamber?'

There are times when the injuries Gorgone Locke did to my
face on Gudrun have their benefits. My face simply couldn't
show the reaction they were hoping to see. But inside, I
balked. Their intelligence was good, good enough to have
cracked Glossia, if only partially. I was sure of the source.
They had already mentioned that weasel von Baigg. Months
before, on Thracian right before the atrocity, I had begun to
suspect von Baigg. At that time, I merely assumed he was Lord

Rorken's plant to watch over me. Now I realised he was happy to talk to anyone. I had recognised von Baigg's weakness and stalled his career. Clearly he had decided to seek advancement from other inquisitors by selling me out.

'If you are telling me Fischig is the operative I know as Hound, I am truly surprised,' I replied levelly, choosing my words with extreme care.

'We will talk to him in time,' said Palfir.

'Not while he is my recognised second. That would break the code of prejudice. If you wish to interview him, I must be allowed a new second. Of my choosing.'

'We will get to that,' said Riggre.

'Why did you survive the Thracian horror?' asked Moyag.

'I was lucky.'

'Explain lucky?'

'I had stopped to honour the tomb of the admiral. The Spatian Gate protected me from the air strikes.' After the lies Cherubael had told me on Eechan, I dreaded this question coming up again under psychic interview. The lies, or at least my attempts to screen them, would be picked up.

'The atrocity was simply cover to allow you to liberate and remove from Thracian the heretic psyker Esarhaddon.'

'I would normally address that notion with scorn. If the entire event had been staged simply to "launder" the psyker, then it was inhumanly wasteful. However, I believe in some regards you are right. That's what the atrocity was engineered to do. But not by me.'

Moyag licked his yellowing teeth eagerly. 'You maintain that it was in fact Interrogator Lyko who executed the event?'

'In collaboration with the daemonhost.'

'But Lyko cannot answer those charges, can he? Because you killed him on Eechan.'

'I executed Lyko on Eechan as a traitor-enemy of the Imperium.'

'I submit to you that you killed him because he was on to you. You killed him to silence him.'

'Do I really have to be here? You're doing a fine job of making up your own answers.'

'Where is Esarhaddon?'

'Wherever Cherubael took him.'

'And where is that?' asked Palfir.

I shrugged. 'To his master. Quixos.'

All three of them laughed. 'Quixos is dead. He died long ago!' Moyag chuckled.

'Then why did the inquisitor general and I find that he had been manipulating her codes to gain access to Cadian airspace?'

'Because that's how you made it look. You say Quixos used his power to steal her authority code. If that's true, then it's a crime any deviant inquisitor of renown could manage. You could manage it. And using a dead man's code means no one is going to object.'

'Quixos isn't dead.' I cleared my throat. 'Quixos is Hereticus and Extremis Diabolus. He has perverted inquisitors such as Lyko and Molitor into his service. He uses daemon-hosts. He triggers holocausts to cover his theft of alpha-plus class psykers.'

The three interrogators fell silent for a moment.

'We are wasting time here,' I said. 'I am not the man you want.'

But the time-wasting continued. A week, passed, then a second. Every day, I was taken to the great hall and subjected to anything from two to six hours of First Action interview.

The questions were repeated so many times, I became sick of hearing them. None of the interrogators seemed to listen to my statements. As far as I knew, no part of my story was being checked out.

They were clearly wary of escalating to physical or psychic means of extraction. Because I was a psyker, I could at least make things difficult enough so that they'd never know how much of what they were getting out of me was true. Osma had evidently decided to wear me down with endless cycles of verbal cross-examination.

For fifteen minutes each evening, with the ocean light fading, I was allowed to speak with Fischig. These conversations were pointless. The cell areas were undoubtedly laced with vox-thieves and listening devices, and as far as we knew, Glossia was compromised.

Fischig could tell me little, although I was able to learn that Medea, Aemos and the gun-cutter were not in Osma's hands, and neither was the *Essene*.

There had been no further sighting of Prophaniti-Husmaan, and Fischig was certain that the mystery starship that had delivered Prophaniti to Cadia had not been intercepted that fateful night.

Through Fischig's agency, I sent petitions to Osma, to Rorken and to Neve, protesting my arrest and urging them to take further action regarding Quixos. No word came back.

Candlemas was long past. Three more weeks went by. I realised that the year had turned. Outside the thick, bleak walls of the Carnificina, it was 340.M41.

At the end of my third month of detention and interrogation, I was led into the great hall for my daily interview and found Osma waiting for me instead of the usual interrogators.

'Sit,' he said, gesturing to the chair in the centre of the stark room.

It was dark and cold. Bitter, late winter storms were pushing in from the east, and though it was day, no light came from the high windows. They were muffled with snow. My breath steamed in the air, and I shivered. Osma had arranged six lamps around the edges of the room.

I sat down, pushing my hands into the pockets of my coat against the chill. I didn't want Osma to see my distress. He stood, warm and insulated in his burnished power armour, reviewing a data-slate.

I could see myself, reflected in the polished panels of his backplate. My clothes were ragged and filthy. My skin pale. I had dropped a good seven kilos, and now sported a thick beard as unruly as my hair. The only item in my possession was the Inquisitorial rosette in my coat pocket. It comforted me.

Osma turned to face me. 'In three months, your story has not changed.'

'That should tell you something.'

'It tells me you have great reserves of strength and a careful mind.'

'Or that I'm not lying.'

He put the slate down on one of the lamp tables.

'Let me explain to you what is going to happen. Lord Rorken has persuaded Grandmaster Orsini to have you extradited to Thracian Primaris. There you will stand trial for the charges in the carta extremis before a Magistery Tribunal of the Ordo Malleus and the Officio of Internal Prosecution. Rorken isn't happy, but it is all Orsini would allow. Rorken, I have heard, feels that your innocence – or guilt – can be ascertained once and for all in a formal trial.'

'The result of that trial may embarrass you and your master, Lord Bezier.'

He laughed. 'In truth, I would welcome such embarrassment if it meant the exoneration of a valuable inquisitor like you, Eisenhorn. But I don't think it will. You will burn on Thracian for this, Eisenhorn, as surely as you would have done here.'

'I'll take my chances, Osma.'

He nodded. 'So will I. The Black Ships will arrive in three days time to conduct you to Thracian Primaris. That gives me three days to break you before the matter is taken out of my hands.'

'Be careful, Osma.'

'I'm always careful. Tomorrow, my staff will begin Ninth Action examination of you. There will be no respite until the Black Ships arrive or you tell me what I want to hear.'

'Two days of Ninth Action methods will probably guarantee I won't be alive when the Black Ships come.'

'Probably. A shame, and questions will be asked. But this is a lonely prison and I am in charge. That is why, today, I'm just talking to you. Just you and me. A last chance. Tell me the whole truth now, Eisenhorn, man to man. Make this easy on us both. Confess your crimes before the pain begins tomorrow, spare us the trial on Thracian, and I'll do everything in my power to ensure your execution is quick and painless.'

'I'll gladly tell you the truth.'

His eyes brightened.

'It's all there, on that slate you were reading. Exactly as I have been saying these last three months.'

When the guards took me back to my frigid cell, down stone hallways where the ocean gales moaned, Fischig was waiting for me. Our daily fifteen minutes.

He had brought a lamp, and a tray with my night meal: thin, tepid fish-broth and stale hunks of rusk bread with a glass of watered rum.

I sat down on the crude bunk.

'I'm to be extradited for trial,' I told him.

He nodded. 'But I understand tomorrow the painwork begins. I've filed a protest, but I'm sure it'll be accidentally lost in the trash.'

'I'm sure it will.'

'You should eat,' he said.

'I'm not hungry.'

'Just eat. You'll need your strength and from the look of you, you've precious little of that.'

I shook my head.

'Gregor,' he said, dropping his voice. 'I have a question to ask you. You won't like it much, but it's important.'

'Important?'

'To me. And to your friends.'

'Ask it.'

'Do you remember – God-Emperor, but it seems so long ago! – last year, when we met up again, at that grave field outside Kasr Tyrok?'

'Of course.'

'In the shrine tower, you said to me that you couldn't conceive of doing anything that would please or benefit a daemon. You said, "I can't ever imagine myself that insane."'

'I remember it clearly. You said that if you ever thought I was, you'd shoot me yourself.'

He nodded, with a sour chuckle. There was a moment of silence, broken only by the crackling of the lamp and the boom of the sea outside the prison ramparts.

'You want to be sure, don't you, Godwyn?' I asked.

He looked at me, reproachfully.

'I can understand that. I expect total loyalty from you and all my staff. You have the right to be assured of the same from me.'

'Then you know my question.'

I fixed him with my eyes. 'You want to ask if I'm lying. If there's any truth to the charges. If you have been working for a man who consorts with daemons.'

'It's a stupid question, I know. If you are those things, you won't hesitate to lie again now.'

'I'm too tired for anything but the truth, Godwyn. I swear, by the Golden Throne, I am not what Osma says I am. I am a true servant of the Emperor and the Inquisition. Find me an eagle and I'll swear on that too. I don't know what else I can do to convince you.'

He got to his feet. 'That's enough for me. I just wanted to be sure. Your word has always been enough, and after all the years we've been together, I was sure that you'd tell me if... even if it was...'

'Know this, old friend. I would. Even if I was the scum Osma believes me to be, and even if I could hide it from him... I couldn't lie to a direct question from you. Not you, Chastener Fischig.'

The guard rapped on the cell door.

'One minute more!' Fischig shouted. 'Eat your supper,' he said to me.

'Did Osma put you up to this?' I asked.

'Hell, no!' he snarled, offended.

'It's all right. I didn't think so.'

The guard hammered again.

'All right, damn your eyes!' Fischig growled.

'I'll see you tomorrow,' I said.

'Yeah,' he replied. 'Do one thing for me.'

'Name it.'

'Eat your supper.'

The cramps began just after what I guessed was midnight. They woke me from a bad sleep. Pain surged through my body and my mind was numb. I hadn't felt this bad since Pye's handiwork on Lethe Eleven, during the Darknight almost two whole years before.

I tried to rise, and fell off the bunk. Spasms wracked me, and I cried out. I vomited up the dregs of the dire supper. Bouts of fever-heat and death-chill twitched through me.

I don't know how long it took for me to crawl to the cell door, or how long I lay there beating my fists against it until it opened. Hours, possibly.

Consciousness ebbed and flowed with the cramping and the rising agony.

'Holy Emperor!' the guard exclaimed as he opened the door and saw me by the light of his rush-lamp.

He called out and feet came beating down the cell way.

'He's sick,' I heard the guard say.

'Leave him till morning,' said another.

'He'll be dead,' the first guard answered nervously.

'Please...' I stammered, reaching out my hand. It was frozen in a claw-shape, paralysed and ugly.

Others were arriving. I heard Fischig's voice.

'He needs a doctor. Trained medicae help,' Fischig said.

'It's not allowed,' complained a guard.

'Look at him, man! He's dying! An attack of some sort.'

'Let me through,' said another voice.

It was the prison medic, accompanied by Interrogator Riggre, who looked as if he had been roused from his bed.

'He's faking it, leave him!' Riggre said contemptuously.

'Shut up!' Fischig snarled. 'Look at him! That's no act!'

'He's a master of deception,' Riggre returned. 'Maybe he's been licking the lead-paint off the door to aid his act, more fool him. This is a sham. Leave him.'

'He's dying,' said Fischig.

'He looks bloody sick,' said a guard uncomfortably.

More cramping spasms twisted me involuntarily.

The doctor was hunched over me. I could hear the beeping of the medicae auspex he'd taken from his pharmacopoeia.

'This is no act,' he muttered. 'His body's in seizure. You can't fake muscle binding like that. Blood-oxygen is down to thirty per cent and his heart is defibrillating. He'll be dead in less than an hour.'

'Give him a shot. Fix him!' Riggre yelled.

'I can't, sir. Not here. We haven't got the facilities. Ahh! Emperor, look! He's bleeding out now, from the eyes and nose.'

'Do something!' Riggre screamed.

'We have to get him to an infirmary. Kasr Derth is the nearest. We have to get him there quickly or he's dead!'

'That's ridiculous, doctor!' said Riggre. 'You must be able to do something...'

'Not here.'

'Call up a flight, Riggre,' Fischig said.

'He's a primary level prisoner of the Inquisition! We can't just take him out of here!'

'Then get Osma–'

'He's gone back to the mainland for the night.'

Fischig's voice was low. 'Are you going to be the one to tell Osma you let his prize captive die on the floor of his cell?'

'N-no...'

'I'll tell him, then. I'll tell Osma that his man Riggre cheated him of the greatest prosecution of his career because he couldn't be bothered to authorise transport and thus let Eisenhorn die of toxic shock in this prison stack!'

'Call up transport!' Riggre shouted at the guards. 'Now!'

They carried me up to the stone-cut landing pad on a stretcher. Voices yelled and argued in the biting wind and blizzard-filled darkness. The medic had fixed up an intravenous drip and was trying to slow my symptoms with a few drugs from his kit.

The pad lights flickered on, cold and white, and backlit the swirling snow into black dots.

A Cadian shuttle came in low, its attitude thrusters shaking the pad and swirling the snowfall in random directions.

They carried me into the green-lit interior, and the worst of the cold and weather was stolen away as the hatch shut. I felt the sudden yaw of the ship as we lifted up and turned away towards the mainland. Fischig loomed over me, adjusting the restraining straps that held me into the shuttle's cot. Over the roar of the engines, I could hear Riggre shouting at the pilot.

Covertly, Fischig slid an injector vial from his coat and fixed it into the intravenous rig in place of the prison doctor's injector.

I began to feel better almost at once.

'Stay still, and breathe slowly,' Fischig whispered. 'And hold on tight. Things are about to get... bumpy.'

'Contact! Three kilometres and coming in hard!' I heard the co-pilot blurt.

'What the hell is that?' Riggre demanded.

There was a pinging sound from the shuttle's transponder.

'Throne of Earth! They've got a target-lock on us!' exclaimed the pilot.

'Attention, shuttle,' a voice crackled over the open vox. 'Set down on the islet west five-two by three-six. Now, or I will shoot you out of the air!'

My vision was settling now. I looked across the green-lit cabin and saw Riggre pull a laspistol.

'What treachery is this?' he asked, looking at Fischig.

'I think you should do as you were asked and set down right now,' said Fischig calmly.

Riggre made to fire the pistol, but there was a searing flash of light. Fischig burned Riggre with a blast from the digi-weapon built into the jokaero-made ring on his right index finger. An item of Maxilla's jewellery, I realised.

Fischig fired another shot that vaporised the vox-system.

'Down!' he ordered the pilot, pointing the ring at him.

The shuttle made emergency groundfall in a snowstorm on the rocky beach of the uninhabited islet.

'Hands on your heads!' Fischig ordered the crewmen as he bundled me out of the hatch and into the blizzard.

I could barely walk and he had to support me.

'You poisoned me,' I gasped.

'I had to make it convincing. Aemos prepared a dose that would reactivate the binary poison in your body. Pye's poison.'

'You bastards!'

'Hah! A man who can curse is far from dead. Come on!'

He half-carried me across the shingle into the oceanic gale, snowflakes stinging our faces. Lights swooped down ahead of us as the gun-cutter came in, executing a perfect, Betancore-style landing on the icy shingle.

Fischig bundled me up the landing ramp into the arms of Bequin and Inshabel.

'Dear lord, have you thought this through?' I wheezed.

'Of course we have!' Bequin snapped. 'Nathun! Get a booster shot of antivenin!'

For the second time in under two years, I was dead. From binary poison at the hands of Beldame Sadia's henchmen on Lethe, and now, dead in a shuttle-crash, brought down in a winter-storm over the Caducades on Cadia.

The gun-cutter lofted from the beach, ran the length of it, and then came back towards the downed shuttle.

May the Emperor forgive me and my staff for the deaths of Riggre and the two flight crew. Their deaths were the only way I could maintain my security.

'Fire,' I heard Nayl tell Medea.

The gun-cutter's ordnance strafed the Cadian shuttle and blew it apart. By dawn, the jetsam along the remote islet's shore would suggest nothing but a tragic crash caused by the hellish storms.

We banked up through the cover of the storms towards orbital space. Though no one told me, I knew our flight plan was covered by someone else's authority code.

Neve's was my guess. Probably with her permission.

The *Essene* was waiting for us.

'Now what?' I asked Fischig hoarsely.

'Dammit, I've risked everything I count dear to get you this far,' he replied. 'I was kind of hoping you'd know what to do now.'

'Cinchare,' I said. 'Tell Maxilla to get us to Cinchare.'

There are some secrets that are worth keeping.

'What's at Cinchare?' Bequin asked.

'An old friend,' I said.

'Not a friend, exactly,' added Aemos.

'No. Aemos is right. An old associate.'

'Two old associates, to be specific,' Aemos added.

Bequin pulled a particularly angry face. 'You pair and your old intimacies. Why don't you ever give a straight answer?'

'Because the less you know, the less the Inquisition can harm you if we're caught,' I said.

'The new lean you,' syruped Maxilla as I walked onto the *Essene*'s bridge.

I had shaved away my beard, had my ragged hair clipped back, and dressed in a suit of black linen after my shower. I was still terribly weak on my feet and in no mind for Maxilla's foolery.

'Course is set for Cinchare,' Maxilla said stiffly, apparently recognising my mood. His gold-masked servitors chimed in agreement. His hooded Navigator, all senses fixed on some different, quite other place, said nothing.

'I have a question,' said Inshabel. He was seated at secondary navigation position, reviewing the star-maps. 'Why Cinchare? A mining world out in the edges of the Segmentum, almost a Halo Star. I thought we'd be trying to find Quixos.'

'There's no point.'

'What?' Maxilla and Inshabel asked, almost in unison.

I sat down on a padded leather seat. 'Why make the endeavour to find Quixos when he would surely kill us at a stroke? We've barely survived individual encounters with two of his daemonhosts. We haven't the strength to fight him.'

'So?' asked Inshabel.

'So the first thing we do is find the strength. Prepare. Arm ourselves. Make ourselves ready to take down one of the most powerful evils in the Imperium.'

'And for that we need to go to Cinchare?' Inshabel whispered.

'Cinchare's the start, Nathun,' I said. 'Trust me.'

SEVENTEEN

Rogue star
Doctor Savine, Cora and Mr Horn
In the annex

Even at full warp, it took the *Essene* thirty weeks to reach Cinchare.

True, we took a circuitous route, avoiding all possible encounters with the forces of the Imperium. I hated that. For once, I hated the subterfuge.

We learned, indirectly, a few weeks into the voyage, that my escape from Cadia had been discovered. The Inquisition – and other agencies – were hunting me. I had been formally declared Heretic and Extremis Diabolus. Lord Rorken had finally counter-signed Osma's carta.

I was now something I had never been before.

A fugitive. A renegade. And in aiding me, my band of comrades had made themselves fugitives too.

We had a few scrapes. Refuelling at Mallid, we were discovered and pursued by an unidentified warship which we lost in the empyrean. At Avignor, a squadron of Ecclesiarchy battle-boats, standing picket watch along the border of the diocese, tried to run us to ground. We only escaped that one thanks to a combination of Maxilla's shipcraft and Medea's fighting nous.

On Trexia Beta, Nayl and Fischig ran across a band of Arbites hunters while they were trying to hire an astropath. They never told me how many they had been forced to kill, but it sat badly with them for weeks.

On Anemae Gulfward, Bequin succeeded in obtaining the services of an astropath, a sickly female called Tasaera Ungish. When Ungish found out who I was, she begged to be returned to her backwater world. It took a long time to convince her that she was in no danger from me. I had to open my mind to her in the end.

At Oet's Star, we were discovered by an Inquisitor Frontalle during a resupply layover. As it was with Riggre and the Cadian pilots, I will always be haunted by those necessary deaths. I tried to reason with Frontalle. I tried very hard. A young man, he believed that taking me down was the key to a famous career. Eisenhorn the Heretic, he kept calling me. They were the last words on his lips when I pitched him into the geothermal heating exchanger.

From Trexia Beta onwards, there was an almost permanent rumour that a kill-team of the Grey Knights was hunting us. And the Deathwatch Chapter too.

I prayed to my God-Emperor that I could complete this task before the forces of righteousness overtook me. And I prayed to him that my friends might be spared.

Between those escapades, there were only the long, slow weeks of transit in the deep warp. I filled my time with study, and with weapons practice with Nayl, Fischig or Medea. I battled to get myself healthy again. The Carnificina had wasted me, both in body and spirit. The weight I had lost would simply not go back on, despite Maxilla's generous banquets.

And I felt slow. Slow with a blade, slow on my feet. Slow and clumsy with a gun.

Even my mind was slow. I began to fear that Osma had broken me.

Tasaera Ungish was a semi-paralysed woman in her fifties. The arduous rituals of the warp had left her broken and all but burned out, consigned to a life as a junior telepath in the class-chambers of Anemae Gulfward. Her raddled body was supported by an augmetic exo-skeleton. I believe she might have been beautiful once, but her face was now hollow and her hair thin where the implant plugs of her calling had been sited.

'That time again, heretic?' she asked as I walked into her quarters. This was about the twentieth week of the voyage.

'I wish you wouldn't call me that,' I said.

'Coping strategy,' she purred. 'Your woman Bequin connived me out of a safe life on Anemae Gulfward, and made me party to a heretic's private crusade.'

'A safe life, Ungish? A bad end. You'd have been dead in another six months, the strain of the traffic they were making you process.'

She tutted, her augmetic chassis whirring as she poured us two glasses of amasec. Hers was laced with fitobarrier enhancers, and her room stank of lho-leaf. I knew the rigours of her life had left her in constant pain, and she fought that pain off with everything she could lay her hands on.

'Dead and buried on Anemae Gulfward in six... or dead in agony in your service.'

'It's not like that,' I said, nodding as I took the glass she proffered.

'Is it not?'

'No. I've let you see my mind. You know the purity of my cause.'

She frowned. 'Maybe.' She was having difficulty manipulating her own glass. The mechadendrites that governed her right hand were old and slow.

She waved me off when I tried to help.

'Maybe?' I asked.

She took a big swig of her drink and then poked a lho-stick between her crinkled lips.

'I've seen your mind, heretic. You're not as clean as you like to think you are.'

I sat down on the chaise. 'Am I not?'

She lit the lho-stick and exhaled a deep lungful of its narcotic smoke with a sigh.

'Ah, don't mind me. A ruined worn-out psyker who talks too much.'

'I'm interested. What do you see?'

Her exo-skeleton made soft whines as it walked her over to the other couch and the hydraulics hissed as they settled her into the seat. She took another deep puff.

'I'm sorry,' she said. 'Would you like one?'

I shook my head.

'I have served the Astropathicus all my life, such as it is, on guild tenure and as a freelance, as now. When your woman came to me with a job offer and real money, I took it. But, oh me, oh my...'

'Astropaths are supposed to be neutral,' I countered.

'Astropaths are supposed to serve the Emperor, heretic,' she said.

'What have you seen in my mind?' I asked, bluntly.

'Too, too much,' she responded, blowing a magnificent smoke-ring.

'Tell me.'

She shook her head, or that's what I supposed the hissing action of her head-cage was supposed to convey.

'I suppose I should be grateful. You took me from a dead life to this... an adventure.'

'I don't need you to be grateful,' I said.

'Dead and buried on Anemae Gulfward in six... or dead in agony in your service,' she repeated.

'It won't be like that.'

She blew another smoke ring. 'Oh, it will. I've seen it. Clear as day.'

'You have?'

'Many times. I'm going to die because of you, heretic.'

Ungish was stubborn and defeatist. I knew she had seen things she wouldn't talk about. Eventually, I stopped asking. We met every few days, and she psychometrically captured images from my mind. The Cadian pylons. Cherubael. Prophaniti, and the ornaments he wore.

By the time we reached Cinchare, I had a sheaf of psychometric pictures and, thanks to the crippled astropath, a grim sense of the future.

Cinchare. A mineral rock orbiting a rogue star.

Plagued by gravitic storms, the Cinchare system wanders sloppily through the fringes of the Halo Stars at the edge of Imperial space. Ten thousand years ago it had been a neighbour of 3458 Dornal, and had nine planets and an asteroid belt. When we finally found it, it was lurching through the

Pymbyle systems, major and minor, and had suffered two serious cosmological collisions. Now it had six planets and radiating sheets of asteroid belts. Cinchare's rogue star was locked in a drunken dance with Pymbyle Minor, a flirtatious encounter of gravities that would take another million years to resolve.

Cinchare itself, or more properly Cinchare rogue system/ planet four X181B, was a blue nugget of rock swaggering along an almost figure-eight far orbit around the clashing stars, following the vagaries of their impacting gravity wells.

Rich in ultra-rare metals including ancylitum and phorydnum, it had been a miner's plunder-haven for as long as it had been identified.

'No watch ships. Precious little in the way of guidance buoys,' Maxilla said as he steered the *Essene* in-system. 'I've got a habitation hot-spot. The mining colony, I'll bet.'

'Park us in orbit,' I told him. 'Medea, fire up the cutter for landfall. Aemos, you're with me.'

'Whoo!' whispered Medea, tightening the grip of her circuit-inlaid hands around the bio-sensors of the cutter's steering yoke. Another hard buffet had shaken the craft.

'The gravity-tides are all over the place. I keep hitting eddies and anti-trojan points.'

'Small wonder,' Aemos muttered, easing himself into a deck-seat and connecting the restraint harness across his lap. 'The rogue star and its planet-herd have made a disaster area of this system.'

'Hmmm...' said Medea, showing no concern as she rolled the cutter up and over on its back to avoid a jagged black asteroid that tumbled across our path. The close approach to Cinchare was a debris field, full of rock matter and collision slag, all swirling around in complex and exotic orbits. Parts of this field had formed into thin ring systems around Cinchare, but even the rings were buckled and warped by gravity-clashes. The space around us was a bright misty gold where starlight was catching the banks of dust and micro-litter. The cutter's shields could handle most of the larger rocks that swirled through it, but some were giants and required evasive manoeuvres.

Through the gold dust-light, we began to see Cinchare more clearly: an irregular, glittered blue object, spinning fast along a stricken axis. It was half in shadow, and the peaks of its mineral mountains made pre-dawn flashes as they caught the early light coming up over the daylight terminator.

'The closer we get to the body, the worse the gravitic disturbances will become, of course,' Aemos mused aloud. Medea didn't need the advice. Even I knew that an irregular body – and especially an irregular body composed of varying densities – would have a near-space lousy with abnormal gravity effects. I think Aemos was just chatting to keep his mind off things.

Medea banked us around the searing trails of three bolides, and into what felt like a chute of high gravity. Cinchare's surface, a revolving, pitted cold expanse, rushed up to meet us and filled the main ports. The descent and proximity alarms started to sound, and Medea killed them both with an impatient sideways stab of her hand. We levelled out a little.

'The mining facility beacons just woke up,' Medea cleared her throat. 'I've got a pre-lock telemetry handshake. They're requesting ident.'

'Give it.'

Medea activated the cutter's transponder and broadcast our craft's identifying pulse. It was one of the disguise templates

we stored in the codifier for covert work, a delicate piece of
fakery designed by Medea and Maxilla. According to its signature, we were a research team from the Royal Scholam
Geologicus on Mendalin.

'They've cleared us to touch,' Medea reported, easing us
past another buffet of gravity turbulence. 'They've activated
the guide pathway.'

'Any vox contact?'

She shook her head. 'It could all be mechanical.'

'Take us in.'

Cinchare Minehead was a cluster of old industrial structures plugging the cone of an upthrust impact event. Flight
approach was down a rille in the crater edge. The buildings
seemed at first sight to be rude and unfinished, rough-hewn
from the blue rock, but I quickly realised they were standard
Imperial modular structures caked with accretions of blue
dust and gypnate. As far as records showed, Cinchare Minehead had been here for nine hundred years.

We set down on a cleared hardpan surrounded by serially
winking marker lamps. The braking jets kicked up a swirling
halo of eluviam into the air-less sky. After a short wait, two
monotask servitors, heavy-grade units on caterpillar tracks,
emerged into the hard starlight from the shadows of a docking barn, attached clamps to our front end and silently towed
us back into the barn.

It was a grim place of dirty bare metal and lifting gear. Two
battered prospector pods sat in berthing bays, and in the
gloom at the far end was a cargo shuttle that had seen better days.

The barn doors closed behind us, and flashing hazard
lamps in the berthing dock moved from amber to green as

the atmosphere was cycled back in. Apart from the servitors, there was no sign of life.

'Cutter's systems show green on outside conditions,' said Medea, swinging out of her seat.

'Are we ready?' I asked.

'Sure,' said Medea. She had switched her regular Glavian pilot's gear, with its distinctive cerise jacket, for a much more anonymous set of grubby flight overalls. Heavy, tan and baggy, they were actually the quilted liner of an armoured void-suit. The surface was covered in eyelets, laces and stud-connectors where the armour segments would lock on and there were umbilical sockets in the chest. Medea had removed the helmet ring and allowed the heavy collar to hang open. She wore workgloves and steel-capped military boots, and tucked her hair up under a billed cap with the Imperial eagle on the front.

Aemos had adjusted the hydraulic settings of his augmetic exo-skeleton to hold him in the stiffest, most upright stance possible. With a long tunic-cloak of black bagheera, a white skull cap and an engraved data-cane, he looked every centimetre a distinguished scholam academic.

I lacked any trace of my usual Inquisitorial garb. I wore leather breeches and high, buckled boots, an old flak-armour jerkin with dirty ceramite over-plates, and a full-face filter mask with tinted eyeslits that resembled nothing so much as a snarling skull. Nayl had lent me a motion tracker unit from his personal kit, which I had strapped over my right shoulder, and a heavy, snub-nosed laspistol that hung in an armpit rig under my jerkin. A combat shotgun rested in a scabbard between my shoulder blades, and I had a belt of shells for it around my waist. I looked and felt like hired thug-muscle... which was precisely the point.

Medea popped the hatch and we descended into the barn.

It was cold, and the air was parched from too many automatic scrubbings. Odd mechanical noises sounded sporadically in the distance. Squat, short-base servitors were busy tinkering with the old shuttle's exposed engine-guts.

We clanged up the grille stairs to the interior hatch. It was marked with a bas-relief symbol of the Adeptus Mechanicus, and an enamelled sign below it announced that the tech-priesthood was the supreme authority at Cinchare Minehead.

The heavy hatch whirred back into its wall-slot revealing a gloomy prep-tunnel lined with empty void-suits that swung on their hooks in the breeze. Beyond that, there was a dank scrub-room, a darkened office with a padlock on the door, and an empty survey suite with a deactivated chart table.

'Where is everybody?' Medea asked.

We followed the echoing hallways through the complex. Grubby mining equipment was scattered or piled in corners. A small first-aid station had been stripped of surgical equipment and stacked with crates of pickled fish. A side room was empty except for hundreds of broken wine bottles. A disused walk-in freezer store exuded the stink of spoiled meat through its open door. Water spattered from the dark, lofty ceilings of some vaults. Chains swung from overhead hoists. Cold, dry breezes gusted down the halls.

When the wall-speakers boomed, we all started.

'Allied Imperial Minerals! Duty rotation in fifteen minutes!'

The voice was an automatic recording. Nothing stirred in response.

'This is most perturbatory,' murmured Aemos. 'According to Imperial records, Cinchare Minehead is an active concern.

Allied Imperial has a workforce of nineteen hundred running their deep-cast mines, and Ortog Promethium another seven hundred at their gypnate quarries. Not to mention independent prospectors, ancilliary service workers, security and the personnel of the Adeptus. Minehead is meant to have a population of nearly three thousand.'

We had reached a main concourse, a wide thoroughfare lit by overhead lamps, many of which were smashed. Abandoned merchant shops and bars lined either side.

'Let's look around,' I said. We fanned out. I walked to the north end of the trash-littered concourse and found steps leading down into a wide plaza full of more empty shops and businesses.

I heard the whine of an electric motor from down to the left, and followed it. Round the corner of a boarded-up canteen, a fat-tyred open buggy was pulled up outside the unkempt entrance of a claims registry. I went inside. The floor was covered in spilled, yellowing papers and dented data-slates. A snowdrift of used and mouldering ration cartons filled a side door into a filing room.

Nayl's motion detector clicked and whirred. It projected its display on the inside of my mask's right lens. Motion, the rear office, eight metres.

I edged to the door and peered in, my hand on the grip of the holstered las.

A long-limbed man in filthy overalls was crouching with his back to me, rummaging through a foot locker.

'Hello?' I said.

He jumped out of his skin, turning and rising in the same frantic motion, then crashed backwards against a row of metal cabinets. His long, gawky face was pale with fear. His hands were raised.

'Oh crap! Oh dear God-Emperor! Oh, please... please...'

'Calm down,' I said.

'Who are you? Oh, crap, don't hurt me!'

'I'm not going to. My name is Horn. Who are you?'

'Bandelbi... Fyn Bandelbi... Mining superintendant second class, Ortog Promethium... Crap, don't hurt me!'

'I'm not going to,' I repeated firmly. At least the frayed nametag on his dungarees agreed with him: 'BANDELBI, F. SUPER 2nd O.P.'

'Put your hands down,' I said. 'Why did you think I was going to hurt you?'

He lowered his hands and shrugged. 'I didn't... sort of... I don't know...'

He regained a little composure and squinted at me. 'Where did you come from?' he asked. He was an ugly, lantern-jawed fellow with unkempt greasy hair and stubble. There was the hint of a raw pink birthmark on the side of his throat.

'Off rock. Just got here. I was wondering why there was no one around.'

'Everyone's gone.'

'Gone?'

'Gone. Shipped out. Left. Because of the Gravs.'

'The Gravs?'

I don't know if he was going to answer. My motion tracker suddenly flashed an alert up on my lens and I wheeled around to find a man standing in the registry's entrance. He was a big man with dark skin and a white stubble of hair and beard. The autopistol in his right hand was aimed at my face.

'Nice and slow,' he said. 'Lose the guns. And the mask.'

'What's going on? Who's in charge here?' demanded a voice from outside. It was Aemos.

The man with the gun glanced outside and then waved me

ahead of him. Aemos, looking very haughty and dignified, stood in the streetway behind the parked buggy.

'Well? I am Doctor Savine, from the Royal Scholam Geologicus on Mendalin. Is this the way Cinchare Minehead greets its guests?' I was impressed. There was a querulous tone of piqued authority. Aemos had acting talents I had never imagined.

'You got papers?' asked the man with the gun, still covering me. Bandelbi had emerged and was watching the exchange.

'Of course!' Aemos snapped. 'And I'll show them to someone in authority.'

The man with the gun reached his free hand down into the neck of his mesh-reinforced coat and pulled out a polished silver badge on a neck chain. 'Enforcer Kaleil, Cinchare Minehead Security Service. I'm the only authority you'll find round here.'

Aemos tutted and rapped the tip of his data-cane down on the rockcrete ground. The cane-head clicked around and cast a small hologram into the air above it: identity details, the seal of the Royal Scholam Geographicus, and a slowly revolving 3-D scan of Aemos's head.

'Okay, doctor,' nodded Kaleil. He gestured to me with the gun. 'What about this goon?'

'You think I'd travel out to this misbegotten rock without a bodyguard? This goon is Mr Horn.'

'This goon was putting the squeeze on my friend Bandelbi.'

Aemos looked at me sternly. 'I've warned you about that, Horn! Dammit! You're not in the Mordian gang-wars now!'

Aemos turned back to Kaleil. 'He is somewhat enthusiastic. One testosterone-stimm too many, somewhere along the line. But I needed muscle, not brains, and he was cheaper than a cyber-mastiff.'

Be thankful you can't see my face behind this mask, old friend, I thought.

'Okay. But keep him on a leash,' said Kaleil, holstering his weapon. 'Let's go to the security station and you can tell me what the hell you're doing here.'

'And you can tell me where the hell everyone is,' replied Aemos. Kaleil nodded and gestured for us to lead the way down the street.

'So you don't need me to detonate anyone's skull, Doctor Savine?' said a voice.

Kaleil and Bandelbi froze. Medea slunk from cover in a shutterway across the street, a Glavian needle pistol held in an unwavering two-handed grip and aimed at Kaleil's head.

'Crap!' Bandelbi gasped.

'My pilot,' Aemos said, deadpan. He flapped a hand sidelong at Medea. 'No, Cora. We're all friends here now.'

Medea grinned and winked at Kaleil, sliding her weapon away inside her flight suit.

'Had you cold, Enforcer Kaleil.'

Kaleil gave her a murderous glare and led us towards the security station.

The station was on the second floor of a round building on the corner of the deserted plaza. A guard-rail ran at hip-height around the office, and beyond that, inwardly-raked windows permitted a wide view down into the plaza area. Kaleil thumbed a wall-control that reduced the tinting in the glass and made the room a little brighter.

Seats were arranged around a central, circular workstation, above which glowed a holo-display. Empty ration pouches and ale bottles cluttered the surfaces of the workstation, and handwritten notes and memos had been taped along the edges of the console. Around the room were couch seats with splitting upholstery, and piles of junk. A door in the rear led through to an armoury and a ready room. The air was humid and smelled of sweat and unwashed clothes.

Kaleil took off his mesh jacket and tossed it onto a couch. He wore a grubby vest that showed off his physique and the Imperial Guard tattoos on his upper arms.

His badge of office hung down over his chest like an athlete's medal.

'Get 'em refreshment,' he told Bandelbi. The miner began swishing each of the ale bottles standing on the cowling of the workstation to find one with some contents left.

'Fresh ones,' Kaleil scolded. 'And I'm sure the doctor would prefer something softer... or harder.'

'Amasec, if you have it,' said Aemos.

'Ale's fine,' smiled Medea, flopping onto a couch and folding her legs up under her.

I shook my head. 'Nothing.'

Bandelbi disappeared.

Kaleil sat down backwards on one of the workstation chairs so he could fold his arms on the top of the backrest.

'Okay, doctor. What's the story?'

'I am the head of the metallurgy department at the Royal Scholam. Do you know Mendalin?'

Kaleil shook his head. 'Never been there.'

'A fine world, a noble world. Famed for its academia.' Aemos carefully took a seat next to Medea.

I stood back, by the windows. I could tell Kaleil had one eye on me.

'We are engaged in a twenty year program, commissioned by Archduke Frederik himself, to investigate the inner transition qualities of the rarest metals for... well, the applications are classified, actually. The results may improve the industrial health of Mendalin's engine yards. The archduke is a keen amateur metallurgist. He's the patron of the Royal Scholam, in fact.'

'Do tell,' murmured Kaleil.

'Phorydnum is one of the metals to be covered in our program. And this planetoid is one of the nearest sources of it. The Administratum has kindly issued me with a bond to visit Cinchare and obtain samples, and I have letters from the Lord Director of Imperial Allied to inspect the phorydnum workings. Do you wish to see them?'

Kaleil waved a dismissive hand.

'I also hoped to meet with the tech-priests stationed here in order to discuss their understanding of the properties of this precious substance.'

'You're on a fact-finding trip?'

'A research mission,' said Aemos.

Bandelbi returned with three ales and an enamel cup. He carried them on a dented locker door which he was using as a tray.

'It's not good stuff,' he told Aemos, handing him the cup. 'Just ration issue grade.'

Aemos sipped it without the hint of a shudder. 'Rough, but bracing,' he announced.

Kaleil took his bottle and tugged a swig from the neck.

'You've had a wasted journey, I'm afraid,' he said. 'Emperor knows what Imperial Allied were playing at when they gave you those letters. They must know their people have pulled out.'

'Explain,' I said. Kaleil shot me a glance.

'This rock's been worked pretty consistently for the last nine centuries. It's hazardous work, but the rewards are great. As you said, Cinchare's a rich source of many metals that are very hard to come by.'

He took another swig.

'These last twenty years, the authorities here have been getting worried about the conditions. The gravity distortions. Cinchare moving ever closer into the grav fields of Pymbyle. Reckoning was that the place would be unviable in another eighty, ninety years. Imperial Allied and Ortog stepped up their work, trying to strip out as much as they could before Cinchare passed into a gravity envelope that would make it untouchable for the next few thousand years. The indie prospectors too... they came flocking. Regular old fashioned ore-rush, the past few years.'

'So what happened?' asked Medea.

'The Gravs,' said Bandelbi. He was clearing a seat for himself on one of the paper-stacked couches. He looked up and saw Medea's quizzically raised eyebrow.

'Gravity sickness,' he said at once in response to her unasked question. He scratched the birthmark on his neck nervously. He'd been keeping a keen eye on her. She was probably the first woman he'd seen in a while. Kaleil was more composed.

'Gravity sickness,' Bandelbi continued, 'weight distemper, lead-head, the Gravs... you know.'

'Chronic Gravitisthesia, also known as Mazbur's Syndrome. A progressive disorder caused by exotic gravitational flux. Symptoms include paranoia, loss of co-ordination, bursts of anxiety or rapture, memory loss, hallucination and sometimes, in extremis, homicidal urges. The condition is usually accompanied by myasthenia gravis, osteochondritis, osteoporosis, scoliosis and leukaemia,' Aemos finished.

Kaleil widened his eyes. 'I thought you were a doctor of metals, doctor, not a medicae.'

'I am. But gravity, that invisible power, is a fundamental part of the life of all elements. So I take an interest in it.'

'Yeah, well... the predictions said Cinchare might become unviable due to gravity in ninety years. But the human body is softer than a hunk of mineral ore. The Gravs first showed up about two years back. Workers getting sick. A few cases of violence and insanity. Then we realised what was going on. Imperial Allied pulled out nine months ago. Ortog seven.'

'It's ironic,' Aemos said. 'Cinchare is mineral rich precisely because of the exotic gravities it has been subjected to in its billion year life. Elements have been transmuted and rearranged here in ways that may be unique. Cinchare is a precious philosopher's stone, my friends, an alchemist's dream! And now mankind cannot benefit from its gifts for precisely the same reason they exist in the first place!'

'Yeah, doc, ironic is what it is,' said Bandelbi, knocking back his ale.

'That doesn't explain why you're still here,' I said.

'Skeleton crew,' said Kaleil in a tone that said it was none of my business. 'The Adeptus Mechanicus pulled out too, about three months ago. But one of theirs stayed behind. Some sort of vital research that had to be finished. And we were ordered to stay behind and keep Cinchare Minehead open until he finished.'

I moved round and looked out of the station windows. The plaza was empty of everything except trash. 'And how many is "we", Enforcer?'

'Service crew of twenty. I'm in charge. All volunteers.'

'The techlords promised us triple pay!' Bandelbi told Medea, clearly trying to impress her.

'Gee whiz,' she smiled.

'Where are the others? The other eighteen?' I pressed.

Kaleil got up off his chair and tossed his empty bottle at an overflowing litter basket in the corner. It bounced off and broke on the floor. 'Around about. This is a big place. What you see is just the tip. Like a... what's it called, those frozen lumps of water they have in the sea on some planets?'

'Iceberg?' Medea suggested.

'Yeah, like one of those. Ninety per cent of Cinchare Minehead is sub-soil. That's a crap of a lot of space to patrol, maintain and keep ticking over.'

'You're in vox contact with the rest of the skeleton crew?'

'We keep in touch. Some I don't see for weeks.'

'This tech-priest, the one who remained?' Aemos said. 'Where is he?'

Kaleil shrugged. 'Gone rockside. Into the karsts and the mines. I've not seen him for two months.'

'When do you expect him back?' Aemos said, as if it didn't matter.

Kaleil shrugged again. 'Never.'

'What was his name?' I asked, turning to look directly into the enforcer's dark eyes.

'Bure,' he said. 'Why?'

'Well, this is all most perturbatory!' Aemos blurted, rising from his seat. 'The archduke will be very put out. It has cost a deal of time and money to venture this mission. Mr Kaleil... since we've come this far, I'd like to do what little I can.'

'Like what, doctor?'

'Obtain some samples, inspect the phorydnum workings, study the minerology ledgers?'

'I don't know... Cinchare Minehead's meant to be closed up now. Officially.'

'Would it really be too much to ask? I'm sure the Lord Director of Imperial Allied would be pleased if you co-operated
with me. Pleased enough to proffer a bonus if I made a report
to him.'

Kaleil frowned. 'Uh huh. What are we talking about?'

'A day to overview the ledgers and the mineralogy database,
perhaps another day to examine the sample archives from
the quarries. And... well, how long would it take to arrange
a visit to the phorydnum face? The latest one?'

'I call my staff in, maybe two days round trip.'

'So... excellent! Four days total and we'll be gone.'

'I dunno...' said Bandelbi.

'Don't you want me hanging around for a few days?' asked
Medea, reading Bandelbi's body language as acutely as any
trained inquisitor, and revealing as much latent acting ability as Aemos.

'I shouldn't allow it,' said Kaleil. 'This place is off limits now.
Company orders. You didn't ought to stay here.'

'You stay here,' I pointed out.

'I get danger money,' he said.

'And you could get more,' said Aemos. 'I promise you,
I'll speak highly of your co-operation to the Lord Director of Imperial Allied... and my old friends at the Adeptus.
They would reward well anyone assisting a servant of the
archduke.'

'Get me an ale,' Kaleil told Bandelbi. He looked at us, rolling his chin. 'I'll talk to my staff, see what they think.'

'Good, good,' said Aemos. 'I do hope we can reach an
arrangement. In the meantime, we'll need quarters. Are there
spare beds here?'

'Cinchare's been fulla empty beds since the workforce
moved out,' Bandelbi told Medea through a nasty smile.

'Find them a hab,' Kaleil told the miner. 'I'll get on to the crew.'

'Something's not right,' I said, pulling off my mask and tossing it onto the floor.

'These cots are really rather cosy,' Aemos replied, adjusting the tension of his exo-frame and reclining on the mattress.

We were in a dry, stuffy rec-room above the miners' welfare. The artificial lamplight from the plaza outside slanted in through sagging blinds. Bandelbi had provided three metal cots with subsiding mattresses and sleeping bags that smelled like they had been used to sieve motor fuel and cabbage.

'You always worry,' Medea said, uninhibitedly shrugging off her flight suit and kicking it into a corner. She was clad in nothing but her vest and briefs, and her shoulder holster, which she was now unclasping.

Aemos rolled over and looked the other way.

'It's my job to worry. And stop getting undressed. We're not finished.'

Medea looked at me, and rebuckled her gun rig with a dark frown.

'Okay, my lord and master... what? What's not right?'

'I can't quite put my finger on it...' I began.

Medea tutted and flopped down on her cot.

'Yes, you can, Gregor,' Aemos said.

'Maybe I can.'

'Try.'

'This stuff about the Gravs. Even if the corporations were suckered, it's not like the Adeptus Mechanicus to fail in a prediction. Any cosmologist would know if Cinchare was entering a gravitation wilderness that would be harmful to humans. They'd know it years in advance. Emperor protect me, stellar objects move far slower and more predictably than human minds!'

'A good point,' said Aemos.

'And one that you'd already thought of, I'm sure,' I said.

'Yes,' he confirmed. 'Kaleil is clearly lying about something.'

'And you don't think anything's wrong?'

'Of course I do,' Aemos muttered. 'But I'm tired.'

'Get up,' I told him brusquely.

He sat up.

'At least we know Bure's still here,' I said.

'This is the guy we came to find?' Medea asked.

I nodded. 'Magos Bure.'

'So how do you two know him? A tech-priest magos?'

'Old story, my dear,' said Aemos.

'I've got time.'

'He was a loyal ally of my master, Inquisitor Hapshant, Aemos's old boss,' I said, cutting to the chase before Aemos could get going.

'A blast from the past, huh?' she grinned.

'Something like that.'

'Still, it's a lo-o-ong way to come just to catch up with an old friend,' she added.

'Enough, Medea!' I said. 'You don't need to know the particulars yet. Maybe better for you if you don't.'

She blew a raspberry at me and began to pull her flight suit back on.

'You tried to reach the *Essene* recently?' I asked.

'My vox hasn't got the range,' she sulked back, fiddling with the zipper. 'Gravity distortions are too much. We expected that. I could go back to the cutter and use the main 'caster.'

'I need you here. We need to scare up some answers fast. I want you to sneak Aemos down to the Administratum archive, and see if you can coax anything out of the data banks, if they're still functioning.'

'While you...'

'I'm going to the annex of the Adeptus Mechanicus. Meet back here in three hours. We're looking for any clues, but particularly any traces of Bure's whereabouts.'

Aemos nodded. 'What if we're challenged?'

'You couldn't sleep, you went for a walk, and you got lost.'

'And if they don't believe me?'

'That's why Medea's going with you,' I said.

The annex of the tech-priesthood lay in the western sector of Cinchare Minehead's jumbled maze of pressurised habs and processing sheds, about two kilometres from the plaza. At first, I hadn't known where I was going, but the tunnels and transit ways were marked with numbered signs and symbol-coded notices, and after a while I found a large, etched-metal directory map screwed to a pillar beside a bank of dusty public drinking fountains.

A twist of the tap on one of the fountains produced nothing but a dry rasp.

Approaching the annex, the whitewashed tunnel walls were overpainted with dark red stripes, and there were numerous caution signs and warnings that demanded correct papers and identities on pain of death.

Still, the whole place was bare and empty, and thick with dust and litter.

At the end of the red-striped access tunnel, the vast adamantite blast-gates to the annex stood open. There was an eerie silence.

The annex was a colossal tower of hewn rock dressed in red steel, filling a side chimney of the crater that housed

Cinchare's minehead. A sealed glass dome covered the paved yard between the blast-gates and the annex, and the building itself rose up beyond the glass to the top of the crater rim. High above, I could see the blue rock and the starlit void beyond. Meteors streaked overhead

The doorway of the annex was a giant portal taller than three men, framed by thick doric columns of black lucullite. Above it leered the graven image of the Machine God, its eyes clearly carved in such a way that they would flare ominously with gas burn-offs piped up from the mines. They were cold and dead now.

And the burnished metal doors of the portal were open.

I stepped inside. Fine sand covered the floor of the grand prothyron. Dust motes glittered in the bars of light spearing into the high hallway through deadlights up near the ribbed roof. Both walls were entirely panelled with banks of codifiers and matriculators, all dormant and powered down. Crescents of dust bearded every single switch and dial.

I knew at once this was a bad sign. The tech-priests treasured machines more than anything else. If they had evacuated as Kaleil described, there was no way they would have left such a wealth of technology here... especially as each unit was clearly designed to slot out of its alcove in the black marble walls.

The chamber beyond the prothyron was a veritable chapel, a cathedral dedicated to the God-Machine, the master of Mars. The floor was creamy travertine slabs, so tightly laid not even a sheet of paper could be slipped between the stones. The chapel itself was triapsidal with walls of smooth, cold lucullite and a roof thirty metres above my head. There was yet more precious technology arranged in six concentric circles of intricate brass workstations around a central plinth. All of it was dead and unpowered.

I crossed the chamber towards the plinth, painfully aware of how loud my footsteps rang back from the emptiness. Chilly starlight shone down through an opaion in the centre of the roof, directly above the massive grandiorite plinth. The huge, severed head of an ancient Warlord Titan hung above the plinth where the starlight shafted down. I realised that nothing supported the head – no cables, no platform, no scaffolding. It simply hung in the air.

As I got close to the plinth, gazing up at the Titan's face, my hair pricked. Static, or something like it, bristled the atmosphere. Some invisible, harnessed force – perhaps gravity or magnetics, certainly something beyond my understanding – was at play here, suspending the multiple tonnes of the machine-skull. It was a silent marvel, characteristic of the tech-priesthood. Even with the power shut down, their miracles endured.

On one workstation console – a brass frame full of intermeshed iron cogs, silvered wires and glass valves – I saw a length of canvas-sleeved neural hose, one end plugged into the display, the other frayed and severed. That was more than just a case of someone leaving in a hurry.

Over the years, my dealings with the Adeptus Mechanicus had been few. They were a law unto themselves, like the Astartes, and only a fool would meddle with their power. Bure – Magos Geard Bure – had been my closest contact with them. Without the Priesthood of Mars, the technologies of the Imperium would wither and perish, and without their ceaseless endeavours, no new wonders would ever be added to mankind's might.

Yet here I stood, unmolested and uninvited, in the middle of one of their inner sanctums.

My vox-link pipped. A voice, Medea's, badly distorted by gravity flux, said 'Aegis wishes Thorn. By halflife d–'

It cut off.

'Thorn attends Aegis,' I said. Nothing.

'Thorn attends Aegis, the whisperless void.'

Still nothing. What little I had caught of Medea's brief message troubled me – 'halflife' was a Glossia code word that could be used in phrases to disclose an important discovery or indicate a grave predicament. But what troubled me far more was the fact she had cut off. My reply, if she had heard it, indicated her transmission had been incomplete or garbled.

I waited a full minute, then another.

Without warning, my vox pipped quickly three times. Medea had test-keyed her transmitter in a non-vocal code form that indicated she couldn't talk and that I should stand by.

I brushed the thin skin of dust off one dead workdesk and gazed at the worn, rune-marked keyboard and the small display screens of thick, convex glass, wondering what secrets I could possibly unlock from it.

Little, I decided. Aemos, who frankly knew more than it was healthy to know, might have a chance. He had worked closely with Bure years before, and I fancied he had more experience of the mysterious tech-priests and their ways than he cared to admit.

My motion-tracker suddenly clicked around, and I tensed, pulling my stub-nose laspistol. The tracker's display on my mask's right lens indicated a movement or contact seventeen paces to my left, but even as I turned, it flashed up more. Multiple contacts, all around, coming so fast that they overlapped and utterly confused the tracker for a moment. The lens display showed a default 'oo:oo:oo' for a second as it struggled to compute the vectors, and then it scrolled a tight column of coordinates in front of my eye.

But by then, I knew what it had sensed.

The sanctum was coming to life.

In swift succession, each workstation chattered into action, cogs whirring, valves glowing, screens lighting, pistons hissing. Pneumatic gas-pumps exhaled and communiqué flasks began to pop and whizz through the network of elegant glass-and-brass message tubes that ran between the consoles and up the walls. Several desks projected small hologram images above their hololith hubs: three dimensional strata maps, spectroscopy graphs, sonar readings and oscillating wave-forms. Powerful underlights ignited on the plinth-top beneath the floating head of the Titan and threw its features into malevolent relief.

I sank down behind one of the stations, which vibrated and chattered against my back. The sudden, inexplicable life was daunting and alarming. Somewhere close by, one particular machine was rattling and repeating like an old machine gun on full auto.

As suddenly as it had started, the life died away. Stations fell silent and their lights went out. The throb of power leaked away into the darkness. The Titan's underlights dimmed and died. One by one, the holograms extinguished and the desks fell dormant. The chirring of cogs and servos and the throb of valves ebbed into stillness.

The last sound to go was that autogun racket. It continued for a good few seconds after everything else had stopped, then it too ceased abruptly.

The chapel was then as dark and quiet as it had been when I first entered.

I got to my feet. There had been no power in this place, no

feeding source. What had started and woken the machines? It had to have been some signal from outside.

Using commonsense and guesswork, I went around the circle of stations nearest to me, hunting for the one that had chattered like a stubber. The most likely candidate was a bulky desk that seemed to have external and general gain vox functions. But its keys were dead to my touch.

On a whim, I got down on my knees and peered behind the desk. There were fixings where a basket hopper should have been sitting to catch the print-outs. The hopper was missing. The sheaf of print-out had fallen down into the dust under the desk.

I scooped the sheaf out. It was about nine metres long, punch-cut by the printer's jaws into shorter sections. Clearly this desk had been disgorging print-outs for some time without anyone around to collect them. The sections at the bottom of the spool were beginning to yellow.

I looked them over, but they meant nothing. Tabulated columns of machine code in close, regular bands. Carefully, I laid them out on the travertine floor and rolled them tightly into a thick scroll.

I was nearly finished when my vox pipped.

'Aegis wishes thorn. By halflight disabused, in Administratum by heart. Scales fall from eyes. Multifarious, the grasp of changelings. Pattern thimble advised.'

'Pattern thimble acknowledged. Thorn arising by heart.'

Medea's words had told me all I needed to know. They had found something in the Administratum, and they needed me back swiftly. There was danger from Chaos all around. I should trust no one.

I holstered my laspistol and tucked the print-out scroll into my waistband.

As I ran out of the annex and down the red-striped tunnel, I tugged my combat shotgun out over my shoulder and racked the slide.

EIGHTEEN

Pattern thimble
Going rockside
Geard Bure's translithopede

Glossia's not so hard to understand. It uses subliminal symbols and 'head words'. Don't look for a mystery in it, it isn't there. That's why it works so well as a private code. There is no encryption – at least no mathematical encryption – to be calculated and broken. It is idiomatic and visceral. It is verbal impressionism. It uses the uncalculable, unregulated mechanisms of poetry and intimacy to perform its functions. There have been times in the last – well, the increasing years of my career, let's say – there have been times when an ally or retainer of mine has sent me a Glossia message using terms and words that have never been used before. And still, I have understood them.

It's a knack. It's knowing how to use, and improvise, a shared cant. There are basic rules of construction and metaphor, of course, but Glossia's strength lies in its nebulous vagueness. Its idioms. Its resonance. It is akin to the gut-slang

313

DAN ABNETT

of the Ermenoes, who have replaced language with subtleties of skin-colour.

Pattern thimble, for example.

'Pattern' indicates a course of action or behaviour. 'Thimble'
is a qualifier, disclosing the manner or mode of said action. A
thimble is a small tin cap that you might use to protect your
finger from the short, sharp stabs of a needle during darn-
ing. It wouldn't fend off, say, an atomic strike or a horde of
genestealers. But, in the idiom of Glossia, it would seal you
against sudden, spearing, close attacks. It is also quiet and
unremarkable.

And so, quietly, unremarkably, I slipped down the tunnel ways of Cinchare Minehead towards the officium of the
Administratum. I was stealthy and secretive, and my motion
tracker and shotgun were my thimble.

Pattern thimble. Gideon Ravenor had coined that particular phrase, adding it to the vocabulary of my Glossia.

I thought of Ravenor, alone in his plastic-sheeted cot on
Thracian. My anger, dimmed these last few months, welled.

My motion tracker warned me into cover at a junction of
transit tunnels about half a kilometre from the plaza. Hidden behind a stack of empty promethium drums, I watched
as two electric buggies buzzed past, heading towards the concourse area. Bandelbi was driving the lead one. There were
two miners with him, and three more in the buggy behind.
They all looked grimy and slovenly.

There were more buggies in the plaza, parked out in front of
the security office. I saw a couple of labourer-types lounging
in the building doorway, smoking lho-sticks.

I slipped into the miner's welfare through the back. Medea

and Aemos were waiting for me in the shabby rec-room billet.

'Well?'

'We nosed around the Administratum,' said Aemos. 'It wasn't even locked.'

'Then the place started to crawl with Kaleil's people and we skedaddled,' said Medea. Both of them looked tense and pensive.

'They see you?'

She shook her head. 'But there is a damn sight more than twenty of them. I counted thirty, thirty-five at least.'

'What did you find?'

'Recent archives are non-existent, or they've been erased,' said Aemos. 'Nothing for the last two and a half months, not even a caretaking log, the sort of thing you'd expect Kaleil to have been obliged to keep.'

'He could be recording it at the security office.'

'If he was following official protocol, it would have been automatically copied to the central archives. You know how anal the Administratum is about keeping full records.'

'What else?'

'Well, it was a cursory examination – we didn't have much time. But Kaleil told us Imperial Allied pulled out nine months ago and Ortog Promethium followed them two months later. According to the archive, both corporations were active, working and fully crewed as recently as three months ago. There's no record of any "Grav" cases, nor any filed reports or memos about the possibility of such a problem.'

'Kaleil was lying?'

'In all respects.'

'So where is everyone?'

Aemos shrugged.

'Do we leave now?' Medea asked.

'I'm determined to find Bure,' I replied, 'and there's something afoot here that really ought to–'

'Gregor,' Aemos murmured. 'I hate to be the one to point this out, but this isn't your concern. Although I know full well you are as loyal to the Golden Throne now as you ever were, in most respects that matter, you're no longer an inquisitor. Your authority is no longer recognised by the Imperium. You're a rogue... a rogue with more than enough problems of your own to sort out without involving yourself in this.'

I think he expected me to be angry. I wasn't.

'You're right... but I can't just stop being a servant of the Emperor, not just like that, no matter what the rest of mankind believes me to be. If I can do any good here, I will. I don't care about recognition, or official sanction.'

'I told you he'd say that,' Medea sneered at Aemos.

'Yes, you did. She did,' he said, looking back at me.

'Sorry to be so predictable.'

'Moral constancy is nothing to apologise for,' said Aemos.

I took the scroll of paper I'd recovered from the annex and showed it to my old savant.

'What do you make of this?' I told them what had happened in the sanctum of the Machine-God.

He studied the curling sheaf for a few minutes, checking back and forth.

'There are elements of this machine code that I can't make out. Adeptus encryption. But... well, look at the text breaks. These are the filed records of regular transmissions from outside the minehead. Every... six hours, to the second.'

'And the sanctum's dormant systems would wake up the moment an external transmission came in?'

'In order to record it, yes. How long were the machines in life?'

I shook my head. 'Two, maybe two and half minutes.'

'Two minutes forty-eight seconds?' he asked.

'Could be.'

He ran his finger along a line of header text above the last code-burst. 'That's exactly how long the latest transmission lasted.'

'So someone's out there? Outside the minehead on Cinchare somewhere, sending regular transmissions back to the Adeptus annex?'

'Not just someone... it's Bure. This is the Adeptus code-form for his name.' Aemos leafed back through the sheets and studied the yellowest and oldest. 'He's been broadcasting for... eleven weeks.'

'What is he saying?'

'I've no idea. The main text is too deeply codified. Mechanilingua-A or C or possibly some modern revision of one of the hexadecimal servitoware scripts. Possibly Impulse Analog version nine. I can't–'

'You can't read it. That's enough for me.'

'All right. But I know where he is.'

I paused. 'You do?'

Aemos smiled and adjusted his heavy augmetic eyewear. 'Well, no. I don't actually know where he is. But I can find him.'

'How?'

He pointed to a vertical strip of coloured bars that ran down the side of each transmission burst. 'Each broadcast is routinely accompanied by a spectrographic report on the location of the transmitter. These colours are a condensed expression of the type, mix and density of the rock surrounding him. It's like a fingerprint. If I had a good quality strata map of

Cinchare, and a geologicae auspex, I could track him down.'

I smiled. 'I knew there was a reason I kept you around.'

'So we're going after him?' asked Medea.

'Yes, we are. We'll need transport. A prospecting pod, maybe. Can you handle one of those?'

'Piece of cake. Where do we get one?'

'Imperial Allied has an excursion terminal full of them,' Aemos said. 'I saw a schematic guide of the minehead screwed to a wall.' I had seen just the same sort of thing, but I didn't recall a detail like that. It reminded me of the extraordinary photo-memory Aemos possessed.

'What about the chart and auspex you said you'll need?' Medea asked.

'Any prospector machine will have an on-board mineral-ogicae or geologicae scanner,' said Aemos. 'That will suffice. A comprehensive chart, though, that'll be less of a certainty. We'd better make sure we have one before we set off.'

He sat down on his cot and began to adjust the settings of his wrist-mounted data-slate.

'What are you doing?' I asked, sitting down next to him.

'Downloading a chart from the security office's cogitorum.'

'Can you do that?' Medea asked.

'It's simple enough. Despite the gravitics, my slate's vox-link has enough range to communicate with the office's codifier. I can make a text-bridge and ask it to send its chart files.'

'Yeah, yeah, but can you do that without knowing the sys-tem's user-code?' Medea asked.

'No,' said Aemos. 'But fortunately, I do know it.'

'How come?'

'It was on a note taped to the edge of the central control desk. Didn't you see it?'

Both Medea and I shook our heads and smiled. Just sitting

there with Kaleil, talking and sipping fifth-rate amasec, Aemos
had soaked up and memorised every detail of the place.

'One question,' Medea said. 'We don't know what's going on
here, but it's probably a safe bet your friend is no friend of Kaleil
and his pals. If we can find him using this, why haven't they?'

'I doubt even an experienced miner could make much sense
of this spectroscopy expression. It's an Adeptus code,' Aemos
said, proudly.

'It's simpler than that,' I said. 'They haven't found it. The
annex was covered in dust, undisturbed. I don't think Kaleil
or any of his people have been into the annex. Fear of the
Adeptus Mechanicus is a strong disincentive. They don't know
what we know.'

In the night, they came to kill us.

Once Aemos had downloaded the chart – and several other
files of data besides – we resolved to get a few hours' sleep
before making our move.

I had been asleep for about a hour when I woke in the dark
to find Medea's fingers stroking my cheek.

As soon as I stirred, she pinched my lips shut tight.

'Spectres, invasive, spiral vine,' she whispered.

My eyes became accustomed to the half-light. Aemos was
snoring.

I rose off my cot and heard what Medea had heard: the
stairs outside the rec-room creaking. Medea was pulling on
her flight suit, but keeping her needle pistol aimed at the door.

I pulled my laspistol from its holster on the floor and then
leant over to Aemos, putting my hand over his mouth.

His eyes flicked open.

'Keep snoring but get ready to move,' I whispered into his
ear.

Aemos struggled up, snorting out fake snores as he collected up his robe and cane.

I had stripped down to my vest. My jacket and motion tracker were on the floor at the foot of the cot. There was no time to reach for them.

Someone kicked the door in. The bright blue lances of two laser sights stabbed into the rec-room, and a tight burst of stubber fire blew holes in my vacated cot and puffed padding fibres up from the wounds in the mattress.

Medea and I returned fire, bracketing the doorway with about a dozen shots between us. Two dark shapes toppled backwards. Someone screamed in pain.

A flurry of gunfire from ground level outside slammed up in through the windows, blowing one of them right out of its mounting in a shower of glascite. Ruined slat-blinds rippled and jiggled with the impacts.

'Back!' I cried, firing twice at a shape in the doorway. A triple pulse of answering las-fire scorched past my head.

But light flooded in behind us as a rear door crashed open. Medea swung around, lithe and long-limbed, and broke in the face of the first intruder with a high kick that sent him reeling back.

Figures charged in from the doors before and behind us. I shot two, but then was carried over onto my back by two more who struggled frantically to rip the laspistol out of my hand. I kneed one in the groin and shot him through the neck as he coiled away.

The other one had his hands on my throat.

I speared my mind right into his and triggered a massive cerebral haemorrhage that burst his eyeballs and sent him slack.

The smell of blood and cordite and the miners' unwashed

bodies was intense. Medea danced back, and delivered a forearm slam to the face of another assassin that made him stumble and gasp.

She flexed and delivered a spin-kick which hit him so hard he smashed back out of the window.

Another was coming at her from behind. I saw a knife blade flash in the gloom.

Aemos, slow but steady, swung round and broke the knife-man's neck with a single punch. Another thing too easy to underestimate about my old savant was the inhuman strength his augmetic exo-chassis provided.

There was a little more wild gunfire, and then the spitting sound of Medea's Glavian pistol.

I curved my back and sprang back onto my feet in time to gun down a man with a shotgun who was coming in through the door.

Silence. Drifting smoke.

Voices were shouting below on the plaza.

'Grab your things!' I ordered. 'We're going right now!'

Half-dressed and lugging the rest of our kit, we scrambled down the back stairs. The body of one miner shot by Medea lay crumpled on the steps under the first landing. The front of his Ortog Promethium overalls was soaked with blood.

There was a livid birthmark on the side of his awkwardly twisted neck.

'Look familiar?' asked Aemos.

It did.

'Didn't that creep Bandelbi have a birthmark too?' Medea asked.

'Most certainly,' I replied.

* * *

We broke our way through a series of cluttered storerooms
and came out in an access alley behind the shops adjoining
the welfare. A ginger-haired miner posted as rearguard for the
ambush turned in surprise as we emerged, his hands fumbling with the shotgun slung over his shoulder on a leather
strap.

Drop it and come here! I said, using my will.

He tossed the weapon down and trotted over to us, his eyes
glazed and confused.

Show me your neck! I willed again.

He brushed up his tousled hair with one hand and tugged
his worksuit's neckline down with the other. The birthmark
was there, centred on his nape.

'We haven't got time for this!' Aemos said. Running footsteps were pounding through the building behind us and we
could hear shouts and curses.

'Where did you get this mark?' I willed at the ginger-haired
man.

'Kaleil gave it me,' he said slackly.

What does it mean?

Driven by my undeniable will-force, he tried to say something that the rest of his mind and soul simply forbade. It
sounded like 'Lith' but it was impossible to say for sure as
the effort killed him.

'Dammit, Gregor! We have to go!' Aemos roared.

As if to prove his point, two miners burst out of the doorway we had come through, aiming autorifles. Medea and I
whipped around as one and dropped them both, one kill
shot each.

Aemos's faultless recall led us through the winding sub-streets
of Cinchare Minehead to the massive, dank bulk of Imperial

Allied. There was a hue and cry behind us, mixed with the whine of electric buggies.

We ran across the plant's wide, metal drawbridge, through a rockcrete gatehouse festooned with razorwire, and on down through the echoing entrance hall.

Footsteps followed.

The excursion terminal was a semi-circular barn of corrugated steel overlooking the mouth of the main working. Six prospecting pods sat in oily iron cradles under the barn's roof. They were slug-shaped machines, painted in the silver and khaki colours of Imperial Allied. Each one had a rack of flood and spotlights mounted above the cockpit, and several large servo arms and locator dishes arrayed under the chin.

'That one!' Medea yelled, heading for the third in line. She was still trying to fasten her flight suit properly. I carried my jacket and motion tracker. There had been no time to stop and get dressed.

'Why this one?' I yelled, following her.

'The power hoses are all still attached and it's showing green across the board on the telltales! Unclamp the hoses!'

I threw my stuff to Aemos, who hurried aboard behind Medea through the small side hatch, and ran to where three thick power cables were attached to the multi-socket in the flank of the pod. Just as Medea had noticed, all the indicator lights above the socket were green.

I twisted the valves and pulled them free, one by one. The last one was reluctant and needed a moment of brute force.

Las-shots spanked into the hull casing beside me.

I jerked the hose free and then turned, firing back down the length of the barn terminal. The pod's attitude thrusters began to cough and wheeze as Medea brought the craft to life.

Solid and las-shots peppered around me. I ran to the hatch and climbed in. Medea was at the helm in the cramped cockpit.

'Go!' I cried, slamming the hatch shut.

'Come on! Come on!' Medea cursed at the pod's controls. The over-urged engines whined painfully.

'Cradle lock!' Aemos spluttered desperately.

Realising her mistake, Medea swore expertly, eased the power down a tad, and threw a greasy yellow lever on the right-hand bulkhead. There was a jarring clank as the locking cuff that held the pod tight in the cradle disengaged.

'Sorry,' she grinned.

Freed, the pod lifted out of its landing cradle, swayed to the right as gunfire hunted for it, and then accelerated away, into the lightless mouth of the mine tunnels.

The upper workings of the Imperial Allied mines were huge excavations reinforced with rockcrete and filled with abandoned mining machines. Medea kicked in the pod's lamp array and illuminated our path with hard spot-beams of clear white light. At the far end of one reinforced spur, the lamps picked out a sudden, wide gradient where the horizontal incuts of the surface mines began their descent. Running down the steep slope were derelict cable-trams of filthy ore-hoppers and a funicular railway for transporting work-crews to the lower faces.

Aemos sat behind us in the pod's small cabin, reviewing the charts he had obtained from the security office. 'Continue down,' was all he said.

The steep access bore descended for about a kilometre and a half, occasionally flattening into work-shelves with entries to side seams. The view through the front screen seemed to be in black and white: the fierce white light piercing the blackness and revealing only pale grey dust and rock, and the occasional sparkle of druse.

Medea slowed us as we passed over more fragmented and extensive piles of breakdown and then, under Aemos's instruction, manoeuvred us down into the throat of an almost vertical chimney. This chimney – a pitch in mining terms – was a natural formation, possibly an ancient lava tube. Slowly revolving laterally, we hovered down into it. Flowstone caked the walls like swathes of creamy drapery, and quilled bushes of volcanic glass sprouted from outcrops. The space was small, even for a compact pod like the one we had borrowed. Occasionally, Medea would nudge or clip an out thrust of quills and the glass fragments would fall silently, glittering, into the pit below.

About two kilometres down, the pitch opened out into a complex series of curving tubes, sub-caves and sumps. It was like moving out of an oesophagus into the complex chambers of an intestinal tract. The flowstone started to show more colour: steely blues with milky calcite swirls, mottled reds glinting with oolites. Flinty black druse and other clastic litter covered the smoothed folds of the ancient floor.

Medea pointed my attention to the small scanner box mounted below the main petrographic assayer. The little screen was awash with an almost indecipherable graphic of ghosting strata layers and reflecting lithic densities. Three bright yellow cursors showed clearly in the upper quadrant.

'They're coming after us,' she said.

'They seem to know where we are right enough. How are they tracking us?'

'Same way we're getting such a clean return on their position.'

'Are the locators on this crate that powerful?'

Medea shook her head. 'They're fine for the immediate locality, but they've got nowhere near enough gain to penetrate the rock.'

'So?'

'I think all these prospector pods have high-powered beacons, probably built into flight recorders. They'd need them for routine search and recovery.'

'I'll take a look.'

I swung out of my seat and moved back down the pod, stooping, and using the overhead hand-rails to support myself. Aemos was still at work. He'd fired up the pod's mineralogicae auspex, and was running a complex cross-search for the spectographic fingerprints that appeared on the Adeptus Mechanicus transmissions. He didn't even have the scrolls open any more: the complex subtleties of the colour bars had long since been committed to memory.

Every few minutes, he consulted the main chart and called a course-correction to Medea.

At the rear of the pod, between racks holding old rebreathers with perishing rubber visor-seals, I found a small crawl space into the engine bay.

I stuck my head and shoulders inside, and shone around with a lamp-pack I'd unbuckled from one of the rebreather sets. A simple process of elimination directed me to a fat metal drum clamped to the underside of the gravitic assembly and the housing for the kinaesthetic gyroscopes. Adeptus Mechanicus purity seals secured its cover.

I slid back out into the cabin, selected a medium plasma cutter from the tool web, and went back in. The hot blue tongue of the cutter sliced the drum's cover off and fused its pulsing innards.

Back in the cockpit, I saw we were now travelling down a

wide cavern that was barbed with oily dripstones and varnished with incandescent blooms of moon-milk and angel's hair.

'They look lost already,' Medea remarked, nodding at the scanner box. She was right. The yellow cursors were moving with nothing like the same confidence. They were milling, trying to reacquire our signal.

We travelled for two more hours, through small flask-chambers gleaming with cavepearls, across vast low seas of chert and lapilli, between massive stalactites that bit tunnels in two like the incisors of prediluvial monsters. Domepits and sumps sheened with brackish alkaline water and the smoke snaking from nests of fumaroles betrayed the fact that there was now a rudimentary atmosphere: methane, sulphur, radon and pockets of carbon monoxide. Venting cases from Cinchare's active heart and the gas-products of chemical and gravito-chemical reactions built and collected here, far below ground, leaking only slowly up to the airless surface. Hull temperature was increasing. We were now about fifteen kilometres down, and beginning to feel the effects of the asthenosphere.

'Hey!' said Medea suddenly.

She slowed the pod, and swung it around, traversing the lights. We were in a gypnate chamber where the chert-covered floor was scalloped by several gours formed by water eons before. Several side spurs led away into tight pinches or were revealed on the chart to pinch out no further than twenty metres in.

'What did you see?' I asked.

'There!'

The spot-lamps framed a black shape that I thought for a

moment was just a jagged pile of boulders and stalagmite bosses. But Medea roved us in.

It was a prospecting pod, similar to ours, but bearing the crest of Ortog Promethium. It had been crushed and split like an old can, the stanchions of its cabin protruding from the metal hull like ribs.

'Hell...' Medea murmured.

'Mining's a dangerous job,' I said.

'That's recent,' Aemos said, appearing at our shoulders. 'Look at the tephra.'

'The what?' asked Medea.

'It's a generic term for clastic materials. The dust and shale bed the wreck's lying on. Move the lamp round. There. The tephra's yellowish-white gypnate all around, but it's scorched and fused under the wreck. Mineral smoke from the fumaroles we passed just now vent back down here and cover everything with oxidised dust. I'd wager if it's been there more than a month, the powder would have overlaid the scorching... and coated the wreck.

'Pop the hatch,' I said.

The subterranean atmosphere seemed scalding hot and I began to sweat freely the moment I jumped down from the sill. I could hear nothing except my breath rasping inside my rebreather mask. I trudged round to the front of the hovering pod into the cones of its lights, and saw Aemos and Medea in the lit cockpit, both hidden behind rebreather masks of their own.

I waved once and crunched off over the dusty sill, my bootcaps catching the occasional geode which scattered and flashed in the light.

There was no mistaking the blast holes in the wreck's hull.

Sustained fire from a multi-laser had split the pod wide open. I shone my hand torch in through the rents and saw a blackened cabin space, burned out.

The three crew members were still in there, at their posts, reduced to grimacing mummies by the acidic air, and by the hundreds of glistening white worms that writhed and burrowed as my light hit them. It figured that with its hot, wet, gaseous interior, Cinchare was a far from dead world.

More troglobyte things scurried and squirmed around my feet. Long-legged metallic beetles and inflated, jelly-like molluscs, all drawn to this unexpected source of rich nutrients.

Something moved beside me and slammed into my left hip. I fell hard against the broken hull, cursing that I hadn't been wearing my motion tracker. It came in again, and this time I felt a sharp pain in my left thigh. I kicked out with a mask-muffled curse.

It was about the size of a large dog, but longer and lower, moving on lean hind limbs. Its skin was nearly silver, and its eye-less head was just a vast set of jaws filled with hundreds of transparent fangs. All around the maw, long sensory bristles and tendrils twitched and rippled.

It lunged again, its thin, stiff tail raised high as a counterbalance. This thing, I guessed, was top of the food chain in Cinchare's lightless cavities. Too big to force its way inside the wreck to get at the corpses, it had been lurking outside, feeding on the carrion worms and molluscs that had congregated on the crash.

With a twist of its head, it had a good grip on my left ankle. I could feel the tips of its teeth biting through the heavy leather of my boot.

I managed to tug my shotgun from the scabbard on my back and shoot it through the torso at point black range. Viscous tissues and filmy flesh scattered in all directions and the thing flopped over. By the time I had prised its jaws off my boot with my knife, the carrion-eaters had begun to swarm over it and feed.

We moved off again, down a gour-lined spur and into a cavern breathtakingly encrusted with glass-silk and billions of cavepearls.

'There's been fighting down here,' I told Aemos and Medea, raising my voice to be heard over the re-cycling cabin air as we pumped the last of the coarse Cinchare gas-soup out.

'Who's fighting who?'

I shrugged, and sat back to tug one of the predator's broken fangs out of my boot leather.

'Well,' said Aemos, 'you'll be interested to know that the cavern with the wreck in it matched one of the spectroscope traces from the Mechanicus transmissions exactly.'

'How long ago?'

'About two weeks.'

'So... Bure could have been the one who did the shooting.'

'Bure... or whoever's sending transmissions back to the annex.'

'But why would he take out a prospector pod?' I wondered aloud.

'Rather depends on what the prospector pod was trying to do to him,' said Medea.

Aemos raised his tufty eyebrows. 'Most perturbatory.'

Another three hours, another two kilometres down. It was damn hot, and the air outside was thick with venting steams and gases. Fumaroles, some large, some in scabby clusters, belched black smoke into the caves, riddling some areas like honeycomb. Several caverns and domepits were home to luminous acidic lakes, where the geothermals steadily simmered the water. Gorges and the occasional pitch showed flares of red light from lava rivers and asthenospheric cauldrons of molten rock.

We no longer had to rely on the lamps. The cave systems were lit by streams of glowing magma, flaming lakes of pitch and promethium and thick, sticky curtains and rafts of bio-luminescent fungi that thrived in the heated ducts. The pod's air-scrubbers were no longer able to remove the scent of sulphur from the cabin air, and the cooling system was inadequate. We were all sweating, and so were the interior walls of the cabin. Condensation dribbled down the bare metal of the hull's inner skin.

'Dead stop, please,' Aemos said.

Medea cut the thrusters and let us coast slowly over a seething lake of lava that radiated a glare of almost neon brilliance from beneath its blackened crust.

Aemos checked the chart against the spectroscope readings that the mineralogicae assayer was sending to a small repeater screen in the cabin bay.

'This is it. The source location for the last transmission.'

'You're sure?' I asked.

He gave me a withering look. 'Of course.'

'Swing us around, slowly,' I told Medea. We craned to look out of the pod's front ports, playing the lamp array up and down to make sense of the stark shadows in the cavern walls.

'What are those? Tube tunnels?'

'Auspex says they pinch out in a few hundred metres. God-Emperor, it looks pretty primordial out there!' Medea wiped a trickle of perspiration out of her eyes.

'What's that the lights are catching there?'

Aemos peered to where I was pointing. 'Amygdules,' he said. 'Cavities filled with quartzes or other secondary minerals.'

'Okay,' said Medea, unscrewing the stopper of a water-flask. 'Seeing as how you know everything... what's that?'

'Well, I... most perturbatory.'

It was a hole, perfectly circular, thirty metres in diameter, cut into the far rock wall.

'Edge closer,' I said. 'That's not a natural formation. It's too... precise.'

'What the hell made a hole like that?' Medea murmured, nudging us in.

'An industrial mining drill could–'

'This far down? This far from any mine infrastructure?' I cut Aemos short. 'Look at this place. Only sealed units like this pod can function at this depth.'

'Barely,' Medea commented, ominously. She was keeping a weather eye on the hull-integrity read-out. Amber runes were twitching on and off.

'It's deep,' I said. I looked at the display for the forward scanners. 'Goes off as far as we can read and maintains its shape and size.'

'But it's cut sheer through igneous rock... through the side of a forty kilometre square batholyth! That's solid anthragate!' There was a note of confusion in Aemos's frail old voice.

'I've got tremors,' said Medea suddenly. The needles on the rolling seismograph had been scratching away for a good hour or more, such was the background instability this deep down. But now they were skritching back and forth wildly.

'There's a pattern to them,' Aemos said. 'That's not tectonic. That's too regular... mechanical almost.'

I paused for a moment, considering our options. 'Take us into the shaft,' I said.

Medea looked at me, as if she was hoping she'd misheard me.

'Let's go.'

The cut shaft was so perfectly circular it was scary. As we sped down, we could see that the inner surface of the tube was fused like flowstone, with radiating patterns of furrows scooped into it.

'This was plasma-cut,' said Aemos. 'And whatever cut it, left an impression of its motivators in the rock before it cooled and hardened.'

The tube snaked occasionally, whilst maintaining its form. The bends were long and slow, but Medea took them cautiously. The seismograph was still jiggling.

I took out a holoquill and wrote a phrase down on the back of a chart-pad.

'Can you convert this into simple machine code?' I asked Aemos.

He looked at it. 'Hmmm... "Vade elquum alatoratha semptus"... you have a good memory.'

'Can you do it?'

'Of course.'

'What is that?' asked Medea. 'Some kind of sorcery?'

'No,' I smiled as Aemos got to work. 'It's like Glossia. A private language, one that hasn't been used in a long time.'

'There,' said Aemos.

'Punch it into the voxponder and set it to continuous repeat,' I said.

'I hope this works,' said Aemos. 'I hope you're right.'

'So do I,' I said.

Instrumentation pinged. 'We're approaching the end of the bore-hole!' Medea called. 'Another kilometre, and then we're out into a huge cavity!'

'Get that signal going!' I urged my elderly savant.

We were on it almost before we were ready. A massive tube of machined metal, thirty metres in diameter and seventy long, with a huge plasma cutting-screw at the front end and rows of claw-like impellers that cycled down its flanks like the active teeth of a gigantic chainsword. It had cut its way from the tube and was grumbling across the clastic silt of the chamber floor away from us, pumping thick clouds of vapour-ised rock and steam out behind it.

'Emperor protect me! It's huge!' Aemos exclaimed.

'What in the name of the Golden Throne is that?' gasped Medea.

'Slow down! Slow down!' I cried, but she was already brak-ing us back behind the leviathan.

'Oh crap!' said Medea. Recessed hardpoints along the giant's flank had swivelled and opened, and multi-laser batteries had popped out to target us.

I grabbed the vox-set's hand-mic.

'Vade elquum alatoratha semptus!' I yelled into the mic. 'Vade elquum alatoratha semptus!'

The weapons – which could have obliterated us in a single salvo – did not fire. They remained trained on us, however. Then heavy shutter doors on the back end of the enormous machine opened slowly, revealing a small, well-lit hangar space.

'We won't get another invitation!' I told Medea.

With a worried shrug, she steered us inside.

* * *

I led the pair of them out of the pod into the arched dock-bay. The shutters had locked shut behind us, and pungent sulphurous fog pooled around our feet as it was pulled out of the bay by chugging air processors.

The bay was of a grand design, fluted with brass fittings and brushed steel. There was a brand new prospector pod, painted oxide-red, in the docking cradle next to the one that had received our singed specimen. Three other cradles, new and black with oil, lay vacant. All the light came from phosphorescent gas filaments in caged glass hoods around the room, and the effect was a flickering, lambent glow. An iron screwstair with padded leather rails led up to a boarding platform above us.

'That's a good sign,' I said. The bas-relief roundel of the Adeptus Mechanicus was visible above the inner door lock on the platform.

We all started as long servitor arms whirred out from compartments in the walls. In a second, six were trained on us: two with auspex sensors, sniffing us, and four with weapon mounts.

'I suggest we don't move,' I whispered.

The inner lock clanked and opened. A hooded figure in long orange robes seemed to hover out onto the platform. It grasped the handrail with both hands and looked down at us.

'Vade smeritus valsara esm,' it growled.

'Vade elquum alatoratha semptus,' I replied. 'Valsarum esoque quonda tasabae.'

The figure pulled back its hood, revealing a mechanical skull finished in oil-smudged chrome. Its lens-like eyes glowed bright green. Fat black cables under its jaw pulsed and the vox-caster screwed into its throat spoke.

'Gregor... Uber... It's been a long time.'

NINETEEN

Walking through stone
Lith
The Inmate

'This is Medea Betancore,' I said, once Geard Bure's strong mechanical grip had finally released my hand.

'Miss Betancore,' Bure bowed slightly. 'The Adeptus Mechanicus of Mars, holy servants of the God-Machine, bids you take sanctuary in this, its worthy device.'

I was about to hiss at Medea and explain that she had been greeted formally, but, typically, she needed no prompting.

She deftly made the machine-fist salute of the Mechanicus and bowed in return. 'May your devices and desires serve the God-Emperor until time runs its course, magos.'

Bure chuckled – an eerie sound when it came from a prosthetic voice-box – and turned his unblinking green eye-lights to me.

'You've trained this one well, Eisenhorn.'

'I–'

'He has, magos,' said Medea quickly. 'But that response I learned from study of the Divine Primer.'

'You've read the Primer?' Bure asked.

'It was basic study in air school on my home world,' she replied.

'Medea has a... considerable aptitude for machines,' Aemos said. 'She is our pilot.'

'Indeed...' Bure walked around her and uninhibitedly caressed her body with his metal fingers. Medea temporarily humoured him.

'She is machine-wise, yet she has no augmentation?' Bure questioned me.

Medea stripped off her gloves and showed him the intricate circuits inlaid into her hands.

'I beg to differ, magos.'

He took her hands in his and gazed in hungry wonder. Drool-like ropes of clear lubricant oil trickled out between his chrome teeth like spittle.

'A Glavian! Your enhancements are... so... beautiful...'

'Thank you, sir.'

'You've never thought to permit any other augmentation? Limbs? Organs? It is quite liberating.'

'I... get by with what I've got,' smiled Medea.

'I'm sure you do,' Bure said, suddenly swinging round to face me. 'Welcome to my translithopede, Eisenhorn. You too, Aemos, my old friend. I must admit I can't conceive what brought you here. Is it the Lith? Has the Inquisition sent you to deal with the Lith?'

News of my disgrace clearly hadn't reached him, and for that, I was thankful.

'No, magos,' I said. 'A stranger quirk has brought us here.'

'Has it? How odd. When I first detected your signal – in dear Hapshant's old private code – I couldn't believe it. I nearly shot you down.'

'I took a chance,' I said.

'Well, that chance has led you to me and I'm glad. Come, this way.'

His skeletal silver hands ushered us towards the door lock.

Bure had no lower limbs. He floated on anti-gravity suspensors, the hem of his orange robe hanging a few centimetres above the plated deck. We fell in step behind him and walked the length of a long, oval companionway lined with brass bulkheads and more gas filament lamps.

'This burrowing machine is a wonder,' Aemos said.

'All machines are wonders,' Bure replied. 'This is a necessity, the primary tool of my work here on Cinchare. There were, of course, a number of lesser prototypes before I made the necessary refinements. This translithopede was engineered from my designs by the Adeptus fabricatory on Rysa and shipped here for my use three standard years ago. With it, I can go where I please in this rock, and unlock the secret lore of Cinchare's metals.'

Magos Bure had been a metallurgy specialist for two hundred years, his knowledge and discoveries almost worshipped by his brethren in the tech-priesthood. Before that, he had been a fabricator-architect in the Titan forges of Triplex Phall. To my certain knowledge, he was almost seven hundred years old. Hapshant had occasionally hinted that Bure was far older than that.

Not a shred of the magos's flesh remained. The vestigial organic parts of Geard Bure the human being – his brain and neural systems – were sealed inside his gleaming mechanoid body. I had never learned if this was a matter of design or necessity. Perhaps, as is the case with so many, disease or grievous injury had forced such extreme augmentation upon him. Or perhaps, like Tobias Maxilla, he had deliberately discarded the weakness of flesh in favour of machine perfection. Knowing the technophiliac disposition of the Mechanicus priesthood, the latter seemed more likely to me.

My late mentor, Inquisitor Hapshant, had encountered Magos Bure in the early part of his career, during the celebrated mission to secure the STC Lectionary from the ashrams of Ullidor the Techsmith. As I have remarked, the Inquisition – indeed most august bodies of the Imperium – find dealings with the Cult Mechanicus problematic at best. Its power is legendary and its insularity notorious. The cult is a closed order which guards the secrets of its technologies jealously. But Bure and Hapshant developed a beneficial working relationship based on mutual esteem. On several occasions, Bure's specialist wisdom assisted my mentor in the prosecution of important cases, and on several others, the favour was returned.

That is why, a century before, I entrusted an item of particular importance to his expert custody.

The control chamber of the wheezing translithopede was a split-level chapel where a raised command podium, like a giant brass pulpit, overlooked two semi-circular rows of busy control stations. The riveted iron walls were painted matt red and etched with the various aspects and runes of the Machine God. The forward wall was shrouded in long drapes of red velvet.

Six oil-streaked servitors worked at the chattering control stations, their hands and faces plugged directly into the systems via thick, metal-sleeved cables or striped flexes marked with purity seals and parchment labels. Glass valves and dials flickered and glowed, and the air was heady with the scent of oils and sacred unguents.

Two relatively human tech-adepts in orange robes were overseeing the activity. One was linked directly into the vehicle's mind-impulse unit through a trio of neural plugs, and he murmured aloud the rites and scriptures of the Adeptus. The other turned and bowed as we came onto the podium.

He had a wire-mesh speaker where his mouth should have been. When he spoke, it was in a pulse of binary machine code.

Bure responded in kind, and for a few moments they exchanged tight bursts of condensed data. Then Bure floated over to a brass lectern built into the podium's rail and opened his robe. Two probing neural cables extended from his chrome sternum like sucker-worms hunting for prey and connected swiftly with the polished sockets on the lectern.

Now Bure was also conjoined with the translithopede's mind-impulse unit.

'We make good speed,' he told us. He twitched, and the velvet drapes at the far end of the chamber drew aside automatically, revealing a large holographic display. Secondary images overlaid the main one, showing three-dimensional charts and power/speed graphics. The main image was just a dark rushing blur laced with crackles of blue energy.

This was the view directly ahead of us, the rock disintegrating before the awesome destructive force of the plasma cutting-screw. We were travelling straight through solid rock.

'Perhaps it's time we discussed what's going on here,' I said.

'We hunt,' sad Bure.

'You've been hunting for a long time, magos,' said Aemos. 'Eleven weeks now. What are you hunting for?'

'And why is Cinchare minehead derelict?' I added.

Bure paused as he selected the correct electrograft memory. He was almost lost in the euphoria of mind-impulse union.

'Ninety-two days ago, as far as I am able to reason it, an

independent prospector called Farluke, working under license for Ortog Promethium, returned from a long tour of assay rock side and presented his masters with a unique discovery. They tried to keep it secret for a while, hoping, I believe, to exploit it for their own ends. That error in judgment was costly. By the time they realised their mistake, and shared their data with the Adeptus, it was already too late.'

'What had Farluke found?' asked Aemos.

'It is called the Lith. I have not seen it, but I have studied extracts recovered from the bodies of tainted men.'

'Recovered?' breathed Medea, unnerved.

'Posthumously. The Lith is a hyper-dense geode of approximately seven hundred tonnes. It is, as I understand it, a perfect decahedron four metres in diameter. Its mineral composition is exotic and inexplicable. And it is alive.'

'What? Magos! Alive?'

'Sentient, at least. It is infused with the wretched filth of Chaos. How long it has lain undiscovered in the depths of this world, I do not know. Perhaps it has always been here, or perhaps it was hidden in pre-Imperial times by unknown hands to keep it safe... or to dispose of it. Perhaps, indeed, it is the reason Cinchare has broken from the order of its stellar dance and drifted, rogue and wild, through the stars. I had hoped, initially, to find it and recover it. Its composition alone promised a wealth of precious knowledge. But now I hunt for it... simply to destroy it.'

'It has corrupted this world, hasn't it?' I said.

'Completely. As soon as it came in contact with men, it began to twist their minds with its malign power. It subjugated them. The Ortog work teams sent down to examine it were the first. What is, to all intents and purposes, a cult sprang up spontaneously. Each initiate had a splinter of rock shaved from the Lith buried beneath his skin in a simple, brutal ritual.'

'We've seen the marks.'

'Disorder spread through Cinchare minehead as the cult grew. The Lith couldn't be moved, but splinters were brought up and used to infect more and more of the workforce. Once tainted, the workers began to disappear, setting off on pilgrimages down into the mines to make worship to the Lith. Many never made it. Most have simply vanished. I've tried to follow their tracks, sometimes encountering hostile cult elements bent on protecting their deity. But Farluke's original data is unreliable. I cannot find the Lith's true location. I fear it is just a matter of time before the cult manages to extend its reach beyond Cinchare. Or...'

'Or?'

'Or they will complete some arcane task instructed by the Lith and awaken its power in full... or allow it to connect with its own kind.'

We considered this grim possibility for a moment. Aemos quietly pulled up an entry on the screen of his data-slate, unclipped the device from his wrist, and handed it to Bure.

'Does this help?' he asked.

Bure stared at the slate. His green eyebeams dilated into hard, bright points.

'How in the name of the Warpsmiths did you–'

'What is it?' I asked, stepped forward.

'The location of the Lith,' said Aemos proudly.

'How did you get this?' Bure cried, his vox undercut by excited binary chatter.

'The cult needs to know where it is. The reference was clearly marked in the charts I downloaded from the security office. I didn't realise its significance until now.'

'You just downloaded this?' Bure said.

'I believe they thought they had no reason to hide it. It wasn't encrypted.'

Bure threw back his chrome skull and laughed, a screeching, mocking cackle. 'Eleven weeks! Eleven weeks I have scoured and searched and fought my way through the bowels of this rock, hunting for clues, and the answer was up there all the time! In plain sight!'

He turned to Aemos and laid a steel hand on the savant's stooped shoulder. 'I have always admired your wisdom, Uber, and recognised why Hapshant valued you so... but now I realise that great wisdom comes from simplicity.'

'It was luck, nothing more.'

'It was bold simplicity, savant! A moment of direct, clear thought that quite dwarfs my labours down here.'

'You're too kind...' Aemos mumbled.

'Kind? No, I am not kind.' Bure's eye-lights swelled and flashed. 'I will cut my way to the heart of the Lith, and then its spawn will see how unkind my soul can be.'

Two hours later, after Bure's servitors had taken us to a sparely furnished cabin and provided us with flavourless, odourless nutrient broth and hard cakes of fibre bread, we were summoned back to the control chamber.

Outside, a small war was going on.

I had already sensed we had decelerated from tunnelling speed by the reduced throb of the impellers, and now I saw why. We had bored out of the rock into a towering vault lit by spurting pools of magma and flaming spouts of gas. On the chamber's holographic screen, I could see distorted, jarring images of the cavern outside. Silent laser fire was jabbing at us.

Bure was linked to the podium's lectern.

'We've found their nest,' he said. 'They resist.'

As I watched, two soot-stained prospector pods powered in towards us, firing small arms from their open hatches.

Bure nodded to one of his tech-adepts, and the shriek of multi-laser blasts rang through the hull. One pod exploded in a ball of light, the other tumbled away, shredded and burning.

I realised there were men on the ground too: miners in armoured worksuits scurrying forward and firing at the translithopede.

Bure increased magnification, and we saw that some of them carried pallets of mining charges, hoping to get close enough to breach our hull.

'Stalkers,' Bure said. It was evidently an order. There was a clank and a thud as hatches opened somewhere below us, and then new shapes began to move into view on the screen.

They were combat servitors. Heavyweight and burnished silver, they strode on powerful, backward-jointed legs, puffing black exhaust from their upthrust smoke stacks. Cannons in their upper limbs jerked with pneumatic recoil as they systematically targeted and cut down the cultists.

'Stalker 453, left and target,' Bure murmured. They were all slaved to his direct control.

One of the stalkers retrained its weapons and gunned four more cultists down. The charge-load they had been hefting exploded in a bright flash that blacked out the display for a second. When the holo-image returned, the stalker was already pacing on after new targets.

'Stalker 130 and Stalker 252, fan right. Opposition in cover behind that stalactite mass.'

'Oh great Emperor,' said Aemos suddenly. 'Some of them are unarmoured.'

It was true. A good many of the men assaulting us wore no

shielding or environment armour. Their clothes were charred to black rags and their flesh was blistered and raw. Some force was keeping them active and functioning in this great infernal depth where no living thing should have been able to survive unprotected. Not the pressure, the extreme heat, not even the toxic, corrosive atmosphere was stopping them. The taint of the Lith had transmuted them into denizens of this underworld.

The wave of stalkers strode forward inexorably, and the translithopede followed them slowly, its impelling lines of adamantium cilia dragging it across the cavern rock. The multi-lasers fired again, destroying another vehicle – a large ore transporter that had been attempting to crash itself into our machine.

The mighty plasma screw churned again and ruptured apart a curtain of massive dripstones. Drizzles of dust obscured our picture for a few seconds.

When it cleared, we saw the true horror, and realised the ultimate, blasphemous fate of Cinchare minehead's population.

The blasphemy was huge, a writhing mound of baked, raw flesh and cooking bone. One by one, the tainted workers of Cinchare, even Bure's corrupted brethren from the Adeptus, had come down here to willingly contribute their organic matter to this mass.

As the translithopede came into view, it rose up, forming a great, rearing worm of red ooze and blackened meat fifty metres high. A ghastly mouth, big enough to swallow a prospecting pod, gaped wide in its cresting head, and it belched a vast ball of flaming gases at us.

The translithopede shook, warning hooters sounded, and the picture was lost. One control station below exploded, throwing its servitor to the deck. Smoke billowed through the chamber.

'Such power,' Bure marvelled, emotionless. The whole machine lurched again, more violently, and we stumbled, despite the internal gravity systems and inertial dampers.

The screen image restored, jumping, for a brief moment, enough to see that the blasphemy seemed to be coiling itself around us. The hull creaked and protested. Minor explosions rang out from lower decks. Plated seams bulged and several rivets flew out like bullets.

'Bure!'

'I will break it! I will cast it out!'

'Bure! In the name of the Emperor!'

He wasn't listening. All his efforts were focussed on the mind-impulse link driving the translithopede, on the orchestration of his stalkers as they rallied to counter-attack the monstrosity. His confidence in the supremacy of the Machine over all things was blinding him to the very real possibility that the formidable Cult Mechanicus had just met its match.

I turned to Medea and Aemos.

'Come on!' I cried.

We were halfway down the translithopede's main companionway, heading towards the rear of the great machine, when a still more violent impact shook it. Without warning, the inertial dampers failed and we tumbled as the burrower was rolled onto its side. The glass mantles of the gas lights smashed, and weak flame sputtered and danced along the walls. There was a further series of terrific impacts.

We got to our feet, now forced to use the curving wall as a floor. The pulsing shriek of the multi-lasers was by then a constant noise outside.

Red warning lights were flashing in the arched dock-bay. Our pod had been torn from its cradle by the latest impact and lay crumpled on its side, reclining against part of the roof arching. But the oxide-red pod was still safely locked in place.

Medea and I jumped down from the dock's inner hatch onto the ceiling, but Aemos called after us.

'I can't make that jump,' he protested. I knew he was right.

'Then seal the hatch and get back to help Bure!'

'The Emperor protect you both!' he shouted as the hatch closed.

Power cables that had once lain on the deck now dangled like ropes. Grabbing one each, we began to rappel up towards the pod in its cradle. We were halfway there when the world seemed to shudder again and the translithopede righted itself violently. Medea and I went sprawling, loose debris skittering all around us. I had barely enough time to dive and heave Medea aside before our own wrecked pod came crunching back down the wall, slamming sideways onto the floor.

Another lurch and the deck tipped the other way, out of true by about twenty degrees. The unanchored pod began sliding across the deck towards us.

'Get in!' Medea yelled. 'Get in!' She had the side hatch of the red pod open and dragged me halfway inside. A moment later, and the translithopede rocked back thirty degrees in the other direction.

The loose pod immediately squealed back across the deck and crashed into the wall bulkheads. I was dangling by my hands from the open hatch.

'Crap! Get in! Get the hell in!' Medea wailed, fighting to hold on to me. I grunted and swung my legs up so that my toe caps caught the door sill. With a further effort, I managed to pull myself up, and Medea slammed the hatch.

There was still more shaking and rocking. We clambered in to the seats of the pilot station in the low cockpit, and strapped on the harnesses. Medea was keying the pod's drive ignition when the translithopede inverted again and left us hanging in our seats by the safety straps. The pod was now locked in its cradle on the roof.

'This'll be fun,' Medea laughed aggressively. She had sent a remote command to open the dock-bay's shutter doors. Then she powered the pod's engines to full thrust and disengaged the cradle lock.

For a dizzying second, we dropped, upside down, like a rock. Then she hit the thrusters and looped us. We missed the dock-bay roof by a handsbreadth and flew out through the opening shutters even as the entire translithopede rolled over again.

The blasphemy had wrapped itself around Bure's great sub-terranean burrower with constricting coils. It thrashed and shook the machine, and I could clearly see the armoured hull beginning to buckle and crumple. There were smoking sockets where some of the multi-laser batteries had been ripped away. The stalkers were converging on the wrestling giants, strafing the Chaos worm with furious barrages. The remains of several lay crushed where the translithopede had rolled on them.

Medea banked us around, trying to speed-familiarise herself with the control layout.

'What do we do? I take it you've got a plan?'

I shook my head. 'I'm working on it.' Bure's pod was unarmed – I know this because I checked feverishly the moment we were airborne – and there was nothing that might be turned into an offensive weapon apart from a mining laser under the chin of the cockpit. A mining laser with fierce cutting power and a range of about five metres.

'Take us deeper into the cavern,' I said, consulting the display on the pod's geologicae auspex.

'Away from the fight?'

'We can't engage that thing... so we find the Lith instead. And that return has got to be it.'

There was a pulsing cursor on the screen: big, unmistakable.

Cultists on the cave floor blasted at us as we zipped over them and headed off down the long, volcanic cavern. Spumes of pyroclastic wrath detonated up from the lava lakes and threatened to envelop us.

Then we saw the Lith.

It had been buried in a plug of obsidian jutting from the cavern wall, but serious excavation work had been done to reveal it.

Heavy mining pods and anti-grav drill platforms sat on the ash slopes below it, and the ground was covered in fragments of obsidian.

It was, as Bure had described, a perfect decahedron four metres across, dark green and glassy like water-ice. It glowed with an inner light. Even from a distance, it felt malevolent. I sensed an unnerving tickling at the edge of my psychic range. Medea looked sick.

'I don't want to get any closer,' she said suddenly.

'We have to.'

'And do what?'

I wondered if we could cut it with the mining laser. I wondered indeed if that would do any good. I doubted we would make much of dent in it even if we power-dived the pod at it.

Yet, the cultists had shaved splinters from it to promulgate their evil. It was vulnerable... unless it had somehow allowed the splinters to be removed.

We certainly couldn't move it.

I could feel it now, whispering in my head. There were no words, just a murmur that chilled my spine. Insidious, slow... slow like eons of geological time, slow like a glacier or a tectonic plate. It spoke softly and without haste, gently unfolding its seductive message. It had no need to rush. It had all the time in the galaxy...

The pod yawed wildly. I started and looked around. Medea had lost partial control because she had turned to be violently sick over the side of her seat. Her skin was blanched and she was panting and sweating.

'I... I can't...' she gasped. 'Don't make me go any closer...'

She had reached her limits. I leaned over and put my hand against the side of her head. 'Sleep,' I said softly, using the will.

She sank into merciful unconsciousness.

I took the controls.

I was no flier like Medea Betancore, and for a moment, I thought I was going to dive us nose-first into the lake of bubbling magma as I fumbled with the actuators.

But Medea's late father had trained me well enough. I swooped low over the pool of molten rock, creating a shockwave vortex in the brimstone, and banked around a massive anthragate column that rose up into the jagged roof. There was just a last wide lake of fire between me and the ash shore where the Lith was exposed.

It was whispering again, but I shook it off. I had trained my mind hard to resist the ministrations of Chaos and its psychic wiles. This was how it turned weak minds. This was how it had polluted and tainted the population of Cinchare minehead. The whispering... the formless, shapeless words of power that drew mankind into the embrace of the warp...

An idea struck me. I like to think it was an idea born out of the same pure simplicity that Bure had celebrated in Aemos. A perfect, simple possibility.

I shrugged from my mind my fears for the life of Aemos and the magos. The blasphemy might already have torn the translithopede apart in the cavern far behind me. If they were not beyond hope, then this was the best I could do for them.

Risking a free hand, I reached sideways and activated the pod's voxponder, setting it to record. Then, concentrating on my steering once more, I began to speak, clearly and loudly, dredging words up from my memory. Long ago, on my birth planet, DeKere's World, as a child, standing in the long hall of the primary scholam with the other pupils, reciting together...

A collision warning blared, and I veered to the left in time to glimpse a prospecting pod that filled my cockpit windows for a moment before racing past.

Two bright yellow cursors had appeared on my auspex display. The beacon locators of prospecting pods, like the ones that had chased us into the mine system.

The one that had tried to collide with me was turning wide over the lava lake. The other was coming in on an intercept course. I swung round to face it and then gulled away at the last minute. The pass was close, close enough to see the Ortog Promethium symbols on its flank. Close enough to see Enforcer Kaleil's face through the cockpit ports.

The first pod, an Imperial Allied symbol just visible through the heat-flaked paint, came in and blocked my route to the shore and the Lith. Its driver, unidentifiable, had smashed the window lights out and was firing a lascarbine out from the cockpit. Despite our comparative speeds, I felt several shots land home, banging into the pod's fuselage. I steered away, trying desperately not to break my recitation as I concentrated on the air duel.

I began to chant the words like a mantra.

As I turned from the Imperial Allied pod, I met Kaleil's vessel head on. I rolled hard to evade, but still we clipped and the whole pod shook. Warning lights lit up across the control console. I had thruster damage and reduced manoeuvring ability. The lava lake flashed up to consume me but I climbed hard, away from the ash beach.

All the while, my recitation continued.

The Imperial Allied pod was on my tail, streaking the air with las-shots. We whipped hard around the anthragate pillar, but I couldn't shake him. I tried to think what Medea would do. What Midas would have done. For a moment, my words faltered as I planned and executed my frantic response.

The pod was right behind me. I braked hard, and managed to spin the anti-grav machine in place using the attitude jets, dropping my nose as if curtseying to my attacker. And I ignited my mining laser.

The Imperial Allied pod was far too close to my rear to effect a turn or a brake. I think he was trying for a collision, but I was just too high for him. He ran in under my hull at full thrust, so close he tore the lighting array and the auspex antennae off the underside of my pod.

He also ran straight through the incandescent spear of my mining laser. It sliced the Imperial Allied pod lengthways and sent the disintegrating halves spinning away into the white hot magma below.

My pod was half crippled now from the pair of impacts. I continued my recitation, hoping the brief lapse wouldn't matter.

With its antennae gone, the auspex was blind, but I could see Kaleil anyway. He was gunning across the lake straight for me.

I hovered in place. There was a time for action and, as I had already gambled, a time for words. I switched off the vox-ponder and keyed the open channel.

'Kaleil?'

'Horn!'

'Not Horn... Inquisitor Eisenhorn.'

Silence. He was two hundred metres and closing at a speed that would wipe us both out.

I pressed the vox-mic close to my mouth and used every shred of my will.

'Don't,' I said.

The Ortog Promethium pod veered and then dived straight down into the lava lake. A halo of fire broke up from the slow, undulating splash it made in the liquid rock.

I limped my pod over to the ash beach and set down about twenty metres short of the Lith. Medea moaned in her sleep. I dreaded the dreams that might be boiling through her subconscious.

'Get out of my head!' I snarled aloud at the Lith's persistent whispering.

It took me a moment to rewind the voxponder recording and set it to a continuous loop. Then I diverted its signal into the echo-sounding sonar system that the pod used to supplement its auspex in assay and location work. I twiddled the dials until the powerful sonar was aimed directly at the malevolent decahedron.

Conveyed in fierce ultrasonic pulses, my recording blasted the Lith. The Emperor's Prayer of Abrogation Against the Warp, learned by rote by every good schoolchild of the Imperium. An innocent blessing against the darkness, a banishment of Chaos. I doubted it had ever been used so actively. I doubted my scholam tutors had ever conceived of such a use for that simple, sing-song declaration.

'Words,' I murmured. 'Your corrupt whispers against my words of power. How do you like that?'

I pushed the sonar gain to maximum. In terms of sonics alone, the pulses would have stunned a man to unconsciousness and snapped his bones.

For a good minute or more, I feared it was having no effect.

Then the whispering ceased. It became a subsonic moaning of rage and anguish, and finally agony.

TWENTY

Interview with the Damned
Bure, warsmith
Orbul Infanta

'Let me make sure I understand you, Eisenhorn,' said the dis-embodied voice of Pontius Glaw, slowly and contemptuously. 'You think I'm going to help you?'

I cleared my throat. 'Yes.'

Pontius laughed. Synapse leads connected to the gold circuits of his engram sphere flashed in series. 'I didn't think a man of such studied dullness and sobriety as you would have the ability to surprise me, Eisenhorn. My mistake.'

'You *will* help me,' I said, quietly but emphatically.

I brushed frost from the grilled steps and sat down facing his casket. It was claw-footed, rectangular, compact and filled with complex technology designed for one purpose: the support and operation of the engram sphere, a rough-cut nugget the size of a clenched fist in which resided the intellect – and perhaps the soul – of one of the most notorious heretics in the Imperium.

Pontius Glaw, dead in body for nigh on three hundred years, had been in his physical life one of the more unwholesome products of the powerful Glaw dynasty. That family line, part of the high nobility of Gudrun, had whelped many heretics in its time, the last of whom had been instrumental in the affair of the Necroteuch. Supported by the considerable efforts of Imperial Navy Security, I had all but crushed their poisonous lineage, and in the process had captured the engram sphere of Pontius Glaw. His family and their minions had attempted to sacrifice thousands of innocents in order to restore him to physicality. That, too, I had denied.

Once the affair had ended, I had been left with this casket full of heretical spite. In terms of technology alone, it was a wonder, and there was no telling what secrets the Pontius might have in it. So instead of destroying it, I had passed it into the safekeeping of Magos Geard Bure. Bure, I knew, would have the time and skill enough to unlock its technical marvels at least. And he was trustworthy.

But from time to time in that past hundred years, I had questioned the validity of that decision. In all honesty, I should have surrendered the Pontius to the Ordo Hereticus for examination and disposal. The fact that I hadn't some-times played on my conscience, for it suggested deceit and unwholesome subterfuge on my part. In the light of events in the past year, I found myself fighting back the notion that perhaps my accusers were right. Had it been the act of an unsound man to secret away such a radical entity?

Aemos had consoled my spirits, reminding me that the casket utilised mind-impulse technology undoubtedly stolen from the Cult Mechanicus. There was, he said, no question that such a device should be in the custody of the Adeptus priesthood.

'Go on then,' Pontius said. 'Make your case. Why would I help you?'

'I require specialist information that I'm certain you have. Certain lore.'

'You are an inquisitor, Eisenhorn. All the resources of the Imperium are at your disposal. Am I to understand that, well, that your scope has become somewhat limited?'

I was damned if I was going to tell this monster of the straits I was in. And even though he was right in a way, there was no Imperial archive I knew of that could answer my questions.

'What I need might be regarded as... proscribed knowledge.'

'Ahhhhh...'

'What? "Ah" what?'

Even without features or body language to read, Pontius seemed insufferably pleased with himself. 'So you've finally reached that place. How wonderful.'

'What place?' I felt uncomfortable. I had been planning this interview for months, and now control was slipping entirely to Glaw.

'The place where you cross the line.'

'I hav-'

'All inquisitors cross the line eventually.'

'I tell y-'

'All of them. It's an occupational hazard.'

'Listen to me, you worthless-'

'Methinks Inquisitor Eisenhorn protests too much. The line, Gregor. The line! The line between order and chaos, between right and wrong, between mankind and man-unkind. I know it, because I've crossed it. Willingly, of course. Gladly. Skipping and dancing and delighting. For the likes of you, it is a more painful process.'

I rose. 'I don't think this conversation is going anywhere, Glaw. I'm leaving.'

'So soon?'

'Perhaps I'll be back in another century or two.'

'It was on Quenthus Eight, in the spring of 019.M41.'

I paused at the cell hatchway. 'What was?'

'The moment I crossed the line. Would you like to hear about it?'

I was rattled, but I returned to my seat on the steps. I knew what he was doing. Imprisoned in his casket without touch or smell or taste, without any sensory stimulation, Pontius Glaw craved company and conversation. I had learned that much during my long interrogations of him aboard the *Essene* ten decades before during the voyage to the remote system KCX-1288. Now he was simply feeding me morsels to make me stay and talk to him.

However, in a hundred years of captivity, he had never come close to revealing such intimate details of his personal history.

'019.M41. A busy year. The buttress worlds of the far eastern rim were resisting a holy waaagh! by the greenskins, and two of the High Lords of Terra had been assassinated in as many months by disaffected Imperial families. There was talk of civil war. The sub-sector's trader markets had crashed. Trade was bad. What a year. Saint Drache was martyred on Korynth. Billions starved in the Beznos famine.'

'I have access to history texts, Pontius,' I said dryly.

'I was on Quenthus VIII, buying fighters for my pit-games. They're a good breed, the Quenthi, long in the hams and quite belligerent. I was, perhaps, twenty-five. I forget exactly. I was in my prime, beautiful.'

There was a long silence while he considered this reflection. Light-sparks pulsed along his wires.

'One of the pit-marshals at the amphitheatre I was visiting advised me to see a fighter who had been bought in from the very edges of the Ultima Segmentum. A great, tanned fellow from a feral world called Borea. His name was Aaa, which meant, in his tongue, "sword-cuts-meat-for-women-prizes". Isn't that lovely? If I had ever sired a son, a human one, I mean, I would have called him Aaa. Aaa Glaw. Quite a ring to it, eh?'

'I'm still on the verge of leaving, Glaw.'

The voice from the casket chuckled. 'This Aaa was a piece of work. His teeth were filed into points and his fingertips had been bound and treated with traditional unguents since his birth so that they had grown into claws. Claws, Eisenhorn! Fused, calcified hooks of keratin and callouses. I once saw him rip through chainmail with them. Anyway, he was a true find. They kept him shackled permanently. The pit-marshal told me that he'd torn a fellow prisoner's arm off during transit, and scalped a careless stadium guard. With his teeth.'

'Charming.'

'I bought him, of course. I think he liked me. He had no real language, naturally, and his table manners! He slept in his own soil and rutted like a canine.'

'No wonder he liked you.'

The frost crackled around the casket. 'Cruel boy. I am a cultured man. Ha. I *was* a cultured man. Now I am an erudite and dangerous box. But don't forget my learning and upbringing, Eisenhorn. You'd be amazed how easy it is for a well-raised and schooled son of the Imperium to slide across that line I mentioned.'

'Go on. I'm sure you had a point to make.'

'Aaa served me well. I won several fortunes on his pit-fights. I won't pretend we ever became friends... one doesn't become friends with a favourite carnodon now, does one? And one certainly never makes friends with a commodity. But we built an understanding over the years. I would visit him in his cell, unguarded, and he never touched me. He would halt out old myths of his home world, Borea. Vicious tales of barbary and murder. But I'm getting ahead of myself. The moment, the moment was there on Quenthus, in the amphitheatre, under the spring sun. The pit-marshal showed me Aaa, and tempted me to purchase him. Aaa looked at me, and I think he saw a kindred soul... which is probably why we bonded once he was mine. In his simple, broken speech, he implored me to buy him, telling me graphically what sport I would have of him. And to seal the deal, he offered me his torc.'

'His torc?'

'That's right. The slaves were allowed to keep certain familiar items provided they weren't potential weapons. Aaa wore a golden torc around his neck, the mark of his tribe. It was the most valuable thing he possessed. Actually, it was the only thing he possessed. But no matter... he offered it to me in return for me becoming his master. I took it, and, as I said, I bought him.'

'And that was the line?' I sat back, unimpressed.

'Wait, wait... later, later that same day, I examined the torc. It was inlaid with astonishing technology. Borea might have been a beast-world by then, but millennia back, it had clearly been an advanced outpost of mankind. It had fallen into a feral dark age because Chaos had touched it, and that torc was a relic of the decline. Its forbidden, forgotten technology focussed the stuff of the Darkness into the wearer's mind. No wonder Borea, where every adult male wore one, was a savage waste. I was intrigued. I put the torc on.'

'You put it on?'

'I was young and reckless, what can I say? I put it on. Within

a few hours, the tendrils of the warp had suffused my recep-
tive mind. And do you know what?'

'What?'

'It was wonderful! Liberating! I was alive to the real universe
at last! I had crossed the line, and it was bliss. Suddenly I saw
everything as it actually was, not as the Ministorum and the
rot-hearted Emperor wanted to see it. Engulfing eternity! The
fragility of the human race! The glories of the warp! The fleeting
treasure of flesh! The incomparable sweetness of death! All of it!'

'And you ceased to be Pontius Glaw, the seventh son of a
respectable Imperial House, and became Pontius Glaw, the
sadistic idolator and abomination?'

'A boy's got to have a hobby.'

'Thank you for sharing this with me, Pontius. It has been
revealing.'

'I'm just getting started...'

'Goodbye.'

'Eisenhorn! Eisenhorn, wait! Please! I–'

The cell hatches clanged shut after me.

I waited two days before I returned to see him. He was sullen and moody this time.

I entered the cell and set down the tray I was carrying.

'Don't expect me to talk to you,' he said.

'Why?'

'I opened my soul to you the other day and you... walked
out.'

'I'm back now.'

'Yes, you are. Closer to that line yet?'

'You tell me.' I leaned over and poured myself a large glass
of amasec from the decanter on the tray. I rocked the glass a
few times and then took a deep sip.

'Amasec.'

'Yes.'

'Vintage?'

'Fifty year old Gathalamor vintage, aged in burwood barrels.'

'Is it... good?'

'No.'

'No?'

'It is perfect.'

The casket sighed.

'You were saying. About that line?' I asked.

'I... I was saying I was most annoyed with you,' Pontius returned, stubbornly.

'Oh.' I casually slid a lho-stick from the paste-board tub I had backhanded from Tasaera Ungish's stateroom. I lit it and took a deep drag, exhaling the smoke towards the infernal casket. Nayl had injected me with powerful anti-intoxicants and counter-opiate drugs just half an hour earlier, but I sat back and openly seemed to relish the smoke.

'Is that a lho-stick?'

'Yes, Pontius.'

'Hmmm...'

'You were saying?'

'Is it good?'

'You were saying?'

'I... I've told you of my slip. My crossing of the line. What else do you want of me?'

'The rest. You think I've crossed the line too, don't you?'

'Yes. It's in your bearing. You seem like a man who has understood the wider significance of the warp.'

'Why is that?'

'I told you it happens to all inquisitors sooner or later. I can imagine you as a young man, stiff and puritanical, in the scholam. It must have seemed so simple to you back then. The light and the dark.'

'Not so obvious these days.'

'Of course not. Because the warp is in everything. It is there even in the most ordered things you do. Life would be brittle and flavourless without it.'

'Like your life is now?' I suggested, and took another sip.

'Damn you!'

'According to you, I'm already damned.'

'Everyone is damned. Mankind is damned. The whole human species. Chaos and death are the only real truths of reality. To believe otherwise is ignorance. And the Inquisition... so proud and dutiful and full of its own importance, so certain that it is fighting against Chaos... is the most ignorant thing of all. Your daily work brings you closer and closer to the warp, increases your understanding of orderless powers. Gradually, without noticing it, even the most puritanical and rod-stiff inquisitor becomes seduced.'

'I don't agree.'

Pontius's mood seemed to have brightened now we were engaged in debate again. 'The first step is the knowledge. An inquisitor must understand the basic traits of Chaos in order to fight it. In a few years, he knows more about the warp than most untutored cultists. Then the second step: the moment he breaks the rules and allows some aspect of Chaos to survive or remain so that he can study it and learn from it. I wouldn't even bother trying to deny that one, Eisenhorn. I'm right here, aren't I?'

'You are. But understanding is essential. Even a puritan will tell you that! Without it, the Inquisition's struggle is hopeless.'

'Don't get me started on that,' he chuckled. Then paused. 'Describe the taste of that amasec in your mouth. The quality, the scent.'

'Why?'

'It is three hundred years since I have tasted anything. Smelt anything. Touched anything.'

I had feared my gambit with the amasec and the opiate too obvious, but it had drawn him in. 'It feels like oil on my tongue, soft, body-heat. The aroma precedes the taste, like peat and pepper, spiced. The taste is a burn in the throat that lights a fire behind my heart.'

The casket made a long, mournful sound of tantalised regret.

'The third step?' I prompted.

'The third step... the third step is the line itself. When the inquisitor becomes a radical. When he chooses to use Chaos against Chaos. When he employs the agencies of the warp. When he asks the heretical for help.'

'I see.'

'I'm sure you do. So... are you going to ask me to help you?'

'Yes. Will you give me that help?'

'It depends,' the casket murmured. 'What's in it for me?'

I stubbed out the lho-stick. 'Given what you've just said, I assume your reward would be the satisfaction of seeing me cross that line and damn myself.'

'Ha ha! Very clever! I'm enjoying that part already. What else?'

I turned the glass in my hand, swilling the amber spirit around. 'Magos Bure is a talented man. A master of machinery. Though I would never release you from imprisonment, I could perhaps ask him for a favour.'

'A favour?' Pontius echoed with trembling anticipation.

'A body for you. A servitor chassis. The ability to walk, reach,

hold, see. Perhaps even the finessing extras of sense actuators: rudimentary touch, smell, taste. That would be child's
play for him.'

'Gods of the warp!' he whispered.

'Well?'

'Ask. Ask me. Ask me, Eisenhorn.'

'Let us talk for a while... on the subject of daemonhosts.'

'Do you know what you're doing?' Fischig said to me.

'Of course,' I said. We had taken over the security office in
Cinchare minehead as our base. Bequin and Aemos had set
the place straight and got it running properly, and Medea,
Inshabel, Nayl and Fischig patrolled the area regularly. Bure
had provided servitor-stalkers as additional guards, and a
vox-uplink had been established with the orbiting *Essene* to
forewarn us of any arriving space traffic.

It was late one afternoon in the third week of our visit to the
mining rock. I had just returned from my daily visit to Glaw's
cell in the Mechanicus annex and I stood with Fischig by the
windows of the office, looking down into the plaza.

'Really sure?' he pressed.

'I seem to remember him asking us the same thing when we
sprang him from the Carnificina,' said Bequin, coming over
to join us. 'Thanks to Osma and his ridiculous witch-hunt,
we've been forced into a corner. If we can come through this
successfully, we will redeem ourselves.'

Fischig snorted. 'I just don't like it. Not dealing with that
butcher. Not promising him anything. I feel like we've crossed
the line–'

'What?' I asked sharply. I had told them only the very spar-
est details of my conversations.

'I said I felt like we'd crossed the line. What's the matter?'

I shook my head. 'Nothing. How are the rest of the preparations going?'

I sensed Fischig wanted to have it out, but it was really too late for that. I deflected him with the subject change.

'Your magos friend is working. Nayl took him the blade yesterday and showed him your notes and diagrams,' he said.

'The communiqués are all written, encrypted and sealed, ready to be sent,' said Bequin. 'Just give the word, and Ungish will transmit them. And I have the declaration here.' She handed me a data-slate.

It was a carta extremis formally declaring Quixos Heretic and Extremis Diabolus, naming his crimes and given in my authority. It was dated the twentieth day of the tenth month, 340.M41. There was no location of issue, but Aemos had made certain all the other particulars were phrased precisely according to High Imperial Law and the statutes of the Inquisition.

'Good. We'll send that in a few days.' I knew that the moment the carta was published, my agenda would be known. The scheme I was embarking on might take years to complete, and all that time I would be hunted. I really didn't want to stir things up so soon.

'How much longer will we be here?' Bequin asked.

'I don't know. Another week? A month? Longer? It depends on how forthcoming Glaw decides to be.'

'But you've got things from him already?' asked Fischig.

'Yes.' Not too much, I hoped.

I walked through the empty streets of the minehead for an hour or two that evening to clear my mind. I knew damn well that I was choosing a dangerous path. I had to remain focussed or I risked losing control.

Once I'd got the upper hand with Glaw, I'd been playing with him during those early conversations. His talk of the line, his three-step description of the corruption that awaited an imprudent inquisitor... that was nothing new to me. I had indulged him so that he might feel superior and smug. Any inquisitor worth the rosette knew the perils and temptations that surrounded him.

But it didn't stop his words from cutting me. Every puritanical Commodus Voke was a potential Quixos. When Glaw said that the line was often crossed without it being recognised, he was right. I'd met enough radicals to know that.

I had always, always prided myself on my puritanical stance, moderate and Amalathian though it might be. I deplored the radical heresies. That's why I wanted Quixos.

But I worried still. I considered what I was doing to be risky, of course, but also pragmatic given my difficult situation. To destroy Quixos, I had to get past his daemonhosts, and that required power, knowledge and expertise. And I could no longer turn to the Holy Inquisition for support. But had I crossed the line? Was I becoming guilty of sins that could so easily escalate into radical abomination? Was I so obsessed with bringing Quixos to justice that I was abandoning my own principles?

I was sure I was not. I knew what I was doing, and I was taking every precaution I could to manage the more dangerous elements I was employing. I was pure and true, even now.

And if I wasn't, how could I tell?

I climbed an observation mast that rose above the mine settlement and lingered for a while in the caged glass blister at the top, looking out across the town's skyline to the ragged blue landscape of Cinchare, and the gliding stars beyond it. Shoals of meteors burned bright lines down the sky.

There was a noise on the stairs behind me. It was Nayl.

He put away his sidearm. 'It's you,' he said, joining me in the blister. 'I was patrolling and I saw the tower door open. Everything all right?'

I nodded. 'You fight dirty sometimes, don't you, Harlon?'

He looked at me quizzically and scratched his shaved scalp. 'Not sure I know what you mean, boss,' he said.

'All those years, bounty hunting... and I've seen you fight, remember? Sometimes you have to break the rules to win.'

'I suppose so. When all's said and done, you use whatever works. I'm not proud of some of my more... ruthless moments. But they're necessary. I've always been of the opinion that fairplay is overrated. The bastard trying to skin you won't be playing fair, that's for sure. You do what you have to do.'

'The end justifies the means?'

He raised his eyebrows and laughed. 'Now that's different. That kind of thinking gets a man into trouble. There are some means that no end will ever justify. But fighting dirty, occasionally, is no bad thing. Neither's breaking the rules. Provided you remember one thing.'

'Which is?'

'You have to understand the rules in the first place if you're going to break them.'

Apart from my daily visits to Glaw in the annex, I also spent time with Bure. He was labouring in his workshops, assisted by servitors and his tech-adepts. He had thrown himself totally into the tasks I had set him. Though he never said, I think he saw it as returning with interest my efforts in the battle with the Lith.

He had also listened without alarm when Aemos and I had related the history of the recent past. It felt like a confession. I explained the carta out against me, my rogue status. He had accepted my innocence without question. As he put it, 'Hapshant wouldn't have raised a radical. It's the rest of the galaxy that's wrong.'

That was good enough for him. I was quietly moved.

One day in the sixth week of our increasingly prolonged stay, he called me to his workshop.

It lay beneath the main chapel of the annex and was two storeys deep, a veritable smithy alive with engineering machines and apparatus the purposes of which baffled me. Steam-presses hammered and banged, and screw-guns wailed. Quite apart from my own projects, there was much work to do repairing the annex and the translithopede. I walked down through the swathes of steam and found Bure supervising two servitors who were machining symbols into a two-metre long pole of composite steel.

'Eisenhorn,' he said, raising his bright green eye-lights to look at me.

'How goes the work?'

'I feel like a warsmith, back in the foundries of the forge worlds, when I was flesh. The specifications you have asked for are difficult, but not impossible. I enjoy a challenge.'

I took several sheets of paper from my coat pocket and handed them to him. 'More notes, taken during my last interview with Glaw. I've underlined the key remarks. Here, he suggests electrum for the cap piece.'

'I was going to use iron, or an iron alloy. Electrum. That makes sense.' He took my notes over to a raised planning table that was littered with scrolls, holoquills, measuring tools and data-slates. Pages of notes that I had already provided him with were piled up, along with the psychometrically captured images Ungish had drawn from my mind of the Cadian pylons, Cherubael, Prophaniti, and the ornaments he had worn.

'I'm also pondering the lodestone for the cap. I considered pyraline or one of the other tele-empathic crystallines like epidotrichite, but I doubt any of them would have the durability for your purposes. Certainly not for more than one or two uses. I also thought of tabular zanthroclase.'

'What's that?'

'A silicate we use in mind-impulse devices. But I'm not convinced. I have a few other possibilities in mind.' It was a measure of the trust Bure showed me that he felt he could mention such Cult Mechanicus secrets so freely. I felt honoured.

'Here's the haft,' he said, showing me to the etching bench where the two servitors were machining the decoration of the long pole.

'Steel?'

'Superficially. There's a titanium core surrounded by an adamantium sleeve under the steel jacket. The titanium is drilled with channels that carry the conductive lapidorontium wires.'

'It looks perfect,' I said.

'It is perfect. Virtually perfect. It's machined to within a nanometre of your measurements. Let me show you the sword.'

I followed him to a workbench at the far end of the smithy where the sword lay on a rest under a dust sheet.

'What do you think?' he asked, drawing the cloth back.

Barbarisater was as beautiful as I remembered it. I admired the fresh pentagrammatic wards that had been etched in the blade since I had last seen it, ten on each side.

'It is a remarkable artifact. I was almost unwilling to make the alterations you requested. As it was, I wore out eight adamantium drill bits on this side alone. The hardened steel skin of the blade around the solid core has been folded and beaten nine hundred times. It is beyond anything we can manufacture today.'

I would owe Clan Esw Sweydyr for this weapon, as I already owed them for Arianrhod's life. I should have returned it to their care, for it was part of their clan legacy and *usuril*, or 'living story'. It was mine to safeguard, not to take, and certainly not to deface this way. But face to face with Prophaniti at Kasr Gesh I had learned two things. Indeed, that monstrous thing had told them to me. Pentagrammatic wards worked against daemonhosts, but they were no stronger than the weapon that bore them.

To my certain knowledge, there were few finer, stronger blades in human space. I would make my peace and apologies to the clans of Carthae in time, fates permitting.

I went to touch it, but Bure stopped me. 'It is still resting. We must respect its anima. In a few days, you can take it. Train with it well. You must know it intimately before you use it in combat.'

He accompanied me to the door of the forge. 'Both weapons must be blessed and consecrated before use. I cannot do that, though I can ceremonially dedicate their manufacture to the Machine God.'

'I have already planned for their consecration,' I said. 'But I would welcome your ceremony. When I go against Quixos, I can think of no more potent a patron god to be looking down over me than your Machine Lord.'

'We will be leaving in a few days,' I told him.

The casket was silent for a while. 'I will miss our conversations, Eisenhorn.'

'Nevertheless, I have to go.'

'You think you're ready?'

'I think this part of my readiness is complete. Is there anything else you can tell me?'

'I have been wondering that. I cannot think of anything. Except...'

'Except what?'

The lights around the engram sphere twinkled. 'Except this. Apart from everything you've learned from me, the secrets, the lore, the mysteries, you must know that going after this foe is... dangerous.'

I laughed involuntarily. 'I think I've worked that much out already, Pontius!'

'No, you don't know what I mean. You have the determination, I know, the ambition, I know that too – you have the knowledge, we assume, and the weapons too, we hope – but unless your mind is prepared, you will perish. Instantly, and no ward or staff or blade or rune will save you.'

'You sound like... you care if I lose.'

'Do I? Then consider this, Gregor Eisenhorn. You may deem me a monster beneath contempt, but if I do care, what does that say about me? Or you?'

'Goodbye, Pontius Glaw,' I said, and closed the cell hatches behind me for the last time.

I will record this thought now, because I feel I must. For all that Pontius Glaw was... and for all that came later, I cannot shake my bond to him, though I try. There, in the cell on Cinchare, and a century before in the dim hold of the *Essene*, we had spoken together for hundreds of hours. I had no doubt that he was an unforgivably evil thing, and that he would have killed me in a second during those times had he been

allowed the chance. But he was a being of extraordinary intellect, wit and learning. Admirable in so many, strange ways.
But for that torc, Aaa's torc, back on that spring day on Quenthus, his life may have been different.

And if it had been different, and we had met, we would have
been the greatest of friends.

We had stayed on Cinchare for three months. Too long, in
my opinion, but there had been no way to speed the preparatory work.

We celebrated Candlemas in the little chapel of the Ministorum off the plaza, lighting candles to welcome the new
Imperial year, and lighting others to commemorate the town's
dead. Aemos and Bequin read the lessons, for all of the Ecclesiarchs were amongst the remembered dead. Bure and his
tech-adepts worshipped with us, and he hovered to the choir
rail under the great statue of the God-Emperor to lead us in
the devotional prayers.

I was fretful and edgy. Partly because I was anxious to get
underway now, but also because of the lore in my head, the
mysteries to which Glaw had introduced me. So much, so
much of it dark. I knew I was a changed man, and that change
was permanent.

But I considered that a year before – just a year, though
it felt much, much longer – I had been a helpless prisoner
in the bleak Carnificina, and Candlemas had passed me by
before I had realised it.

I was not that man any more either, and that change had
been nothing to do with Pontius Glaw's whispered secrets.
For all the darkness swilling in my head, it was better to be
here, strong and ready, fortified, in the company of friends
and allies.

There was no choirmaster to play the organ, so Medea had brought her father's Glavian lyre, and played the Holy Triumph of the Golden Throne so that we could all sing.

That night, we feasted in the refectory of the Cult Mechanicus to honour the start of 341.M41. Maxilla, who remained on duty aboard the *Essene*, sent a banquet to us on a shuttle, along with servitors to wait upon us. One of them reported that a vast storm of meteors had swarmed across the sky at the stroke of midnight, lighting the night side of Cinchare with their fires. Nayl growled that this was a bad omen, but Inshabel insisted it was a good one.

I suppose it rather depended which part of the vast spread of the Imperium you came from.

The others spent the next two days packing up and making ready to leave, but Aemos and I attended the dedication ceremony in the cimeliarch of the Adeptus Mechanicus annex.

Machine Cult servitors chanted in a modulated binary code and beat upon kettledrums. Magos Bure was clad in his orange robes with a white stole over his shoulders.

He blessed the weapons he had made in turn, taking one then the other from the two tech-adepts who stood in attendance.

Barbarisater, the pentagrammatic power sword, lifted to the light that speared down from the eyes of the Machine God's altar. Then the runestaff, Bure's masterpiece.

He had fashioned a cap-piece for the rune-etched steel pole out of electrum in the form of a sun-flare corona. In the centre of it was a human skull, marked with the thirteenth sign of castigation. The skull was the lodestone, carved by Bure himself into a perfect facsimile of my own skull, as measured by radiative scans. He had tried and rejected over twenty

different tele-empathic crystals before finding one he trusted
would be up to the task.

'It's beautiful,' I said, taking it from him. 'What crystal did
you use in the end?'

'What else?' he said. 'I carved that copy of your skull from
the Lith itself.'

He came to see us off, to the docking barn where the gun-cutter
had sat for so long. Nayl and Fischig were carrying the last
things aboard. We had broken astropathic silence at last the
night before, and informed Imperial Allied, Ortog Promethium, the Adeptus Mechanicus and the Imperial authorities
of the fate that had befallen Cinchare minehead. We would be
long gone before any of them arrived to begin recovery work.

Bure said farewell to Aemos, who shuffled away to the cutter.

'There's nothing adequate I can say,' I told the magos.

'Nor I to you, Eisenhorn. What of... the inmate?'

'I'd like you to do what I asked you. Give him mobility at
least. But nothing more. He must remain a prisoner, now
and always.'

'Very well. I expect to hear all about your victory, Eisenhorn. I will be waiting.'

'May the Holy Machine God and the Emperor himself protect your systems, Geard.'

'Thank you,' he said. Then he added something that
quite took me aback, given his total belief and reliance on
technology.

'Good luck.'

I walked to the cutter. He watched me for a moment, then
disappeared, closing the inner hatch after him.

That was the last time I ever saw him.

* * *

From Cinchare, the *Essene* ran back, fast and impatient, into the great territories of the Segmentum Obscurus, a three-month voyage that we broke twice.

At Ymshalus, we stopped to transmit the prepared communiqués, all twenty of them. Inshabel and Fischig left us too at that point; Inshabel to secure passage to Elvara Cardinal to begin his work there, and Fischig for the long haul back to Cadia. It would be months, if not years, before we saw them again. That was a sorrowful farewell.

At Palobara, that crossroads on the border, busy with trading vessels and obscura caravans guarded by mercenary gunships, we stopped and transmitted the carta declaration. There was no going back now. Here, I parted company with Bequin, Nayl and Aemos, all of whom were heading back to the Helican sub-sector by a variety of means. Bequin's goal was Messina, and Aemos, with Nayl to watch over him, was bound for Gudrun. Another hard parting.

The *Essene* continued on for Orbul Infanta. This was now a lonely, waiting time. Each night, the remains of my company gathered in Maxilla's dining room and ate together: myself, Medea, Maxilla and Ungish. Ungish was no company, and even Medea and Maxilla had lost their sparkle. They missed the others, and I think they knew how dark and tough the time ahead would be.

I spent my days reading in the cabin library of the cutter, or playing regicide with Medea. I practised with Barbarisater in the hold spaces, slowly mastering the tricks of its weight and balance. I would never match a Carthae-born master, but I had always been good enough with a sword. Barbarisater was an extraordinary piece. I came to know it and it came to know me. Within a week, it was responding to my will, channelling it so hard that the rune marks glowed with manifesting psychic power. It had a will of its own, and once it was in my hands, ready, swinging, it was difficult to stop it pulling and slicing where it pleased. It hungered for blood... or if not blood, then at least the joy of battle. On two separate occasions, Medea came into the hold to see if I was bored enough for another round of regicide, and I had to restrain the steel from lunging at her.

Its sheer length was a problem: I had never used a blade so long. I worried that I would do my own extremities harm. But practice gave me the gift of it: long-armed, flowing moves, sweeping strokes, a tight field of severing. Within a fortnight, I had mastered the knack of spinning it over in my hand, my open palm and the pommel circling around each other like the discs of a gyroscope. I was proud of that move. I think Barbarisater taught it to me.

I worked with the rune staff too, to get used to its feel and balance. Though my aim was appalling, especially over distances further than three or four metres, I became able to channel my will, through my hands, into its haft and then project it from the crystal skull in the form of electrical bolts that dented deck plating.

There was, of course, no way I could test it for its primary use.

We reached the shrine world of Orbul Infanta at the end of the twelfth week. I had three tasks to perform here, and the first was the consecration of the sword and the staff.

With Ungish and Medea, I travelled down to the surface in one of the *Essene*'s unremarkable little launches rather than the gun-cutter. We went to Ezropolis, one of Orbul Infanta's ten thousand shrine cities, in the baking heartland of the western continent.

Orbul Infanta is an Ecclesiarchy governed world, famously blessed with a myriad shrines, each one dedicated to a different Imperial saint, and each one the heart of a city state. The Ecclesiarch chose it as a shrine world because it lay on a direct line between Terra and Avignor. The most popular and thriving shrine cities lay on the coast of the eastern continent, and billions of the faithful flocked to them each year. Ezropolis was far away from such bustle.

Saint Ezra, who had been martyred in 670.M40, was the patron saint of undertaking and setting forth, which I took to be appropriate. His city was a shimmering growth of steel, glass and stone rising from the sun-cooked plains of the mid-west. According to the guide slates, all water was pumped in from the western coast along vast pipelines two thousand kilometres long.

We made planetfall at Ezra Plain, the principal landing facility, and joined the queues of pilgrims climbing the looping stairs into the citadel. Most were clad in yellow, the saint's colour, or had tags or swathes of yellow cloth adorning them. All carried lit candles or oil lamps, despite the unforgiving light. Ezra had promised to light a flame in the darkness to mark all those setting forth, and consequently his hagial colour was flame yellow.

We had done the necessary research. I wore a suit of black linen with a sash of yellow silk and carried a burning votive candle. Ungish was draped in a pale yellow robe the colour of the sun at dawn, and clutched a plaster figurine of the saint. Medea wore a dark red bodyglove under a tabard on which was sewn a yellow aquila symbol. She pushed the small grav-cart on which Barbarisater and the staff lay, wrapped in yellow velvet. It was common for pilgrims to cart their worldly goods to the shrine of Ezra, in order that they might be blessed before any kind of undertaking or setting forth could properly get underway. We blended easily with the teaming lines of sweating, anxious devotees.

At the top of the stairs, we entered the blessed cool of the streets, where the shadows of the buildings fell across us. It was nearly midday, and Ecclesiarchy choirs were singing from the platforms that topped the high, slender towers. Bells were chiming, and yellow sapfinches were being released by the thousand from basket cages in the three city squares. The thrumming ochre clouds of birds swirled up above us, around us, singing in bewilderment. They were brought in each day, a million at a time, from gene-farm aviaries on the coast, where they were bred in industrial quantities. They were not native to this part of Orbul Infanta, and would perish within hours of release into the parched desert. It was reported that the plains around Ezropolis were ankle-deep with the residue of their white bones and bright feathers.

But still, they were the symbol of undertaking and setting forth, and so they were set loose by the million to certain death every midday. There is a terrible irony to this which I have often thought of bringing to the attention of the Ecclesiarchy.

We went to the Cathedral of Saint Ezra Outlooking, a significant temple on the western side of the city. On every eave and wall top we passed, sapfinches perched and twittered with what seemed to me to be indignation.

The cathedral itself was admittedly splendid, a Low Gothic minster raised in the last thirty years and paid for by subscriptions generated by the city fathers and priesthood. Every visitor who entered the city walls was obliged to deposit two high denomination coins into the take boxes at either side of the head of the approach stairs. A yellow robed adept of the priesthood was there to see it was done. The box on the left was the collection for the maintenance and construction of the city temples. The one on the right was the sapfinch fund.

We went inside Saint Ezra Outlooking, into the cool of the marble nave where the faithful were bent in prayer and the hard sunlight made coloured patterns on everything as it slanted through the huge, stained glass windows. The cool air was sweetened by the smoke of sweetwood burners, and livened by the jaunty singing from the cantoria.

I left Medea and Ungish in the arched doorway beside a tomb on which lay the graven image of a Space Marine of the Raven Guard Chapter, his hands arranged so as to indicate which holy crusade he had perished in.

I found the provost of the cathedral, and explained to him what I wanted. He looked at me blankly, fidgeting with his yellow robes, but I soon made him understand by depositing six large coins into his alms chest, and another two into his hand.

He ushered me into a baptism chancel, and I beckoned my colleagues to follow. Once all of us were inside, he drew shut the curtains and opened his breviary. As he began the rite, Medea unwrapped the devices and laid them on the edge of the benitier. The provost mumbled on and, keeping his eyes fixed on the open book so he wouldn't lose his place, raised and unscrewed a flask of chrism with which he anointed both the staff and the sword.

'In blessing and consecrating these items, I worship the Emperor who is my god, and charge those who bring these items forth that they do so without taint of concupiscence. Do you make that pledge?'

I realised he was looking at me. I raised my head from the

kneeling bow I had adopted. Concupiscence. A desire for the
forbidden. Did I dare make that vow, knowing what I knew?

'Well?'

'I am without taint, puritus,' I replied.

He nodded and continued with the consecration.

The first part of my business was done. We went out into the
courtyard in front of the cathedral.

'Take these back to the launch and stow them safely,' I told
Medea, indicating the swaddled weapons on the cart.

'What's concupiscence?' she asked.

'Don't worry about it,' I said.

'Did you just lie, Gregor?'

'Shut up and go on with you.'

Medea wheeled the cart away through the pilgrim crowds.

'She's a sharp girl, heretic,' Ungish whispered.

'Actually, you can shut up too,' I said.

'I damn well won't,' she snapped. 'This is it.'

'What? "It"?'

'In my dreams, I saw you foreswear in front of an Imperial
altar. I saw it happen, and my death followed.'

I watched the sapfinches spiralling in the air above the yard.

'Deja vu.'

'I know deja vu from a dream,' said Ungish sourly. 'I know
deja vu from my backside.'

'The God-Emperor watches over us,' I reassured her.

'Yes, I know he does,' she said. 'I just think he doesn't like
what he sees.'

We waited until evening in the yard, buying hot loaves, wraps
of diced salad and treacly black caffeine from street vendors.
Ungish didn't eat much. Long shadows fell across the yard in

the late afternoon light. I voxed Medea. She was safely back
aboard the launch, waiting for us.

I was waiting to complete the second of my tasks. This
was the appointed day, and the appointed hour was fast
approaching. This would be the first test of the twenty communiqués I had sent out. One had been to Inquisitor Gladus,
a man I admired, and had worked with effectively thirty years
before during the P'glao Conspiracy. Orbul Infanta was within
his canon. I had written to him, laying out my case and asking for his support. Asking him to meet me here, at this place,
at this hour.

It was, like all the messages, a matter of trust. I had only
written to men or women I felt were beyond reproach, and
who, no matter what they thought of me, might do me the
grace of meeting with me to discuss the matter of Quixos. If
they rejected me or my intent, that was fine. I didn't expect
any of them to turn me in or attempt to capture me.

We waited. I was impatient, edgy... edgy still with the dark
mysteries Pontius Glaw had planted in my head. I hadn't slept
well in four months. My temper was short.

I expected Gladus to come, or at least send some kind of
message. He might be detained or delayed, or caught up in
his own noble business. But I didn't think he'd ignore me. I
searched the evening crowds for some trace of his long-haired,
bearded form, his grey robes, his barb-capped staff.

'He's not coming,' said Ungish.

'Oh, give it a rest.'

'Please, inquisitor, I want to go. My dream...'

'Why don't you trust me, Ungish? I will protect you,' I said.
I opened my black linen coat so she could see the laspistol
holstered under my left arm.

'Why?' she fretted. 'Because you're playing with fire. You've crossed the line.'

I balked. 'Why did you say that?' I asked, hearing Pontius's words loud in my head.

'Because you have, damn you! Heretic! Bloody heretic!'

'Stop it!'

She got to her feet from the courtyard bench unsteadily. Pilgrims were turning to look at the sound of her outburst.

'Heretic!'

'Stop it, Tasaera! Sit down! No one's going to hurt you!'

'Says you, heretic! You've damned us all with your ways! And I'm the one who's going to pay! I saw it in my dream... this place, this hour... your lie at the altar, the circling birds...'

'I didn't lie,' I said, tugging her back down onto the bench.

'He's coming,' she whispered.

'Who? Gladus?'

She shook her head. 'Not Gladus. He's never coming. None of them are coming. They've all read your pretty, begging letters and erased them. You're a heretic and they won't begin to deal with you.'

'I know the people I've written to, Ungish. None of them would dismiss me so.'

She looked round into my face, her head-cage hissing as it adjusted. Her eyes were full of tears.

'I'm so afraid, Eisenhorn. He's coming.'

'Who is?'

'The hunter. That's all my dream showed. A hunter, blank and invisible.'

'You worry too much. Come with me.'

We went back into the Cathedral of Saint Ezra Outlooking, and took seats in the front of the ranks of carrels. Evening sunlight raked sidelong through the windows. The statue of the saint, raised behind the rood screen, looked majestic.

'Better now?' I asked.

'Yes,' she snivelled.

I kept glancing around, hoping that Gladus would appear. Straggles of pilgrims were arriving for the evening devotion.

Maybe he wasn't coming. Maybe Ungish was right. Maybe I was more of a pariah than I imagined, even to old friends and colleagues.

Maybe Gladus had read my humble communiqué and discarded it with a curse. Maybe he had sent it to the Arbites... or the Ecclesiarchy... or the Inquisition's Officio of Internal Prosecution.

'Two more minutes,' I assured her. 'Then we'll go.' It was long past the hour I had asked Gladus to meet me.

I looked about again. Pilgrims were by now flooding into the cathedral through the main doors.

There was a gap in the flow, a space where a man should have been. It was quite noticeable, with the pilgrims jostling around it but never entering it.

My eyes widened. In the gap was a glint of energy, like a side-flash from a mirror shield.

'Ungish,' I hissed, reaching for my weapon.

Bolt rounds came screaming down the nave towards me from the gap. Pilgrims shrieked in panic and fled in all directions.

'The hunter!' Ungish wailed. 'Blank and invisible!'

He was that. With his mirror shield activated, he was just a heat-haze blur, marked only by the bright flare of his weapon.

Mass panic had seized the cathedral. Pilgrims were trampling other pilgrims in their race to flee.

The backs of the carrels exploded with wicked punctures as the bolt rounds blew through them.

I fired back, down the aisle, with tidy bursts of las-fire.

'Thorn wishes Aegis, craven hounds at the hindmost!'

That was all I was able to send before a bolt round glanced sidelong into my neck and threw me backwards, destroying my vox headset in the process.

I rolled on the marble floor, bleeding all over the place.

'Eisenhorn! Eisenhorn!' Ungish bawled and then screamed in agony.

I saw her thrown back through the panelled wood of the box pews, demolishing them. A bolt round had hit her square in the stomach. Bleeding out, she writhed on the floor amid the wood splinters, wailing and crying.

I tried to crawl across to her as further, heedless bolt-fire fractured the rest of the front pews.

I looked up. Witchfinder Arnaut Tantalid disengaged his mirror shield and gazed down at me.

'You are an accursed heretic, Eisenhorn, and that fact is now proven beyond doubt by the carta issued for you. In the name of the Ministorum of Mankind, I claim your life.'

TWENTY-ONE

Death at St Ezra's
The long hunt
The cell of five

Precisely how he had found me was a mystery, but I believe he had been on my tail for a long time, since before Cinchare. The fact that he had come to Saint Ezra Outlooking at that hour and that day convinced me that he had intercepted my communiqué to Gladus. And he might have triumphed over me, right there, right then, if he'd but pressed the advantage and finished the job with his boltgun.

Instead, Tantalid holstered his bolt pistol and drew his ancient chainsword, Theophantus, intent on delivering formal execution with the holy weapon.

I fired my laspistol, powering shot after shot at him, driving him backwards. His gold-chased battle suit, which gave his shrivelled frame the bulk and proportions of a Space Marine, absorbed or deflected the impacts, but the sheer force knocked him back several paces.

I jumped up, firing again, and retreating down the epistle

side of the cathedral, towards the feretory. Bystanders and church servants were still fleeing. Its iron teeth singing, Theophantus swung at me. Tantalid was barking out the Accusal of Heresy, verse after verse.

Be quiet! I yelled, enforcing my will.

The psychic sting shocked him into silence, but he was generally protected by psi-dampers and ignored my next will-driven order to 'desist' completely.

The chainsword revved around and I threw myself aside as it cleft a bench pew in two. The backswing nearly caught me, but I dodged behind a pier column that took the force of the blow in a splintering shower of sparks and stone chippings.

Ungish was still crying out in pain. The sound chilled and infuriated me. I fired my laspistol again, but the last few shots fizzed and spluttered, underpowered. The power cell was exhausted. I dived again, feinting past his slow-moving bulk, and grappled with him from behind. It was a desperate ploy. Unarmoured as I was, I stood little chance of overwhelming his brute force or hurting him. He got a steel-gloved paw round behind himself, grabbed me by the coat and tore me off him.

My coat ripped. I bounced hard off a pillar and crashed awkwardly through the delicate fretwork of a confessional screen. I had barely pulled myself out of the flimsy wooden wreckage when the chainsword swooped in again and chewed a deep gouge in the cathedral floor.

I ran from him then, across the south aisle towards the feretory. Two men of the cathedral's Frateris Militia, clearly seeking advancement by coming to the aid of the fearsome Ministorum witch-hunter, closed in to block my escape. They were both clad in Ezra's yellow and carried short stave-maces in one hand and temple lanterns in the other.

I think they both quickly regretted their enthusiastic involvement.

I didn't even bother with the will. I think my rage was too great to have used it cleanly anyway. I side-stepped the first mace, caught and broke the wrist that wielded it, and kicked the man down. The mace turned in the air as it flew from the sprawling oaf's useless hand, and I caught it and turned it cross-wise in time to block the down-stroke of the other man's club. As he bounced back with the recoil of his own, negated strike, I smacked him in the side of the knee with my captured weapon. He fell over with sharp wail of pain, losing hold of his own mace and trying to beat me with his temple lamp instead. I took the lamp away from him and kicked him in the belly so he doubled up on his side, sobbing and trying to remember how to breathe.

The first man was back up, running at me. I spun and smashed the temple lamp in his face, sideways. Both its light and his went out.

The paving shook as Tantalid hove down on me. I used the captured mace like a sword, double-handed, to deflect his first strokes. It was iron-banded hardwood, and tough, but no match for a chainsword. After three or so clashes, the mace was chewed and mangled. I threw it aside and tore a church standard down from the wall beside the feretory door. Theo-phantus immediately shredded the old embroidered cloth and wood-frame titulus from the end, but that left me with three metres of cast-iron pole.

I held it like a quarterstaff, striking Tantalid hard on the side of the head with one end and then square on the opposite hip with the other. Then I stabbed the end at him viciously, like a spear-thrust, and managed to dent the chest-plate of his armour.

In response – and frothing mad with anger himself now – he put up Theophantus and shortened my pole by about half a metre. I wrenched the remaining pole around one-handed and struck him on the other side of the head. Blood was spilling from his ears. He howled and made an attack that almost took my arm off.

My third attempt to clip his miserable head missed. He was wise to it now, and blocked with his chainsword. The chain teeth caught in the pole and plucked it from my hands, throwing it up ten metres into the air. It landed behind some pews with a loud, echoing clang.

I rocked back from the follow up, but the murderous saw caught my right shoulder and gashed me deeply. Clutching the wound, I ducked again, and Theophantus decapitated a statue of Saint Ezra's pardoner.

No matter what I did, it was going his way. He had the weapons and the armour on his side. And now I was bleeding badly, which meant I would progressively slow and weaken, and it was just a matter for him to keep pressing the onslaught and he would triumph.

I became aware of another commotion near the main doors of the great church. Many startled worshippers and hierarchs had retreated and gathered there to watch the holy combat. Now they were spilling aside, their huddle breaking. A figure stormed through them.

Medea.

She ran down the main aisle, calling to me, firing her needle pistol over the tops of the pews at Tantalid. The lethal rounds pinged and clicked off his armour, and he turned in annoyance.

Tantalid dragged out his boltpistol and fired at this new attack. Medea hurled the object she had been carrying in her

MALLEUS   393

other hand and then disappeared from view as she dived to
evade the hammer blows of the bolt rounds. At least, I prayed
it was a deliberate dive. If he had hit her...

The object she had thrown bounced off a pew near me and
landed on the floor, spilling from its yellow cloth.

Barbarisater.

Risking dismemberment from the chainsword, I hurled
myself at the Carthaen blade. My hands found its long grip
and I rolled twice to avoid the next downstrike of Theophantus.

Barbarisater purred in my grip as I came up. The runes
blazed with vengeful light.

Tantalid realised that the nature of the battle had suddenly
changed. I saw it in his eyes.

My first swing severed his wrist, cutting clean through the
power-armoured cuff, dropping his hand to the floor, still
clutching the smoking boltgun.

My second met Theophantus and destroyed it, spraying disintegrating chain-teeth and machine parts into the air.

My third cut Witchfinder Tantalid in two from the left shoulder to the groin. Neither half of him made a sound as they
fell apart onto the cathedral floor.

Barbarisater was still seething with power, and twitched as
Medea emerged unhurt from behind a choir stall. I forced the
hungry blade down.

'Come on!' she said.

Ungish was dead. There was nothing I could do for her. And
there was so much I should have done. She had been right.
Right about this. Right about her fate. I dreaded to think how
much more of what she had said might prove to be true too.

Hearing my frantic glossia call when Tantalid first attacked,
Medea had taken the launch up from Ezra Plain outside the
city, despite all official warnings for her to abort, and flown

it right in, setting down in the courtyard outside Saint Ezra Outlooking.

As we ran out now, into the evening, through crowds of stunned onlookers who leapt out of our path, the city Arbites and the Frateris Militia were rising in alarmed response. There was no point waiting to face them.

The launch shot us skywards, back towards the *Essene*, to leave Orbul Infanta as fast as we could.

It was a mess, and I was terribly disheartened. The confidence with which we had all set out from Cinchare seemed to have dissolved. Orbul Infanta had been just the first part of a long stratagem, and thanks to Tantalid, it had ended badly. I'd failed to contact Gladus, and discovered that as careful as I had been, my communiqués were not secure. The third task I had planned to undertake on Orbul Infanta, a search of the Imperial archivum for certain information relating to Quixos, hadn't even been started.

At least the weapons were consecrated. And Barbarisater had more than proved itself in combat.

Frigates of the Frateris Militia, along with several Imperial Navy guard boats, attempted to block the *Essene*, but Maxilla's Navigator got us out of the system and real space before they could even close range. Some ships pursued us into the warp, and we were chased for eight days, finally losing our pursuers through a series of real-space decelerations and redirections.

We went to ground. A month at a low-tech depot on a farming world, another two at the automated station at Kwyle. I was jumping at shadows by then, expecting enemies and rivals to loom out of every doorway. But it was quiet and we were unmolested. Maxilla had made a career out of passing

unnoticed and avoiding attention. He lent that practiced art
to our cause now, and reassured me into the bargain.

Three months after leaving Orbul Infanta in such haste, we
risked a run to Gloricent, an outlying but prosperous trade
world in the Antimar sub-sector, another division of the
Scarus Sector, just two sub-sectors over from the Helican sub
itself. Though worlds like Gudrun and Thracian Primaris were
a good four months away by starship, it felt a little like being
home. Disguised, Medea and I visited the sea-lashed stone
piles of one of the main trade-hives, and procured a pair of
astropaths, hiring their services from the local commercial
guild on an open-ended lease.

Their names were Adgur and Ueli, both young males, both
psychically capable but dull-witted and emotionless. Their
young heads were shaved and their plugs shiny and new, and
they spoke to me in overly formal ways that sounded like
the parrot-learned etiquette it sadly was. But their eyes were
ringed with darkness and their flesh was losing its youthful
lustre. The rigour of the astropathic life was already taking
its toll.

Using them, I sent fresh communiqués that superceded the
original ones and revised certain aspects of my scheme. None
of the messages now suggested the sort of trial meetings I had
attempted with Gladus. I would not give so much away now.

After a week, and no reponses, we left Gloricent and went,
via Mimonon to Sarum, the capital world of the Antimar
sub-sector. I managed to do some useful work in its libraries, but backed off when a sour little confessor on a research
sabbatical took to following me as if he recognised me.

While at anchor off Sarum, I got my first responses, all

coded: from Bequin on Messina, and from Aemos on Gudrun. Both reported that their parts of the plan were going much more smoothly than mine had. Two days later, a partially scrambled astropathic message came from Inshabel on Elvara Cardinal. What parts I got of it seemed to indicate some success. I was impatient to know more.

The week before we left Sarum, I received two more, both anonymous, one from Thracian Primaris, the other from a cluster of slave-worlds that owed fealty to the Salies Province of the Ophidian sub-sector. From the careful code and language of both, I recognised their senders.

My spirits lifted.

After that improvement, things again seemed to slow and stagnate. There was no progress, and no further communications. We were forced to quit Lorwen, our next stop after Sarum, with unseemly haste, when a flotilla of warships from Battlefleet Reaver arrived. I know now that the Battlefleet manoeuvres at Lorwen – and incidentally at Sarum and Femis Major too – were part of a major precautionary deployment against a pair of space hulks that had suddenly roamed into the sub-sector. But they caused us over thirteen weeks of anxious hiding amongst the brown and black dwarf stars of an extinguished stellar nursery.

Another Candlemas went by while we were in the empyrean, en route to the Drewlian Group. Medea, Maxilla and I marked it together, just the three of us. The two astropaths and the Navigator were not invited to attend. I raised a glass to toast the continued success of our mission. I don't think I would have been so hearty if I had known it would be another full year before the final act of the plan would play out.

* * *

I spent the first four months of 342 fruitlessly engaged in a search for the celebrated precog-hermit Lukas Cassian in the stinking marshes of Drewlia Two, only to learn that he had been murdered by a Monodominant cult four years earlier. During that quest, I terminated the activities of a plague-daemon sect infesting the marshlands. That was quite an undertaking in its own right, but my full account of it is filed in the Inquisition archives separately, and it has no bearing on this record. Besides, I still regard it bitterly as an interruption and waste of time. Neither will I set down here the full story of Nathan Inshabel's ventures on Elvara Cardinal, or Harlon Nayl's frankly extraordinary experiences on Bimus Tertius, though both tales connect to this record. Inshabel has written his own, refreshingly witty account of his exploits, which may be accessed by those with the appropriate clearance, something I recommend as illuminating and rewarding. Nayl asked me not to include his story, and has never committed it to record. It may be learned only by those with the temerity to ask him and the money to pay for a long night's serious drinking.

All this while, I remained an Imperial outlaw, wanted by the Inquisition for my heresies. It is interesting to note that at no time during this period did the Inquisition formally refute or overturn the carta I had declared on Quixos.

The year 343.M41 was half gone already by the time the *Essene* took me to Thessalon, a feudal world near Hesperus in the Helican sub-sector. It had been chosen by Nayl as the point for our secret congregation. Commanding a twenty-man field team selected from my staff on Gudrun, he arrived a week before the rest of us to secure the location and make sure we were not compromised. His preparations were thorough and ingenious. No one entered the area without him knowing it, nor could anyone have done so. At the slightest sign of outside interruption or official interference, we would have ample time to withdraw and flee.

As a final precaution, I was the last to arrive.

Thessalon is a tough little world whose population lives in a dark age and knows nothing of the Imperium or the galaxy beyond its skies.

The meeting place was a ruined keep in the north of the second continent, two thousand kilometres from the nearest indigenous community. A few lonely animal herders and subsistence farmers undoubtedly saw the lights of our ships in their heavens, but to them they were just the portents of the gods and the bright eyes of fabulous beasts.

Medea deposited me at the edge of a conifer forest at nightfall, and then took the gun-cutter back to stand off as air-cover, ready to redeploy at a moment's notice. For the first time in over two standard years, I was dressed as an inquisitor in black leather, storm coat and proudly displayed rosette. I also wore my faith-harness with the engraving *Puritus*. Damn anyone who believed I wasn't worthy of it.

Nayl, in combat armour, with a laser carbine cradled over one arm, appeared out of the trees and greeted me. We shook hands. It was good to see him again. His men, who were all around I was sure, were invisible in the gathering darkness.

Nayl led me through the black woods into a break in the trees where the pine tops framed a perfect oval of starfilled mauve. The keep, a jumbled pile of grey stone, stood in the clearing, with hooded lamps glowing from the lower slit windows.

Nayl walked me past and around the alarm-sensors, the

tripwires and the beams of motion detectors that webbed
the structure. Servitor-skulls from my personal arsenal hovered in the shadows, alert and armed.

Bequin and Aemos met me under the broken entrance arch.
Aemos looked pale and worried, but his face broke into a
warm smile as he saw me. Bequin hugged me.

'How many?' I asked her.

'Four,' she said.

Not bad. Not great, but not bad. It rather depended who
those four were.

'And everything else?'

'All the preparations are now set. We can begin this undertaking at any time,' Aemos said.

'We have a target?'

'We do. You'll learn how when we brief everyone.'

'Good.' I paused. 'Anything else I should know?'

All three of them shook their heads.

'Let's do it then,' I said.

Despite all the precautions, I was taking my life in my hands.
I was presenting myself, voluntarily, to four members of the
Inquisition. I was trusting that my previous friendships and
allegiances with them would count for more than the accu-
sations Osma had laid at my door. These four were the only
four who had responded out of the original twenty communiqués. Nayl had vetted each one, but there was still a very
real chance that any or all of them had attended simply to
execute the declared heretic Gregor Eisenhorn.

I would soon know.

As I stepped into the main, candlelit chamber, a hush killed
the small talk and six men turned to face me. Fischig, imposing

in black body armour, nodded me a half-smile. Interrogator Inshabel, in a bodyglove and lightweight cloak, bowed his head and smiled nervously.

The other four stared at me levelly.

I walked into their midst solemnly.

The first lowered the hood of his maroon cape. It was Titus Endor. 'Hello, Gregor,' he said.

'Well met, old friend.' Endor had been one of the first two to contact me anonymously the previous year, from the Salies slave-worlds. The other, who had written from Thracian Primaris, stood next to him.

'Commodus Voke. You honour me with your presence.'

The wizened old wretch sneered at me. 'For the sake of our history, and damn-his-eyes Lyko, and other matters, I am here, Eisenhorn, though the Emperor knows I am very suspicious of this. I will hear you out, and if I don't like what you have to say, I will withdraw... without breaking the confidence of this meeting!' he added sternly with a raised finger. 'I will not betray this congress, but I reserve the right to leave and quit if I find it worthless.'

'That right is yours, Commodus.'

To his left stood a tall, confident man I didn't recognise. He wore brown leather flak armour under a long blue coat of cavalry twill and his silver rosette was fixed on the left breast. His domed head was shaved, but there was a violet glint in his eyes that told me he was a Cadian.

'Inquisitor Raum Grumman,' said Fischig, stepping forward. Grumman took my proffered hand with a curt nod.

'Inquisitor General Neve acknowledges your communiqué to her, and asks me to express her true sadness that she could not join you here. She personally requested me to take her place, and render you the service I freely render her.'

'I am grateful for it, Grumman. But right from the start, I want to be sure that you know what we're about here. Just being here because your provincial chief requested it isn't enough.'

The Cadian smiled. 'Actually, it is. But to reassure you, I have reviewed the matter carefully with Neve herself and your man Fischig. I have no illusions about the danger of being here and siding with you. Given the evidence, I would have been here anyway.'

'Good. Excellent. Welcome, Grumman.'

The identity of the fourth and final guest took me aback. He was clad in polished battleware plating that looked custom-made and exorbitantly expensive. With gauntleted hands, he lifted the scowling houndskull helmet off his head. Inquisitor Massimo Ricci, of the Helican Ordo Xenos. He was hardly an old friend, but I knew him well.

'Ricci?'

His handsome, haughty face displayed a wide smile.

'Like Grumman, I am here to extend apologies from another. For numerous reasons that I'm sure you can appreciate, Lord Rorken cannot answer your request in person. It would be political suicide for him to participate in this matter. But my lord has faith in you still, Eisenhorn. He has sent me to act as his proxy.'

Ricci was one of Lord Rorken's most valued and admired inquisitors. Many said he was a likely successor for the post as a Master of the Ordo Xenos. For him to be here was an enormous compliment, both from Lord Rorken, who had seen fit to send one of his most illustrious men, and from Ricci himself, who was risking a high-profile career just by being here. Clearly both of them had taken my proposal and cause very seriously.

'Gentlemen,' I said. 'I am pleased, and honoured, to see you all. Let us discuss this matter, freely and openly, and see where we stand.'

The Thessalonian night winds moaned through the ruined cavities of the keep as I briefed them. Inshabel and Nayl had carried chairs in, and erected a heavy trestle table. Bequin and Aemos provided data-slates, charts, papers and other pieces of evidence as I called for them.

I talked for about two hours, taking them through the entire matter of Quixos as it was known to me. Much of what I said had been laid out in the initial communiqués, but I filled in all the details, and answered questions as they arose. Endor seemed satisfied, and hardly spoke. It was good to have a true friend here, one who simply trusted my word and purpose. Grumman was also generally non-committal. Voke and Ricci asked plenty of questions, and required clarification on the smallest points.

All three ordos were represented around that table: Voke was Ordo Malleus – though thankfully not a tight member of Bezier's inner circle – Ricci and I were Ordo Xenos, and Grumman and Endor were Ordo Hereticus. All of us apart from Grumman were assigned servants of the Ordos Inquisitorae Helican. Only Titus Endor, who I knew to be famously demure, wasn't wearing his rosette openly.

I believe I spoke eloquently and well.

We broke after two hours to stretch our legs, ruminate and take refreshment. I went outside, taking in the cold night air, listening to the wind swish the conifers. Fischig joined me and brought me a glass of wine.

'It's bad with Neve,' he said, just getting right into it. He had

travelled back to Cadia from Cinchare to collect more data
and to specifically recruit the inquisitor general.

'Because of me?'

He nodded. 'Because of everything. Osma made big trouble
after we sprung you from the Carnificina. He had the combined clout of Bezier and Orsini behind him, after all. That
made Neve's superior, Grandmaster Nunthum of the Ordos
Cadia, sit up and take notice, I can tell you. They were after
her for her job. But they couldn't prove a thing. Neve's very
good at being slippery. And she fought your corner like a
she-bear too, believe you me.'

'She's safe?'

'Yeah. Thanks to a massive incursion of the Enemy eight
months ago. The Cadian Gate's on a war footing and utterly
in turmoil. Last thing anyone's worrying about is what part
Neve may have played in the Eisenhorn Conspiracy.'

'That's what they're calling it?'

'That's what they're calling it.'

I sipped the wine, expecting something rough and local. It
turned out to be a damned good Samatan red. From my own
cellars, I guessed.

Bequin would have taken care of such things and chosen
the very best to mollify our guests.

'Grumman: what do you make of him?'

'I've got plenty of time for him, Gregor,' Fischig said. 'Smart
mind, knows what he's doing. Given the scrutiny she was
under, Neve knew she couldn't get away, so she picked Grumman, and I don't think she would have if he wasn't worth
his salt.

'The pair go back a long way, and Grumman's doing this
out of respect for her. But we spent a long time talking on the
voyage back here, and I think he's in it for himself now too.'

'Good. The others?'

'Voke's full of surprises,' he snorted. 'When you said he was going to be on your list of contacts, I thought you were mad. Not as mad as writing to Lord Rorken, of course, but anyway... I never thought the old bastard would show, or even deign to answer you. He's so stiff even the rod up his arse has got a rod up its arse. That's one bet I would have lost. He must like you more than he lets on.'

'We have an understanding,' I said. I'd saved Voke's life on the flagship *Saint Scythus*, but he'd returned that favour on the Avenue of the Victor Bellum. Maybe that was enough.

'He needs convincing,' said Fischig, 'but I think he's in for the long haul.'

'You do?'

'You see that creep Heldane anywhere?'

I knew what Fischig meant. Heldane would have opposed this mission without question, and taken great delight in bringing me in, dead or alive. Voke had clearly come here without his old pupil knowing. Fischig was right. That was a good sign.

'Endor, well, he's safe, isn't he?' said Fischig. 'Given your history, he'd have come anyway.'

'It's good to have him here. What about Ricci?'

Fischig's voice suddenly dropped to a hiss. 'Speaking of whom.'

He withdrew. Clutching a goblet of wine, Ricci walked out of the archway behind us and joined me, gazing up at the staggeringly bright star-field.

'I hope you realise how lucky you are,' Ricci said.

'Every day.'

'You took a risk contacting Lord Rorken. He's always liked you, but given the current climate, liking you is a dangerous habit. He was at loggerheads with Bezier and Orsini over your case.'

'And still he sent you?'

'Let me be direct, Gregor. I think it will help. Lord Rorken, may his fortunes multiply in the face of the God-Emperor, sent me to assist you in the unmasking and destruction of the heretic Quixos. But if, along the way, I should discover anything that confirmed the generally-believed allegations of your own heresy...'

'What?'

'I think you understand.'

'You're his hatchet man. You'll help me... but if I cross the line in your eyes, Rorken has sanctioned you to execute me.'

He raised his glass. 'I think we know where we stand.'

We did. Now it made much more sense that Rorken had sent so senior an agent to my side.

I said nothing. Ricci smiled and went back inside.

We sat down around the table again and debated some more. I found most of the questions – especially those from Voke and Ricci – wilfully small-minded.

At last, after another hour, Grumman voiced a pertinent query.

'Supposing we agree to this. Agree that Eisenhorn is wrongly charged and that Quixos deserves our sternest censure... how do we do that? Do we know where Quixos is?'

'Yes,' I said, though I didn't know the answer myself. My people had enjoyed the best part of two years to do their work, many dozens of agents sifting data from hundreds of worlds.

Unbidden, Bequin stepped forward and took a seat with us at the table.

'About three months ago, our research discerned a pattern

in the data surrounding the near-mythical life of Quixos. And that pattern centred on Maginor.'

'Capital of the Niaides sub-sector, Viceroy sector, Ultima segmentum,' announced Voke.

'Your astronomical knowledge is humbling, sir,' Bequin said smoothly. She handed out data-slates.

'As you can see from the file of data marked "alpha", Quixos certainly visited Maginor almost two hundred years ago, and became involved with a cartel of trade interests and noble families known as the Mystic Path. The Path was a network which was already utilising prohibited and forbidden lore and technologies. Quixos should have closed them down and burned them. It is clear he did not. Instead, he fed and supported them. He nurtured them until they became a power base for his invisible empire of dark belief. No longer a cartel but a cult. A cult of Quixos.'

'Why do we think he's still there?' asked Ricci.

'We think he's made his hidden fastness there, sir,' said Bequin. 'The reaches of the Mystic Path now spread throughout the segmentum and beyond. Maginor is its heart. In 239. M41, Inquisitor Lugenbrau and a warrior band numbering some sixty individuals disappeared on Maginor. No trace of them was ever found, though Interrogator Inshabel was able to... ah... recover an incomplete verbal transcript of a pict-recording apparently made during Lugenbrau's raid.'

I speed-read the transcript. It was harrowing. 'You got this from Elvara Cardinal, Inshabel?' I asked.

Inshabel was at the back of the room. He stepped forward, blushing. 'Not directly, sir. It actually came from the Inquisitorial data-library on Fibos Secundus. How is a damn good story, but it's probably wasting valuable time to repeat it just now.'

Inshabel was right, as I have already said. It was a damn good story, and I enjoyed it when he told it to me later. I urge you to access it.

'We believe Lugenbrau was hunting Quixos, although he may not have known it,' continued Bequin. 'He and his entire band were wiped out by Quixos's forces.'

'Lugenbrau,' murmured Voke, setting his slate down and looking off into space. 'I never met him, but he was a trusted pupil of my late comrade, Inquisitor Pavel Uet. When Lugenbrau went missing, Uet took it hard. The loss shortened his life.'

Voke looked at me with his rheumy eyes. 'If I wasn't decided before, Eisenhorn, I am now. Quixos must pay.'

'I agree,' said Endor, tossing his slate onto the table and looking grim. 'At the very least, the Inquisition demands vengeance for this.'

'Maginor, then?' Grumman asked.

'It's still his base of operations, sir, we are sure of that,' said Bequin. 'And until a week ago, we were all set to prepare for a strike against Maginor. Then we received this.' She held up an astropathic transcript.

'I will read it, if I may.' She carefully put on her half-moon glasses. They suited her, but I knew her vanity made her hate them. It said a lot about the situation that she was willing to wear them in front of these men.

'It begins... "Gregor, my friend. I have been kept up to date with the data concerning your quarry. It gives me something to do, these winter afternoons. I agree that Maginor may be the seat of the evil, and certainly requires the attention of the Inquisition. But, if you'll pardon me, I suggest that Maginor be left to the Ordos Niaides. Using pointers Aemos gave me, I have assessed the following. My full findings are on the data-files attached below, but in short, I think you should be looking at Farness Beta. Quixos's fascination with the pylons of Cadia made me think, you see.

"'See below, that I have traced massive stonecutting orders to the limit-world of Serebos, which lies galactically south of Terra. The masonic guilds of Serebos are famously secretive about their contracts. They provide an inert, obsidian-like black glass-stone called serebite, a beautiful substance that is in high demand right across the Imperium. Serebite is, as far as reckoning goes, as close to the material used on Cadia for the pylons as it is possible to get. As I have said, the masonic guilds are close about their contracts, but there is little hiding the transportation of a massive copy of one of those pylons by shipping guild bulk-lifter. Three-quarters of a kilometre long and a quarter square! Quixos has ordered the manufacture of a perfect copy of the Cadian pylons, and has had it shipped to Farness Beta.'"

Bequin paused and looked up at us.

"'If you've ever trusted my advice, trust this now,'" she continued. "'Quixos is on Farness. And if you're going to stop him, it must be now. Your devoted friend and pupil. Gideon.'"

Gideon. Gideon Ravenor. Crippled as he was, he had found this insight, which totally altered our plan of attack. I was speechless. I felt almost tearful.

'There is a postscript,' said Bequin. 'He writes, "The daemon-hosts will be your foulest problem. I know you are prepared, but I send you these. One for each of the twenty you have summoned."'

Bequin took off her half-moon glasses and rose. Nayl brought in a crate and set it down on the table. Inside were twenty scrolls of daemonic protection, each sealed inside a blessed tube of green marble, and twenty consecrated gold amulets of the God-Emperor as a skeletal relic. It was so typical of Ravenor to attend to such details. Nayl handed them out, a heavy scroll tube and an amulet to each of us.

'I'm convinced,' Ricci said, getting to his feet and hanging the amulet around his neck so that it hung between the purity seals of his armour.

'I am glad. Grumman?'

'I'm with you,' said the Cadian.

'A toast,' I said, raising my glass. 'To this cell of five. And to the others who have assisted in getting us this far.' Bequin, Aemos, Nayl, Fischig and Inshabel also saluted with their glasses.

'To Farness Beta. To the end of Quixos.'

The five inquisitors in the drafty keep clinked glasses.

'Farness Beta,' said Ricci. 'Remind me. Where is that?'

'In the throat of the Cadian Gate,' said Grumman. 'Right on the edge of the Eye of Terror.'

TWENTY-TWO

Farness Beta
Cherubael and Prophaniti
Quixos

It was early in 343.M41 before we reached Farness Beta. By then, war was bifurcating the Cadia sub-sector, and armies of sheer horror were spewing out of the Eye of Terror. Like a whirlpool of fire, the Eye dominated the skies of most gate-worlds, distended and angry, flaring more savagely than at any time in living memory. Every flash and pulse of its maelstrom was another warp hole opening, another flotilla of death unleashed. That spring was known as the Staunch Holding of the Cadian Gate, and entered the history books, as every scholar knows.

During the first months of 343, the Cadians saw off the greatest incursion of Chaos suffered in three hundred years.

It was almost as if the Archenemy knew something.

The *Essene* brought me to Farness champing and eager to get on. We were escorted through the immaterium by two other ships: Ricci's stately steeple of a cruiser and Voke's ancient porcupine of a warship. Endor and Grumman, along with their retinue bands, travelled aboard the Essene with me. It had been a long time since the Essene had carried so many people.

The Imperial Navy taskforce, a ten-ship squadron seconded from Battlefleet Scarus for special operations under the remit of the Battlefleet Disciplinary Detachment, was waiting for us.

The taskforce had already been on station for a fortnight, and its reconnaissance and intelligence operations had comprehensively prepared the ground for us.

'We have a confirmed location for Pariah,' Lord Procurator Olm Madorthene told me over a vox-pict link from his own ship.

Pariah was the operational word we had set for Quixos. 'Or at least his seat of activity, anyway. I'm relaying the data to you now. Site A is what you're looking for.'

I turned from my seat on the *Essene*'s elegant bridge and Maxilla nodded to one of his beautiful servitors. The map display flashed up on the secondary screen of my console.

'I have it,' I said, turning back to look at Madorthene's slightly fuzzy image on the main bridge display.

'It's a table mountain called Ferell Sidor, literally the "altar of the sun", up in one of the remote northern wards of Hengav province. Provincial government has declared the whole ward a Sacred Territory because the area is riddled with Second Dynasty tholos tombs. Access is supposed to be restricted to the Ecclesiarchy, the Farnessi royal families and sanctioned archaeologists. We believe Pariah obtained licenses to excavate on Ferell Sidor about six years ago, in the guise of an archaeological mission from the Universitariate of Avellorn.

The local authorities are supposed to monitor such missions, but frankly they have no idea what he's up to there. If you look at the detail map...'

'Yes, got it.'

'You can see the extent of the workings. Pariah's constructed a small town up there, alongside the pit.'

'The excavation is considerable...'

'We think that's where he's buried or sited this facsimile pylon. It's difficult to get a clear view. We didn't want to get too close and tip him off.'

I rose from my bridge throne and stood facing the enormous image of the lord procurator's face. 'You're set?'

'Absolutely. You have a copy of my assault strategy there. Make any amendments you like.'

There was no need. Madorthene's plan was economical and efficient. Officially, this was an operation by the Battlefleet Disciplinary Detachment, prosecuting leads gathered during the inquest into the Thracian Atrocity. Lord Procurator Madorthene had entered into a co-operative pact with Commodus Voke to execute the plan. In reality, his pact was secretly with me. Olm was the only non-inquisitor I had written to.

We encrypted the call-signs and command authorities for the operation, agreed the zero-hour, and wished each other luck.

'The Emperor protects, Gregor,' he said.

'I hope so, Olm,' I replied.

Two hours before sunrise the next day, five hundred Imperial Guard from the Fifty-First Thracian moved in towards Ferell Sidor – Site A – from covert forward assembly points in the surrounding hills where they had been dropped by troop ships the day before. They advanced, silently, in three prongs, the first securing the single trackway that gave land-vehicle access to the table mountain. When all three were in position, we woke Ferell Sidor up.

The frigates *Zhikov* and *Fury of Spatian* bombarded the mountain for six minutes, raising a ball of fire that lit the landscape as if the sun had come up early. In its afterglow, thirty Marauder bombers overflew Site A at low level and delivered thirty thousand kilos of high explosives.

Another false dawn.

Despite this punishing overture, when the ground troops went in eight minutes after the last bomb, resistance was furious. Madorthene had feared that the best part of Quixos's strength lay underground, wormed inside the mountain, resistant to the worst aerial assaults.

In the blazing ruins of the excavation township, the Thracian troops found themselves engaging fanatical and well-armed cultists. Most wore the insignia and colours of the Mystic Path. Many were mutants. Initial reports estimated over eight hundred enemy warriors. Madorthene committed the taskforce reserve: another seven hundred Thracian assault soldiers.

By then, we were already deploying in the second wave. Medea landed Inshabel and myself on the edge of the strike zone, along with Endor and his two weapon-servitors. Ricci's shielded pinnace settled in close by, kicking up dust and delivering him and Commodus Voke, along with a bodyguard of twenty Inquisitorial troops. Grumman, using a Navy dropship loaned by Madorthene, was the last to make groundfall, but the first to engage. Grumman's ten-man squad were all ex-Kasrkin specialists.

As we hurried forward through the backwashing smoke,

our landing ships rising back into the pre-dawn sky behind us, there was a tremor and a palpable upwelling of psychic force. Frighteningly powerful waves of psyker power erupted from the epicentre of Site A, killing over thirty of the forward troops... and then suddenly cut off.

We had all anticipated Quixos would have vast psychic defences – he had, after all, been collecting psykers like Esarhaddon – and it seemed likely that active psychic assaults would be a key element of his resistance, perhaps even more significant than his daemonhosts. I had taken no chances.

In two groups, my entire Distaff of untouchables, some fifty individuals all told, had moved in alongside the first ground-troop advances. Bequin, guarded by Nayl and twelve of my warrior staff, led one group, and Thula Surskova, protected by Fischig and a dozen more fighters, led the other.

The Distaff had never been used on such a scale before, but it proved to be the weapon I had always suspected. The blankness they generated contained and negated the engulfing psychic storm, effectively bottling it inside Site A and preventing it from threatening our closing forces.

With Inshabel, I moved underground, down the rock-cut steps into the inner sectors of Site A. For almost an hour we fought our way through the smoked-swathed surface structures, a metre at a time. Now, with the sun rising, we found our first access point to the lower levels: a stairwell exposed by a bomb crater.

The place was strewn with smouldering debris and a few unidentifiable bodies. In places, power cables were hanging, sparking, from the rockcrete roof. We both wore motion trackers, and switched left and right, gunning down cultists as they appeared. My boltgun was already running short of shells, and Inshabel was on to his second-to-last power cell. The level of resistance was unbelievable.

At a junction in the seemingly random jumble of tunnels, we encountered Endor. He had a couple of Thracian troopers and an Inquisition guardsman with him, but he'd lost both of his slow-moving attack-servitors. I knew what he was thinking just by the look in his eyes. We had come in strong and confident, but perhaps not strong enough. I thought I had anticipated the worst Quixos could throw against us. Maybe I had underestimated him after all.

Ferocious bursts of shooting alerted us to a firefight in a larger chamber to the left. We arrived in time to meet four wounded, terrified Thracian troopers fleeing towards us.

'Back! Go back!' they were screaming.

I pushed past them.

The chamber beyond was massive and half-filled with veiling smoke. Green, unnatural flames were licking up the walls. At the far end, the already huge chamber seemed to open out into something much, much vaster.

But that was not what occupied my eyes.

Surrounded by over fifty bodies, most of them Imperial Guard, Commodus Voke was standing his ground against Prophaniti.

The old inquisitor was shuddering, his robes stiffening with psychic ice. Corposant fire glowed from his mouth and eyes. The daemonhost, its cruel features just recognisable as a distortion of poor, lost Husmaan's face, hovered in front of Voke, struggling at an invisible barrier of telekinetic wrath.

We ran forward, abruptly drawing fire from cultists spreading into the chamber from the right. The Thracian beside me bucked and twitched as he was hit twice, and Inshabel cursed as he was winged.

Endor urged the remaining men to advance on his lead, and took the fight to the cultists, his laspistol blazing and his chainblade swinging.

Voke was close to breaking. I could see him wavering under the immense pressure.

I holstered my boltgun and stumbled across the bodies and debris to aid him, praying that my runestaff would do what it was supposed to.

And a dizzying blast of white light and scourging heat blew me back through the air.

I tried to get up, half-realising that I had been blown clean out of the chamber, through a flakboard partition into some kind of dank chute. Invisible forces lifted me to my feet. Light bathed me.

Cherubael hovered before me.

'Gregor,' it said. 'You've come so far. I knew you had it in you.'

I held the runestaff in front of me. The green marble scroll of daemonic protection that Ravenor had sent had already been reduced to a shattered remnant by the force of Cherubael's opening attack.

'I've waited for this moment for such a long time,' said the daemonhost. 'Remember on Eechan I said you'd have to make things up to me? Well, this is the time. Now. This is the moment that everything's been about. The one I have seen coming since our paths first crossed. Destinies... our destinies, intertwined, remember that?'

'How could I forget?' I spat. 'You claim to have been using me all along! Guiding me! Even protecting me! I watched you kill Lyko on Eechan! So that I would live... for this moment? Why?'

Cherubael smiled. 'When the warp is in you as it is in me,

you see time from all angles. You see what will be and what will come, what someone here now will do in a century or two, what someone there has done a thousand years in the past. You see the possibilities.'

'Riddles! That's all you ever speak!'

'No more riddles, Eisenhorn. From the moment I first met you, I saw you were the only one, the only one with the tenacity, the skill and the opportunity to give me what I want. What I want most of all. I saw that if I kept you safe, you would come and give me that most precious thing here, on this world, at this hour.'

'I would never help a daemon like you!'

Cherubael grinned, blank-eyed and utterly serious. 'Then destroy me, if you can.'

It lunged. I raised the runestaff and channelled my will down through the psi-conductive pole into the lodestone. The carved fragment of the Lith blazed with blue light.

Pontius Glaw knew a thing or two about daemonhosts. Their greatest weakness was the strength of the will that had bound them as slaves. The runestaff, so carefully prepared and constructed, so painstakingly etched with the ancient symbols of control, was a lever to topple that binding will by amplifying my own to levels that would overwhelm it.

For a brief moment, I felt how it must feel to be an alpha-plus psyker.

The scintillating spear of energy that shot from the lode-stone struck Cherubael in the chest.

The daemonhost smiled for a second, and then its flesh-vessel ruptured open, billowing a storm of Chaos-fire in all directions. I had cast it out of its binding and banished it back into the warp.

And in the moment as my amplified mind overmastered his, I saw the years of enslavement it had endured at Quixos's hands, the torments of its binding, the great, forbidden text of the *Malus Codicium* whose arcane knowledge Quixos had used to create his daemonhosts.

And I realised that I had given Cherubael exactly what it wanted after all.

Freedom.

I stumbled back into the main chamber. By then, Voke, whose resistance to Prophaniti had been astonishing, was dead.

I remembered Voke's words after the atrocity on Thracian: 'I will make amends. I will not rest until every one of these wretches is destroyed, and order restored. And then I will not rest until I find who and what was behind it.'

He could rest now. That work was done.

The daemonhost was casting the valiant old man's empty husk of a body aside and gliding towards Endor and Inshabel, who were both already on their knees in agony. Cyan flames washed from Prophaniti's fingertips and wrapped my two friends in tight, burning psychic shackles. They were trapped morsels for it to feed off at its leisure.

Prophaniti froze when I appeared, instinctively knowing I posed a more serious threat. The Lith-stone was still smoking with blood-red light.

The daemonhost surged through the air at me, teeth bared, arms spread, incandescent with light, baying my name. It was like facing the attack run of a supersonic warcraft firing all guns. I know so. It is my misfortune to have experienced that too.

Prophaniti whooped with glee.

'At Kasr Geth, you told me to make my weapons sounder

next time, monster!' I howled, and impaled its charging form on the steel pole of the runestaff. 'Is this sound enough?'

Prophaniti screamed and exploded, blowing me off my feet. I don't think I banished it. I think I obliterated its essence forever.

The runestaff was, miraculously, unscathed, and lay amid the rubble. But Prophaniti's dissipating being had made it white hot from base to cap, and I could not pick it up again.

I ran across to Titus Endor and Inshabel, both of whom lolled weakly on the floor.

Inshabel was dazed but intact. Endor had daemon gashes across his chest and neck. He looked up at me blearily.

'You got them both, Gregor...'

'I pray there are no more,' I replied, trying to staunch his bleeding. His rosette slid out of his coat pocket and I leaned to pick it up.

The Inquisitorial symbol was decorated with the ornate crest of the Ordo Malleus.

'Malleus?' I hissed.

'No...'

'When did you transfer, Endor? Damn you, when did you change ordos?'

'They forced me...' he wheezed, 'Osma forced me! When he had me on Messina... there were certain matters from a case a few years ago. He'd got his hands on them somehow... He... he promised I would burn if I didn't help him get to you.'

'What matters?'

'Nothing! Nothing, Gregor, I swear! But he had Bezel's backing! He could have made anything look heretical! I transferred orders to stop him breaking me. He said I would be rewarded, advanced. He said Ordo Malleus was a better prospect for me.'

'But you were to keep an eye on me?'

'I told him nothing! I never sold you out. I did just enough to keep Osma satisfied.'

'Like coming here. No wonder you hid your rosette. He wanted you to take me down, didn't he?'

Endor was silent. Inshabel looked on in stark disbelief.

'I... I was to go along with this operation, in the hope that it might be successful. Orsini's under no illusions that Quixos is a menace, and this was an expedient way, perhaps, of eliminating him. If you were still... alive at the end of it, I was told to arrest you on the carta charges. Or, if you resisted...'

'Get him up to ground level,' I told Inshabel quietly. 'Find him a medic. Don't let him out of your sight.'

'Yes sir!'

'Gregor!' Endor gasped as Inshabel lifted him. 'By the God-Emperor, I never meant–'

'Get him out of here!' I growled.

The assault on Ferell Sidor was three hours old when Grumman, Ricci and I entered the undervault of the excavation pit. Madorthene's forces were still locked in a monumental struggle with the renegade's warriors throughout the warren of tunnels and chambers in the table mountain.

Ricci was weak from a blade wound, and all of his bodyguards were dead. Grumman had just two Kasrkin left with him, both of them armed with lasrifles.

The vast undervault was an excavated pit almost a kilometre deep, open to the sky. The serebite copy of the Radian pylon rested in the base of it, surrounded by adamantite scaffolding. Gibbet cages, hundreds of them, hung from the scaffolding on chains. In each one, trapped and helpless, was a human body.

They were Quixos's carefully collected arsenal of rogue psykers, secretly acquired from all over the Imperium. It must have taken him decades to accumulate so many. One of them, I had no doubt, was Esarhaddon

'What is he doing?' Ricci asked, a touch of awe in his voice.

'Something we have to stop,' said Grumman, with a direct simplicity I appreciated. It was the only answer any of us needed.

We had been living at our nerve ends since the assault began, and were wired with combat sharpness. Even so, despite our combined experience and skill, what happened next took us all totally by surprise.

One moment there was nothing. The next, a robed, armoured form was in amongst us, moving so fast it was simply a blur.

So fast. So accursedly fast.

Instantly, Ricci was split open down the length of his spine. As he was still in the process of falling on his face, choking on his own blood, one of the Kasrkin was severed at the waist, and toppled in halves, his gun firing spasmodically. The other Kasrkin folded up around the impaling thrust of a long, dark blade, spontaneously combusting from the belly out.

Grumman pushed me out of the way as the devastating blur turned again, and fired his laspistol at it three times. Snapping round faster than my eyes could follow, the long, dark blade the blur was wielding deflected each crackling shot.

Grumman's head left his shoulders.

Quixos, the arch-heretic, the renegade, the unforgivable radical, whirled on me before Grumman's butchered body had even started to slump.

I had one fleeting glimpse of the long daemonsword, Kharnagar. It was gnarled and knotted and thick with abominable runes and irregular claw-like serrations.

That's all I saw as it came whistling towards my face.

TWENTY-THREE

The heretic
Afterwards

A bare hand's breadth from my head, the blood-red blade came to a dead stop, blocked by the gleaming steel of Barbarisater.

Time seemed to stand still for a heartbeat. We faced each other, our blades locked together. Quixos had been a speed-distorted phantom until our swords had struck. Now he was frozen, glaring between the crossed blades at me.

The renegade's armour was ragged and filthy, and ornate with warp-signs. His Inquisitorial rosette was displayed, incongruously, on his right shoulder guard. It revolted me to see it worn amongst such corruption.

His ancient face was a misshapen, pustular horror. Rudimentary antlers bulged from his brow. His skin was dark like granite. Wheezing augmetic cables and implants bulged at his throat and under the dirty head-cloth he wore. His eyes were shining balls of blood.

In honesty, he was a disappointing little monster compared to the notion of him that had built up in my mind. But there was no denying his inhuman strength and speed.

Eisenhorn, he said. It was psychic. His twisted mouth didn't open.

Barbarisater felt him move before I did. It lurched in my hands. In the time it takes to draw a breath, we had exchanged a flurry of twenty or more blows. The talon-edged blade of Kharnager rang dully off the Carthaen steel. Barbarisater's pentagrammatic runes flashed and flared with discharging energy. Kharnager groaned softly.

Heretic! Slave of Chaos! his raw, broken mind-voice railed in my brain.

You speak of yourself! I returned. Our blades continued to ring off one another, hunting for a gap, mutually denied.

Why would you try to end my work here if you were not a minion of the warp?

Your work? This thing?

We broke, and then came in again, blades striking so fast the noise became one long ringing tone. I barely made an *ulsar* in time to stop one of his rapid down-stabs. He blocked my response of a *tahn wyla*, and the *uru arav* that I followed it with.

This is just the test, the prototype. Once the trials with it are conducted, then my work will flower!

You carve up a mountain... for a prototype? A prototype of what?

The pylons of Cadia pacify the warp, he spat. *By amplifying them using extreme-level psykers, they could be made into a weapon. A weapon to destroy the warp! A weapon to collapse the Eye of Terror in upon itself!*

He was raving, insane. What patches of truth or sane notions might lurk in his words, I had no idea. There was no way to distinguish them from his lunatic fancy. All I knew was that a pylon, psychically super-charged, might do all manner of things, but its side-effects would be catastrophic. It could lay waste to the continent, the planet.

I think, and here lay the true horror of it, I think Quixos knew that. I think he considered that to be an acceptable price to pay, just as he had considered the atrocity on Thracian a necessary cost to obtain a psyker of such peerless quality as Esarhaddon. What other abominations had he caused in acquiring the others?

As Grumman had said, just before his death, this simply had to be stopped.

I looked at his face.

This was where radicalism led. This was the true face of one who had reached the place and crossed the line. This was the obscene reality behind Pontius Glaw's jaunty glorifications of Chaos.

We rained blows at each other, drawing sparks and little curls of vapour from the blade edges. I tried a low swing, but he leapt over it, and alternated a series of scissoring blows that drove me backwards across the dusty ground. I thought my feet would slip. He was a whirlwind.

I saw my moment. Barbarisater saw it too. A slight under-swing on his blade return that opened a gap for a *sar aht uht*, a slice to the heart, just for a microsecond.

I thrust in, putting all my will into the blade. Somehow, dazzlingly, he still managed to turn Kharnager and block me.

Barbarisater struck the daemonsword and broke in half.

And it was the ultimate failure of the ancient Carthaen blade that gave me victory. If it had stayed intact, the block would have stopped it and the fight would have continued.

Breaking around Quixos's sword-edge, the truncated half

of Barbarisater in my hand continued on, with all my mus-
tered force behind it, until the broken end plunged through
his cloak, his body armour, his augmetic implants and ran
him through the torso.

The *ewl caer*.

It took almost equal force to break the suction of his flesh
around the blade and rip it out.

Quixos staggered backwards, polluted blood spurting from
the wound, his augmetics shorting out and exploding.

Then he fell to the dusty floor of the undervault, and became
dust himself, until there was nothing left but rotting augmetic
devices and empty armour twisted under his lank cape.

Heretic! his mind screeched out as he died.

Coming from him, the word felt like a compliment.

Site A was dismantled and destroyed by the taskforce, and the
faux pylon smashed by sustained orbital fire. Quixos's psykers,
and his surviving servants, were imprisoned, and then turned
over to the Black Ships of the Inquisition, six of which arrived
a few days later, once we had published news of our achievement. Most of the captives were deemed too dangerous or
too tainted to keep, even under the closest guard, and were
executed. Esarhaddon was one of those.

Many precious texts and artifacts were recovered from Site
A, and many more that were diabolic and abominable. He had
accumulated a vast resource of esoteric material, and there
was supposed to be a great deal more at his fastness on distant Maginor. A further purge would reveal the truth of that.

As the report has it, no trace was ever found of the *Malus
Codicium*, the foul grimoire on which his power had ultimately been based.

* * *

By the time I had returned to Gudrun with my followers and allies, the carta issued against me had been abolished. None of Osma's allegations could stand up in the face of the evidence gathered at Farness, or the many statements collected by the Inquisition, statements pleading my innocence made by such individuals as Lord Procurator Madorthene, Inquisitor General Neve, Interrogator Inshabel and, God-Emperor help him, Titus Endor.

I was never offered any sort of official apology, not by Grandmaster Orsini, or by Bezier, and certainly not by Osma. His career didn't suffer one bit. Twenty years later, he was elected Master of the Ordo Malleus Helican after Bezier's sudden, unexpected death.

Grumman's remains, and the remains of his Kasrkin, were buried in one of the lonely field-grave plots on Cadia, to be remembered as long as the Law of Decipherability allowed. Ricci had a library named after him on his home world of Hesperus. Voke was buried with full honours at the Thorian Sacristy adjoining the Great Cathedral of the Ministorum on Thracian Primaris. A small brass plaque commemorating the achievements of his long and dedicated career remains on the sacristy wall to this day.

He and I had never been friends, but I own that in the years after he was gone, I missed his caustic manner from time to time.

EPILOGUE

Winter, 345.M41

The voice was like the sound of some eternal glacier – slow, old, cold, heavy.

It asked simply, 'Why?'

'Because I can.'

The silence lasted for a long time. The thousand candle flames flickered and rippled the carefully inscribed stone walls with echoes of their moving glow.

'Why? Why... have you done this... this wretched thing to me?'

'Because I have power over you where once you had power over me. You used me. You orchestrated my life. You moved me like a regicide piece to the place where I best served your desires. Now, that is reversed.'

It thrashed against its chains and shackles, but it was still too weak from the ordeals of the snaring, the entrapment.

'Damn you...' it whispered, falling limp.

'Understand me. I said I would never help a thing like you, but you tricked me into doing so and almost got away with it. That's why I have done this. That's why I have expended the considerable time and effort involved in raising you, snaring you and binding you. This is a lesson. I will never, ever allow my actions or my life to benefit the Archenemy. You said that from the outset, you knew I was the one who would free you from Quixos's service. It's a shame for you that you failed to see what I might do to you instead.'

'Damn you!' the voice was louder.

'There will be a time, Cherubael, daemon-thing, when you will wish with all your putrid soul to be Quixos's plaything again.'

Cherubael threw itself at me as far as it could before the chains went taut and snapped it back. Its scream of rage and malice shook the cell and blew every last one of the candles out.

I sealed the vacuum hatch, engaged the warp dampers and the void shield, and turned the thirteen locks one by one.

From far away in the house, Jarat was ringing the bell for dinner. I was bone-weary from my exertions, but food and wine and good company would refresh me.

I climbed the screwstair from the deep basement stronghold, code-locked the door and wandered to my study. Outside, the snows had come early to Gudrun. Light flakes were blowing in through the twilight, across the woods and paddocks, and settling across the lawns of my estate.

In the study, I returned the items I had been carrying to their places. I put the bottles of chrism back on the shelf, and the ritual athame, mirror and lamens in the casket. The Imperial amulet went back on its velvet pad in the locking draw, and I slid the tube-scrolls back into their catalogue rack.

Then I placed the runestaff on its hooks in the lit alcove above the glass case containing the broken pieces of proud Barbarisater.

Finally, I opened the void safe in the floor behind my bureau, and gently laid the *Malus Codicium* inside.

Jarat was ringing the bell again.

I sealed the safe and went down to dinner.

ABOUT THE AUTHOR

Dan Abnett has written over fifty novels, including *Anarch*, the latest instalment in the acclaimed Gaunt's Ghosts series. He has also written the Ravenor and Eisenhorn books, the most recent of which is *The Magos*. For the Horus Heresy, he is the author of *Horus Rising, Legion, The Unremembered Empire, Know No Fear* and *Prospero Burns*, the last two of which were both *New York Times* bestsellers. He also scripted *Macragge's Honour*, the first Horus Heresy graphic novel, as well as numerous audio dramas and short stories set in the Warhammer 40,000 and Warhammer universes. He lives and works in Maidstone, Kent.